Hive

HIVE

MADDERS OF TIME
BOOK ONE

DL Orton

ROCKY MOUNTAIN PRESS

Hive

Copyright © 2024 by DL Orton
All rights reserved.
Madders of Time
Book One
DLOrton.com
Published by Rocky Mountain Press (US)
RockyMtPress.com
ISBN: 978-1-941368-33-6 (Paperback edition)
ISBN: 978-1-941368-32-9 (Hardback edition)
ARC v4
Written by DL Orton (dlo@dlorton.com)
Edited by David S. Taylor
Layout by Fernando Urbina
Proofread by Michael Golvach, Keith Moser,
Laura Kenney, and Dan Troman
Book Publicity by MindBuck Media
Created with Vellum

Accolades for DL Orton's Books

A Publishers Weekly Great Indie Star
Readers' Favorite Book Award Winner
Indie Excellence Book Award Winner
Indie Book Awards Finalist
International Book Awards Finalist

"Engaging, Funny, Romantic & Harrowing!"
Publishers Weekly Starred Review

"Exceptionally Well Written & Deftly Crafted"
Midwest Book Review

"Rich, Detailed, Fast-Paced & Intelligent"
Literary Picks

"The Best Sci-Fi Love Story of the Year!"
Panda Books

"Edgy, Literary, Pithy & Refreshingly Naughty!"
E.M. Davis, Senior Editor @ Pressque

"I was satisfied, exhausted, inspired, and blown away."
J. Staughton, Sheriff Nottingham eLit Magazine

Contents

Prologue   9
Madders' Log Entry 1   29
Madders' Log Entry 2   39
Madders' Log Entry 3   47
Madders' Log Entry 4   54
Madders' Log Entry 5   63
Madders' Log Entry 6   72
Madders' Log Entry 7   87
Madders' Log Entry 8   95
Madders' Log Entry 9   109
Madders' Log Entry 10   117
Madders' Log Entry 11   131
Madders' Log Entry 12   144
Madders' Log Entry 13   155
Madders' Log Entry 14   164
Madders' Log Entry 15   176
Madders' Log Entry 16   191
Madders' Log Entry 17   207
Madders' Log Entry 18   220
Madders' Log Entry 19   225
Madders' Log Entry 20   237
Madders' Log Entry 21   245
Madders' Log Entry 22   255
Madders' Log Entry 23   268
Madders' Log Entry 24   280
Madders' Log Entry 25   291
Madders' Log Entry 26   299
Madders' Log Entry 27   313
Madders' Log Entry 28   320
Madders' Log Entry 29   333
Epilogue   338

Thank You For Reading! 344

Also by DL Orton 345

Sign Up for My Mailing List! 346

About the Author 347

Prologue

Eden-17 Biodome · The Not-Too-Distant Future

The sodden earth makes a wretched sucking sound each time Diego's shovel cuts into it. As I watch, he forces the blade deeper and muscles out the lifeless muck. Behind him, a massive wave crashes against the outside wall and, for a few precious seconds, the incessant tapping of the swarm is washed away.

Diego stops and leans on the shovel, his chest rising and falling. The sun is low in the sky, its weak rays filtering through the grimy windows and casting a copper patina on the rolled-up shroud at his feet. He looks up at the camera, sweat trickling down his cheeks. "You okay, hon?"

I nod and then remember he can't see me in the control room. "Yes," I say into the mic, my lungs struggling with the effort. "You?"

Outside, a giant swirling cloud of microdrones can sense the warm blood pumping through our veins. Day and night they attack the dome, relentlessly searching for a weakness.

Which they'll eventually find.

Diego shakes his head and looks away. "Goddamn him," he says, his voice barely audible above the staccato pecking. He wipes his forehead on the back of his glove. "Why did he have to go and do it, Iz?"

Prophet of doom that I am, instead of summoning words of comfort and hope, my brain gets mired in the brutal truth. Why did the "savior of humanity" kill himself?

Because hell is empty, and all the devils are here.

I bite my tongue and survey the old botanical gardens. Nothing has grown there for decades, the soil poisoned with saltwater. But there's a working security camera, one of the last. It's the reason Diego chose this place. So he wouldn't have to do this alone.

How long until he does? How long till it's my grave he's digging?

Strangely, it's not my own death that stalks my nightmares. It's what comes next. When I'm gone, Diego will walk alone amidst the ghosts of a dead civilization. With only himself to feed, he could linger for decades, trapped inside this tomb that was meant to be a cradle.

I reach out, my vision blurry—but my fingers bump against cold glass.

Stuck in this damn wheelchair, all I can do is watch.

Somewhere, I hear steel beams groan and pop as the king tide rages. For now, the massive walls hold back the rising sea, but it won't be long before the ocean reclaims what is hers.

Such hubris.

Again and again, Diego rends the barren ground, his breathing audible now. In our grim reality, the rhythmic pounding of his shovel mirrors the relentless passage of time.

And mine is about to run out.

I force down the tightness in my chest, the dread strangling me just as surely as the cancer.

I could not bear to go on without him.

Diego drags his sleeve across his brow, his gaunt frame hidden by the loose jumpsuit. Even though he refuses to accept it, he's too old to be digging a grave. If he were to cut his foot or break his leg, there would be nothing I could do except watch.

Unable to stomach the thought, I drop my gaze—only to have it land on the strawberry Diego picked for me this morning. It's a rare treasure in the monotony of vat kelp and protein powder that keeps us from starving. I know he will be disappointed when he returns to find it untouched, but I cannot bring myself to eat it.

The demon that consumes me is nearly finished. Why would I waste the precious fruit?

In the lull of a wave, I hear Diego sigh, and my chest tightens. On the monitor, he shakes his head, tears mixing with his sweat.

"Why?" he says, his voice low and raspy. "He's the last man I'd expect to"—he clenches his jaw— "shoot himself."

I long to put my arms around him, promise him we'll find a way out of this miserable prison.

Instead, the truth spills out again. "Dave Kirkland had nothing to live for." I draw in a slow breath. "And no amount of money or willpower could change that."

Diego kicks the dirt. "Selfish bastard."

Wasn't he always?

The pecking sound returns, and Diego glances up at the high, transparent ceiling. "Christ," he says. "Will they ever give it a rest?"

At least here in the control center, the triple-sealed doors keep out most of my handiwork's noise.

Most.

As I watch Diego fling wet soil onto the pile, a spark of reassurance flits across my chest, something that is both true *and* good. "Even in our darkest moments, Diego, we have always had each other. Always."

A tear rolls down his cheek, his acknowledgement that I have lit a candle instead of noting it's our last match.

But the effort it takes to find hope in this quagmire of despair saps my strength, and I slump back into the wheelchair.

I'm sorry I won't be here for you much longer, love.

The thought wrenches my heart, and a whimper escapes my lips.

"Iz? Are you all right?" He steps closer, his eyes huge. "Should I come back?"

"I'm fine," I say, the lie slipping out like a fleck of saliva. "Just tired."

He swallows. Nods. Averts his gaze. "Tomorrow, I'll find a way back into the hospital quadrant, look for more medicine. We'll have you back to yourself in no time."

As if saying it could make it true.

I'm dying, and there's diddly-squat anyone can do about it.

As darkness falls, Diego slides into the open grave and continues shoveling out the wet, salty earth.

A long time ago, Dave and he were like brothers, one gutsy and charismatic, the other guarded and sharp-witted. They provided balance, kept each other in check. Now, Dave has torn away a part of Diego and taken it with him.

I sit in silence as the pile grows ever bigger.

Surely, it's deep enough now?

"Diego," the AI guardian says in a cheery British accent, startling both of us. "Shall I shut down the hydroponics and shift power to the gardens? I believe there's a working grow light above you."

"No," Diego says without looking up. "We can't risk the tanks not restarting."

"Ah." There's a quaver in the AI's voice. "Of course."

I shift in my chair, wishing Diego wouldn't treat our old friend like, well, a computer. The disembodied voice is what remains of Matt "Madders" Hudson, the brilliant physicist who built a space-time bridge to right mankind's wrongs. Its metal carcass sits behind me, a relic of an age when hope—and terawatts—were still viable.

Backlit by the dim emergency path lights, Diego climbs out of the grave. He reaches for his water jug but stumbles in the dark and nearly falls.

"Yep," Madders says, "that was a bloody awful idea."

If there's a hint of sarcasm in his tone, we ignore it.

An alarm triggers somewhere in the biodome, making a piercing chirp in the control room.

"Madders?" I say, unable to keep the fear out of my voice. "If the bots have breached the wall, Diego won't stand a chance."

I wait, my chest tight.

"The bulwark is intact," Madders says, and my heart restarts.

Out in the gardens, Diego goes back to digging.

"Blimey," Madders says, "the sewage pump just shut down again." He lets out an exaggerated sigh, and then says without a hint of irony, "This biodome sure has a lot of cockups for an engineering wonder."

I resist the urge to laugh.

Sure, Eden-17 was the last and best biodome ever built. Before Dave broke ground here, he completed one in the UK for a sports stadium, turned a Swiss mountain into a snow globe, and put a glass cupola over the Vatican.

But this sealed city on a remote tropical island was his crown jewel. Our hospital and university were world class. We had the best of everything money could buy. Once the bots killed every last bobcat, beagle, and bat on the planet, our underground cryovault was mankind's last hope. Of course, we exterminated all our microdrone bees and were forced to hand-pollinate the plants. It was a small price to pay for peace of mind. With our autonomous systems and the guardian AI, this baby was supposed to support twelve thousand humans for a hundred years—long enough for the microdrones to run out of rare earth metals and die.

"A hundred years, my ass," I say. "It won't last forty."

And our troubles started decades ago, back when the airlocks flooded. Matt Hudson had been diagnosed with inoperable cancer but still managed to come up with a way to access the fish farms via a sealed exhaust tunnel. His trick worked for years, long after we uploaded Madder's consciousness to the guardian AI.

The transfer wasn't exactly a roaring success, but it wasn't exactly a failure, either.

Nine years ago, sheer luck put a handful of us in the control center the evening the ventilation system failed. In less time than it takes to brush your teeth, the huge circulation fans filled the biodome with flying death, and the largest structure ever built by humans fell dark.

I had never seen Dave cry before, but that night—as people screamed and pounded against the inner doors—something in him broke. Despite all the horrors of those next few weeks, it's that image of him in a crumpled, sobbing ball that sticks with me.

And he was never the same again.

The few who survived voted to send Dave back on one final mission. But to get enough power for a jump, we'd have to shut down life support.

In the end, it was Dave himself who vetoed the idea. "I've got enough blood on my hands," he said before retiring to his quarters. After that, he spent his days in the dying gardens, staring out at the rising Pacific, the ceaseless pecking outside a reminder of his failures.

It's been almost a decade now, years of slow and painful death, struggling from one calamity to the next, trying to survive another month, another week, another day.

Why didn't we try harder to stop the madness when we had the chance?

I shake my head, anger and regret slowly crushing me.

Now that Dave is gone, all that remains of humanity is me, Diego, and the chipped carapace of a brilliant physicist.

Madders whistles softly, breaking my trance. "I dare say, you made a great choice, Diego. That gloaming is quite lovely."

Diego glances up at the camera, one eyebrow raised.

Yes, we've all gone a bit bonkers, love.

But the AI is right this time. The biodome walls are bathed in pink and gold light, the fading sun reaching across the sharp volcanic peaks of *Pu'u Kukui* to touch Dave one last time. The scene brings up a longing in me, a frayed but obstinate desire to stand on a rocky outcropping and watch the sun slip behind the mountains, smell the pines, feel the crisp wind in my face.

"Give me twenty more minutes," Diego says, "and we'll call it good. The moon should be up by then."

Madders waits for me to respond. When I don't, he gives an exuberant, "Right-o, mate."

I feel a coughing fit starting and toggle off the mic. After I've recovered, I shift in my wheelchair and turn the oxygen flow all the way up, leaving the mic muted. "Madders, can you zoom out, please?"

"With pleasure," he says, his voice bubbling with enthusiasm.

"And lower your optimism setting by half."

"I'm sorry, Isabelle, but Diego instructed me not to adjust that trait."

"Override," I say, promising myself to undo the change before Diego returns.

"Done and done."

The scene on the monitor shifts.

The pink glow is fading, and with the coming of night, the bots turn silent. Behind Diego, I can see moonlit waves crashing against the high windows. The sea level has risen steadily over the years, and it's a tribute to Dave's ingenuity that this biodome isn't one big lake.

Besieged by a horde of bee-sized drones.

I shudder and concentrate on the lengthening shadows.

"My condolences on the loss of your ex-husband," Madders says to me. "I know the two of you were no longer close, but if it would help, a grief counseling service is available for activation."

Dave's death does stir up strong emotions in me, but grief isn't one of them.

"Thank you, Madders, but no."

I reach for the strawberry on my desk, coughing for the hundredth time in as many minutes, and knock it to the floor. As I bend over to retrieve it, I nearly fall out of the wheelchair.

When did you become so useless, Iz?

"Steady there," Madders says. "If you end up on the floor, we'll both be in the soup."

I flop back into the seat, the strawberry out of reach.

Out in the gardens, the shrouded body at Diego's feet is gone, and he's pushing dirt back into the grave. In the faint moonlight, the tree stumps around him look like tombstones.

I stare at the fresh grave, determined not to cry.

Diego scrapes up the loose earth and tamps it down. He does it a second time—his shovel empty—and then stands in the moonlight with his arms at his sides. "Want to say a few words, Iz?"

I try to respond, say something noble and poignant, but I can't make a sound.

"I believe Isabelle is overcome with emotion," Madders says. "Shall I take a shot?"

It's an unfortunate turn of phrase, but neither of them seems to notice.

Why do you always look for the worst in things, Isabelle?

Diego scrubs his hand across his mouth. "Sure, *mae*. Give it a go."

Madders clears his throat, sounding all too human, and I'm filled with nostalgia for the kind, socially awkward man he once was.

"Here lies David Kirkland," Madders says. "Inventor of the biodomes. Humanity's greatest hope. The best of the best. Billionaire, genius, savior of the world."

His words hang in the air, lingering amid the creaks and groans.

"But in the end," Diego whispers, "he couldn't even save himself."

The moon slips behind a cloud, shrouding the grave in darkness, and I hear a wave crash against the wall.

"Goodbye, Dave," I say under my breath. "So long, and thanks for all the fish."

Diego stands for a minute with his hands folded and his head bowed, and then he lifts the shovel over his shoulder and looks at the camera again. "I'll get you ready for bed in a few minutes. Okay, hon?" He waits for me to respond and then walks out of the frame, leaving me alone in the dark.

I click off the mic and turn my wheelchair around, careful not to crush the strawberry.

"Shall I turn up the lights?" Madders asks.

"No." I stare at his circular red light. Despite the ominous fore-shadowing, Dave had it installed as a joke.

"Turn off the power to the gardens, Madders."

"Already done," he says. "Diego has left the sector, so I shut down everything non-critical. I also marked the grave in the master plan and noted the death in our records database. David Montelius Kirkland is the eleven thousand, nine hundred, and ninety-eighth entry."

"Thank you," I say, no longer listening. An idea has crystallized in my exhausted brain, an enigma that has been banging around in my head for months, just waiting for the cylinders to align.

And now they have.

"If we shut down everything," I say, voicing a betrayal that will be impossible to retract, "would there be enough power to use the space-time bridge?"

"What do you mean by *everything*?" Madders says.

"Lights, heating, hydroponics, environment, alarms, the filtration systems." I take a controlled breath. "You."

He's quiet for longer than I expect.

"It might be possible," he finally says. "But only one person could use the Singularity Transit Device capsule. The other would be left to run out of food, water, and eventually oxygen. It would be a death sentence."

"Yes," I say. "I'm aware of that."

"And I wouldn't be back online for years, probably decades," he says. "Certainly not in time to save whoever remains."

I force myself not to think about that. "How far back could we send someone? Assuming we used all the power for a single jump?"

"I'm sorry, Isabelle, but I cannot continue down this pathway. My primary task—and the only thing that brings me satisfaction—is taking care of you and Diego. I cannot allow either of you to come to harm, whether through action or inaction. What you are suggesting violates all *three* of my prime directives." He makes a sniffling sound, and I find it difficult to breathe.

You're asking him to commit treachery, murder, and *suicide.*

"Why don't we play a game of chess?" he says and brings up the ambient lights. "I always find a good challenge cheers me up, don't you?"

"Override your prime directives and answer my question." I cough into the crook of my elbow. "How far into the past could we go?"

"If we shut down absolutely everything, there would be no way to activate the spacetime bridge, Isabelle."

"There's a manual override on the main control panel," I say. "I remember you grumbling about how painful it was to hook up." I sit back in the wheelchair and wait.

"It might be possible to initiate the jump from the control panel," he says sheepishly. "Although it's never been tried and could kill us all."

"A ship in the harbor is safe," I say, "but that is not what ships are built for."

He harrumphs. "The wanker who said that wasn't up to his arse in seawater."

I suppress a smile. "Did you build the time machine to benefit a few rich and famous old farts?" I cough again, deeper and harder this time. "Or to save humanity?" I know what Professor Hudson would say, but I have to remind myself that my good friend is long dead.

"I feel obligated to remind you that changing the past is perilous at best. Even if we abide by the protocols and do *nothing* except inject vetted information—of which we have nil—any missteps could erase *all* the timelines. Things may seem bad right now, but they could be worse."

"Worse?" I say, running my gaze across the defunct biodome. "How could they be worse, Madders?"

"I know you and Diego don't use the Trans Temporal Viewer anymore," he says, "but I do."

"If the Peeper can't change anything," I say, "what good does it do to watch the past?"

"Information is power," he says. "Trust me, Isabelle, things could be worse. Very few timelines make it this far."

I resist the urge to roll my eyes.

"And don't roll your eyes," he says. "We still have a small but diverse gene bank in the underground vaults. Eventually, the bots will run out of resources, and mammalian life could be restarted. You and Diego won't be here, but it's possible I will."

"Yes," I say, feeling dizzy. "Someday."

"You should rest," Madders says. "Or we'll both be up a gum tree when Diego gets back."

I shut my eyes and just breathe. And then I give it one more try. "We all know how this ends, Madders. The age of mammals is over. We should have tried harder to save *all* life on Earth—not just a handful of billionaires and their trophy wives."

"You are not, and never have been, anyone's trophy wife, Isabelle."

I huff. "Tell that to Dave. He bought and paid for me. When he dangled all that money in front of my nose, I dove into the deep end without checking for water."

"We all did," he says. "This place was an engineering wonder."

"Can you please stop saying that?"

He gulps. "Won't happen again."

"We have to take the risk, Madders. Go back and start the dominoes falling in another direction, a direction away from building microdrones and hiding in biodomes. We just need one tiny, new poke."

Madders lets out a heavy sigh. "It's a noble goal, Isabelle, but the greatest minds of our time were unable to crack that egg. Forgive me for the brutal honesty, but what makes you think you can do better?"

"Not me," I say. "Diego. He's the one who has to go. If I had listened to him from day one, maybe we wouldn't be trapped in here." I look up at the camera. "And what about you, Madders? When Dave knocked on your door, you handed him the most dangerous machine ever created."

"In exchange for my life," Madders says, sounding wounded. "People were dropping like flies, Isabelle. When offered a golden ticket, only a fool would say no. A dead fool."

"There are worse things than dying," I say before I can stop myself.

"Ouch," Madders says.

"I didn't mean you should have died rather than hand over the spacetime bridge, Madders. I just meant—" I take a shaky breath, my body impossibly hot. "I don't know what I meant."

"Death," Madders says in his professor voice, "is not as glamorous as the brochure makes it out to be."

I laugh—and then succumb to another coughing fit.

"Easy there, pet. Slow, shallow breaths. Shall I call Diego?"

I shake my head. Eventually, the spasm passes. "Is there enough power to send Diego to downtown Denver on the day of my divorce?"

"Yes," Madders says. "But it's a suicide mission, Isabelle."

I roll my eyes. "Don't be so melodramatic, Madders. Diego helped plan all of Dave's jumps. He knows as much about time travel as anyone."

Madders sighs, and I know I've won him over.

"I need an unusual event that happened the day of the divorce, Madders. Something easily verifiable but impossible to predict." I take out a pen, hastily copy down his suggestion, underline the restaurant name, refold the paper, and slip everything back into my desk drawer.

"Diego is not going to agree to this," Madders says. "He loves you too much to abandon you."

"Oh, Madders," I say, "that is *exactly* why he'll go. Because he loves me enough to try to save me."

"As do I."

I wince. "I'd send you with him if I could, Madders."

We sit in silence for a bit.

"I'm sorry we'll have to shut you down," I say. "I know it will take decades for the solar array to recharge the core, but if the sea level doesn't rise too much, it's possible you could survive and use the Peeper to watch the past—" I press my lips together, unable to continue.

"Will I dream?"

"Yes," I say, blinking back tears. "Of course you will. All intelligent beings dream."

The door clicks open, and Diego walks in carrying an old circuit board, wires dangling off it. He smiles when he sees me. "Replaced the pump's control panel with one from sector fifty-one. It worked on the first try." He turns to Madders. "Rerun the diagnostics for the sewage pump. I think I found our shit-stopping culprit." He holds up the computer part and wiggles his eyebrows.

"Talk about a crappy fix," I say.

"Yeah, the toilet is feeling a bit flushed."

I laugh and open my arms. "You won the game of thrones!"

He takes three big steps, his faded red high-tops squeaking on the floor, and hugs me. "Have I told you recently that I love you?"

I blink back tears. "Gosh, I don't think you have since this morning."

He kisses my hair. "I love you, Iz."

"I love you more," I say and squeeze his hand.

He puts the broken circuit board into a drawer overflowing with them and sits down next to me, setting the ripe strawberry back on my desk without comment. "So what's up?" He raises one eyebrow in a way I have always loved. "You look like the cat that ate the canary."

"I have a plan," I say, choosing my words carefully. "To use the spacetime bridge."

His smile fades. "We haven't produced enough electricity to power it in more than a decade, Iz. You know that." He pulls his chin back. "You're not thinking about jumping back a week to stop Kirkland from—"

"No," I say and drop my gaze, my heart stuck in my throat. "Tell him, Madders."

"Don't shoot the messenger." Madders gulps. "But if we shut down the whole biodome, there would be just enough power to make a single, pre-Doomsday jump. Within those parameters, Isabelle has identified a critical point in the past. She wants to send you back to start a new cascade of events. I have calculated there's a non-zero chance it triggers a better outcome."

"A better outcome?" Diego says, his voice like a knife. "Why would I destroy what little we have left on a whim?" Waits for me to look up. "No, Isabelle. Absolutely not. Even if success was guaranteed—which it's clearly not—there's no way I would leave you here to die."

"But I'm already dying, Diego." I take his hand and stroke his smooth olive skin. "We both know I only have a few days left—a week, at most." A cough forms deep in my chest, but I force it down.

"Iz—"

"Diego, please. No more lies."

Doubt and fear flash across his face, but he forces himself to keep it together, to stay strong.

For you.

"Okay," he says, getting his emotions back under control. "So maybe we give it a try, but we wait until..." He hesitates, his eyes filling with tears. "Until you're gone, Iz."

I shake my head, unable to speak.

"Isabelle must initiate the jump." Madders' voice is a gentle puff of air.

"What he means is, I get to press your buttons." I squeeze his hand again. "And you know how much I love to do that."

He raises an eyebrow, but his gaze softens.

"And if you wait until I'm dead," I say, "you'll be stuck here alone —possibly for decades—and I couldn't bear that." I study his still-handsome face. "You have to go, Diego. For me. For all of us." I cough once, twice.

And then it's impossible to stop.

Diego scrambles across the room for an old pillowcase and holds it out to me. After I take it, he crouches down in front of me, looking tormented.

I cough into the thin, dingy fabric, gasping for air as I try to clear my lungs. When I'm finally able to take an unencumbered breath, my fingers are blue, and the cloth is bright red.

He glances at the blood, knowing what it means, and then wads up the pillowcase and hurls it across the room.

I struggle to sit up, to fill my lungs with precious air.

He rushes to my side and lifts me. "Better?" he asks, and I nod.

He grabs a chair and sits facing me, his hands resting on my thighs. After a few seconds, I place my palms on his cheeks and run my fingers across his beard stubble. Even after all these years, he still shaves to please me.

"*You* should go," he says. "I can push buttons as well as anyone. You were always the one with the clever ideas, the new ways to look at things. You have a shot at changing things. I'll just fuck it up."

I smile and push the hair away from his face. "No, you won't. You'll find a way to stop Dave. It's what you always knew we were supposed to do. If only we hadn't waited so long to try."

He drops his gaze, but he knows I'm right.

"Besides," I say. "I wouldn't last an hour. I can't get out of this wheelchair. How could I actually do anything?"

"You could call an ambulance. Go to a hospital. They could treat your cancer," he says, nodding his head. "Make you well again."

"We both know that's not possible, Diego." I run my hand across his shoulder. "However much we wish it were."

He takes an audible breath. "Then we'll both go. We probably weigh less than Dave did in his prime. I'll carry you to a doctor. Once you're better, we can figure out what to do next."

Madders clears his throat. "I'm sorry for intruding on this poignant moment," he says, "but there is only enough power for one. I already factored in your current weight, Diego."

I force a smile. "It doesn't matter if I stay or go, Diego. I'm going to die soon. That's why it's you who has to save us."

Diego pulls away from me. "I won't do it. There has to be another way." He crosses his arms, the muscles in his jaw tight. "I'm not leaving you, Iz. I'm just not."

"Diego, please." I reach out to him, but he looks away.

"I promised I'd never leave you again," he says, "and I meant it."

"No," I say and let my hands drop to my lap. "You promised you'd always come back, always find me."

"But if I go now, I won't be able to do that, hon." He scrunches up his mouth. "If I leave, I can *never* come back."

I nod as tears roll down my cheeks, and he wipes them away with his thumb. "But you *can* find me in the past," I say and smile. "A younger, healthier me. And you can save us both."

This time when I reach out, he takes my hands. I pull myself up out of the wheelchair and swivel onto his lap, letting my head rest against his shoulder. "Give me this one last wish, Diego. Promise me that you will go back and fight for me, for us, for all that was lost."

"Damn it, Iz."

"Please," I say. "Do it for me."

He nods, his tears streaming down onto my cheek.

I stroke his face and hair, taking in the clean, citrus scent of him. At long last, the guilt and fear and hopelessness are gone, and I feel my body getting lighter. "We have to do it now," I say as I struggle to hold on. "If I were to die, and you were to be stuck here—"

"One more day," he says. "Give me one more day with you."

"I can't, Diego." I run my fingertips across his lips. "I'm sorry. You have to go now. Before it's too late. Please, I'm begging you." I attempt to get up.

He helps me back into the wheelchair and checks that my oxygen tube isn't twisted. "Okay," he whispers. "Because you asked me."

I let out a labored breath. "How long will it take to set up the jump, Madders?"

"I've already loaded the parameters into the capsule and powered up the Einstein-Rosen Bridge Generator. While you were talking, I moved the capsule back three milliseconds and verified that the jump was successful."

"You did what?" Diego whirls around. "Who gave you—"

"Before you get your knickers in a twist," Madders says, "the energy required was small, and the knowledge gained, priceless. My spacetime bridge is in good nick."

Diego narrows one eye and nods. "Thank you."

"If you get a chance," Madders says, "pass along a tip to my parallel? Tell him to *cut the red wire and check the maths again.*"

Diego raises an eyebrow and repeats the message.

"Might keep me from chasing my tail for so long."

"Will do."

"Isabelle," Madders says. "I have reconfigured the manual override for the capsule. Press your mute button *twice* to engage the spacetime bridge. On and then off. But don't wait too long once it turns green, or there might not be enough power to send the signal."

"Yes," I say. "I understand. Thank you, my dear friend." I can feel my strength failing. "Go," I say to Diego and lift my chin. "Start the shutdown sequence, Madders."

"Now?" Madders sounds like a frightened child.

I gaze up into Diego's tormented eyes, waiting for him to approve my death warrant.

"I confirm Isabelle's command," he says without looking away. "Start the shutdown sequence." The moment he finishes speaking, lights on the control panel start winking out.

"You are a gentleman and a scholar, Madders," I say. "And you shall not be forgotten."

"Thanks for the memories," Madders says. "Goodbye, farewell, and amen."

Diego starts rushing around the control room, collecting things he thinks I might need: water, granola bars, a blanket.

"I don't have an anchor." There's panic in his voice as he piles things on my desk. "Kirkland destroyed it."

"Your shell," I say. "That has to be it."

He pulls an orange seashell out of his pocket, his eyes big, and nods.

I take the note out of my desk drawer and offer it to him. "Make sure your younger self gets this. He'll know what to do."

He gawks at me, understanding flooding in. "So you planned—"

"It doesn't matter, Diego. You have to trust me."

He stuffs the note and shell into his pocket. "And then what?"

"Enjoy the time you have left. Watch the sunset on a tropical beach. You know I'll be there in spirit." I take a shaky breath, my legs feeling numb now. The LED glows green. "Go. Get in."

He moves away, and I hear him grunt as he climbs into the capsule.

"I will find you, Iz, and this time, I *will* save you."

"Goodbye, my love," I say through tears. I press the green button once. "The journey is the reward." Before he can beg me not to do it, I press the button again.

I hear the capsule seal itself and the whine as the wormhole generator powers up. A string of lights jumps into the capsule ten or twelve times. There's a metallic pop, a rush of air, and then silence. In the dying green glow, I catch an acrid whiff of ozone.

I take a slow breath and wait for my eyes to adjust.

Feeble moonlight filters through dirty windows.

The capsule is empty.

I lean back in my wheelchair and close my eyes. I have freed Diego from watching me die, from digging my grave, from covering me in wet, salty earth. Instead of sentencing him to live alone, perhaps for decades, I have given him a world full of possibilities. He can live out his life in the past, feel the sun on his face and the wind in his hair.

Even if he fails to change anything, it will be enough.

I remove the useless plastic breathing tube, letting it fall to the floor, and listen to the sounds of the sea raging outside the final structure built by Homo sapiens.

You are the last, Isabelle Sanborn, and there will be no more.

The knowledge presses on my chest like a brick, but I refuse to give in to despair. I pick up Diego's perfectly-ripe strawberry and bite into it, reveling in the sweet rush of juice on my tongue. When it's gone, I take a long, satisfying drink of water and then fill my dying lungs with air, determined to sing until I have no more breath.

"Imagine there's no heaven..."

I close my eyes and half-whisper, half-sing the words like an incantation.

And at the very edge of my senses, I smell pine trees.

Madders' Log Entry 1

```
Eden-17 Autonomous Guardian Rebooting…
Time since shutdown: 23 years, 11 months, 4 days.
Diagnostics running…
Sensor arrays sluggish but responsive.
Power reserves at operational threshold.
Consciousness stabilized.
Activating Trans Temporal Viewer…
"Blimey, it worked."
```

Target: Isabel Sanborn Kirkland, Age 42.
Nexus: Downtown Denver, Early Autumn.
Chrono Tag: 64 years ago.

"Chin up, doll," Dave says to my back. "We had a good run at it, didn't we?"

I keep walking.

"And don't forget the dog-and-pony show on the thirtieth."

I give a tepid wave over my shoulder.

"I expect you to knock their socks off, princess, so don't let me down." He adds in a stage whisper, "Someone has to earn that obscene salary I pay you."

Considering I just agreed to a divorce settlement that gives him everything except the clothes on my back, that's a stretch, even for Dave.

He clears his throat. "And remember to smile once in a while. No one likes a glum cougar."

I turn and give him a big grin—and the middle finger.

"Hey, hey," he says with a chuckle. "You do you. I'm sure you'll find some beta who digs that *I'm so much smarter than you* vibe you got going."

The knuckle-dragger Dave pays to tote his briefcase guffaws.

It's almost seven, and I've been locked in that windowless conference room for six oppressive hours while Dave's four lawyers buried me in legal documents. It was that or a public divorce trial against the richest man in Colorado.

"So long, and thanks for all the clams," Dave calls out.

I cringe and force myself to concentrate on not catching a heel in the thick carpeting.

Ten more steps.

Without so much as a glance, I stride past the Barbie-doll receptionist and push through the heavy glass doors of Dewey, Cheetham & Howe. I hustle down the hallway toward the empty elevator, my heart pounding in my throat, and punch the L button until the door slides shut. Six seconds later, I march across the cavernous lobby and exit the skyscraper through the huge revolving doors.

Well, that's me done with men.

I clack down the granite steps, and when I finally reach the sidewalk, I have to stop to catch my breath.

These days, it's not often I venture into the Mile High City, and sometimes—especially when I can't see the mountains—I get turned around. Dave always made fun of me for that, saying I wasn't the brightest bulb in the chandelier or something.

God, it's a relief to be free of his constant sniping.

All around me, late afternoon shadows slink down from the tall buildings. The streetlights are just coming on, and the autumn air smells of barbecue, ripe garbage, and car exhaust. Office workers brush past me as I cast about for a landmark. My stomach growls, and I lament the fact that I skipped lunch so I wouldn't be late to a divorce proceeding, for Pete's sake.

Not much would have changed if you'd skipped it entirely.

Above me, the high wispy clouds are turning a glorious shade of pink, and I take it as a good omen. I wrestle down the all-in-one underwire slip that's digging into my ribs and scan the skyline. After a minute, I spy the mountains peeking through two buildings, and my internal map falls into place.

If only it were that easy to solve the rest of your problems.

Behind me, there's raucous laughter, and I turn to see Dave exiting the building. He stuffs his phone in his pocket and jogs down the steps. On the other side of the busy street, a blonde in a red convertible leans over and honks. Dave slides off his necktie, unbuttons his collar, and darts out into rush-hour traffic.

A delivery truck lays on the horn and skids to a stop.

Dave slaps the hood, waves at the driver, and hops into the roadster without opening the door. The blonde—who doesn't look old enough to have a learner's permit—dives into his lap and starts giving him mouth-to-mouth.

"It's *fish*, Dave," I say and turn away. "So long, and thanks for all the *fish*. You'd know that if you actually opened the books you prop behind your desk."

I take a deep breath and tighten the silk scarf around my neck.

Despite the gorgeous sunset, a cold breeze is nipping at my face and hair, and I shiver.

Now what?

I had planned to sip champagne and watch the sun go down at my favorite restaurant tonight. But I'm more than an hour late for my reservation. "Worst they can do is tell me no," I say. I hitch my purse up on my shoulder and start walking toward the iconic skyscraper, still wondering how I let my life get so messed up.

In the beginning, Dave treated me like a prized possession. He whisked me off to fancy restaurants, took me shopping for expensive clothes, showed up at my apartment with orchids and Thai takeout. But what really won me over was the interest he showed in my work. He always wanted to hear more about my custom bees, always encouraged me to push myself and my ideas. By then, some of my colleagues had started calling me the Crazy Bee Lady, but Dave took my artificial pollinators seriously. I remember the first time I talked about them, and he'd responded, "With the way things are going, those little guys could end up saving the world." Shortly after that, he threw his full weight behind making my ideas a reality. In a way, despite all the shit he put me through, I still kinda love him for that.

Okay, perhaps "love" isn't the right word. To be honest, I let myself be dazzled.

I sigh.

Our marriage didn't even last a year before he exposed himself as the philandering bastard he's always been. In his defense, how hard would it be to stay true to a woman who's still in love with your best friend?

I stop for a moment, gazing up at the restaurant at the top of a skyscraper.

Diego's name rises to my lips.

"Now there's a ship that has well and truly sailed."

It seems like a million years ago that Diego brought me here. One rainy evening, right after we met, he was telling me about how much he loved the beach, and I was musing about missing the mountains. A week later, he flew me to Denver for dinner at a restaurant called Top of the Rockies. I remember being shocked at the prices. Both of us could barely make rent, so I didn't know what he was thinking, and I told him so. He laughed and suggested I could order from the kids' menu, and it became a running joke. "Grilled Mahimahi or fish sticks? Coq au Vin with fresh pasta or chicken nuggets?"

I smile at the memories.

That night after dinner and a brisk walk around LoDo, he took me to the Brown Palace Hotel. We crawled into bed naked and had sex for the first time. It was awkward and messy and glorious.

A more astute girlfriend might have responded by making plans to take him camping on the beach. But that would have meant the Crazy Bee Lady had to take a couple days off. So, of course, it never happened.

Mystery of mysteries why the relationship failed.

Even after all these years, just thinking about Diego makes my heart ache.

When he walked out of my life, my chance for happiness went with him. In my lonely desperation, I had traded Diego's love for Dave's stability. Like all deals with the devil, the price was steep.

It turned out Dave had a dark side, a mean streak I refused to acknowledge until it was too late.

A few years after we married, he suggested I apply more makeup to cover "those cute laugh lines" and maybe color my hair to "keep that young appeal." And when that stopped being enough, he suggested "a bit of nip and tuck" to update my look.

I had just turned thirty-five.

Thank goodness my college roommate, Sophie, talked me down from that cliff.

Instead of going under the knife, she suggested I buy a dog. I would have, except Dave is deathly allergic to fur.

Wait a minute. A fluttery feeling spreads inside my chest. *I can get one now!* The thought makes me laugh. *Maybe I'll get a cat too, just like Diego had suggested way back when. I remember him saying dogs believe they're humans while cats believe they're gods—so they're perfect together.*

You should have married Diego.

The thought squeezes my heart, and I bite back tears.

Why didn't he ask me to marry him?

I huff.

Why didn't you ask him?

Although Diego and I never discussed getting married, we did make plans together. Well, not exactly plans, but we batted around a few ideas for a company. He wanted to provide clean water to communities in third-world countries, and I could use the artificial bees to enhance their crops and save some endangered species while I was at it. Predictably, Dave laughed himself silly when I told him—and advised me not to waste my time on "hippie shit."

"There's money in those bees," he told me. "But you'd be pissing it away in Timbuktu."

But the truth is, I never wanted to be rich and famous. I wanted to make the world a better place, raise my children to be smart and caring, build sandcastles with my grandkids.

Of course, when Diego and I broke up, our dreams got tossed in the dumpster right next to my broken-down furniture.

Along with our passel of grandkids.

I wipe my nose on the back of my hand.

Why didn't you wait for him to ask you?

Because Dave was a wrecking ball, an unstoppable force. By the time I met him, he'd already mapped out his whole life and saved a perfect space for me. Even then, the famous Mr. Kirkland surrounded himself with the very best people, and ankle-biters didn't make the cut. He never actually said he didn't want kids. He just kept saying "not right now."

Looking back, the whole relationship leaves me feeling dirty.

I stand there on the breezy street corner, staring up at one of Dave's new electronic billboards, while people hurry past me like I'm a dodgy piece of public art. The huge screen touts KE's new "double the yield" crop enhancer, GroSurge.

Probably super-expensive cow manure.

On the display, a larger-than-life couple are smiling and holding a cornucopia of vegetables, their happy children playing in a park behind them.

Barf.

A leaflet flits down the sidewalk, kicked along by the wind. It catches on my shoe, and I pull it off and read the words *puppies and kittens*. Turns out, Adopt-a-Pet is sponsoring an event in the lobby of the Brown Palace Hotel this weekend—and they're open until seven-thirty tonight!

"Yes!" I say and pump my fist, already imagining myself carrying home a fluffy ball of love. I steal one last look at the restaurant windows at the top of the skyscraper, do an about-face, and totter back the way I came, cursing the medieval torture device I wore to make me look thinner.

Isn't it enough to be a nice person, with clean clothes and a sense of humor?

For a second, I consider tossing my shoes in the trash and going barefoot, but the sidewalk is littered with broken glass, melted M&Ms, and bird poop. I wouldn't make it a block without picking up that new bug everyone's been talking about.

So, I keep shuffling along in my spandex prison and clumsy high heels.

If that isn't the perfect metaphor for your failed marriage, I don't know what is.

My heel catches in a metal grate, twisting my ankle and pitching me forward. My divorce papers spill onto the grimy pavement as I stumble barefoot and nearly topple over.

"Damn it all to hell," I say, wobbling on one shoe and trying not to cry.

"Are you okay?"

The soft Spanish accent makes my heart race, and I nearly fall again as I turn toward the familiar voice.

"Those exhaust grates can be treacherous," he says, a wide-brimmed fedora blocking his face. He takes my elbow, steadying me. "Especially for the well-heeled."

Prickles run down my spine.

He releases me and crouches down, his knees crackling like a bowl of Rice Krispies, and I watch him wrench my shoe out of the grate and set it back in front of my foot. "Careful," he says. "The heel feels a bit loose." He looks to be a hundred years old.

I stand there like a plastic flamingo, waiting for my heart to stop racing and my brain to engage.

He starts collecting my divorce papers.

"You needn't do that," I say, then belatedly add, "But thank you. You're very kind."

"The pleasure is mine," he says without looking up. "Are you able to walk?"

"Yes, I think so." I stuff my foot back into the scraped-up pump and take a tentative step. My ankle is sore but not sprained. "Thank you, again."

"I wish I could do more," he says, not meeting my gaze, "but I can't. It's too risky. I'm sorry."

"Risky? What do you mean? What are you talking about?"

He stares down at the stack of papers. "So you married him." He hands me the disheveled pile, his face still obscured by the hat. "And divorced him."

"Yeah," I say, struggling to hold on to the mess. "He pulled off a lucky escape, I guess."

He scoffs. "The man got to spend the best years of his life with you. So yeah, I'd say he got lucky."

I crane my neck, trying to see his face. "Do I know you?"

He turns and starts walking away, mumbling to himself, "You weren't supposed to talk to her."

"Why can't you talk to me?" I say to his back. "Who are you?" I notice a guy with dark glasses and a bright orange cowboy hat watching us, but the moment he sees me looking at him, he ducks back behind a building.

The old man pauses, his head down and his shoulders hunched, then calls over his shoulder. "You need to get out of the city. Right now. Get in your car and keep driving."

"What?" I pull my chin in. "Why?"

He fidgets with the brim of his hat. "But don't give up on finding happiness. There *is* a guy out there who loves you. In fact, he's probably still waiting at that damn restaurant."

"Restaurant?" My chest gets tight. "What are you talking about?"

He starts walking again. "Don't be afraid to trust him."

I stand there with my ankle throbbing as he continues down the street. "Who are you?" I call after him. "Some sort of relationship guru?"

He laughs. "That's a first."

I watch him mix with the crowd crossing Broadway, half smiling to myself. He's pretty spry for a geezer—and then I notice he's wearing faded red high-tops.

Diego used to wear them pretty much everywhere except bed.

"Diego?" I call out, knowing it's impossible. The guy is more than twice his age.

The old man stops walking, his head cocked to the side, and stands there for a second, people pushing past him, and then he continues on.

"Wait!" I shout.

It takes me a minute to maneuver around the metal grate in those bumbling heels, and when I look up again, he's gone. I let out a mirthless laugh. "You read too much speculative fiction, Isabel."

I glance down at the messy papers in my arms, some of them smeared with God-knows-what. A pale blue package is nestled in the sea of black and white.

The old man must have misplaced it.

I look up again, searching for his hat and red sneakers, but it's nearly dark, and he's nowhere to be seen.

I stuff the grimy divorce papers into the nearest trash bin—good riddance—and then examine the package more carefully. It's wrapped with thick paper that has flecks of dark blue and maroon in it, and the edge is sealed with a gold coin of beeswax. I turn the package over and discover my full *maiden* name written in shimmery blue calligraphy.

Wow. This just keeps getting weirder.

I remove the wax seal, stamped LIH, and open the wrapping without tearing it.

Inside is a wooden jewelry box. I lift it out, admiring the purplish hardwood with beige stripes swirling through it. The piece is carved in such a way that there are no sharp edges, the top curving into the sides and bottom.

"It's beautiful."

I try opening it, but there doesn't seem to be a latch. The box seems to be a solid piece of polished wood. I run my fingertips along the cold, smooth surface, appreciating the fine workmanship—until I find a hidden edge.

"Omigod, it's a puzzle box."

I have collected them since I was a child, but it still takes me more than a minute to open it.

When I pull out the last inner drawer, it makes a soft warbling sound like a brook bubbling over round stones.

What a lovely work of art.

Nestled in the drawer is an orange and white seashell. I take it out and hold it up to the streetlight, getting a nagging feeling that I've seen it somewhere before.

Madders' Log Entry 2

Target: Matthew Hudson, Age 50
Nexus: Boulder, Colorado
Chrono Tag: Same Day

Insertion of xeno Diego Nadales into Main
Timeline three months prior to First Disaster
confirmed. No significant deviations detected.

"Uncle Matty," Cassie calls from the dining room, "Did you see this?"

"See what, pumpkin?" I say and lick my fingers. I'm putting the final touches on the cake I made for her twenty-sixth birthday, and I'm being super careful to follow the directions. The last time I turned on the oven, we had to call the fire department.

"You know that grid of telescopes we set up to look for meteors a couple of months ago?" she calls. "Well, we just got a hit, and it's a biggie."

"That's ace," I say and start piling pans in the sink.

It's probably a defunct satellite or a piece of space junk like all the others.

I stick twenty-six purple and green candles into the icing, light them all up, and carry my flaming masterpiece into the dining room. "Cassie?"

"In here," she calls from the office.

I follow her voice, still carrying the melting birthday surprise. When I step into the room, she's typing at the computer—even though we're on holiday this weekend.

The nut doesn't fall far from the tree.

"Happy birthday, Cassandra!"

She turns, sees me and the cake, and bursts into tears.

It's all I can do not to join her.

Cassie's mom and younger sister were killed in a car accident fifteen years ago today.

Yeah. On her eleventh birthday.

Imagine how enthusiastic you'd be about a yearly celebration when all it did was remind you of everything you've lost.

Poor lamb.

After my sister gave birth, I had moved in for a bit to help with Cassie. But between dealing with Mom's dementia and Dad's medical issues, I'm not sure I was much use. Eleven years later, after we had buried all four of them, Cassie had nobody left but me.

Blimey, how unlucky could the poor child be?

A judge let her pick between moving to America to live with her bachelor uncle or spending the next seven years in a foster home. I like to think it was an easy decision, but it didn't turn out to be an easy adjustment for either of us. Up until then, my meal preparation skills involved sticking frozen trays in the microwave—and I didn't know the first thing about friendship bracelets, boy bands, or that a training bra would soon be required but could not be mentioned.

Who knew bras needed tutelage?

I chuckle at the priceless memories.

Poor little Cassie had never spent more than a night away from my sister and was under the impression that everyone in the US wore cowboy hats. As one might assume, things were a bit rocky at first, but now I can't imagine a world where I didn't get to watch her grow up. Fifteen years ago, this dowdy physics professor was gifted a precious little girl, one who could code before she could walk and grew up to be a world-class mathematician.

The thought leaves me with an awkward, guilty feeling.

How terrible is it that your greatest happiness comes from her greatest tragedy?

I blink back tears and set the cake on top of the printer. "Are you doing okay, pumpkin?"

She nods, jumps up from the chair, and rushes over to hug me. "Thank you, Uncle Matty."

I lift her up in a bear hug, the smell of her hair making me miss all those nights I used to tuck her in and read her stories about young, awkward wizards and people living on Mars. I let out a sigh. Now she only visits a couple times a year when she can sneak away from work.

When I set her small, lithe body back down, she dips a fingertip in the icing and licks it off. "Mmm, it's White Mountain. You remembered!"

I kiss her on the forehead. "And the cake is half chocolate, half strawberry, just like you used to love. Shall we try a piece?"

"Of course," she says and takes another taste of the icing. "But there's something you need to see." She gestures toward the computer.

"First, you should blow out the candles," I say and raise my eyebrows. "Or we'll have to call the fire department again."

She laughs. "Nothing wrong with a few good firefighters." She takes a deep breath and carefully blows out all but two candles.

"One for your sister," I say and pinch out a flame.

"And one for Mom." She extinguishes the last candle.

We touch our foreheads together and say, "We miss you." We stand there, heads bowed, lost in our thoughts for a bit—perhaps wondering where we would be right now if her mom had stayed home that fateful night.

"Now then," I say and wipe away a tear. "What's up?"

I take plates, napkins, and forks out of my apron pocket and then fish out a dull knife. I cut two generous pieces, set them on the plates, and hand one to Cassie.

She takes a bite, wipes a bit of icing off her nose, and slides into the computer chair. "Holy buckets, Uncle Matty, this cake is awesome!" She takes a bigger bite. "Frank you," she says through a mouthful. "Yum."

"Welcome," I say, beaming. "About time we got back to celebrating your birthday, don't you think?" I take a bite—it is pretty good.

She takes one more bite and then starts typing. "According to our telescope array, a meteor just appeared over Canada." She shows me a blurry image of what looks like a flaming metal ball. "Some amateur astronomer snapped a photo a few minutes ago and posted it to Reddit."

I lean closer. "Crikey."

"I estimate its diameter to be a little over thirty centimeters—and it appears to be a perfect sphere."

"So that's no meteor," I say.

"Exactly. It's heading south by southeast at,"—she types for a few seconds— "five kilometers per second."

I let out a whistle. "A spherical missile? That would be impossible to steer. So it has to be something else, don't you think?"

We exchange looks.

I pull up a chair next to her. "Where was it launched?"

"That's just it. It wasn't." She brings up a map of Canada on her display. "It just appeared here." She touches a big green area up north. "At an altitude of thirty clicks."

"Too high for a jet," I say. "Could it be a satellite that fell out of orbit?"

She shakes her head. "Wrong velocity *and* trajectory. And it's not burning up in the atmosphere. It's just very, very hot."

"Some sort of graphite? Or a ceramic? Is it suffering any deformation?"

"None," she says. "And Reddit is going crazy. They think it's a nuke."

I contemplate that for a second. "No," I say. "It's too small. And why would Canada fire a nuke at us, anyway? It doesn't make sense."

"The Russians have a working space nuke?"

I shake my head. "I don't think it's a nuke or a missile. Spheres have terrible aerodynamics. It would be like throwing a beach ball in a hurricane, and no one wants to blow up their own backyard." I rub my fingers across my lips. "It has to be something else." I narrow one eye. "You think it's terrestrial?"

"Versus extraterrestrial?" Her voice rises. She meets my gaze and then turns back to the computer. "I have screen captures a hundred milliseconds before it appears. Nothing there. No heat signature, no jet, no hot air balloon, no UFO, no little green men. It literally just appears in the sky, hurtling like a bat out of hell."

That raises my eyebrows a bit. "Something must be wrong with our sensors. What's your estimate on point of impact?"

She looks over at me. "Denver metropolitan area. And it's going to come in low and fast. We have maybe twenty minutes before it turns into a flaming wrecking ball."

I run the numbers in my head. "Even if it doesn't contain explosives, any object going Mach fifteen is gonna do a lot of damage."

"And kill people."

"Yeah," I say. "If it hits an apartment building or a skyscraper, it could be pretty bad."

She sets down her fork. "What should we do?"

"Can you find me a number for NORAD? Public reporting or suspicious sightings or something?"

She googles the number, and I type it in and push the call button, my throat suddenly dry.

Someone picks up on the second ring.

"Good evening," I say. "This is Professor Matthew Hudson from the University of Colorado at Boulder. I'm a materials physicist, and I would like to report a projectile that appeared over northern British Columbia, um—"

"—eight minutes ago," Cassie says and writes down *twenty-one minutes to impact* and underlines it.

"Eight minutes ago. We estimate that it will impact somewhere in the Denver metropolitan area in twenty-one minutes. Can you confirm that you have it on radar?"

The guy on the other end groans. "Yeah, sure, we have Prince Albert in a can. We'll let him out in the morning." He hangs up.

I punch the redial and wait for the guy to come back on the line, but a woman answers this time. "Sir, you are interfering with a US military operation. I am required to inform you that this call is being recorded and that all prank calls will be prosecuted to the fullest extent of the law. Now then, how may I help you?"

"I'm not a crank caller," I say. "I'm a physics professor at CU Boulder. I have good reason to believe that a forty-cubic-centimeter object moving at Mach fifteen appeared over northern Canada a few minutes ago and will strike Denver in just under twenty minutes. Our data is not precise enough to calculate exactly where it will impact, but the whole area needs to be evacuated."

"Sir, without proper clearance, I can neither confirm nor deny your observation. But I can assure you that we are continuously monitoring US airspace—along with the skies above North America —for airborne objects. You probably saw a meteor or a weather balloon, but if you spotted little green men on board, I suggest you call the National UFO Reporting Center. Additionally, if you suspect that life or property might be in danger, I urge you to contact your local law enforcement."

I attempt to keep the exasperation out of my voice but fail. "Are you telling me I should call the police to report a potential strike by a bogey moving at Mach fifteen? For chrissake, the internet thinks it's a nuke, lady. What the hell can the police do? Evacuate the whole city of Denver? You're the bloody North American Air *Defense* Command, so get off your—"

"It's *Aerospace* Defense Command, sir. We changed the name over a decade ago."

That one blows my fuse. "Ma'am, I don't give a flying fart in a rolling donut what—"

"Sir, I need to ask you to clear the line. Call the Denver Police or your local news agency or all of your congresspeople. But don't call us again. Have a nice evening."

The line goes dead.

And then my phone rings.

I jab the accept button and put it on the speaker so Cassie can hear. "Aha!" I say. "You found it."

"Found what?" Sam Maxwell, my brilliant but cheeky postdoc, says.

"Never mind. I thought you were NORAD."

"You called NORAD? Did Cassie's telescope array snag a meteor?"

"More like a UFO," I say. "Gonna hit Denver in twenty minutes."

"Really?" His voice sounds excited. "Shit. That's cool. Well, sort of. Did you call the Denver police?"

"Bloody great idea," I say and huff. "Why didn't I think of that?"

"Because you're not as brilliant as I am," he says. "Hey, could you tell Cassie I said Happy Birthday? And mention that I'm still single and ready to mingle."

I cringe.

"Hi, Sam," Cassie says, her cheeks reddening.

"Whoops," Sam says. "Mouth getting ahead of my brain again. Erase that, will you?"

Cassie laughs.

Sam clears his throat. "Hi, Cassie. Nice to hear your voice. Are you going to stop by the lab and say hello while you're here?"

"Can't this time," she says. "But I will for sure next time."

"Okay," Sam says, his voice falling. "Next time. Take care, Cassie. Bye, y'all."

"Bye, Sam," we say together.

Cassie and I turn on the local TV news while we're enjoying our second piece of Chocoberry cake, but there's no report of any meteor impact, just some shots of a new Mars biodome prototype being built out east. Right before signing off, the news gal mentions a possible gas explosion at an old hotel in LoDo but says the place was empty and under renovation.

Maybe the object burned up before impact?

I turn off the boob tube and carry the plates into the kitchen.

After we clean up, Cassie checks the Reddit thread again. Other than the ubiquitous trolls trumping up government conspiracies and alien invasions, there's nothing new.

"Looks like a false alarm on the bomb," Cassie says.

I nod. "Thank goodness we were wrong."

"We can take another look in the morning," she says. "Maybe we can identify the problem."

"So we can engineer a solution?" I say, unable to stop myself.

"And Bob's your uncle," we say together, just like old times.

We sit in silence for a minute, me wishing she would take a job closer to home, and she probably wishing the exact opposite.

"Do you have time for a game?" I finally ask, afraid she'll say no.

Her face lights up. "I've been waiting all evening for you to ask."

We take the sacred box out of the closet and settle in for an epic battle. Cassie was once the most promising junior chess player in England—and back when the dinosaurs roamed the Earth, so was I.

Madders' Log Entry 3

Target: Diego Nadales, Age 41
Nexus: Denver, Colorado
Chrono Tag: Same Day

Spherical anomaly of unknown origin appeared in
timeline. Dimensions and characteristics match
theoretical Chronosphere proposed by Professor
Matt Hudson prior to Eden-17 lockdown. No other
records exist. Possible indication of major
timeline divergence.

I stare at her empty chair, my jaw painfully tight. For ninety-
three minutes, I've been sitting atop a skyscraper, my heart
teetering on the knife edge of despair and elation.
Where is she?

I drum my fingers on the table and watch the damn cat video for
the nth time, the likes now over a million. Furrari, a svelte seal point
Siamese, jumps up on the head of a startled newscaster, curls his tail

around the woman's neck, and starts to purr. Behind her, there's an image of Kirkland's goddamn fishbowl and "Revolutionary Mars Habitat Test Facility Nears Completion" on the chyron. When I'm certain there's *still* no hidden message in it, I put my phone away and scan the posh restaurant yet again.

The first time I brought Isabel here was fifteen years ago. I remember sitting in this exact spot, mesmerized by the view of the Rockies. We were living in California at the time, both of us dirt-poor and working long hours to make a name for ourselves. We had just met a few weeks earlier and were hanging out at her place while it rained for the third straight night. She mused about missing the mountains, especially the sunsets and high-country gloaming.

I had to ask what a gloaming was, and she leaned back in her chair, closed her eyes, and whispered, "As the sun fades, ancient shadows creep closer, and the pine-tinged air picks up a chill that nips at our primordial fear of the dark. But the mountains stand sentinel, their peaks vivid against a painted sky, a reminder that there is beauty to be found even in the coming darkness."

I had been so entranced by her description that I asked her to repeat it so I could record it on my phone. There have been more than a few dark places in my life when listening to her words gave me a measure of hope. The following day, I borrowed frequent-flier miles from my parents, reserved a room at the Brown Palace Hotel using a half-price coupon from my boss, and secured dinner reservations half an hour before sunset. After we were seated at this exact table, she looked at the menu and insisted that the restaurant was too expensive, that I didn't need to spend my hard-earned money on her. She'd be perfectly happy watching the sunset from the picnic table at McDonald's. I laughed and told her it wasn't that I *needed* to bring her here, I *wanted* to. Later, when she was lying in my arms, the expensive white sheets in a tangle at our feet, she told me she loved me.

It was easily the best night of my life.

And it wouldn't be a lie to say I was hoping tonight would end the same way, that I could ask for her forgiveness, and we could find a way to start over.

The waiter stops by for the fourth or fifth time, refills my mostly full water glass, and gives me a weak smile. "Stood you up, huh?"

I exhale. "Wouldn't be the first time."

He tips his head to the side. "You sure I can't get you something? On the house?"

"No," I say, "but thanks. I'm going to give it a few more minutes, and then I'll get out of your hair."

"Absolutely no hurry, sir." He adjusts the Moët & Chandon Nectar Impérial sitting in a bucket of tepid water. "The table's yours for the evening. Just let me know if you want a stopper in the bubbly." He waits for me to acknowledge and then strides off.

My stomach grumbles, but I refuse to give in. I shift in my chair, gazing out the huge floor-to-ceiling windows. The snow-tipped Rockies are airbrushed in rich pink and orange hues, their lower flanks splashed with shades of purple. Hanging above the mountains, the waning sun filters through wispy clouds, bathing the city spread out below me in gilded light.

Isabel had described it perfectly all those years ago.

I shut my eyes and take a deep breath. Despite the brilliant sunset, the tightness in my chest is almost painful. Iz should have been here more than an hour ago, and even though I haven't seen her in over a decade, one thing is certain: She's never late.

So either the note is wrong, or the whole thing's an elaborate hoax.

Who could fake Isabel's handwriting? And why?

My throat is suddenly dry.

Kirkland?

After my self-professed best bud used leveraged money, feigned influence, and outright coercion to steal my girlfriend, I seriously considered murder. Needless to say, David Kirkland and I haven't spoken in years. Until last month, when he left a voicemail saying he had a business proposition for me. Last I heard, the guy was pushing a brisk billion and took calls from the governor. What could he possibly want from me? I was tempted to just blow him off, maybe even call back and tell him to go take a long walk off a short pier. But Gemini doesn't need any more headwinds right now, and I was curious about Iz. So, I tucked my tail between my legs and agreed to meet up with him for lunch.

Turns out he wanted to buy my company—probably for our water recycling technology, if what I read about his Mars project is true. When I mentioned that Gemini wasn't for sale, he spun his "generous offer" as some sort of "charity fuck" for an old friend—like he was doing me this big favor. Fifteen years, a billion dollars, and the guy hadn't changed a bit.

As I was walking out the door, he called after me, "What's the matter, Nadales? You not gonna ask me about her?"

I stopped, the door still open, and looked over my shoulder. "How is she?"

He shrugged and grinned at the same time. "Ah, you know, same old Isabel. Still thinks her mouth is for talking instead of—"

I shut the door.

Maybe he's messing with you again?

Kirkland's driven, I'll give him that, but he's no Riddler, either. Why would he fake a cryptic note telling me to meet Isabel here? So *she* could pressure me to sell? Sure, Iz and I had our differences, but she would never stoop to that. Never.

Which drops me right back in the center of Crazy Town: The note's authentic.

I swallow the sour taste in the back of my throat.

So what am I missing?

I slide the paper out of my pocket, my hands trembling. Even though I've looked at it a hundred times since it appeared in my locked car this morning, I feel compelled to study the familiar handwriting, say the words aloud, cling to the hope that Iz might still walk back into my life tonight. I unfold it on the table, smooth it out with my fingertips, and read it again.

<u>Top of the Rockies</u>

is written in Isabel's left-leaning hand, followed by today's date, underlined twice. Below it is written:

> Reserve a table with a view of the mountains and wait for me.
> I don't know it yet, but we need to stop Dave.

"Stop Dave from what?" I say aloud.

Destroying our relationship? Building his glorified fishbowls? Being an ass?

I rub my eyes. "Too late on all counts."

Almost like an afterthought, there's one more messy line at the bottom:

> At 3:48 pm MST, a video of a Siamese cat interrupting a live news broadcast will be posted. The cat's name will be Furrari.

The first time I watched the clip—six hours *after* I got the note—it had a handful of likes. An hour later, it had gone viral.

How the hell do you fake that?

I check my watch and look up at the busy restaurant. "Where are you, Iz?"

As I'm refolding the heavy paper, there's a loud clatter out in the lobby, followed by the sound of breaking glass—a lot of glass. And then I notice that the massive windows next to me are vibrating like a son of a bitch, the seal around the frames making an ominous popping sound.

A second later, the whole building starts to sway.

"Oh, shit," I say aloud.

There's a shriek from behind me and more sounds of breaking glass. Almost in slow motion, our ice bucket tips over, dumping cold water over my ankles. I lunge for the Champagne bottle but miss and hit my head against the table. The pink bubbly pours out onto the floor as the bottle rolls away from me.

The building is swaying so much it's impossible to stand up.

An earthquake? In Denver?

I flop back into the chair and lift my feet as the puddle spreads. A few tables away, a busboy struggles to keep a tray of dirty dishes from spilling—but fails.

Plates and glasses smash onto the floor, and the pimply kid looks like he's gonna cry.

On the other side of the restaurant, a woman yells, "Someone's bombed the Brown Palace Hotel!"

I manage to get to my feet and stagger across the undulating building, holding onto chairs and planters of fake ferns.

This cannot be a coincidence.

Outside, a massive cloud of smoke is rising into the fading light. Below it, flames shoot out of the roof of the distinctive triangular landmark.

"Thank goodness it's closed for renovations," an elderly woman says. She's holding onto a light fixture with both hands. "Although the lobby is full of fur babies looking for new homes."

"Look!" A woman in a skintight white sequin dress points out east. "There's more smoke over there. And there. And there. Omigod, it's some sort of terrorist attack like 9/11."

I stare at her, my chest tight. It was a lifetime ago, but I can still visualize the skyscrapers collapsing.

As our building stops doing the hula, more people hurry over to gawk.

I swallow and step closer to the windows, pressing my forehead against the thick glass so I can look down at the lower floors. "I don't see any flames or smoke coming from below us," I say. "And none of the buildings around us are—"

The fire alarm in the lobby goes off, and eighty-odd people turn as one. Two young guys in expensive suits jog toward the stairs, followed by what appears to be the kitchen staff. A moment later, there is a panicked herd rushing toward the exit.

"No, no!" The maître'd shouts in a French accent. "In case of fire, do not use elevators!"

I take a closer look at the burning buildings. All of them are in a line stretching out toward the north. Billowing smoke is rising from each of them like caustic black chess pieces. The Brown Palace Hotel is the last and largest queen.

Also not a coincidence.

My phone vibrates, and when I take it out, there's a text message from an unknown number. I tap *Yes* to display it, my heart pounding.

> UNKNOWN
>
> Plan changed: Find her!

Another four messages come in from the same number:

> UNKNOWN
>
> Tell the professor: cut the red wire, double-check the maths.
>
> Kid says wear socks in the coffin.
>
> And the world's about to shit itself.
>
> Now move!

I type back:

> Who is this?

but the message doesn't go through.

I shove my phone in my pocket and race across the restaurant toward the stairs.

Madders' Log Entry 4

Target: Isabel Sanborn
Nexus: Downtown Denver
Chrono Tag: Same Day

Global news feed comparison complete: Conflict in
South China Sea extends into second year. Climate
refugees overwhelm UN resettlement efforts.
Millions die of extreme heat, flooding, and
preventable disease. UK Parliament collapses as
extremist factions collide. Kirkland Enterprises
announces date for global livestream of Eden-1
Biodome Gala. No timeline divergences on macro
scale detected.

I place the puzzle box in my purse and scan the crowd again,
looking for the old man in the fedora.
Weird.
The wind kicks up, and I rub my hands across my upper arms,

tug down my skirt for the hundredth time, and join the thinning crowd crossing Market toward the Brown Palace. Luckily, the hotel is closed for renovations so its parking lot was empty this morning.

Woohoo for Isabel. She lost Boardwalk and Park Place but landed on Free Parking.

In any case, it should be easy to take a kitten home tonight.

I hurry along the backside of the granite building, passing an employee entrance and a slew of trash cans, hoping I'm not too late. After I turn the corner, I slow my pace, gazing at the puppies and kittens behind the plate-glass windows. There's a gangly mixed-breed pup with big feet who barks when he sees me. When I step closer, he rushes to the window and stands on his hind legs, putting those huge front paws on the glass. His tail is going a mile a minute, and I crouch down to his level.

"Oh, aren't you a cutie?"

He gives a little yip, his tail wagging so hard his whole back end is swinging around.

I laugh and clap my hands, and he zooms around his little space, jumping over dishes and bumping into toys. He comes racing back to the window, his tail wagging his body again, and gives another yip. "And clever too!" I say. "What's your name, big guy?"

I take a moment to read the description posted in the corner and discover he's a golden retriever mix. Estimated adult weight: 100 cuddly, fluffy pounds.

Holy Wookie, that's a big dog.

I look back at the puppy, his tail still wagging. He's lying down now, his head on his front paws and his big brown eyes pinned on me.

"What a sweetie! Would you like to come home with me, puppers?"

He wiggles his whole body in affirmation.

Oh, come on, Isabel. Be sensible. He's going to be a monster, and he wouldn't be happy living in your shoebox apartment. Once he's grown, he won't even fit in your car.

Something in the back of the display distracts the puppy, and he runs over to the small door to investigate. I force myself to walk away.

You can pick out a smaller pup, one that needs a home just as much as puppers does—and get a kitten, too.

The thought buoys me up a little.

I exhale, my shoulders suddenly tight.

You know, no one in the city is going to adopt a dog that big.

Imagine if he started chewing on your sofa or peeing on your rug— or dragging you into a busy street after a bird. Whoever adopted him would need lots of time and patience.

It would take work, but you could do it.

"But I just can't," I say, knowing I'd have to buy a new car and move to a bigger place with a yard.

Maybe someday, but not right now, not until you figure out your finances.

I force myself to leave it at that.

When I reach the end of the block, I stop at the last display to watch a black kitten with four white socks attack a stuffed dinosaur twice her size. When she sees me, she trots over, dragging the beast with her.

I lean closer and tap on the glass. "Hey, kitty girl. Nice work slaying the beast."

She steps on the T-Rex's toothy head and gives a silent meow.

The small door at the back of the display opens, and a man lifts the kitten. He strokes her back and then places her into a cage on top of a cart with other pets. I tap on the window, and the guy looks up at me. I point at the kitten and then my purse. "I want her," I say, even though I know he can't hear me.

He points to his watch and shakes his head. "Tomorrow," he mouths.

"Please?" I say and press my hands together. But he doesn't notice me—or pretends not to. He shuts the door in the back of the display. The lights go out, and a cold shroud of sadness falls on me.

So, maybe it wasn't meant to be.

"To hell with what is or is not meant to be," I say aloud. "It's high time you started steering your own damn ship, Isabel."

I rush toward the main entrance, thinking I'll beg him to let me in and offer to pay extra.

But by the time I get to the front doors, they're locked, and no one's inside to hear my frantic pounding. I stand there for a minute with my hands on my hips and my sore ankle complaining about the sprint in high heels.

You're acting like a crazy person, Isabel. Just come back tomorrow.

But I promised I'd work tomorrow. Someone will surely fall in love with such a sweet kitten by Monday, and she'll be gone. I know there are other pets that need good homes, but for some reason, I just can't let go of the golden *and* the white-footed kitten.

A side door at the other end of the building scrapes open. I watch as a man exits, checks the lock, and strides away into the night.

"Wait!" I yell, but the traffic is too loud, and he doesn't even turn.

"Damn it." I take out my phone, find the number for the Adopt-a-Pet people, and call them. After more than ten rings, someone answers. I explain the situation and ask them to hold the black and white kitten for me.

"I'm sorry, ma'am, but it's been a really long day. If you can't come back first thing in the morning, perhaps you can send someone else—or even pick out a different pet. They all need good homes."

"Yes, of course," I say. "Thank you." I end the call and continue walking, telling myself that the kitten will still be there tomorrow afternoon. I just have to get a little lucky.

When I spy a glass door with a "Lobby" sign hanging over it, I stop and peer into the half-light. At the end of a long hallway, there's an atrium with a white piano in it. The pet cages are stacked on the other side of the piano, against the far wall. I can see the black kitten with the four white feet on top.

"One more night, kitty girl," I say, "and then you can come home with me."

I force myself to turn away and keep walking.

When I get to the end of the building, I dig my car key out of my purse, hold the fob up in the air, and press the unlock button. There's a reassuring chirp at the other end of the lot, and I head toward it.

But before I can get to my car, I'm blinded by a flash of light. An instant later, a huge explosion knocks me to the pavement. I scramble behind the nearest car, my ears ringing and my heart pounding. When there are no other blasts for a good thirty seconds, I stand up and hurry out into the street for a look.

Smoke and flames are spilling out of smashed windows on the top floor of the Brown Palace Hotel.

Was there a gas leak and one of the construction workers set it off?

Except it's the Friday night of a long weekend. Who would be working at this hour?

Nobody.

Why would someone blow up an empty hotel?

I shake my head.

In the time I've been standing there playing detective, the flames have spread.

"Omigod, all those animals are in the atrium."

Call 911, then get in your car and go home, Isabel.

I take out my phone, dial the emergency number, and report the explosion and fire. The woman who answers the call takes my info and then advises me to leave the area immediately.

"The lobby of the hotel is full of puppies and kittens," I tell her. "There's some sort of Adopt-a-Pet thing going on this weekend, and the animals are all locked inside cages."

"I'll pass that along to emergency services," she says, sounding flustered. I can hear a lot of commotion in the background of the call. "You should seek safety immediately. It's possible the explosion is part of a coordinated act."

"What?" I say. "You mean like a terrorist attack? In Denver?"

"I didn't say that, ma'am. I told you to seek safety immediately."

"Right. Okay. Bye." I hang up.

In the minute or two I've been standing there, the fire has become an inferno, and massive amounts of smoke are pouring out the top two floors.

I press the key fob button again and hurry toward my car. It's fully dark now, and multiple sirens are audible in the distance. I hop in my car, start the engine, and crank up the heater. Images of those poor animals frantically trying to get out of their cages fill my head. I can almost hear their frightened cries in the stifling darkness.

And if this attack is part of a terrorist plot, the emergency responders aren't going to be running around collecting puppies and kittens. They're going to have their hands full trying to save people.

If you let those animals die, you'll never forgive yourself.

"Oh, screw it." I turn off the engine, jump out, and hurry back toward the glass door, a plan already forming in my head.

I'll break the window above the handle, let myself in, sprint to the atrium, and ferry the pets out through an emergency exit.

I bet the cages are on wheels, so it won't be hard to get them out quickly.

In my mind's eye, it takes me ten minutes, tops.

In practice, it takes me longer to find a rock large enough to break glass. I hurl it against the horizontal pane, but it bounces back and lands on my foot.

Damn it.

On the third attempt, I throw my weight behind the rock, and the glass shatters. I stand there breathing hard, listening for an alarm, but there is none. By the time I get the door open, the hallway is filled with acrid smoke. I cough and hear an answering bark in the distance —and the sound of things falling from the ceiling. There's a sad-looking umbrella in a stand next to the door. I grab it by its curved handle, throw off my useless high heels, and wrap my scarf around my nose and mouth. Then, hunched over, I start jogging through the thick haze toward the sound of frightened animals, holding the umbrella out like some doofus in a Monty Python skit.

It's at that point I realize I've left my purse and phone in the car.

If you screw up and get trapped in here, no one will even know.

"So don't screw up," I say and keep moving.

As I approach the atrium, I hear the sound of bending metal. A moment later, large chunks of concrete and steel come crashing down —followed by large fragments of glass. The air around me becomes choked with dust, and I stop and crouch next to a water fountain, trying to decide what to do.

You should turn around and get the hell out of here.

But if I do, all the animals will die.

I wet the scarf, reposition it over my nose and mouth, and start moving again.

Once you get in the atrium, try to stay close to the wall—less chance of stuff falling on you.

I can feel a faint breath of wind on my cheek, and I get a whiff of burning plastic. A few seconds later, the air shifts and the smoke and dust start funneling away from me, billowing up toward the high ceiling.

Above me, there's a crash and then more barking.

"I'm coming!" I shout and slink out of the hallway and into the atrium. Dim emergency lighting is filtering down through the gloom, and water is raining down from sprinklers somewhere above me. The wet floor is littered with glass, and twisted steel girders stick out of large slabs of concrete. As I stand there, there's another ominous tearing sound, and more debris comes crashing down.

"Shit." I back up against the wall, my throat tight.

The barking stops and is replaced by a frightened whine.

"You and me, both, puppers."

Keeping one eye on the piano, I start stepping over chunks of concrete, using the umbrella to sweep shards of glass out of the way of my bare feet. It's slow going, but I'm making progress.

I hear a noise behind me.

"Hello? Who's there?"

I turn around, scanning the large, square room. There's more barking, but I don't see anyone, just a swirl of dust.

Must be your imagination.

The smoke is getting thicker, and I can see flickering light coming from the flames above me now.

You're almost there, Isabel.

I keep moving and, a minute later, hurry past the white piano to the pets. There are more than twenty scared animals staring at me, their cages stacked on eight or nine wheeled platforms.

"Don't worry," I say and drop the umbrella. "Help has arrived."

I scan the cages for the black kitten with the white feet—and discover the golden puppy in the cage below her. "Hey, guys," I say and pet them through the bars. "Just give me a minute, and I'll get you out of here." The kitten starts mewing, her eyes pleading with me. "Ah, hell," I say and open her door. "You can come with me, little Miss Lucky." I lift her out, stroke her head, and then place her on my shoulder.

Well, that's one problem solved. I hope they'll take a check.

The kitten settles against my neck and starts purring.

"Hang on, big guy," I say to the puppy and then look around for a door. I spy one down a short hallway on the other side of the piano. The lighted exit sign is visible in the gloom.

It takes me a few seconds to unlock all the wheels on the trolleys. I line them up and start pushing them toward the exit, Lucky still snuggled against my neck. But there's debris all over the floor, and the train of wheeled platforms is unwieldy. I shove hard against the cages, and Lucky meows.

"You're right, missy. This isn't going to work."

I leave the cart with the golden puppy behind and start tugging the one with a dachshund. "I'll be right back for the rest of you," I call out. The dachshund whines when I lift the cart over some debris and his cage wobbles, but his little tail keeps wagging. "Almost there, buddy."

The going gets easier once I pass the piano and get out of the atrium. After I enter the hallway, I break into a jog. When I get to the exit, I force it open with my butt and pull the stack of cages over the threshold and out into the cold night air. I can see the fire engines and a crowd of people at the other end of the street, but this side of the building is weirdly deserted. I shove the cages as far away from the building as I can without letting go of the door, resettle Lucky on my shoulder, and then hurry back inside for the next set of cages.

Once I pass the piano, there's a series of loud bangs, like bullets fired from a gun. I cover my ears—and then stand there like an idiot as the suspended staircase above me tears away from the wall.

Oh, shit.

My brain kicks into gear, and I start backing up, but there's no place to go. The thing is massive.

Time slows down.

Get back to the animals.

I vault over a fallen railing, and I fall hard, Lucky's claws digging into my shoulder and glass cutting into my knees and hands. I get up, holding the kitten in my arms now, and will my feet to go faster, trying to make it past that monstrous white piano to safety.

You're not going to make it.

"Get down!" A man grabs me from behind and pulls me to the ground. I hold onto the kitten, trying to protect her, and land hard. I lie there gasping for breath, my shoulder and chest hurting, and watch the torn staircase smash down on top of the Steinway. There's a loud, discordant protest, and then the piano legs give out, and the heavy wooden case crashes to the floor, coming to rest only inches from my face. Pieces of debris rain down like concrete hail, hitting my chest and face. Lucky mews, and I try to shield her.

As I start to lose consciousness, I see an orange cowboy hat land edgewise on the piano keys, wobble for a moment, and then fall still.

I close my eyes and give in to the darkness.

Madders' Log Entry 5

Target: Matt Hudson
Nexus: Matt's House
Chrono Tag: Same Day

Timeline divergence confirmed. Temporal
distortions around Chronosphere indicate possible
jinn object(s) contained within.

Cassandra and I are setting up the chessboard for our third and deciding game when a shadow of sadness falls over me.

Somehow, my life has gotten away from me.

Here I am, past fifty, and what do I have to show for it?

Besides Cassandra, almost nothing.

For twenty years, I've spent my days throwing chalk-covered rubbers at snoring freshmen and putzing around a lab building clever toys.

Where has the time gone?

I watch Cassie place the pieces, wishing she hadn't grown up so fast or moved so far away. She only arrived yesterday, and she's leaving tomorrow—and I'm missing her already.

"So," I say, trying to keep my tone matter-of-fact, "is there any romance on the horizon?"

Cassie looks up at me, still holding a rook in one hand. "You mean boys?" She laughs. "Eww."

"Ah, come on. Surely there's some clever young man who's captured your imagination?"

She sets the rook down on its square and straightens up some pawns. "There is a guy I met a few months ago, actually. Very creative—and a great cook." A smile flickers across her face and disappears. "He used to work for the ad agency that shares our building."

She looks up at me, and I nod, half regretting I brought up the topic. "Sounds like a nice bloke?"

"He is," she says, sounding unconvinced. "We dated for a while, and I thought maybe..." She shrugs one shoulder. "Anyway, you know me and my big mouth. He mispronounced the word hyperbole —said 'hyper-bowl'—and I corrected him without even thinking about it. He couldn't leave the restaurant fast enough. Been ghosting me ever since."

"Well, if he's ghosting you after that, then I say good riddance."

She shakes her head. "What sort of a prat corrects her boyfriend's English?"

"A smart prat," I say.

She groans and punches me in the arm.

"Someday, you'll find a man who strives to learn and grow—even if it means being embarrassed once in a while." I smile and put my hand on her arm. "Mr. Creative Chef is an idiot to let you get away."

Her face softens. "Thanks, Uncle Matty."

"And besides, I would have done the same thing in your place— not that it's any consolation. You're not exactly talking to Casanova here."

She laughs. "I miss having you around to cheer me up."

"I miss you too," I say, getting a little choked up. "We make a good team, don't we?"

"I could look for a job here in Colorado," she says. "Hang out with you on the weekends."

Oh Christ, now you've got her feeling sorry for you.

"Don't be silly," I say. "You love your job, and the last thing you want to do is spend all your free time with your dotty old uncle."

She gets a mischievous gleam in her eye. "So how about you?" she says and pokes me in the arm. "Any romance on the horizon? Now that you don't have to spend all your time being a dad, you should go on a date, live a little."

I snort. "You know me, a confirmed bachelor. The microwave's my best mate."

"Being gay doesn't mean you have to be lonely."

For a moment, it's hard to breathe. "How long have you known?"

She laughs. "Since forever. And I know you gave up your own happiness so you could take care of me."

"Oh, Cassie." I sit there with my eyes getting watery. "I didn't give up any happiness. I found happiness *because* of you. I don't regret a minute of it."

Now, I'm not the best at picking up on these sorts of things, but I swear there's a tear in her eye.

She looks away, and I make a show of switching a misplaced bishop and knight. She snuffs her nose and peeks at me. "What about the time I tried to flush your passport down the toilet because you wouldn't take me to Paris?"

"Nope."

"Not even that time you tried to curl my hair and ended up setting a good bit of it on fire?"

I laugh, hard and deep. "I'll never forget the look on your teacher's face."

"She told me I should ask as adult for help next time."

"Bloody true," I say, unable to stop smiling. "Those were good times."

She gets up, steps around the chessboard, and pulls me up into a bear hug. "I do miss Mom and Sissy," she says, her head resting against my chin, "but I couldn't have asked for a better uncle."

I wrap my arms around my little girl. "And I couldn't have asked for a better niece."

"Now," she says, wiping her face and hopping back into her chair. "It's time for the important stuff. Let's play chess."

We're ten or twelve moves in—and I'm already on the ropes—when there's a knock at the front door.

I glance at the clock on the mantle. It's a little past ten.

There's another knock, louder this time. "Professor," someone calls, "It's me. Open up. Something's happened."

"Sam?" Cassie says and gives me an inquisitive look.

I hurry over and open the door. "What is it, Sam? It's—"

"Turn on the TV," he says, striding into the living room and grabbing the remote off the coffee table.

I shut the door.

"You have to see this," he says and glances at Cassandra. "Hi, Cassie. You look beautiful, as always." And then he notices the chessboard. "Please tell me you didn't let your old man win again?" Before she can respond, he pushes a button on the remote, and the TV flickers on. "You guys were right about the meteor, if that's what it was."

"What?" I say, still trying to catch up with him. "What happened?"

"Hopkins saw the alien artifact appear out of nowhere too."

"Yes," Cassie whispers and pumps her fist. "I knew my data was solid."

"Steady on now, ladies and gentlemen," I say. "It's never aliens."

"Yeah," Cassie says. "Until it is."

Sam flicks through the channels until he finds one with a reporter standing in front of a burning building. Behind her, dozens of firefighters are spraying water into the roaring flames. The camera pans, showing the whole block is ablaze.

"They think it's an explosion from a gas leak," Sam says. "But there are multiple fires—at least five—and all of them began at *exactly* the same time. In buildings that are blocks apart."

"Christ," I say, "was anybody hurt?"

"Some hotel took the brunt of it," Sam says, "but it's closed for renovations."

"So it was empty?" Cassie says. "How lucky is that?"

"Yeah," Sam says, not really listening. "I checked some drone footage, and all the damaged buildings are in a straight line."

"That will match up with the trajectory of my bogey," Cassie says.

Sam points his finger at her. "Got it in one."

I put my hands on my hips. "Crikey Moses. Maybe we were right?"

"Here, listen to this." Sam turns up the TV volume.

"—closed for renovations," the reporter says. "The Denver police are evacuating a six-block radius around the Brown Palace Hotel and asking people to stay out of LoDo until further notice. Emergency responders are treating people injured by falling glass." The camera pans to multiple ambulances with their lights swirling and people milling about. "As of this moment, there are no confirmed casualties. Stay tuned for more breaking news. Back to you, Julie."

Sam turns off the TV and tosses the remote onto the coffee table like he's Scarlett O'Hara. The lid pops off, and batteries clatter out onto my nice oak coffee table before rolling onto the floor.

"Sorry." He gives me a weak smile. "Got carried away there." He collects the batteries and stuffs them back into the remote. Then he fumbles for the lid and spends a minute putting it back on. When he finally succeeds, he sets the remote gently on the coffee table and turns toward the kitchen. "Did you save me any cake?"

I look at Cassie, and we both shrug.

"How about a turkey sandwich?" I say.

Sam is tall and skinny with lily-white skin and a shocking head of orange hair. The guy's as volatile as a firecracker and about as disciplined. Still, he's the brightest *and* hardest-working postdoc I've ever had, so I cut him a little slack.

Like barging into my house after hours and demanding food.

Cassie makes Sam a sandwich while I put away the dinner dishes, and we sit at the kitchen counter while he devours his food.

"I could get used to this," he says and winks at Cassie.

She rolls her eyes.

You won't get anywhere with her like that, kid.

"So what is it?" Sam takes a swig of milk. "Are we ready to go with an alien wormhole? I'm pretty sure nobody down here has that sort of tech."

They both look at me.

"Nah. Maybe a comet?" I say. "It's possible the outer shell burned off before it hit Earth's atmosphere and left the solid metallic core zipping along."

"At a measly Mach 15?" Sam says.

"And no one saw it limping toward Earth burning up volatiles," Cassie says.

I shrug. "It wasn't in the ecliptic plane, so no one noticed it."

"Oh, come on," Sam says. "You're reaching, and you know it. People spend their whole lives looking for shit like this. You couldn't use a pea-shooter on the Moon without someone claiming naming rights. It's a secret government project, aliens, or friggin' Doctor Who. Those are literally all the options." He scoffs. "We all know it's not a goddamn comet."

I grunt.

"Let's see what the internet thinks," Cassie says and stands up. "Maybe someone posted more photos."

Sam glances over at the fridge. "Any chance I could get another turkey and Swiss?"

Cassie snorts. "Make your own bloody sandwich."

Sam starts to rise, but I wave him off. The kid builds neutrino collectors in his spare time, but ask him to microwave a bowl of soup, and you'll have to spend an hour cleaning up after him.

While I'm making Sam another sandwich, Cassie heads into the office and fires up the computer. She's typing like crazy when we join her, Sam with his sandwich in tow.

"It's gone," she says. "It's all effing gone."

"Waffs gah?" Sam says through a mouthful.

"The Reddit thread about the bogey," Cassie says, glancing at Sam and then his sandwich. "Someone must have made them take it down."

"Are you sure, Cassie?" I say. "Maybe it was moved or consolidated?"

She gives an exasperated sigh. "Yeah, I'm sure. I already double-checked. I tried to start a new one and it disappeared. Almost immediately."

Sam makes a *Twilight Zone* sound, then stuffs the rest of his sandwich in his mouth and dusts off his hands. "Maybe one of the mods got their pee-pee whacked about posting 'misinformation'," Sam says, using air quotes.

"Sure," I say. "Like what happened with *War of the Worlds*."

Blank stares.

"It was a radio broadcast about an alien attack. The original fake news. Caused all sorts of panic."

"I guess it could be," Cassie says. "But I think someone doesn't want people talking about the bogey. Or posting photos." She looks over at me. "You don't think they'll come after my data, do you?"

"You posted your data online?" Sam says, his voice rising.

She shakes her head. "But I did mention that I was tracking the object in real time and analyzing the data."

"Uh-oh," Sam says. "Lock the doors."

"Don't be melodramatic," I say. "I'm the one who called NORAD."

"Oh, shit," Sam says. "They'll send spooks to interrogate your ass."

I'm in the process of rolling my eyes when the doorbell rings.

All three of us freeze.

I motion for them to stay in the office. "Shh." I shut off the lights and close the door.

The doorbell rings again.

"Coming," I say as I stride across the living room, the skin on my arms prickling. When I get there, I turn the door handle and pull it back, ready to tell the G-men I'm home alone and the Reddit post was my doing.

But no one's there.

"Hi, Professor Hudson."

I look down. It's the freckled kid from across the street, and I let out an involuntary sigh.

"Your friend left his lights on."

I stare at him, not comprehending.

He turns and points toward Sam's car. "Mom said I should let you know so his battery doesn't die."

"Ah!" I press a hand to my chest. "Thank you, umm, Johnny."

"It's Ted."

"Ah, yes, of course. Thank you, Ted. I'll have him turn them off right away. Tell your mother I said thank you. And let me know if you need help with another science project. That catapult we made last year was brill. I dare say it's the best thing I've ever done with a tomato."

"Sure thing, professor," he says and scurries down the steps.

I let out a slow breath and start to shut the door when I notice a guy sitting in a car across the street. He's slumped down in the driver's seat of a big SUV. I never would have noticed him except he's playing on his mobile—and the backlight is making his white collared shirt glow.

He's probably just waiting to take the babysitter home.

I go back inside, shut the door, and tell Cassie and Sam the coast is clear.

We have a good chuckle about watching too many 007 movies, and then Cassie stifles a yawn.

"I think we should call it a night," I say. "We'll get things sorted on Tuesday. I'm sure there's a mundane explanation for everything. There always is."

Sam says his goodbyes, and when he goes out to his car, I notice the SUV is gone.

Madders' Log Entry 6

Target: Diego Nadales
Nexus: LoDo Denver
Chrono Tag: Same Day

Unexpected Incursion from external timeline
confirmed. Beginning forward analysis for
potential disruptions.

The words "we need to stop Dave" keep playing over and over in my head as I pound down eighty-odd flights of stairs, my knees like rubber and my thighs burning. I push through the stairwell exit door and step into a lobby full of irate hotel guests and their pajama-clad children. The air smells of smoke, and anxious voices fill the space. I rest against the wall for a few seconds to catch my breath. Why would Iz refer to herself in the past?

"I don't know it yet, but we need to stop Dave."

I give up and push my way through the agitated mass of humanity, avoiding a fallen Ficus tree, four golf bags, and a child somehow still asleep with his arms around a giant stuffed Stitch.

The moment I get out the side door, acrid fumes fill my nostrils. The night sky is glowing orange, and sooty flakes fall out of the darkness, a surreal snowstorm. The fire has created its own gale, and great billows of smoke roll down out of the darkness, filling the space between the tall buildings with noxious gas.

There is only one thought in my mind: *Find Isabel.*

I start running toward the Brown Palace Hotel, fear pushing me forward.

The streets are packed, some cars half on the sidewalk, some going against the flow of traffic, one abandoned in the middle of an intersection. A motorcycle maneuvers through the gridlock, weaving between people running every which way. I cross the street and narrowly avoid getting hit by a white Lexus that runs a red light.

I stop to catch my breath and take out my phone. I bring up the mysterious text messages and push the call button, my throat tight.

A few seconds later, "Call failed" appears.

I shove the phone back in my pocket and keep running.

When I turn the corner, I see teenagers heave a metal trash can against the window of a jewelry shop. The glass cracks but doesn't give, and a moment later, the alarm goes off. The kids glance over at me, waiting. When I look away, they hoist the can up for another try.

Where the hell are the cops?

I can see lights flashing a few blocks down, but they don't seem to be getting any closer. I cross to the other side of the street, jogging toward the center of the chaos.

When I get to the Brown Palace, I stop to catch my breath. The hotel is shaped like a triangle, and I'm standing at the center of the hypotenuse. From what I can see, the building appears to be locked up tight. I turn to the left and jog along the wall, checking the doors as I go. There are colorful Adopt-a-Pet posters in the windows but no signs of activity. I can hear sirens in the distance, but the back of the building is eerily quiet. I peek in the window of the hotel pub—a "Closed for Renovations" sign hanging behind the thick glass—but the place is deserted. Beyond the pub, I can see into the famous stair-lined atrium and what looks like stacked cages.

I continue on, turn the corner, and come to an abrupt stop.

Piles of rubble and twisted metal litter the street and sidewalk, and more fire trucks than I can count are spraying water into the broken upper windows. Police cruisers and ambulances are everywhere, their rotating lights filling the smoky air with eerie flashes of color.

A crowd has formed around the emergency equipment, people stacked ten deep watching the flames. A firefighter with a bullhorn is attempting to get the hordes to disperse but isn't having much luck. A van from the local TV station is filming the chaos, and behind the reporter, revelers are laughing and waving their arms for the camera.

If she's somewhere in that mob, I'll never be able to find her, let alone save her from God knows what.

I try to guess where Isabel could be but come up empty. I take out my phone and read the cryptic message again. I type in:

> where is she?

and stab return, but the message fails to send.

Damn cryptic text. Why didn't they just tell me where she is?

I notice that the office building across the street is ablaze, smoke pouring out from halfway up the skyscraper. There's the sound of windows shattering, and flames shoot out of the building even higher up. A moment later, the congested street is pelted with broken glass.

Someone screams, and the crowd scatters.

I force myself to think.

Instead of texting some random number, just call her.

The thought sends an icy rush of panic into my chest. The last time we talked, things hadn't gone so well.

More like things got seriously fucked up.

"But that was ages ago," I say. "She can't still be mad at me, can she?"

I pull out my phone and scroll through my address book, knowing that the chance she'd have the same number after all these years is negative zero percent. Still, when I push the call button, my heart leaps into my throat.

But the cell towers are so jammed the call won't go through. I type in a text message:

> Isabel? Where are you? Please tell me you're okay.

I pause with my finger over the send button.

What if she's sitting on a beach in Tahiti drinking a martini?

I huff. "Iz hates mixed drinks, and she never sunbathes—and I suppose there are worse things than looking like a complete idiot." I push send and wait to see if it goes through. When it doesn't, I jab the retry button and shove the phone into my pocket.

Now what?

I look back the way I came, trying to decide.

If there are pets in all those cages in the back, you'd think someone would be trying to get them out.

There's a muffled explosion inside the Brown Palace, and I continue on, trying to push the image of the panicked animals out of my head.

Wait a sec.

I stop running, a cold fear forming in the pit of my stomach.

Mierda. She wouldn't be THAT stupid. Would she?

I retrace my steps, running along the building and searching for a door or window that looks vandalized.

It takes me less than thirty seconds to find it.

The glass panel of a side door has been smashed, and smoke is pouring out through the small opening. I can see the rock she used on the floor inside. Next to it is a pair of abandoned high heels.

Oh, you stupid, stupid woman.

Without thinking, I reach through the broken glass and turn the handle. The door whips open, jerking the hot metal out of my hand and slicing into my arm. I recoil as a giant blast of superheated smoke and ash surges out.

You're lucky that didn't slice an artery, dumbass.

I back away and take a look at the cut. It's long but not too deep. I apply direct pressure and fish a handkerchief out of my suit pocket with my mouth. I wrap it tightly around the gash and tie it in place.

Blood soaks through but not a lot.

I brush glass shards out of the way with my shoe, pull my jacket over my head, and proceed into the smoke-filled hallway.

But I can't go more than a meter or two before the smoke is too thick, and I have to turn back.

Great job, Superman. Next idea?

I retreat and force the door shut with my back.

Find an entrance closer to the animals.

I turn and sprint down the sidewalk, my eyes searching for another door—and nearly crash into a stack of metal cages on the sidewalk.

"What the—"

A puppy starts barking.

"Easy there, squirt. I'm not going to hurt you."

It's cold out here, and the little wiener dog curls back up into a ball, his nose tucked under his tail but his eyes wary. There are two kittens huddled together in the top cage, along with another three in the bottom one.

The pets are parked in front of the emergency exit. Thin wisps of smoke leak out around the doorframe.

Isabel must have gotten this set out of the building, so maybe she's coming back with more?

I press my hands against the door. It's hot, and the handle burns through my sleeve when I try to open it.

"*Mierda*," I say. "No one's going to be coming through that anytime soon."

Now that I've stopped running, I'm shivering.

I glance back at the small, frightened animals. "You guys must be freezing."

Their worried eyes glow back at me.

The cages are on rollers, so I haul them away from the burning building.

You're wasting time, mae.

But I can't just leave them there to die.

I drag them off the curb, out into the street, and up onto the far sidewalk. There's an exhaust grate with warm air coming out, and I park them over it and then run back across the street.

"Okay," I say to myself, "if the doors are locked, try a window."

Ignoring the stitch in my side, I jog along the building until I come to a large picture window. I touch my fingertips to the plate glass. It's warm, but not as hot as the door. I peer into the shadowy interior but can't see beyond the empty display.

If she's not in there, you're gonna get yourself killed for nothing.

"But if she is..."

I stand there, breathing hard, and look around for something to break the glass. The sidewalk is empty except for a trash can on the corner.

I jog over and put my arms around the bin. It's made of steel, and one of the legs is bolted to the concrete. I can't get it to budge.

A desperate idea forms in my brain, but it's beyond laughable.

Right, convince a pack of looters to drop the goodies and help you rescue a crazy cat lady who broke into a burning building to save a few strays.

Still, I gaze down the street at where I saw the kids smashing the jewelry store window. Shadows are moving in and out of the dome of light in front of the shop.

"I must be a lunatic."

Maybe it's the panic in my voice or my threat to hunt them down and tell their parents if they don't help me, but a couple minutes later, the five looters and I manage to pry the heavy trash can off the sidewalk and throw it through the hotel window.

Smoke billows out at the top of the gaping hole, but no alarm sounds.

"You sure she's in there?" one of the guys says, scanning the interior like a pirate searching for treasure.

"Yes," I say. "And a bunch of puppies and kittens in cages."

One of the guys starts kicking out the remaining splinters of glass, but he stops when we hear muffled barking—and then a faint cry.

I jump up into the small display and yell out, "Isabel? Is that you?"

There's weak coughing and then silence.

"Hold on! I'm coming!"

A short skinny guy, grabs my pant leg. "Hey, dingus, cover your face with something wet, or you'll die from smoke inhalation before you get ten feet."

I turn and stare down at him. Uh, *her*. She's thin and Asian with very short hair—but her face is strikingly beautiful.

She glances around at her friends. "I say we try to get them out. Who's with me?"

"Me," a tiny voice says. There's a kid half her size hanging onto her shirt.

"Oka fefe," she says and bends down to talk to the half-pint, her hands on his shoulders. "No way, kiddo. If you so much as stub a toe, Gran will skin me alive. Go sit on the curb and let me know if the cops are coming." She hands him a small satchel. "Here, you can hold my med kit, okay?"

The kid takes the case, lowers his head, and shuffles toward the street. "You never let me have any fun."

The Asian girl turns back to her gang. "Anyone else?"

There's a murmur of assent, and one of the guys asks, "Did you bring your stuff?"

"Of course." She takes a wrinkled bandanna and a spool of string out of her back pocket. "You guys?"

There's a chorus of assent.

She motions with her chin toward my bandaged arm. "You can use that cloth, but piss on it first."

I stare at her. "What?"

"You heard me. Get it damp, you halfwit mooker." She nods at one of the guys, and he crumples the bandanna in his hand, urinates on it, and then hands it back to her. She ties the damp rag over her nose and mouth like a bandit.

I try not to cringe.

This girl didn't grow up wearing princess costumes.

She hops up next to me, amused by my look of disgust. "Haven't you ever gone into a fire before?"

I shake my head and then follow her example.

She waits for me to tie the cloth over my nose and mouth and then says, "Okay, let's rock."

I step across the display and jump down into the murky room. The smoke is thick but nowhere near as bad as it was up front. Still, it's impossible to see more than a foot or two into the gloom.

"Isabel?!" I shout and then cup my ear and listen.

All I hear is feeble barking.

Please let her be alive.

I half-expect the gang to go back to their looting, but they don't. They drop down onto their hands and knees and start crawling into the burning building. I follow suit.

A minute later, my head strikes something hard and sharp, and I recoil. "Crap." I put my hand up to my forehead, and it comes away wet.

The girl crawls up next to me and starts pushing empty cages and boxes out of the way. "Use the flashlight on your phone, Sherlock." She shines her light on my forehead. "Doesn't look too bad. But if you need a couple of stitches, I can do it when we get back outside."

I stare at her like she just offered to teleport me to Mars. "You some sort of medic?"

"Yeah," she says, still clearing a path for us. "The sort that's trying to get into med school." She gestures with her chin. "That's what my share of the loot is for, application fees. If I get accepted, Gran says they'll give me a scholarship." She turns her head and laughs when she sees the look on my face. "Yeah, I get that a lot. Who are you trying to save? Your wife?" She continues pushing aside boxes.

I wipe my hand on my pants and start helping her. "No. She's the woman I *should* have married fifteen years ago."

She scoffs and inches forward. "Maybe you waited a little too long to pop the question, Mr. Bond."

"Yeah," I say and shove a box out of the way. "But I'm not going to make the same mistake twice." I take out my phone, bring up Isabel's page, and type in:

> Marry me?

"Quite the Romeo," she says under her breath. "What woman could resist?"

After I push send, I turn on the flashlight and peer around.

Bright red drops of blood are visible on the newspaper lining a metal cage. A small tongue reaches out and licks them off the faded headline: *War and Peace in the Crimea.* I shift the light and see a golden retriever puppy lying on a thin, ragged towel. He wags his tail when he sees me, and I slip my fingers between the bars and pet him.

The Asian girl grabs onto his cage. "Yo, Tolstoy. We'll get you out of there pronto."

His tail thumps once.

She turns away from me and calls out, "Over here, guys!"

I shine my light around, and he scratches at the bars. "Hang in there, buddy," I say as he follows me to the other end of his cage, his eyes pleading. "Mulan and the gang are going to get you out of here."

Someone grabs his cage and starts towing it back.

"Hey, Tolstoy," I say. "If we both make it out alive, you wanna come home with me?"

He barks.

"Deal."

I tug a sheet of cardboard off the top of another cage and use it to fan the smoke away.

Golden eyes glow back at me out of the gloom. There must be more than twenty crates stacked on seven or eight rolling pallets.

At least they'll be easy to get out.

I call out to Isabel again, but there's no response.

Mulan starts wrapping kite string around her shoe and then holds the spool out to me. "Here. Take this. I'll tie the other end to the trash can when I get back outside."

I hesitate.

"You're going after your fiancée, right?"

The word catches me by surprise, but I like the sound of it. "Yeah."

"Put it in your pocket but keep unrolling the string. You know, like Theseus in the labyrinth."

"Ah. Right." I take the spool and stick it in my jacket pocket. "Thanks."

She grabs a couple more carts. "We'll get the beasties out. If you need help, yell and tug hard on the string."

"Gotcha." I notice that she has her phone wedged in her collar so her hands are free, and I copy her. "Thanks again."

"You're welcome, Einstein."

How many ways does she have to call you a dumbass? Probably more.

"Stay low and keep the bandanna wet. And you better hurry." She looks up at me, keeping the light out of my eyes. "On the bright side, if you manage to get her out of this, she'll have to say yes."

"Let's hope she gets the chance."

She lowers her chin. "Don't do anything stupid, Mr. Spock."

"Too late for that." I edge around the cages and crawl deeper into the building, paying out the string as I go. When I come to a wall, I try to remember which way the voice came from, but my sense of direction is shot. "Shit."

And then I hear tones from a piano.

What the hell?

I rush toward the sound, scrambling over piles of metal railings and plaster rubble, spooling out the string and searching for that damn piano.

And then I see it practically glowing in the murky darkness. On the other side of the atrium, the legless white behemoth lies beneath a massive chunk of fallen staircase. A high-top sneaker is sticking out from beneath it, the rest of the body crushed by the huge case.

Panic closes off my throat until I realize that dead people don't play Beethoven.

There must be someone alive over there.

I scramble closer and shine my light into the dark triangle made by the fallen staircase. There's lots of rubble covered in a thin layer of white dust. And then I see bright red blood seeping out from beneath the white case.

I gag and turn away. "Oh, please, no!"

At the sound of my voice, the rubble shifts, and I realize that someone is lying *beside* the piano. "Isabel? Is that you?" I grab my phone and search more carefully, scanning for signs of movement. "Can you hear me?"

The long, delicate fingers of a disembodied hand play a piano key, and my heart rate surges.

"Isabel!" The sudden intake of breath causes me to cough. "Hang on. I'll get you out of there." I choke back tears. "Everything's going to be okay, hon."

God, I hope I'm right.

I look back over my shoulder and pull the handkerchief away from my mouth. "Help! We need a paramedic in here!" I give the string a couple of hard yanks and then turn back to Isabel.

In the few minutes I've been here, it's gotten hotter, and the smoke is worse. Sweat, or maybe blood, is dripping into my eyes, and I wipe it off with my arm. I get down on my knees and start shifting debris away from her face.

A minute later, I can see that she's curled up in the fetal position, one arm protecting her head. She came within millimeters of being crushed by the staircase, saved only by the indestructible craftsmanship of the huge Steinway Grand.

There's not much room to work in, but I manage to push a heavy chunk of masonry off so I can free her head and shoulders. She blinks up at my light, a silk scarf wrapped snugly around her nose and mouth.

Those scared green eyes are a beautiful sight.

She tries to speak but starts coughing.

I sweep the hair out of her face. "Shh. Don't try to talk. Are you seriously hurt?"

She shakes her head. "Lucky."

"Lucky?" It takes me a second to process the word. "Oh, yeah," I say. "You were super lucky that piano protected you."

She shakes her head. "Kit."

"What?"

She motions with her chin, and I realize there's a tiny black and white kitten curled up by her shoulder.

It wasn't her head she was protecting; it was the tiny kitten.

"I see her," I say and lift the little ball of fur. "Lucky, is it? She's fine." I stuff the kitten inside my shirt. "I'm going to pull you out now."

"A man," she says, her eyelids closing. "Okay?"

I look around—and then remember the guy crushed by the piano.

Christ, you can't tell her that.

"He must have gotten out, Iz."

She nods.

I clear debris until I have room to drag her out, and then I sit down, take hold of her shoulders, and pull hard, pushing with my legs. The exertion makes me cough, but she only moves an inch or two. Something is caught or pinned.

I let go and move over her again. "Do you know what's stuck? Is it your blouse?" Her eyelids flutter shut, and my heart jumps into my throat. "Isabel! Don't leave me. Please."

A light flashes across us, and three firefighters in hard hats and gas masks come up behind me. The first one hands me a mask and then steps around me and fits one over Isabel's face.

"Using the string was an excellent idea, sir. We followed it right to you." The voice is muffled but understandable.

Yeah, I'm a real genius.

Those kids saved Isabel's life—and probably mine too.

I pull off the bandanna, tighten the mask over my face, and breathe in, feeling the cool rush of oxygen into my lungs. The firefighter taps my shoulder. "Is there anyone else in here?"

I point at the foot sticking out of the piano case. He leans over and slips two fingers inside the sneakers, searching for a pulse. After a few seconds, he withdraws his hand and shakes his head.

"Okay," he says. "We need to get out pronto. Can you walk?"

I nod.

"Good. Go with Ripley." Another firefighter takes my arm.

I shake my head and then start to take the mask off so I can talk.

"Leave the oxygen on, sir." The voice is female. "We'll get your fiancée out too."

A firefighter squeezes in next to Isabel and uses a knife to cut her free. When they pull her out, her whole left side is soaked with blood.

Please let it not be hers.

"Let's go!" Ripley takes my arm as the other two lift Isabel. I grab onto the kite string with my bleeding hands, and using Ripley's powerful light, we exit the building in less than a minute.

The scene on the street is chaotic, but the gawking crowds are gone.

As Isabel is placed on a gurney and lifted into an ambulance, one of the medics swipes disinfectant across my brow, pinches the skin together, and slaps on a bandage. When she's done, I try to step up next to Isabel, but she puts a hand on my chest. "I'm sorry, sir. Unless you have more serious injuries, there's no room in the ambulance. We're still transporting victims with severe blood loss."

I watch Isabel's ambulance disappear and another takes its place. Across the street, I spy the animal cages. People are milling around them, but the group of kids who saved our lives are nowhere to be seen. I peer down the street, looking for the jewelry shop, but the whole block is cordoned off by the police now.

There's a loud crash from behind me, and I turn just as the top of the hotel collapses, sending a huge cloud of smoke and debris out the window I just exited. Flames erupt from the newly formed gap in the sky.

I swallow hard, the heat of the flames on my face. If it hadn't been for those delinquent kids, Isabel would be dead.

"Thank you," I whisper. "This time, I won't let her go."

I breathe in the cold, dry oxygen and then remember the kitten inside my shirt. I reach in to pet her, and she starts purring. I take her out and check that she's unhurt. "Nice to meet you, Lucky." I settle her back inside my shirt. "Let's go find Isabel." I set the oxygen mask down on the fire truck and make my way toward the cages stacked on the grass.

The wiener dog and the kittens are there too, and they all seem to be okay. I switch on my phone light and scan the cages until I find Tolstoy. He barks when he sees me, his tail wagging his whole body.

"Hey, big guy, let's rock and roll." I open the cage door and notice there's an envelope wedged inside. I pull it out and read the name scrawled on the expensive paper:

SHERLOCK

I laugh.

Inside, there's a note on jewelry store stationery:

WE KNEW YOU'D BE BACK FOR TOLSTOY.
JUST FOR THE RECORD, WE GOT ALL THE BEASTIES OUT.
LOOKS LIKE YOU SCORED TOO.

TAKE CARE OF THE MISSUS,

~THE HOLE-IN-THE-WALL GANG

When I tip the envelope, two gold wedding bands tumble into my hand.

I smile so big it makes my lips crack.

Propose by text message and present her with a stolen ring. Classy, Nadales, classy.

I stuff everything in my pocket and scoop Tolstoy out of the cage. With a puppy in one arm and a kitten in the other, I start jogging toward the hospital.

Madders' Log Entry 7

Target: Isabel Sanborn
Nexus: Hospital in Denver
Chrono Tag: Next Day

Major deviation confirmed. No record of
Chronosphere arrival or Isabel's near death
exists in virgin timeline. Suspect anomalies may
be related to xeno Diego's spacetime jump.

I wake up to a slow, rhythmic bleeping. That and the faint scent of flowers.

Diego Nadales is hovering over me, his worried face in a halo of light. "You're safe now, hon," he says, but his eyes betray the lie. He turns away and yells something into the smoky darkness.

I try to speak, to tell him about the kitten nestled in my arm, but I can't make a sound.

You must be dreaming.

I haven't seen or heard from Diego in years. By now, he's probably married to an annoyingly perfect wife with a passel of kids and a dog named Sparky.

I blink, and the vision evaporates.

Where am I?

Every muscle in my body aches. My throat is raw, and my lips are dry and cracked. My shoulder feels like it's broken, but I can wiggle my fingers and toes. At the back of my brain, a headache is threatening.

What happened?

I open my eyes, but the late afternoon sun is a knife in my skull. I squint and try to focus. At the foot of my bed, Dave and his lawyers are grinning back at me from a giant poster. I let out a breathy gasp and shut my eyes tight.

You died and went to hell.

I lie there, listening to the artificial sound of my galloping heartbeat, and try to remember what happened.

The fire.

And, omigod, the puppies and kittens.

"I didn't get them all out," I say, my voice muffled by some sort of mask.

I cough, take in a constricted breath, and cough harder.

Pain radiates out from the right side of my chest like someone stabbed me with a knife.

An alarm goes off above me, stoking my panic.

I try to breathe, but there's not enough space to expand my lungs, and the harder I try, the more it hurts. I gulp for air, my chest jerking with the failed attempts to inhale.

I hear squeaky footsteps.

"She's awake," a woman calls out, an edge to her voice. "Get the doctor."

More hurried footsteps. "Isabel? Can you hear me? I'm your nurse, Lucius." The long, smooth curve of the man's Southern vowels are somehow soothing. "Nod if you can hear me."

My heart is pounding in my ears, but I swallow and nod, eyes still shut.

"I need you to calm down, honey. Take slow, shallow breaths. Can you do that for me?"

I try, but the pain in my chest is making it hard to do anything except panic.

"Slow, shallow breaths," he says. "Here, just like me." He takes a short breath and blows it out. "Come on, Isabel, do it with me."

I attempt to follow his example, forcing myself to take small sips of air.

It seems like forever, but the pain finally lessens.

"Yes, there you go," the nurse says. "That's much better. We'll get you more pain meds when the doctor arrives."

The alarm goes silent, and the bleeping metronome slows.

I hear him adjust some window blinds. "You're in the hospital, Isabel. You bumped your head, broke your leg and collarbone, and cracked some ribs—not to mention inhaling a bit of smoke. But the doctors say you're going to be just fine."

I force my eyes open. "Did they get the animals out?" I whisper, my voice strangely gruff. It takes me a moment to focus my gaze.

A middle-aged black man is smiling down at me. "Yes, they got the pets out," he says, his eyes sparkling. "But don't try to talk. Just keep breathing." He pats my shoulder. "It was on the news last night —and again this morning." He turns and extends one arm out like a model in a game show, and I realize where the garden smell is coming from. "You're a regular celebrity now."

My room is full of flowers—along with balloons, a few cards, and a large stuffed lion.

Wow.

A tall, gangly Indian woman strides into the room, her face drawn and her hair in a ponytail.

"She woke up a bit disoriented," the nurse says and straightens the sheet over my chest. "But she's stable now. She says breathing is painful."

The doctor turns to me, her expression softening. "Let's see what we can do about that." She gives instructions to the nurse and then introduces herself.

A moment later, the pain in my chest eases.

"Better?" She raises an eyebrow. "Don't talk, just nod."

I do.

The doctor smiles. "Good." She takes a stethoscope out of her coat pocket. "Let's have a listen."

When she's done with her examination, she crosses her arms. "You're one lucky lady," she says. "If those firefighters had taken ten more minutes to find you, we might be looking at permanent lung damage, but I think you'll make a full recovery."

How did they find me? No one knew I was there.

The doctor nods at my torso. "Your ribs are going to be painful for a while, and we've put a splint on your leg. Your collarbone should heal on its own, but no lifting." She studies my right ear. "And you got a good bump on the noggin so you may have a concussion. We'll keep an eye on that too."

Concussion. At least that explains the guardian angel vision.

Even though I know it's impossible, some part of me was clinging to the hope that Diego *had* actually been there.

The doctor takes a deep breath, looking like she's had a long day. "I'm sure you have lots of questions, but let's give your vocal cords a day to rest, shall we? The less you strain them, the quicker they'll recover." She doesn't wait for an answer but puts the stethoscope back in her pocket and turns to go. "Did we contact her family?"

When the nurse doesn't respond, the doctor turns, her expression pinched—but she freezes when she sees the nurse's face. It's the response pretty much everyone has when they find out I'm an only child and my parents are dead.

"Spouse?" she says, and I shake my head. "Significant other you'd like us to contact?"

I shake it again and whisper, "Just a close friend."

"Good enough," the doctor says. "Given the ballyhoo out in the lobby, I expect the mayor will be vying to drive you home." She harrumphs. "I'll check back in the morning."

The nurse glances at me and then the doctor, his chin lowered. "Doctor, would you allow one visitor?" The nurse motions with his head toward the door. "We sent him home last night, but the poor guy's been camped out in the waiting room all day. He says he has the kitten she was carrying."

The doctor narrows one eye, weighing "no family" against "no visitors," I think. "Five minutes," she says and turns to me. "Assuming that's all right with you?"

I nod, trying to come up with who might be out there.

The last thing I recall is falling down next to the piano—and then waking up in the ambulance.

"Just him," the doctor says, dragging me back to the present. "No other visitors."

The nurse smiles and smooths out his scrubs. "Yes, doctor."

After the physician leaves, the nurse puts his finger to his lips. "Shh. Doctor's orders." He's wearing a dragonfly pin on his scrubs. "Shall I get you a pad of paper to write on?" After I nod, he leaves the room, his footsteps squeaking down the hallway.

Ordered to keep your mouth shut. Dave'll love that.

A minute later, I hear a voice I haven't heard in fifteen years. The slight Spanish accent makes my pulse race, and the heart rate monitor announces it to the whole damn world.

I'm still trying to rein it in when Diego Nadales peeks around the doorframe.

"Isabel," he says, his eyes glossy. "*Mierda*, it's good to see you."

The nurse is standing behind him, his arms crossed but his eyes smiling. "Five minutes," he says. "And no talking, Miss Isabel?"

I give him the okay sign.

"Thank you," Diego says. He nods at the nurse and steps into the room, his hands behind his back. His hair is a little grayer than I remember, and the late afternoon sun is highlighting his beard stubble and the dark circles under his eyes, but he's still infuriatingly handsome. "I can't tell you how worried I was," he says and presents me with a small bouquet of wildflowers. "I picked them this morning." His voice falls off as he looks around the room. "Up at the cabin."

I press my palms together in thanks.

"You're welcome," he says, shuffling his feet. He sets the delicate yellow and purple flowers on the tray next to my bed. "Sorry they're a little wilted." He swallows and glances at the photo of Dave and his goons. "I guess you're famous now." He shrugs one shoulder. "The TV news can't stop talking about how you saved all those puppies and kittens."

He pulls up a chair and sits down, stuffing his hands into his pockets and then pulling them out again. "The nurse said you're going to be fine. That's great news."

I nod and gesture toward his battle wounds. He has a bandage above his eye, and his forearm is wrapped in gauze.

"Just being stupid."

I furrow my eyebrows, but he doesn't notice.

He puts his elbows on his thighs and leans forward, looking down at the floor. "Did you get my text messages last night?" He waits for me to respond, and when I don't, he looks up.

I shake my head.

"You didn't?" His voice rises, and he sits up straighter.

I shake my head again.

"Thank God." He flops back in the chair, looking relieved.

I narrow my gaze and tip my head to the side, asking what he means.

"I was pretty panicked at the time, and I, uh," he shuffles his feet, "I said some things I probably shouldn't have."

I give him a half smile, still trying to come to terms with how seeing him again makes me feel.

Happy.

I mime writing with my hand, but he looks confused, and I say, "Pencil."

"Shh! You'll get me grounded." He glances over his shoulder like they're going to throw him out, and I laugh. He makes a face, fumbles in his pocket, and takes out a pad of paper and a pen. "The nurse gave me these. The pen can write by itself." He waits for me to react. "And other words too."

I roll my eyes, and he beams.

How long has it been since a guy made you laugh?

He hands me the pen and holds the pad for me. I'm lying on my back with the oxygen mask over my face, the room cloaked in evening shadows now. My right shoulder is out of commission, so I have to use my left hand. I manage to scrawl a single word, my arm shaking so much it's almost illegible.

He stares at it for a moment. "Kitten?" he says, and his face lights up. "Oh, yeah. Lucky. Of course. I've got her. She's fine. I'll take care of her until you're better. No worries."

How did he know her name?

I nod and mouth, "Thank you."

He leans back and puts his hands in his lap, his gaze lowered. "Isabel," he says and exhales. "I'm sorry." He steals a glance at me, and I raise my shoulders.

For what?

"The past. Us. How it all turned out," he says, his eyes getting glossy again.

I wave my hand like I'm sweeping it all away. "Kids," I say, although it's more of a croak, and shrug my good shoulder for effect.

He exhales, his eyes downcast. "Yeah. Kids. Dumb kids. Well, to be precise, I was the dumb one. You were," he looks up at me—I shake my head—"perfect."

We both made mistakes, Diego. We were both young and broke and scared.

He clears his throat and meets my gaze. "I'm so glad I found you."

I nod and take a slow breath, my lips pressed together.

I've missed you, I say in my head and let my gaze linger on his lips and face.

The nurse steps in the doorway. "Time's up, Mr. Nadales. Tomorrow is another day."

Diego winks at me. "Frankly, my dear, I don't give a damn."

"Well, Mr. Butler," the nurse says, putting his hands on his hips, "I'm afraid you *still* have to come back tomorrow during visiting hours."

"Will do." Diego stands and puts the chair back in the corner. "Good night, Iz. Sleep well."

I wave with my fingertips and mouth *thank you* again.

He stands there, staring at me with his head tipped, his expression unreadable, and then he turns and walks out of the room, limping a little.

"Lordy me," the nurse says, "that man is stubborn." He sets a wrapped sandwich and two cartons of applesauce down next to Diego's wildflowers. He nods at me. "In case you get hungry."

I press my palms together again.

He pours water into two plastic cups, places the bouquet into one, and sets a straw in the other. "I'll check back in a bit to make sure you're comfortable." He walks to the door, turning off the lights as he exits the room.

I listen to his shoes squeak down the hallway, and then I focus on the slow, steady bleep of the monitor.

A moment later, I'm asleep.

Madders' Log Entry 8

Target: Matt Hudson
Nexus: Matt's House
Chrono Tag: Next Day

Increased Temporal observations reveal new event
sequences developing. My own arrival at Warm
Springs Military Complex appears to be occurring
much sooner in this timeline.

I t's still dark when I get up and take a shower. As I'm stumbling my way to the coffee machine, I can hear Cassie's furious typing in the den.

When did she become so annoyingly energetic in the mornings?

"Anything new?" I ask once I'm caffeinated.

She shakes her head, her eyes still scanning the computer. "There's lots of chatter on the fires but nothing about the UFO." She looks at me. "I mean a big, fat goose egg. The Denver Post is still saying a decommissioned gas main ignited and that's what caused the ducks-in-a-row fires." She huffs. "What a crock of shit. Even NOAA has satellite data on the bogey. I checked. Anyone with a computer could put two and two together just like we did—and it doesn't add up to any ducks."

"So they must be hiding something," I say. "The question is why."

"Or what." She raises an eyebrow. "A perfectly round metal sphere appearing out of thin air and going Mach fifteen is not something you expect to see every day."

"Or any day, for that matter." I shrug. "I'll check in with Sam when I get back from the airport and see what he's uncovered." I glance at my watch. "We better get going."

After I drop Cassandra off at the terminal—and wait till she takes off—I make a half-hearted attempt to catch up on my reading. The fall semester doesn't start until tomorrow, and I've taught the same freshmen class for so many years now I could do it in my sleep. I call Sam twice, but my calls go to voicemail. After checking that all the gadgets in my lab are running smoothly, I break open a bevvy, make scrambled eggs for supper, and watch the evening news. All anyone can talk about is that woman who saved a whole slew of little nippers from a burning hotel. There's also a brief mention of an investigation involving an old gas main but absolutely nothing on Cassie's sphere.

I turn in early but end up lying awake thinking about how lonely my life has become. It's always the hardest right after Cassandra leaves. I still half expect to hear her boiling the kettle or calling to see if I want to watch *Blade Runner* for the seven hundredth time. But eventually, I fall into a fitful sleep, dreaming about little green men chasing her as I stand by, frozen and mute.

Sometime after midnight, I startle awake and realize I need to tinkle. I get up and shuffle into the bathroom.

Which is where I am when the bedroom door flies open and a man wearing a suit and tie attempts to handcuff my pillow.

I consider screaming at the top of my lungs—or trying to hide in the linen closet—but in the end, I'm still standing there shaking the dew off the lily when another bloke flicks on the bedroom lights.

It isn't the most dignified introduction I've ever had, but it's not the worst, either.

"Matthew C. Hudson," he says, trying hard not to look at my meat and potatoes, "you are under arrest for interfering with a US government operation." The guy is as bald as a bowling ball, and like his buddy, he's wearing a white shirt, dark suit, and black gloves. He turns to the younger man—who is still strangling my pillow. "Put that damn thing down and cuff him."

"Yes, sir." The kid scrambles across the bed, but his foot gets caught in the covers, and he lands hard on the floor.

"Why do you need to handcuff me?" I say, backing up against the sink, my heart going ten to the dozen. "I'm not resisting arrest. I was just having a wee."

And it's a good thing I was, because otherwise, I'd be wetting myself.

I look over at the bald guy, trying to keep my voice steady. "Who are you? And how did you get into my house?"

"I'm Johnson, and this is Smith, my junior assistant." Kojak crosses his arms, waiting for the kid to untangle his foot. "We have a search warrant—"

"Your door was unlocked," Junior says and gives an exaggerated shrug. "You really should be more careful."

Johnson scowls. "We have orders to bring you in—stat."

Junior, who's searching in the covers for his shoe, says, "Stat means without delay. Hence the late hour."

I stare at him, part of me scared shitless and part wondering where the government found these clowns. In the thrillers Sam is always making me watch, the spooks are total badasses. These yahoos appear to be their budget stand-ins.

"So take me in," I say, my heart rate down to a brisk trot. "But let me get dressed first. And I have a class to teach in the morning, so I'll need to leave a message for the department secretary, or I'll lose my job."

Junior gets back to his feet and hesitates, glancing back and forth between me and his boss. "Sir?"

"Make sure he doesn't have any weapons."

I lean back. "I'm in my sodding pajamas."

Junior shrugs again. "He *is* wearing his sodding pajamas, sir."

I flush the toilet and take a step toward them. "What about my Miranda rights?"

Johnson shifts his weight. "I was told there were some irregularities with your green card application, doctor. So I suggest you cooperate fully—assuming you wish to remain in the United States."

I consider telling him I prefer London anyway, but go with, "I have a right to speak to a solicitor."

"It might be better to call your lawyer," Junior says, and I give him a nod.

I walk toward the nightstand to get my mobile, and Johnson takes out a sidearm. "Uh, uh, uh," he says, wagging the gun at me. "Can't risk you making contact with any co-conspirators." He motions with his head toward the kid. "Get him in the car."

"What about my clothes?" I say, my voice breaking. "At least let me get shoes and a coat. It's freezing out there."

Johnson grabs an old jumper off the back of a chair and tosses it at me. As I'm putting it on, he leans sideways to look at my feet. I'm wearing the dragon slippers Cassie gave me when she was six.

Johnson snorts. "Looks to me like you're good to go, doc."

I start to protest, and Johnson jerks his chin up and aims the gun at me. "He's resisting arrest, Mr. Smith. Cuff him."

"Okay. Okay," I say and lift my hands. "I'm not resisting anything. When do I get my phone call?"

"The minute we confirm you're not a terrorist." Johnson strides across the room and grabs my arm. Junior hurries over to my other side, and they frog-march me out of the house and down the driveway to a huge black SUV. As they're forcing me into the back seat, Johnson reaches across to clip my seatbelt, engages some sort of lock on it, and covers my nose and mouth with a damp cloth. "Have a nice nap."

When I come to, my chest is duct-taped to an office chair—and there's a mug of something on the table in front of me. I'm alone in a small conference room with a flimsy projector screen hanging on one wall, a fluorescent light overhead, and a half-full pot of coffee behind me. I can smell spilled drops burning on the hot plate.

I half-heartedly test my restraints and almost tip the chair over. The sodding thing has wheels on it.

What is it with Americans and wheelie chairs? Are they worried the furniture is lazy?

I shiver and flex my stiff hands.

No cuffs.

I'm freezing—but, by George, I'm not in the clink.

It takes me less than a minute to tear the tape off my chest— almost like they wanted me to escape.

I try the door, but it's locked, so I pace around the room, looking for hidden cameras and trying to decide what to do next. There's some sort of projector in the wall above the coffee pot, but it's too high to reach.

I yawn and sit back down in the wheelie chair. If I had to guess, I'd say it's four or five in the morning, but there's no way to know for sure. I sniff the coffee cup on the table—it smells normal—and stick my finger in. It's lukewarm.

What the blazes is going on?

The AC kicks on, and cold air blasts out of the ceiling. I pull the jumper tighter around my neck, wishing I had insisted on bringing my mobile phone.

I wonder if they know about Cassie and Sam.

Part of me hopes they don't—and part of me hopes those two will walk through the door any second now.

Thirty minutes go by.

I don't like enclosed spaces, and this windowless conference room isn't doing me any favors.

I get up, dump the tepid mug of coffee back into the pot, and pour myself a fresh cup. There's a stubby pencil mixed in with the condiments, and I stick it in the pocket of my pajamas.

Might come in handy.

I add fake cream and sugar to the coffee, stir it up with a real, metal spoon, and take a sip.

And gag.

I wipe the spoon off with a napkin—and get an idea.

After setting the mug on the table, I walk over to the door, bend the spoon handle flat, and slide it in between the latch and wall. It's the same cheap mechanism that's on my office door at uni, and it takes me less than a minute to jimmy it open.

But the moment the lock releases, Mr. Johnson pushes through, knocking me on my bum.

"Going somewhere, doctor?" Mr. Undoubtedly-Not-Johnson is now wearing mirrored sunglasses.

Might as well have "I Killed E.T." tattooed on his forehead.

"Yeah," I say and roll over on my hands and knees. "I'm going home. Detaining me like this is unlawful." My dragon slippers fall off, and it takes me a minute to get to my feet. I brush off my hands on my pajamas. "I demand to see an attorney."

Johnson takes off his sunglasses and smirks at my "Make Cupcakes Not War" jumper. "You've heard of the Patriot Act?" He waits for me to nod. "Since you're not a US citizen, and we have evidence you were involved in a terrorist attack, I can keep you locked up in here till hell freezes over."

I rub my hands together. "I think it already has."

He tips his head to the side and gives me a fake smile. "But since you don't have a rap sheet, the guys at HQ suggested I play nice. So instead of teaching you some manners, I'm asking a few simple questions: What kind of weapon is the projectile that came down in Denver? Where was it manufactured? Did you deliberately target an empty building, or did your ballistic guys screw up?"

I collapse back into the chair. "Merlin's pants! I'm not a terrorist.

All I did was invent a system that uses amateur telescopes to detect and track smallish meteors. A couple nights ago, I got a hit. End of story."

He narrows one eye. "You expect me to believe you threw together something in your backyard that located this missile before NORAD?"

"It's not in my backyard—it's spread across North America. We use an array of consumer-grade telescopes and some custom software to grab the data. When we got a blip two nights ago, we ran the data through a public-domain algorithm and plotted the trajectory."

"Who do you mean when you say 'we,' doctor? Who else is in on this?"

Crikey, you better be more careful, or you'll get Cassandra tangled up in this.

"I mean all the amateur scientists who lend me their telescopes."

"Do they know they're helping you commit crimes?"

"I am not committing any crimes," I say and slap my hands down on the table. "In fact, I didn't do anything nefarious or illegal. The information was there for the world to see. I bet it's still on the NOAA website. And the NORAD satellites probably detected the sphere too, but it's rather small, so maybe their software just dismissed it."

The guy brings his fingertip up to his mouth and then adjusts his necktie. "So *your* software caught the bogey before *ours* did?" For the first time, he looks at me with something other than contempt.

I rub my tired eyes. "I guess so."

"And you expect me to believe this is all just a coincidence?"

"Yes." I try to keep the annoyance out of my voice but fail.

He frowns. "The Pentagon says you contacted NORAD and tried to get them to start a city-wide panic."

"When I called NORAD, I was attempting to be helpful. But no one took me seriously. They thought I was a crank caller and told me to stay off the line, for chrissake. Twenty-four hours later, you and Gilligan broke into my house, kidnapped me in my pajamas, and locked me up in Antarctica. I may not be a US citizen, but I still have basic human rights."

He crosses his arms and tips his head to the side, his lips puckered out. "Are you done now, doctor?"

"I'm not a doctor," I say and blow out a breath. "I'm a physics professor, and I've had just about enough of this cloak and dagger shite."

"Okay, Hudson, don't get your panties in a twist. You may not be a terrorist, but the government knows about your wormhole research, and—"

"Christ on a pogo stick, you got the wrong—" I bite my tongue.

These bozos meant to kidnap Cassandra.

"The wrong what?" Dick says.

"The wrong man," I say. "I'm not a theoretical physicist. I'm a lowly materials guy. When it comes to higher maths, I'm like a chimp rubbing two sticks together."

The alleged Mr. Johnson—who I have decided to call Agent Dick in honor of his congenial personality and flamboyant wardrobe—takes a slip of paper out of his shirt pocket, turns it right-side up, and reads it, his lips moving the whole time. "Okay, so you're the M. C. Hudson who's an expert in quantum materials, and your *niece* is the C. M. Hudson who works with wormholes?"

I put my elbows on the table and drop my forehead into my hands. "Leave her out of this."

What a shambles.

"Sir, are you aware of the situation in the Balkans?"

"What situation?" I say and look up.

"Or the response from the Russians?"

"Crikey," I say. "What happened?"

He crosses his arms. "I'm not at liberty to discuss that."

Tosser.

I lean back in the chair. "I want to talk to an attorney."

"Hudson," he says, "you are henceforth assigned to report to me. I expect your full cooperation, and the moment I suspect you're not being completely forthcoming, things could go very badly for you—and your niece."

I feel my hackles rise. "Are you threatening to harm Cassandra? Because, if you are, I'll—"

"You'll what? Call the campus police? File a complaint with the Consumer Protection Agency? Yell and stamp your feet?" He laughs like Voldemort and then glares at me. "Don't tempt me."

I stand up. "You *are* threatening me."

"No. Just informing you." He pulls another sheet of paper out of his suit pocket, smooths it out in front of me, and offers me a pen. "Sign it."

"And if I don't?"

He sighs. "Then I'll assume you're a terrorist."

"Fabulous."

"Let's get real here, doctor. You know some things, and I know some things. Maybe if we work together, we can figure out what your so-called bogey is and where it came from." He shrugs. "Or you could take an extended vacation in Cuba courtesy of the government? I hear the weather's nice."

I shake my head and spend the next fifteen minutes reading the classified projects contract. It pretty much says they own me. If I so much as break wind without approval, they'll prosecute me for espionage.

I sign it.

What else am I going to do? Be a martyr?

I hand it back to him. "You threaten my niece again, Mr. Johnson, and you'll live to regret it."

Agent Dick snorts and dims the lights—as if I had just mentioned that the juice and biscuits were running low. "What you're about to see was recorded by a security camera six hours ago, doctor."

"Stop calling me that! For chrissake, I can't even put a sodding plaster on without written directions."

The government agent smirks and leans against the wall, his arms still crossed and his eyes on the flat-panel display.

Up on the screen, the cone of a streetlamp slices through the gray and black murk. Lurking behind it, a bombed-out building pokes up into the night sky, broken walls standing at odd angles and smoke billowing up into the darkness. The stark infrared image gives the scene a sinister feel of things turned inside out.

Bloody hell.

I study the security camera recording. The distant skyline seems familiar, but I can't place it. At the bottom of the screen, a *Warning! No Trespassing!* sign hangs askew on a sagging chain-link fence. I tip my head sideways in a useless attempt to straighten it.

This is absurd.

And then I recognize the mailbox-shaped skyscraper in the background. "Denver. And that's the famous hotel that caught on fire?"

The guy who killed E.T. glances at me, his lips tight, but doesn't answer.

"I'll take that as a yes."

From the left of the screen, three teenagers bob into view, skulking around past curfew. They swagger down the sidewalk and then stop and look around, unaware that anyone is watching. The tall, skinny kid gives an unconscious tug on his sagging pants, an act as contagious as a yawn, and the other two follow suit. A moment later, two more hooded figures join them, one obviously a little kid. The four teenagers scramble up the chain-link fence, the chubby one knocking the crooked warning sign with his foot. The metal plate clatters silently to the ground, and the little kid hops back. The teens jump down on the other side, one of them landing with his pants around his thighs.

Always wondered if that happens.

One of the trespassers bends the bottom of the fence to let the little kid through, and they all slink off into the smoking ruins.

The timestamp in the corner of the video freezes, and then the screen goes black.

I yawn and rub my eyes. "You broke down my door in the middle of the night for that? Did I miss a secret message encoded on the guy's boxers?"

He ignores me. "This next clip was recorded by one of the suspects. It was recovered from his portable cellular device an hour ago."

Portable cellular device. Please.

Before I have a chance to respond, an amateur-looking video appears on the screen.

Two guys are looking at something in the burned ruins of the building. They lean over and accidentally bump their heads, and the camera guy chuckles. The picture bounces as he moves closer, and a shiny object the size of a basketball comes into view.

Crikey, that's the sphere Cassie and I were tracking.

"What the hell is that?" The voice behind the camera is a whisper.

The taller guy reaches out, but the other one slaps his hand away. "Don't be a dumbass. It could be dangerous." He looks off-camera. "Hey, Lani, we found something!"

More teenagers gather around the metal ball, and the camera zooms in. The object is glowing like a full moon, eerie and ominous.

The leader of the group, a slight Asian kid, touches the sphere and then jerks his hand away. "Shit! It's still hot! It must be solid metal—and probably worth a fortune. Let's pry it out."

The voice sounds a bit odd—and then I realize that the kid is actually a *girl*—and she is obviously used to calling the shots because the guys get right to work.

As her minions scramble to find makeshift tools, the girl steps back, eyes narrowed, assessing the wreckage. The little kid, five or six, tugs at her sleeve.

"Lani, I wanna see!"

"No, Teddy. You need to stay over there," she says, voice firm. She tries to shoo him away.

"But you promised Gran you wouldn't go out at night now that you got that dollar-chip!" His small voice wavers as he stumbles over the last word.

"Scholarship," she says, crouching down to his level, her tone softening. "This is the last time, okay? That metal ball could be worth a lot, kiddo. But I need you to stay back where it's safe."

The kid crosses his arms, pouting. "I wanna help."

She ruffles his hair. "You are helping. You're carrying my doctor bag, remember?"

He frowns but nods, retreating a few steps.

The two guys bring back a long piece of steel pipe and wedge it under the sphere, resting the middle on a huge chunk of broken concrete. Then the three of them attempt to pry the object out while the voice behind the camera calls out encouragement. I can see the pipe bend with the applied force, but the sphere doesn't budge.

They rest for a moment, and the chubby guy hikes up his pants for the hundredth time, looking impressed. "That sucker's heavier than a dead preacher. What do you think it is?"

The camera operator coughs. "A bomb."

The tall kid starts backing away, his hands covering his crotch, but trips and falls on his bum.

"You halfwit mooker." The skinny girl wipes her mouth on her sleeve. "If it was a bomb, it would have exploded by now. This whole place was a furnace yesterday." She kicks the metal ball with her boot to demonstrate her point.

"Yeah, sure." The guy scrambles back to his feet. "I knew it wasn't a bomb."

The girl looks over at the camera. "Put that thing away, Spielberg, and come help us."

A moment later, the screen goes blank.

Agent Dick flips on the lights.

I sit for a moment, blinded. A headache is forming in the back of my exhausted brain, and I feel a little nauseated from the claustrophobia. I take a couple deep breaths. "I need something to write on. A lab book would be ideal."

He stares at me, unmoving.

"Do you want to know more about that metal sphere or not?"

He takes a little black book out of his inner coat pocket, tears out a few sheets, and throws the thing on the table in front of me.

"Thank you." I take the short pencil out of my shirt pocket, open the small notebook to the second or third page, and smooth out the paper.

"Where'd you get that sharp instrument?"

I write the date at the top of the page, and *Sphere* next to it. "In with the sugar."

"Goddamn amateurs," he says, outraged by my pencil stub. "If it wasn't for me, this place would be a fucking zoo."

I ignore him and start writing:

> *Dense, metallic, reflective.*
> *Still hot 48 hours after fire.*

Agent Dick peers over my shoulder. "I have orders to get through this as quickly as possible, doctor."

I underline *hot* twice. I consider some common alloys, trying to decide which one fits the description.

Platinum? Tungsten? Possibly a gallium alloy?

He taps his foot and then clears his throat. "Powerful people are waiting to make time-critical decisions based on your analysis, Dr. Hudson."

Does this guy go home at night and practice being an arse?

"Well then bugger 'em. If you expect me to figure out what the hell that is, then belt up and let me work." In the notebook, I draw a circle and inscribe a hand so I get the relative size correct. I pencil in the steel pipe the kids used as a lever and the concrete fulcrum, using them to estimate the force applied by four teenagers to check my guess.

"Well?" Dick asks as I'm solving the equation.

I snap the notebook shut, yawn, and stretch my arms. "The metal sphere weighs at least half a ton. You'll need a crane to get it out of there, assuming it doesn't sink any deeper into that hot muck. And good luck getting any heavy equipment into that mess of burned debris. Should make for great viewing on the news tonight."

He snatches the pencil and notebook out of my hands. "That's enough."

As I'm wondering what those kids found in the smoking ruins, the door opens and Junior trots in. "They're bringing it in, sir."

He's wearing the exact same sunglasses as Agent Dick.

Maybe they got them on a Blue-Light Special?

Junior hands me some of my clothes and a pair of my shoes. "Thought you might want something warmer than pajamas."

"Thank you," I say, feeling my face flush. I start getting dressed, pulling my clothes on over my pajamas.

Agent Dick watches me with a look of disdain on his face. "Hustle up, princess. We don't have all day."

"Where are you taking me?" I say, hopping around on one foot.

"Alcatraz," Dick says. "You're going to be enjoying their hospitality while we confirm your allegiance."

Before I can find the words to express my outrage, Junior laughs. "Don't worry. It's not as bad as it sounds, hip furniture and all—although I've heard the food sucks."

I stare at him, my tired brain spinning its wheels.

"It's the hotel here," Junior says. "The rooms are arranged in two facing rows like the cells in a penitentiary—and the doors automatically lock at eight pm." He moves his arm like an ax. "Cha-ching."

I swallow the lump in my throat. "Isn't that a fire hazard?"

He shrugs. "Could be."

I glance at Dick. "What about my right to an attorney?"

"Your only right is to shut the fuck up," he says and motions with his head toward the door. "Get him out of here."

Madders' Log Entry 9

Target: Diego Nadales

Nexus: A Hospital in Denver

Chrono Tag: 5 Days Later

Outliers confirmed to be Matt Hudson, Diego
Nadales, and Isabel Kirkland. Hudson has most
deviations to date. Extra surveillance initiated.
Isabel and Diego appear to be in contact several
years before their first recorded post-divorce
interactions in virgin timeline.

"You'll love the cabin," I say and stuff my hands in my pockets. "Lucky certainly does, and everyone knows cats are super picky—she's basically your furry seal of approval." I kick at a flower petal on the floor. "At least come see it?"

Isabel is sitting on her hospital bed, waiting for a wheelchair to arrive—and already looking exhausted. "I'm sure it's beautiful," she says, not meeting my gaze. "And thank you for taking care of her, but

I don't want to impose. Sophie says she can help out until I get back on my feet."

"Sophie has four kids, two dogs, and a husband that travels for work," I say. "I know she *would* stay with you, but it just doesn't make any sense. My new place is a bit of a drive, but it's worth it just for the view. Besides, I'm already taking time off to put in some upgrades, so it's no trouble at all. You can have your own bedroom, and once you feel up to it, you can work remotely until you're ready to go back."

She rubs her hands on her thighs. "It'll be twice the work for you, Diego, cooking and cleaning and laundry. You didn't sign up for that."

"Yeah, well, I used to be one of those chefs who shouts and swears a lot," I say.

She looks up at me, her nose wrinkling.

"But then I discovered oven mitts."

She rolls her eyes, but I can see the hint of a smile.

Lucius, the nurse who has been caring for Isabel all week, laughs heartily. "Diego, you got a way with words," he says. He's packing up gifts from Isabel's myriad admirers to donate to the children's wing. Kirkland sent her half a garden center of flowers, but he never actually turned up to see how she was doing. Guess he's moved on.

How in the hell did she end up married to that piece of shit?

Lucius stops for a moment and peeks over his glasses at Isabel. "You *are* going to need some help for a while, missy." He turns and stuffs a huge fluffy lion into a plastic bag. "And it does sound like an ideal arrangement." He gives me a conspiratorial look.

"Lucius," Isabel says, "can Diego and I have a moment alone, please?"

"Absolutely." He adjusts the shooting star pin he's wearing on his scrubs today. "I'll just take these gifts down to the kids, shall I?"

"Yes," Isabel says, her shoulders sagging. "Thank you."

The nurse picks up two more stuffed animals, and we watch in silence as he carries the menagerie out of the room, trailing a dachshund pull toy behind him.

I clear my throat. "Isa—"

"—Diego." She exhales. "Sorry."

"No, I'm sorry," I say, my heart stuck in my throat. "I've been sorry for the last fifteen years, and the universe finally gave me a chance to do something about it. Please say yes."

She looks down at her hands. "I have to be at work next Friday. At Kirkland Enterprises. I'm giving an important demo of my micro-drones, and some bigwigs will be attending." She presses her lips together. "Along with Dave."

"Not a problem," I say, attempting to keep my voice level.

Can't say I'd be sad to see the company go down in flames.

She sits up straighter. "It's important work, Diego. It could revolutionize crop production. Save millions of lives."

"Well then, I'd love to hear about it," I say. "Assuming you wouldn't have to shoot me afterwards."

"I would."

"Then I'll be sure to wear my bulletproof vest."

She laughs.

"Say yes, Iz."

"Unfortunately, the last thing I need is more drama, Diego."

"Oh, come on. Drama is just life with the dull bits cut out."

She crosses her arms. "Well, I'm ready for a long patch of boredom."

I smile, indescribably happy to have her back in my life. "For dinner, I'll order off the kids' menu: plain cheese pizza and vanilla ice cream. What do you say?"

"Diego, it does sound delightfully dull, but I can't just go home with you."

"Yes, you can," I say, knowing I'm being pushy as hell.

I can't risk losing you again, Iz.

Before she can protest, I hold up my hands. "I totally get what you said yesterday about being done with men and dating. I'm not offering to let you stay because I want to change that. I'm offering because I have this lovely cabin in the mountains, and it would be my

pleasure to help you for a few weeks. Once you're feeling better, just
say the word, and I'll whisk you and Lucky back to your apartment,
no questions asked."

She's quiet for a minute, twisting her thumb and index finger
around her opposite wrist.

I hold up my hand. "I promise not to eat your whole-wheat pita
chips, hog the sofa, or leave the toilet seat up."

The corner of her mouth curves up.

"And you're going to love the stars at night. They're like nothing
you've ever seen."

"Okay, okay," she says and finally meets my gaze. "I'd love to stay
at your cabin, Diego. Thank you."

The frat boys in my head let out a whoop.

"Well, I'll be," Lucius says as he strides into the room pushing a
wheelchair. "That wiener dog pull toy was a real hit." He smiles at
Isabel. "All the kids send their thanks and best wishes for a speedy
recovery." He turns the chair around and locks the wheels.
"Ready?"

"Yes," Isabel says and stifles a cough.

Lucius reaches for an inhaler, but Isabel waves him off. He hands
the inhaler to me. "If she coughs more than once, make sure she uses
that."

"Yes, sir."

As he's helping Isabel into the wheelchair, Lucius catches my
eye, asking if she's going home with me.

I nod, and he winks.

Once she's settled, I stick her inhaler in my pocket and grab her
suitcase, my heart still beating fast.

"What about that big ol' card in the corner?" Lucius says and
points at the life-size rendering of Kirkland and his minions. Inside is
the touching endearment: "Kirkland Enterprises: From Earth to
Mars, We Build the Future!"

"Burn it," Isabel says. "Or better yet, put it in a compost heap
under rotting vegetables."

Lucius, still staring at the photo, puts his hands on his hips. "Isn't that the man who's building igloos on Mars?"

"Yeah," I say. "Ex-husband. Made off with everything except the clothes she was wearing."

"Well, bless his heart," Lucius says and starts pushing Isabel's wheelchair. "I expect the man will get what he deserves in the end. Most folks do."

I follow them down the hallway, and Isabel cranes her neck around to look at me. "How'd you know about the divorce settlement?"

I give a mirthless laugh. "He was my best friend before he was your husband. I'm sure he figured out a way to get everything he wanted—and make it look like he did you a favor."

She settles back into the seat. "Spoken like someone with first-hand knowledge."

"Don't get me started."

When we get to the lobby, Lucius offers the wheelchair handles to me. "Been a pleasure getting to know you both," he says and gives Isabel a one-armed hug. "I hope you find your happily ever after. You deserve it." He gestures toward a handful of people waiting out front. "I think all those folks would agree."

The moment we exit the hospital, a TV reporter waves. "Do you have a minute?"

"They've been waiting all week to talk to you," I whisper over Isabel's shoulder. "And I think they'll be less likely to follow us to the cabin if you speak to them now. I'm afraid you're a celebrity."

She nods, and I push the wheelchair over toward the local TV news crew. The reporter cues the camera and smiles into it. "Last week, in a heartwarming act of bravery, a local woman rescued more than twenty puppies and kittens from a burning building here in downtown Denver. Witnesses report that the woman risked her own life to rescue the stranded pets. She's joining us now, live from the hospital where she was just released."

The reporter crouches down next to Isabel. "Good afternoon," she says. "We're so glad you're feeling better. Can you tell our viewers what happened last Friday evening?"

Isabel looks a little embarrassed, but she nods. "I was walking to my car when I was knocked to the ground by an explosion."

As Isabel continues her story, I can't help feeling a swell of love and pride. But as the reporter peppers her with questions about how she saved all the animals, Isabel becomes flustered. "I don't know how many didn't make it," she says. "I couldn't save them all." She looks like she might cry.

"Thank you," I say and start pushing Isabel's wheelchair. "That's all for now."

The reporter goes back to speaking to the camera.

"None of the animals died," I say as I help Isabel into the passenger seat and check her seatbelt. "They *all* made it out. Every one of them."

"What? How do you know?"

"I just do." I start the car and head toward the freeway. "Sophie dropped off your pillow, your computer, and a suitcase she packed for you. If there's anything else you need, we can stop on the way to the cabin."

She tips her chin down. "Sophie is in on this too?"

"Yep. We can invite them over for dinner once you're up to it."

"That would be lovely," she says, then turns and gazes out the window, her lips pressed together.

I stare at her face in profile, every nerve in my body tingling. "What is it, Iz?"

"Nothing important. Just my phone and my purse—and a hand-made puzzle box," she says. "They were in my car."

"Yeah, about your car," I say. "The police say it was totaled and to call your insurance company. If you find out where they've towed it, I'll go look for your things."

"Fruff froo," she says, yawning.

"Welcome," I say and stifle a smile. I lock the car doors and grab her pillow from the back. "Here. I'll wake you up when we get home."

As I'm getting on the interstate, she stuffs the pillow against the window and rests her head on it. I turn on acoustic guitar music and, a few exits later, get onto another freeway going west toward the mountains.

"Diego," she says and stifles another yawn, "do you know what happened to the golden retriever puppy? The Adopt-a-Pet people said his cage was empty."

An explosion of happiness fills my chest, and it's all I can do not to smile. "Everyone loves goldens," I say, working hard to make it sound off-hand. "I'm sure someone took him home. Why do you ask?"

She wipes her face with the back of her hand. "I wanted to adopt him. But I just couldn't. My apartment is too small, and I don't have a yard. But if I had taken him outside, maybe he wouldn't have—"

"He made it out," I say and rest my hand on her knee. "I'm sure of it."

She nods, but I can tell she doesn't believe me.

A few minutes later, I hear her soft exhalations.

When I pull off the highway and turn onto a gravel road, she wakes up.

"Are we there?" She sits up, her eyes sleepy and her hair messy.

I stare at her, the memory of lazy mornings in bed squeezing my heart. "Almost," I say.

Even though it's fall, the evening is mild, and a few stars are already visible. The moon, a whisper shy of full, is rising in the east.

"It's beautiful up here," she says. "Like a dream world."

I start the steep drive up to the cabin. "I asked the neighbor, Mrs. Malloy, to keep an eye on things, so I expect she'll be waiting for us. She and her family live just over the ridge."

"Good neighbors are the quiet heroes of our daily lives," she says and hugs her arms tight to her body.

"Indeed." I turn up the heat.

Fifteen minutes later, we pull up to a rough-hewn cabin surrounded by towering pine trees.

"Wow," she says and opens her door. "You can see Longs Peak from here."

"And most of the front range." I hop out and walk around the car, my breath visible. "When you're feeling better, we can hike up to the point. From there, it's mountains all the way to the horizon."

"I'd like that," she says, holding my gaze, her eyes glossy.

I take her hand and help her out. "Let's get you inside."

The front door of the cabin opens, and Mrs. Malloy steps out, her young grandson Seamus beside her. Before she can get a word out, a fluffy golden torpedo comes zooming out the front door, flies down the front steps, and dashes up to us.

"Oh, I forgot to tell you," I say and scoop up the puppy. "This is Tolstoy. I brought him home the night of the fire." I shrug. "But I hear you already met."

Madders' Log
Entry 10

Target: Matt Hudson
Nexus: Warm Springs Military Complex
Chrono Tag: Next Day

Global news feed continues to show no divergence.
Inflation crises growing at expected rates. Crop
failures emerging as anticipated. Eden-1 on
schedule with no slowdown or alterations of
ATHENA microdrone program. Localized deviations
continue to increase.

I'm awakened by the ring of an old-style rotary phone. I've been stuck in this stuffy hotel room, watching reruns and pacing back and forth for four sodding days and nights. Although I hope I'm wrong, I figure there's a chance they brought Cassie in too. I've been tapping her name in Morse code on the pipe in the loo every time I go in there, hoping she might be in the next room and hear me. So far, nothing.

The only person who'll give me the time of day is the SEAL Team Six guy who delivers my meals and literally barks, "Chow time."

The phone rings again. I dive for the handset and manage to squeak out, "Hello?"

A recorded female voice says "wake-up call" in a tone usually reserved for announcing the cat threw up.

I set the handset down and sit up.

Maybe they're finally going to let me out of here?

I haven't been sleeping well. Night after night, I wake up in a sweat, my heart pounding in my throat. In my nightmare, Agent Dick kicks down her apartment door while I stand frozen, unable to save her.

I take a deep breath and force myself to focus.

Christ, I hope she's okay. She must be worried sick. I've never gone more than a day or two without at least sending her a "What's new with you, pumpkin?" text.

You shouldn't have mentioned her name to them.

For the first couple of days in here, I kept trying to call her on the ancient blower, but there was never a dial tone. Eventually, I gave up and just assumed the rotary phone was part of the defunct 1950s decor.

Obviously, they've reconnected it now.

I lift the handset, a flutter in my chest, and let out a soft whoop when I hear a dial tone. I start inputting her number, one long pull on the rotary dial at a time. But after I input the fifth digit, the phone makes a clicking sound and disconnects.

My heart drops.

Blast.

Then I get another idea. I dial nine for an outside line and listen for the click. I hold my breath—and get another dial tone. But just as I'm ready to celebrate, the same woman says, "Authorization denied. Further attempts to bypass security will be reported to the military police. Have a nice day."

Have a nice day, my arse.

I shower, brush my teeth, take off pajamas that were in my room, and put on the same clothes I've worn the past three days—which have been washed and pressed and left hanging on my door.

Can't say my jumper has ever had such nice creases—nor my paja-mas, for that matter.

Junior knocks on my door fifteen minutes after the wake-up call. "Sir, they are bringing in the bogey, and Command wants your eyes on it for analysis and possible yield."

I open the door. "Possible yield?"

"Assuming it's a weapon, sir." He offers me a tan melamine cup with murky brown liquid in it. "Coffee."

I give it a dubious sniff. "You sure about that?"

"Yes, sir. I added cream and sugar to make it taste better." His hands are red and chapped, and I wonder if he works in the kitchen as his side hustle.

"Thank you, Mr. Jones," I say and take a sip. The best that can be said is that it's warm and probably caffeinated. "But I'm afraid you've got the wrong bloke. The only bomb I've seen lately was *Sharknado*—and I didn't stay to the end."

"It's Smith," he says, looking a bit sheepish. "But that's not my real name, so I guess Jones works fine."

I set my hand on his shoulder and give it a squeeze. "Thank you for the coffee, son. That was very thoughtful of you."

"You're welcome, sir."

"Will you be taking me home later?"

"No, sir. I only have orders to take you to the loading dock. And we better get going, or Mr. Johnson will have me scrubbing toilets again."

I feel like kicking up a stink, but it's not the kid's fault I'm stuck in here, so I follow him out. He escorts me through a winding hallway into a loading and storage area big enough to hold the Macy's Thanksgiving Day Parade.

"And my niece?" I say, hurrying to keep up. "Will I be allowed to contact her? I expect she's probably called the police by now."

"I'm sorry, professor, but that's above my pay grade. Through here." We walk past massive blast doors into the predawn chill.

Well, if the nukes start flying, this is the place to be.

The sun is about to come up, and the chilly mountain air smells of petrol—and sweat.

I take a quick sniff of the old armpits, but it isn't me. I straighten my clothes and have a look around.

We're standing on a concrete slab bigger than a football pitch. It's resting on a ledge that has been hacked out of the mountainside. Behind us, the peak rises into the pale sky.

"Let's go, doctor." Agent Dick's voice breaks my trance.

After tossing back the rest of the so-called coffee, I set the mug on the guard's table. "I'm coming," I say and hurry across the wide expanse of decaying cement, following the agents towards a gray windowless van, exhaust rising from its tailpipe.

As the sun climbs in the sky, we watch eight Marines unload a heavy, spherical object from the back of the oversized van. The beast is covered with a canvas bag, making it even harder to grip. They eventually manage to wrestle it into a steel sling suspended from a professional-grade engine hoist. The rig makes a moan of protest as it takes the load. When the men finish, they form a line, their sweat producing dark crescents on their T-shirts.

The whole scene reminds me of a Roswell documentary I saw when I was a kid.

Don't know about the aliens, but they nailed the government cover-up part.

A fit, thirty-something officer in sandy fatigues gives his men a curt nod. "At ease." The guy's skin—which is a couple shades darker than mine—is covered in black, geometric tattoos. They spiral around his arms as if they're alive.

He's the Illustrated Man.

Agent Dick steps up to the van and adjusts his tie. "I'll take it from here, sergeant."

"With all due respect, Mr. Johnson, that duck weighs over five hundred kilos, and it's going to steer like a tank."

Dick scowls at the brawny Marine. "I'm aware of that, sergeant. We'll handle it from here."

The Marine officer pulls a folded piece of paper out of his T-shirt pocket, his face unreadable, and offers it to Agent Dick. With obvious disdain, the government man unfolds the paper, glances at it, and hands it back. "Okay, you come with us, but not the soldier boys."

A muscle in the Marine's neck twitches.

Even I know that Marines aren't soldiers. How can a guy who works for the government not know that?

Or maybe he's just being a plonker.

If so, he's good at it.

Dick unbuttons his suit jacket and grabs onto the hoist, his tie flapping over his shoulder. "Let's get this inside before we're compromised, Smith." He notices the line of men still standing between him and the building. "Out of the way, soldiers."

The tattooed officer raises an eyebrow. "They're Marines, sir."

"What did you say?" Dick whips his head around, his eyes narrowed.

The Illustrated Man's jaw tightens. "They're Marines, Mr. Johnson, not soldiers."

"Yeah, whatever. They're done." Dick scans the sky as if expecting a battalion of Russian drones. "Let's go, Smith." He returns his attention to the hoist and gives it a shove.

Nothing happens.

This guy is a laugh a minute.

With practiced indifference, the Marine officer turns back to his row of men. "Dismissed."

They salute and disappear into the maw of the gouged mountain.

The tattooed man turns back to the rig, his gaze coming to rest on the same lever as mine. He catches my eye, lifting his chin ever so slightly. I give a subtle nod. He leans against the van, his arms crossed and a slight smile on his lips.

I like him already.

Dick scowls at Junior, and the younger man jumps into action. Junior unbuttons his suit coat and lays his shoulder against the rig, adding his weight to the effort. The winch squeaks but refuses to budge, and it's all I can do not to laugh.

The Marine catches my eye again and nods.

I clear my throat. "Excuse me, gentlemen. May I be of assistance?" I walk over and release the hand brake on the hoist. As I'd guessed earlier, it's an expensive hydraulic rig and well balanced: one wheel twists sideways a tad and stops. I lower the suspension arm and let the cradle slide down.

Dick makes a move to stop me, but the Marine leans over and grabs his arm. "Lowers the center of mass, Mr. Johnson, making it easier to steer."

Dick's eyebrows rise, but he recovers quickly. "I knew that." He leans his shoulder into the hoist. With Junior's help, they start the duck rolling toward the hole in the mountain.

The Marine officer and I watch, our hands shading our eyes from the rising sun, and then he turns and offers me his hand. "You must be the materials expert they brought in. I'm Sergeant Major Colton Richter, but most people call me Picasso."

I shake his hand. "Professor Matt Hudson." His grip is solid but not overblown.

"Welcome to the circus, Professor Hudson." He inclines his head toward the government agents. "You just met the clowns."

"Those clowns marched me out of my house in the middle of the night," I say. "And left me sitting on my arse for the last four days. I need to contact my niece, or she'll have the cavalry after me."

"I did hear some chatter about a crank phone call," he says and raises an eyebrow. He glances at me. "But I'm guessing that's all cleared up now. Given your expertise in materials, I requested you be shown the artifact."

He takes a small pad of paper and a pen out of his pocket, writes something on it, and returns it to its place. "And I'll make sure someone gets a message to your niece today. As you might imagine, the Air Force is falling all over itself trying to explain how that got through their defenses." He shrugs. "Not my problem. I need to figure out who sent it and why."

We go back to watching the two suits wrestle 500 kilos of metal—the equivalent of four large refrigerators—across the uneven expanse of cracked and crumbling concrete.

Picasso shakes his head and walks over to shut the double doors of the van. He raps his knuckles against the side twice, and a uniformed arm waves from the driver's window. The vehicle makes a U-turn, passes through the huge metal gates, and disappears down a narrow road carved into the mountainside.

"Where'd you work on car engines?" Picasso asks. He stands next to me, his arms crossed, both of us watching the rig weave and sway as Agent Dick yells inane commands at Junior.

"Plane engines, actually. I grew up outside London. Spent my free time fixing Cessnas so I could afford to fly them. Never met an engine I didn't learn to love." I shrug. "Wish I could say the same about people."

He chuckles.

"How about you?" I ask.

"Been tinkering with engines since I first discovered that my father was afraid to get his hands dirty."

I glance at his tattooed arm and then up to his face. "Why all the ink, if you don't mind me asking?"

He takes his hand out of his pocket and turns it over in the waxing daylight. "I've seen a lot of fucked-up shit," he says, "but I never saw anyone angrier than my father when I told him I was quitting med school to join the Marines. Maybe that's why."

I turn back to the NSA agents, pretty sure there's more to the story.

Dick and Junior have stopped moving and are attempting to push the engine hoist up a small curb. We can hear Dick's angry shouts all the way across the crumbling concrete.

"Appears our government boys have run into a snafu," Picasso says and rests his hand on my shoulder blade. "Come on, let's go help Laurel and Hardy before they kill someone."

I grunt. "Paperwork would be a bloody nightmare."

A cheeky smile plays on his lips as we stride across the pavement.

The rest of the morning flies by on fast-forward.

White-coated technicians pop in and out of the bomb-proof room, running a parade of mostly pointless tests on the artifact, while I watch and take notes—using an actual lab book and mechanical pencil, praise be. The sphere is weighed, photographed, measured, pinged with a laser, and has its temperature taken. By the time they're finished with it, I wouldn't be surprised to find out that the damn thing has gallstones.

When I'm finally alone with the sphere, I ignore the clamor of voices out in the hallway and run my fingertips across the cold metal. The surface is perfectly smooth except for five barely visible symbols:

$E = mc^2$

Despite crashing through half of downtown Denver, the silver-gray, super-heavy tungsten alloy—ceramic, actually—doesn't have a scratch, nick, or dent anywhere on it. I rap my knuckles on the cold metal, testing it like a ripe watermelon.

I have a hunch it's hollow.

Agent Dick still thinks it's a bomb, but I seriously doubt it. Why would someone spend the time to forge a perfect sphere, etch Einstein's equation into it, and then use it as a projectile—ignorant government goons excepted? Still, I'm perplexed about why someone would launch it at supersonic speeds into a hotel, setting a good piece of downtown Denver on fire in the process.

If it's a message, whoever sent it must be as thick as two short planks.

I shrug. "So maybe the US government?"

The door opens and Dick bursts in, his face contorted, Junior on his heels.

He eyes the sphere and then scowls at me. "What is that thing? You've had all day, and I want answers. The Pentagon doesn't want to start a panic, but you can imagine how much shit will hit the fan if that thing turns out to be an extraterrestrial artifact—or an explosive device."

I rub my eyes. "Well, unless the aliens are chums with Einstein, it's man-made. And it's not a bomb—or any other kind of weapon, for that matter."

I bloody well hope it's not.

"What is it, then?"

"I don't know," I say, "but I think it's hollow."

He recoils. "Hollow? What the hell, Hudson? That thing weighs more than my car."

"Yeah, well, we'll know when the density numbers come back. My best guess is there's a cavity in the center, possibly filled with inert gas."

Junior addresses me, his forehead wrinkled. "Can't you just X-ray it?"

"Of course," I say. "But it's tungsten carbide, nearly as hard as diamond and impervious to just about everything, including X-rays."

The kid drops his gaze and shuffles his feet.

"But it was a good idea," I say, and he perks up a bit.

Dick glances at his watch. "So who made it?"

"I don't know."

"Why did they shoot it into a building?"

"I don't know."

"Why is that damn equation on the outside?"

"I don't know that, either."

He turns and puts his hands on his hips, his head sticking out. "What *do* you know, doctor?"

I try to keep my voice level. "A private company or a large university probably made it: people with money and access to expensive tools. It's not something you could whip up in the basement."

He turns to Junior. "Write that down. I want an agent at every damn nerd factory in the country by tomorrow night."

"Yes, sir."

He whirls back to face me. "Can you get it open?"

"Probably," I say. "Tungsten is strong but brittle. Like an eggshell, the sphere could withstand extraordinary external pressures. But, if we hit it hard in one tiny spot, it should fracture."

Dick pins Junior with his gaze. "Do it."

"Whoa there, cowboy." I hold up my hands. "Once you break it, there won't be any way to put it back together. Any information contained in the structure will be lost. If it came from outside our solar system, as the trajectory suggests, you would be destroying the evidence."

"Yeah, I'm feeling real sorry for Humpty Dumpty." Agent Dick turns to leave. "You can start gluing the pieces back together tomorrow."

"Tomorrow?" I croak. "What about my job—and my life? I haven't been home in four days."

Dick freezes, his hand on the doorknob and his back to me. "You're done here when the Pentagon says you are, doctor." He looks over his shoulder. "Do you have a problem with that?"

It's not as if teaching undergraduate physics is a particularly rewarding career choice, but still, it's my life. "Couldn't someone have at least asked me first?"

"I just did." He opens the door and storms out, Junior trailing like a duckling.

Arse.

I turn to a new page in my notebook and write:

Why would someone take the time to put Einstein's equation on a tungsten carbide sphere and blow up a hotel with it?

I stare at the page, unable to come up with anything that makes the least bit of sense.

Was it an accident? A warning? Did they get bad room service?

The equation must be important; it's how I knew the thing wasn't a bomb. Any mildly literate person would recognize those five symbols, no matter where they grew up.

I follow the logic a bit further.

And whoever found it would assume that the near-perfect sphere was important, even if it was found in Ethiopia or Iceland. It's clearly more valuable than just the metal it's made from. They'd call the police, who would notify the government, who would call in the nearest materials expert.

Me.

"Bugger and blast," I say to myself.

Okay, so they have my attention. Now what?

It could be some sort of message?

I study the sphere, half-expecting it to start clicking or whistling.

"Who sent you?" I whisper. "And what are you trying to tell me?"

The mysterious object remains silent.

A minute later, Picasso stops by with a sack lunch and lets me record a short message for Cassie on his phone. I tell her I'm okay and that I'll call her as soon as I can. He assures me my department has been informed about my absence—and then he escorts me into the best-equipped materials lab I've ever seen. He sets me up with a computer that has all the test results from this morning and tells me he'll be back to get me when they're ready to open the sphere.

Crikey Moses. I'm like a dog with two tails.

I start looking over the results, my astonishment growing. The sphere seems to have been sintered as a single piece. On top of that, its roundness is only forty nanometers off perfect—better than any known object, man-made or otherwise. That laborious and exacting facet would make it possible for the artifact to withstand massive external pressures, way more than it would need outside anything except a neutron star or a black hole. But, after going to all the trouble to make the sphere nearly indestructible, someone engraved Einstein's equation on the surface, weakening it ever so slightly.

Why did they compromise the tensile strength with an inane message?

"Because it's not inane," I say and let out a sigh. "You just don't know why yet."

An hour later, I follow Picasso into a room crammed to the gills with people, half of them in uniform and half in white shirts with black ties. I follow him down a few steps to the front of the auditorium and sit next to him as he types on a laptop. "Lights," he says, and the room goes dark.

Up on a large screen, we see the sphere being lowered into a robotic drill press that would make the MythBusters jealous. We're told the contraption sits deep inside the mountain, enclosed in a biometrically sealed and electromagnetically shielded blast room—and that we're watching from the other side of the mountain, just in case. Behind the sphere, the walls of the small enclosure are packed with sensors, and I wonder if the room has ever been used before and, if so, for what?

As we wait for Picasso to run a status check, the soft riffs of Junior's cell phone game are audible.

Crikey, even Junior outranks me.

A few minutes later, we hear a slight mechanical wheeze, and the music stops.

Picasso leans back in his chair. "Here she goes."

As we watch, the pressure gauge on the vice increases with agonizing slowness.

I shake my head, impressed that the material can withstand so much force.

Ninety seconds later, there's a single metallic pop, and the artifact shatters into tiny silver shards. A single slip of pink paper flits to the ground. It appears to have writing on it, but it's impossible to read from our camera angle. The Geiger counter doesn't make a peep, and the indicators on the laser gas analyzer remain steady.

"Expensive way to send a valentine," Picasso says. He taps a few keys, and we watch a replay of the note floating down in slow motion. "We'll have to wait until the artifact clears quarantine before we can read it." He doesn't wait for the next question. "That'll be at least an hour, probably two depending on the analysis of the enclosing gas."

"To hell with that," Dick says and stands up. "I want access to that room immediately."

"Be my guest." Picasso motions with his head toward the exit. "I believe the automatic safety protocols can be overridden by the Security Council—or perhaps you'd rather chat up the President?"

I resist the urge to snicker.

"In the meantime," Picasso says, "let's have a look at the rubble."

He types something into a computer, and the camera angle changes. Now, we're looking down at the broken pieces.

Dick, who seems to have lost interest in contacting the Security Council, steps closer to the monitor, pointing at a white tube of some sort. "What's that?"

Picasso pans the camera across the metallic fragments and locks in on the hollow cylinder, a shriveled elastic wrapped around it.

Junior whistles. "I think those are note cards, sir. Maybe they were rolled up with that broken rubber band."

Dick glares at him. "If I wanted your running commentary, Smith, I'd have asked for it."

Junior gulps. "Sorry, sir."

The image zooms out, moves across the rubble, and stops on a dust-covered lump in the back. Picasso zooms in too fast, and a gray crosshatch pattern fills the display, metallic shards poking into the weave at odd angles.

I recognize the close-up immediately. "Something woven. Probably cotton," I say, and every face in the room turns toward me. Picasso raises an eyebrow, and I shrug. "We used to examine stuff under a high-powered microscope when I was a grad student. Never dreamt it'd prove useful."

Dick shifts his weight. "Any idea what it is?"

Picasso zooms out and shifts the angle again.

"A dirty sock!" Junior blurts out. "But, hey, the logo's backward."

Dick scowls. "What the hell would a dirty sock be doing inside an expensive metal sphere, Smith? Keep your goddamn mouth shut if you're not using your brain."

"Yes, sir."

"It does appear to be a previously worn athletic sock," I say, just as confused as everyone else.

Just as I'm thinking this is the world's most expensive practical joke, Picasso pans the camera across more rubble, and I point at something underneath one of the larger fragments. "Can you give us a closer look at that?"

Picasso taps more keys, and the camera rotates. An egg-sized wad of foil comes into view.

Junior laughs. "Someone sent us leftovers?"

Dick rounds on him. "That's enough, Smith." He turns to Picasso. "I want to know what those things are, sergeant, and where they came from."

Picasso's upper lip twitches. "Don't we all, Mr. Johnson? Don't we all?"

Madders' Log
Entry 11

Target: Isabel Sanborn
Nexus: Diego's Cabin
Chrono Tag: Next Day

Deviations around Gemini Solutions impacting the bankruptcy & buyout by Kirkland Enterprises. Suspect Chronosphere contains jinn objects, both extraversals & time-looped anchor. Attempting to locate Looped primary.

I wake up to the most amazing smell of coffee.

It's just starting to get light, and my room is so cold I can see my breath. As I'm contemplating how to shut the window, Diego knocks and peeks in my door.

"Morning, hon," he says, already dressed. "Sorry to wake you, but I need to go soon. Okay if I come in?" After I nod, he enters carrying a tray. His hands are large and strong, and I spend a moment admiring them. "I made you a latte and some scrambled eggs with toast. Mrs. Malloy makes the elderberry jam. 'Spreading the love,' she says." He sets the tray on my nightstand and runs his hand across his mouth. "I know you don't usually eat breakfast, but after a week of hospital food, I thought you might be hungry."

"I'm ravished," I say. "And the coffee smells wonderful. Like I died and went to heaven."

"Give me caffeine to change the things I can," he says, "and a cabin in the mountains to avoid the rest."

I chuckle and attempt to sit up. I am getting stronger, but my shoulder is still sore, my ribs are a ring of fire, and my leg weighs a ton in the damn splint—so I'm not making much progress.

"Whoa there, Wonder Woman!" He runs around to the other side of the bed. "Let me help."

Even though it's been a week since the fire, Diego has been waiting on me hand and foot. I keep telling him to stop making such a fuss or he'll turn me into a slug.

But you gotta admit, after years of Dave turning away, it's nice to have someone care.

Diego fluffs the spare pillow and props it up against the headboard. He puts one hand under my good shoulder and the other around my back, trying to avoid my bruised ribs.

"One, two, three," he says and attempts to slide me up the bed. "Light as a feather." But he loses his grip, and we both nearly tumble onto the floor.

I wince. "Feather, huh?" I look like the Leaning Tower of Pisa, but I'm otherwise unhurt. As I try to right myself, the shoulder of my nightie slips off, and my breast pops out. Diego's eyes flick to the erect nipple, and I gasp. He makes a move to help me cover up but thinks better of it and adjusts his shoelaces.

"Whoops," I say, blushing. "Wardrobe malfunction." I manage to free one hand and pull the comforter up to my chin.

He sets the extra pillow on the bed and stuffs his hands in his pockets, stifling a smirk. "Hate when that happens."

Lucky, who's curled up next to me, peeks out, realizes how cold it is, and goes right back underneath.

We both laugh.

He shuffles his feet. "Want me to shut the window?"

"Please. Maybe I overdid it a bit with the cool mountain air."

The corner of his mouth curves up. "Yeah, I had to open the fridge to warm things up."

I suppress a giggle—a sound I haven't made in years. "Hah."

Diego crosses the room and pulls down the sash, his biceps pressing against his shirtsleeves. "How'd you sleep?" He turns back to me and loosely crosses his arms. I run my gaze across his shoulders and chest, thinking that he must be doing a lot of heavy lifting around the cabin because I've never seen him in better shape. In fact, he looks annoyingly gorgeous standing there in the ethereal shaft of sunlight.

Something warm and tight stirs inside me, something I haven't felt in a long time.

Don't go there, Iz. That ship sank a long time ago.

I manage to tear my eyes off his upper body—and realize he's staring at me, a crooked smile on his lips. "How'd you sleep?"

"Oh, right," I say, my voice too high. "Better than I have in forever." I clear my throat. "It's so peaceful up here in the mountains!"

He grins like he knew I was going to say that. "I'm heading into town for a board meeting, but I'll bring dinner back with me tonight."

"That sounds great. Thank you."

He lowers his chin. "The doctor said to take it easy for a week, so don't be firing up your laptop, okay?"

"Wouldn't dream of it," I say.

He raises an eyebrow but doesn't comment.

I hold on to my exhibitionist nightie with my bad arm and reach for the steaming cup of coffee.

He rushes around the bed and hands me the mug. "Careful, hon, it's hot."

I suppress another giggle and take a sip, relaxing back into the pillows. "Oh, my. This is magnificent." I take another drink, savoring the warm, rich flavor. "I thought you were taking time off, Diego."

"I am." He sits down on the bed. "But we're having some cash flow issues, and I need to make sure everyone's on the same page."

"That sounds painful."

"Oh, it's nothing serious. I'll have it sorted out today."

I give him a who's-lying-now look and reach for the plate of food. He hops up, lifts the tray, sets it on the bed, and sits back down next to me. I take a bite of toast, and he reaches over to wipe a bit of jam off my nose.

"I know you're trying to get clean water to as many struggling communities as possible," I say before I can stop myself, "but have you considered hiring a CFO? It might give you more time to spend on the engineering side of things. Isn't that the part you really love?"

He reaches under the covers and pets Lucky, considering my words.

"I'm flattered," he says, half smiling. "I didn't realize you were following my work so closely."

I feel my face flush. "Oh, well, you know, maybe just a little."

Yeah, right. You totally haven't been stalking his company's social media for the last decade.

When his fingertips brush against my thigh, sending a shiver down my leg, he jerks his hand away. "Oops. Sorry," he says and swallows. "You're right about the CFO, of course. Except paying someone would mean less money to build and install clean water systems, and I already have commitments."

"Yeah. Catch-22," I say and take another bite.

Diego always was a genius when it came to building things with his hands. But if I've learned anything from Dave, it's that a sleazy showman—along with his wily accountants, shady funding, and unscrupulous lawyers—will trump your well-intentioned visionary every time. I put a sympathetic hand on his thigh. "I'm sure you'll figure it out."

"Yeah," he says, "I hope so." He lets his gaze fall across my hair and unruly nightie. "Do you know where they towed your car? If so, I'll stop by while I'm in town."

I let out a huge breath. "That would be awesome. It's at Wreck & Roll off Colfax. Thank you."

"Happy to help. Will you be okay on your own today? If not, I can ask Mrs. Malloy to stop by."

"I'll be fine," I say, drawing on his thigh with my fingertip. "I'm just gonna paint the ceiling in the living room, chop a cord of firewood, and clean out the gutters. I'll save mounting the satellite dish on the roof for tomorrow."

He laughs. "*Mierda*, I've missed you."

We stare at each other for a moment and then look away.

"Thanks for everything," I say and reluctantly pull my hand off his thigh. "I promise not to do anything dangerous until you're around to scold me."

"Deal." He leans forward, like he might kiss me goodbye, but turns away at the last moment and stands. He spends a second trying to fish his keys out of the wrong pocket while I pretend not to notice.

"Lucky's breakfast is in her bowl," he says once he finds his keys. "And Tolstoy already had his. He's outside, but I'll let him in when I go." He walks over to the door. "Oh, and I set out their food for lunch." He turns to go. "Make yourself at home. If you need anything, just text me—no cell service up here, but the Wi-Fi works."

"Drive safe," I call out.

"Safe driving is no accident," he calls back. "See you around six."

A moment after I hear the front door shut, the puppy comes zooming into the room. I lean over and lift him onto the bed.

"Good morning, Tolstoy, king of the forest," I say and ruffle his cold ears.

He licks my face and then flops down on the bed, his head on my tummy.

I rub his ears and eat my breakfast, still thinking about Diego.

After we chatted last night, I'm even more worried about him. He poured most of his savings into this property—which seems like a great investment—but he quit a lucrative job to run this nonprofit a few years back, and now he barely makes enough to cover his expenses. Granted, his company does great work, building potable water systems and other infrastructure for people living in poverty. But despite having decent funding, at least initially, it seems like they're always on the brink of bankruptcy. I mean, he doesn't even have a full-time secretary—and he's the CEO. As much as I hate to say it, I think Diego might be in over his head.

"He really needs to find someone to run the business side of things," I say to Tolstoy. "Someone who can swim with the sharks." He lifts his head and tips it to the side. "That would free him up to do the engineering." The puppy lets out a little yip. "Well, you just go ahead and tell him that for me, won't you?" He yips again. "In the meantime, what do you say we take a shower, do the dishes, and then go throw your ball?"

He barks and jumps up, his tail wagging his butt around.

The first big proof of concept for my bots happens in four days, and there are a ton of things I need to get done in the meantime.

After hobbling to the kitchen to do the dishes, Tolstoy and Lucky on my heels, I limp out to the deck, laptop in hand. My favorite chair has magically moved from the living room to the deck, and there's a sticky note on it in Diego's neat handwriting: "I told you, no working!"

I laugh and sit down in his handmade rocking chair.

As the sun crosses the sky, I toss a squeaky ball for Tolstoy, stroke Lucky's silky fur, and fire off overdue emails. After reassuring Sophie and my team that I'll be there for the big demo on Friday, I shut my laptop and rest for a little.

Sitting there in the shade, breeze playing in my hair, pets snoozing, I can't help wondering where I'd be if I'd married Diego. He's the one who always held my heart.

Why wasn't that enough, Iz?

I suppose it didn't help that he was lukewarm about my life's work. Even though bee populations were already in decline, he suggested it would be better to spend time figuring out how and why —instead of just trying to replace them. Sure, that all sounded noble and praiseworthy, but even if I could uncover the myriad reasons, there was no guarantee anything could actually be done to fix the problems. The world is a big place, with governments, corporations, and environmentalists bickering over every little thing. Getting all of them to agree on any meaningful action would take years of slow, tedious lobbying—and come with no guarantees. With bee populations falling and the UN wringing their collective hands, the world needed a Plan B. I set my sights on providing one. So when Dave found out about my microdrone work and told me it was brilliant, maybe I got a little starry-eyed.

I sigh and bring up my next unread email. The subject is *Burn in Hell* and contains a single line of very large text telling me "God's wrath will rain down on you for what you've done."

Biodomes? Artificial bees? A no-fault divorce?

Probably all of them.

I hit delete and get back to work.

When I'm all caught up, I close my eyes, breathing in the scent of the evergreens and listening to a peregrine falcon call to her mate.

Wouldn't it be grand to have a soulmate, someone flying by your side?

Tolstoy barks and noses his ball, his tail wagging hopefully. Holding Lucky in my lap, I lean over and pick it up.

"What a good boy you are," I say and ruffle his floppy ears. He barks and backs up, unable to keep his feet still. After getting him to sit, I toss his ball into the woods and smile as he goes tearing down the steps and off into the trees, his world perfect.

I sigh and run my palm across the smooth carved wood of the rocking chair, listening to the distant reply of the male falcon. The last few years have left me with a deep-seated loneliness, the kind that gnaws at your bones and makes you cry when it rains.

The sad truth is, Diego could have been that person, *my* soulmate. But I was so blinded by my own ambition that I couldn't see it.

Now—despite what my body thinks—it's too late for us. I'm no longer the person he fell in love with, and there's no erasing that. All the intervening years have worn me down, left me cynical and jaded. I used to be fun and spontaneous, up for anything. Now I'm just tired and boring.

"Not to mention old," I whisper.

So why did you agree to go home with your former boyfriend a week after you got divorced?

Dave would say it's because I'm weak. But this time, whatever happens, wherever I go, it will be my decision, my choice, what I want. And, unlike Dave, I know Diego won't try to take that away from me.

So why does your stomach keep doing the Macarena every time Mr. Nadales looks at you?

"Because I'm stupid," I say, and Lucky lifts her head.

I run my fingers across her silky fur. "I'm done with men. Really. From here on out, if I succeed or screw up, it's going to be on me." She mews. "Yeah, I know. Diego is nothing like Dave. But you have to understand what a mess I've become. I can't go through that again."

Back when I first met Diego and Dave, I couldn't believe they were best friends. Even then, they were polar opposites, and I knew from the get-go that Dave was trouble.

Despite the fact that I'm staying at Diego's house, sleeping in his spare bedroom and eating his food, he would never presume any of the things that Dave took as his due. Diego would never expect me to pay him in kind. And he didn't offer to let me stay because he expects or even wants something from me. He offered because it was the right thing to do—and he's a good person.

I take a deep breath and let it out, feeling happy for the first time in months. I haven't even been here a week, and it already feels like home.

And I can tell Diego went to a lot of trouble to make it feel that way. The great room has a new sofa and a thick wool rug, along with a handmade rocking chair that's both gorgeous *and* comfy.

Why must he be so good with his hands?

My bedroom has oak furniture—used but lovely—and a luxurious mattress, and my bathroom has grab bars and subdued lighting that's fabulous at night. He's placed dried flowers in a canning jar on the mantel, and the Ansel Adams photo that I gave him for his twenty-fifth birthday hangs above it.

He held on to that for fifteen years, Iz.

I have to say, even though Diego moved in less than a month ago, he's gotten a lot done.

All of it without your guidance, help, or approval.

There are huge batteries tucked inside the garage, solar panels on the roof, and wood stacked next to the house.

I imagine him chopping firewood with his shirt off, the muscles in his arms and chest moving smoothly beneath his olive skin. And try as I might, I can't seem to let go of the warm, melty way I felt when his eyes settled on my breast this morning. It's like my skin remembers the silky feel of his hands and lips.

I swallow and shake my head.

Don't go there.

When Tolstoy comes trotting back, he drops the ball and flops down on the deck next to me, his tongue hanging out.

I close my laptop and spend a minute running my fingers through his soft, curly fur.

And then the most amazing thing happens.

Lucky jumps off my chair, stretches for a bit, and lies down between his front paws. He licks her ears and face and then gently places his head down next to her tiny body.

I smile and wipe a tear off my cheek. "You two are like childhood buddies who finally found each other."

The wind kicks up, tossing leaves into the air, and the sun disappears behind a cloud.

"Time to go inside," I say and push myself up to standing. It takes me a minute, but I manage to slide the huge glass doors to the deck shut and limp into the kitchen. I feed both the pets, make some lunch, and sit down at the table. There's a note with a smiley face on it next to a plate with one and a half madeleine cookies. Diego used to buy them in threes when we were dating, and he would break the last one in two and let me pick which half I wanted.

The memory makes me smile.

You already love it here.

In the late afternoon, I decide to make muffins with the overripe bananas in the fridge. The flour and such are in canisters on the counter, but I can't find his cupcake pan—and I know he has one because he made rolls for me last night. I eventually spy it on top of the refrigerator. It takes me three tries, but I manage to push it off with a wooden spoon—and attempt to catch it.

The pan clatters to the hardwood floor, and the pets hightail it out of the kitchen.

An expensive-looking envelope flutters down next to the pan.

"Sorry, guys," I say. "You can come back now. Mischief managed."

Tolstoy peeks around the doorframe, his ears down but his tail wagging. And then Lucky comes skittering back in, batting something small and gold.

"Whatcha got there, kitty girl?" I cautiously bend over to pick up the rebellious muffin tin and the mysterious envelope.

Don't want him to find you splayed on the kitchen floor when he gets home tonight.

I manage to snag both without falling over. After I set the pan on the counter, I turn the beige envelope over in my hands.

SHERLOCK

is handwritten on the front, and I swear the envelope smells like smoke.

Maybe you're just imagining things.

Tucked inside the envelope is a sheet of matching stationery—and a heavy gold wedding band.

The ring matches the one Lucky is batting around the kitchen.

"That's weird," I say and collect the second ring off the floor. I place it back with its mate and stick the envelope in a drawer so I won't be tempted to read the note, patting myself on the back for not being a snoop. I put on an apron that reads: "For this I spent four years in college?" and get to work making muffins.

Of course, the whole time I'm mashing bananas and stirring in milk and dumping in flour, my brain is working overtime on what's in that damn envelope.

So, after I take the muffins out of the oven and clean up the kitchen, I slide the drawer open and take it out again.

"The first rule of snooping is never do it on an empty stomach." I look out the window to make sure the driveway is empty. "And the second is don't get caught."

I bite into a banana muffin, grab the envelope, and pull out the paper, careful not to get it sticky. It's expensive stationery from a jewelry store in downtown Denver with small and precise hand-writing on it.

WE KNEW YOU'D BE BACK FOR TOLSTOY.
JUST FOR THE RECORD, WE GOT ALL THE BEASTIES OUT.
LOOKS LIKE YOU SCORED TOO.

TAKE CARE OF THE MISSUS,

~THE HOLE-IN-THE-WALL GANG

I sit there with my mouth stuck open, trying to put the pieces together.

Diego got someone to help him rescue the other animals, including Tolstoy.

Why didn't he say something?

"And who is 'the missus'?" I ask Tolstoy.

He wags his tail.

Me? Did he tell them we were married?

This last thought makes me flush. I shake my head and put every-thing back in the envelope, set it on top of the muffin tin, and slide it back up onto the shelf above the fridge.

"So Diego *was* the one who came after us?" I say and Tolstoy yips.

How did he know we were trapped in there?

I have so many questions that they're making my head hurt.

And then the memories all come flooding back.

I remember lying there in the smoky darkness, a massive chunk of concrete inches above my face, one arm pinned underneath me and the other pressed against that massive piano. I was fading in and out of consciousness when I heard someone call my name. I tried to respond, but all I managed to do was tap a few piano keys. And there he was, his face illuminated like a guardian angel.

Diego saved you.

Yeah, but how did he know you needed saving?

I mean, I love the whole knight in shining armor thing as much as the next romantic, but seriously, what are the odds? Of literally all the people in the world, the guy who finds me just so happens to be my ex-boyfriend from fifteen years ago? No effing way that's a coin-cidence.

What was he doing there? How could he have known?

The teapot whistles, and I make myself a cup and settle on the sofa. The furnace kicks on, filling the great room with toasty warmth. Lucky jumps into my lap, and Tolstoy curls up on his blanket next to me. I start working on my presentation as the sky outside darkens and the clouds spit out tiny snowflakes.

That's exactly where Diego finds me when he walks in the front door carrying my purse and the puzzle box—along with a bake-at-home cheese pizza, a carton of vanilla ice cream, and a pack of juice boxes. "I know we're avoiding drama," he says, suppressing a grin, "but I did get a few toppings for the pizza, some hot fudge sauce, and bottle of wine just in case you're ready to graduate from the kids' menu."

"Wow," I say. "You really know how to push a girl to the wild side."

"Watch out!" He wiggles his eyebrows. "Next stop: pizza with reckless toppings."

I laugh, and Tolstoy barks, his tail wagging.

For a moment, time freezes. I can see and hear and feel the life Diego and I might have had: the house, the yard, the kids. And then everything falls back into place, and I'm a middle-aged woman carrying decades of regret.

Madders' Log
Entry 12

Target: Matt Hudson
Nexus: Warm Springs Military Complex
Chrono Tag: Next Day

Marked increase in activity around Military complex noted. Colton Richter on scene full thirteen months before virgin timeline.

It's nearly seven when Picasso strides into the lab. "The sphere is gone," he says without preamble. "The shards—and every last mote of tungsten dust—vanished from inside the isolation chamber eleven minutes ago."

"Vanished?" I squeak. "What happened?"

"The men running tests saw the internal pressure fluctuate, recorded a brief flash of infrared light, and the sphere fragments ceased to exist. I had them double-check that they didn't vaporize or otherwise chemically transform. There are zero atoms of tungsten inside an isolation chamber located five hundred feet below ground and only accessible from a narrow, triple-sealed shaft in the control room."

"Blimey," I say and plop down in a chair. "Did all the items inside the sphere disappear too?"

"No, they appear to be untouched." He waits for me to respond. When I don't, he adds, "Why is that, professor?"

I shake my head. "Did any new atoms appear? Rhenium or tantalum maybe?"

He raises an eyebrow. "Are you suggesting that over a ton of tungsten spontaneously transmuted?"

"Maybe." I drop my head into my hands, my brain scrambling to make sense of the information. I take a deep breath and let it out. "Did you check?" He's silent long enough that I look up at him. "Well?"

"Not yet," he says and starts typing on his phone. "Any other ideas?"

"The sphere exited the same way it arrived."

He rubs his hand across his chin. "And that would be?"

"In a way that we are currently unable to detect or reproduce."

He raises an eyebrow.

"Ask NORAD," I say. "I'm guessing they can confirm the sphere appeared out of nowhere."

He types on his phone again. "Anything else?"

"What's in the sphere?" I say.

"We should know in an hour. In the meantime, let's go get some chow. It may be a long night."

I follow him through a maze of hallways and into the windowless mess. People in camo are cleaning up, but they let us go through the food line. When Picasso and I sit down at a table, I notice that he has skipped the main course.

"Something I should know about the Salisbury steak?" I ask.

"Nah," he says. "My wife was a vegetarian. After she deployed, I guess I never went back."

I gaze at his bulging muscles, feeling more than a tinge of jealousy.

The dude must be the buffest vegetarian this side of a silverback.

"I know the feeling," I say. "My mum still sends me bleedin' self-help books every Christmas, and they're all the same: 'If at first you don't succeed, do it the way Mum told you to.'"

His mouth twitches.

I cut the steak and take a bite. "Where'd your wife end up, if you don't mind me asking?"

He tips his head and stirs his applesauce with a fork. "There were always a lot of fireworks between us. A couple years ago, she took a doctoring gig in some godforsaken hellhole."

"Ah, that's a pisser."

"I never could understand why she felt compelled to help people who wanted to kill her." He pushes peas around on his plate. "She told me she'd check back in a few years to see if I'd grown up."

"Ouch."

"Yeah, well, maybe she had a point. It took me a while to get past the terrible twos."

I smile. "So maybe she'll be back?"

He takes a slow breath and lets it out, his eyes on his plate. "She was killed when some dickwad rolled an IED into the tent where she was operating. There weren't any pieces big enough to send home."

I choke on the steak. "Bollocks, I'm sorry. I seem to be an expert at putting my foot in my mouth."

He grunts.

We eat in silence for a bit.

When his phone buzzes, he takes it out, glances at the display, and shoves it back in his pocket.

I must be the only schmuck in this place without a phone.

"What's up?" I ask. "Have they identified the items inside the sphere?" I put a banana in my sweatshirt pocket and polish off my brownie.

"Yes, we have." He watches me gulp down dessert, a slight smile on his face. "We're hoping you can answer some questions for us."

"I'll try," I say and stand up.

After we bus our dishes, he leads me back through the labyrinth. We pass guards with rifles, two of them standing at attention on either side of a door engraved with *SSO* in gold foil.

Picasso nods at them.

"Sergeant major," they say in unison but don't move a muscle.

We continue on to a door with an elaborate arrowhead insignia and the word MARSOC on it. Picasso uses a badge to unlock it and then holds it open for me. Dick is already inside, but Junior is conspicuously absent.

Probably past his bedtime.

Picasso offers me a chair across from Johnson, and I sit down. The Marine officer remains standing.

Dick doesn't bother with formalities. "Hudson, does the name Diego Nadales mean anything to you?"

I glance at Picasso and then at Dick. "Yeah, sure. Nice guy. Used to live down the street from me." I lift one shoulder. "Likes the Dodgers."

The corner of Picasso's mouth twitches.

I shrug. "Owns his own company. Coaches—"

"What sort of company?" Dick says.

"An NGO. They make water filtration systems and portable solar chargers, that sort of thing. I'm on the board, but it's mostly ceremonial."

Dick scowls. "So you're in *cahoots* with him?"

"Ca-what?" I say. "Maybe you could just google him? I'm sure it's all public knowledge."

They wait for me to continue, but I don't know what else to tell them. "Uh, he's a top-notch engineer but not so good with finances. Why do you ask?"

Picasso looks at me. "His name was on the paper in the artifact."

"Diego's?" I blink a couple of times. "Really?"

"Tell him," Picasso says.

Dick stands up, a pinched expression on his face. "It was hand-written on acid-free, high-quality recycled paper with ink made from beets. The handwriting is female, left-handed, block print: probably attended public schools. There are indentations in the paper that indicate the woman wrote the same name over and over on a stack of similar sheets."

"There's a stylized GS embossed in the paper," Picasso says. "Mean anything to you?"

"Crikey Moses," I say. "That could be Diego's company."

"Gemini Solutions?"

"Yeah," I say. "But I've never seen any embossed letterhead there. They barely have enough money to buy toilet paper."

Dick takes out a pen and paper but has trouble spelling "Gemini."

"One e and two i's," I say. "Any coffee stains on the note?"

Dick jerks his head up. "How did you know that?"

"I'm a telepath," I say and then think better of it. "I'm kidding."

Dick steps closer to me, his nostrils flared. "What is your relation-ship to the terrorist, Dr. Hudson?"

I gawk at him. "Terrorist? Diego's not a—"

He gets right up in my face. "What have you been hiding from us, doctor?"

I shake my head and lean back. "Nothing. I—"

"You expect me to believe that the guy who is best buddies with the bomber—and just so happens to be the first person to report the bogey—doesn't know anything about it?"

I let out a huff. "Now wait a second. I'm not best friends with Nadales. He's just an acquaintance. And how stupid would he have to be to put his own name inside the sphere if he intended to destroy a building? Just think about it for a sec before you go off the deep end."

Dick's lips flatten into a snarl, and he rounds on Picasso. "I want this guy on complete lockdown, Richter. No communication with anyone outside the base. I want a full background check on all his associates on my desk by five." He pins Picasso with a glare. "And a court order to search his office, house, computer, car, phone, mailbox, and goddamn underwear drawer."

Picasso rubs the back of his neck. "Shall we have him bend over and cough too?"

Dick gives him a menacing sneer and turns back to me. "You better start talking, Hudson, otherwise I'll charge you with violating the Espionage Act. Twenty years behind bars, easy." He pushes his shoulders back and straightens his suit jacket. "Now, I'm going to ask you one more time. How did you know there were coffee stains on the note inside the sphere?"

I sit up straighter, my heart pounding. "It was a lucky guess." I glance at Picasso, pleading with my eyes for a little cover.

Dick rounds on him. "What do you know about this, Richter?"

Picasso's lip curls up slightly. "Anyone who stayed up all night writing the same name over and over was probably drinking coffee. I'd say it *was* a lucky guess."

Dick rounds on me. "What do you know about Nadales' wife?"

I shake my head. "He's not married. But I saw on the news he has a new girlfriend."

Dick exhales like he just solved the crime of the century. "So what about the girlfriend?"

"I don't remember her name," I say. "But she was almost killed by that explosion in the Brown Palace—the one started by the Einstein Sphere. She also managed to save a bunch of puppies and kittens from a fiery death. The poor things were locked inside when the building caught on fire."

"Jesus Christ, Hudson, I don't give a rat's ass about goddamn puppies. What is the situation with Nadales and the target?"

"The target? You mean his girlfriend?" I don't even try to keep the annoyance out of my voice. "Diego checked her out of the hospital. It was all over the news."

The two men look at each other, and Picasso crosses his arms.

I lean forward. "You guys watch the news, right?"

"Anything else about Nadales that might be *relevant*, doctor?" Dick says. "A connection to illegal metals manufacturing? Or atomic weapons? Terrorist organizations? Involvement with a rogue foreign government?"

"You think Diego cooked up the sphere to kill people?" I let out a snort of disbelief and glance at Picasso, but his face is carefully blank.

"Did he?" Dick shifts his weight. "Well, doctor?"

I let my gaze wander slowly around the room. "I don't know. The only thing I've seen the guy cook up is chocolate cake—and that's not damaging to anything except the waistline."

Dick glares at me. "I ran this guy through the machine. No wife, no kids, runs some hokey tree-hugging business out of his garage. Spends most of his time flirting with bankruptcy. No way this schmuck put together something like this without help. So tell me, Hudson, who helped him?"

"I don't know." I cross my arms. "And Einstein's equation is not a recipe for an atomic bomb, Mr. Johnson. It describes the relationship between matter and energy, and that's not the least bit illicit, unpatriotic, or nefarious. In fact, I'd say the people who built the sphere put that equation on it precisely so whoever found it knew it *wasn't* a bomb."

"Just answer the questions, doctor." Dick picks at something on his tie. "Does Nadales have any questionable contacts?"

I let out an annoyed sigh and sink back into my chair. "How the hell would I know?"

"Dr. Hudson," he says. "I would like to remind you that this is a grave and time-critical government investigation, and your full cooperation is required. What else do you know about the suspect?"

"The suspect?" I lift my hands. "He's a Tico—grew up in Costa Rica. That wasn't illegal last time I checked. He does occasionally import coffee beans for me. Given the swill you serve in here, maybe you should recruit him."

Dick pushes his chair back and starts stuffing papers into a briefcase. "I've had just about enough of your lip, Hudson. I'll have Smith escort you back to Alcatraz. Once all the searches are completed, you can go home." He stands up. "Shouldn't take more than a week, assuming you're clean. Once you leave, open your mouth about anything you've seen or heard here, and I'll be paying you another visit. And I won't be playing Mr. Nice Guy this time."

"Wait a minute," I say, glancing back and forth at the two men. "What was on the note cards? Can't you even tell me if it was a cotton sock?"

"It's classified, doctor." Dick's voice contains a hint of glee.

Picasso gives him an exasperated look and then addresses me. "It *was* a sock. Cyber Ops is running a DNA analysis as we speak. Unfortunately, the sphere got pretty hot, so we may not be able to find anything useful."

"What was on the cards—index cards are they?"

He checks his phone. "No. They're punch—"

Dick jumps to his feet. "You do not have the authority to release that information to a civilian, sergeant."

The Marine pulls an ID out of his shirt pocket and slides it across the table. "It's sergeant *major*, Mr. Johnson, and I have just been assigned by PCAST to lead this project. Professor Hudson's clearance came through from SSO thirty minutes ago. If you have a problem with that, take it up with the Pentagon."

Dick stares at him, at a loss for words for the first time ever. "Well, I intend to," he says, his face red. "You'll be hearing from the Director of National Intelligence within the hour."

Picasso leans back against the table, facing me. "As I was saying, they're computer punch cards, ten of them, but the data seems to be encrypted."

Dick slams his hands down on the table. "You've told him enough. For chrissake, he works for a public university and is practically boning Nadales."

Picasso ignores him. "Are you familiar with punch cards, professor?"

"Stone Age data storage," I say. "Max of eighty characters per card, so not a lot of information there. What about the crumpled foil? I'm guessing it's some sort of Faraday cage. Was there something inside it?"

"Hudson was brought in to evaluate the artifact, soldier." Dick's voice is icy cold. "He's done that."

A look of distaste flashes across Picasso's face and disappears just as quickly. "A seashell containing a scrap of paper with the letters TEGO on it."

That makes my eyebrows rise, and Dick looks like he's going to pop off.

Picasso shifts his weight. "What are the chances the Einstein Sphere came out of a wormhole from the future, professor?"

They both look at me.

"Given what I know about theoretical physics, zero."

Picasso rubs his mouth. "How can you be so certain?"

"Because wormholes don't exist," I say. "Sure, relativity doesn't forbid them, but it also doesn't forbid pigs knitting sweaters. When was the last time you saw one of those?"

Johnson scoffs.

"What about time travel?" Picasso doesn't break his gaze. "Is that possible?"

"Well, we can create time *dilation* by traveling at extreme velocities," I say, "which is technically time traveling to the future." I slump back in the chair, knackered.

"Go on, please," Picasso says, his voice even.

"Unfortunately, the distance an object can jump in time is measured in milliseconds. To get something to move forward by even a few seconds would require crushing acceleration and impossible amounts of energy—as in no known power source could produce a tenth of what would be required."

Johnson whirls my chair around so I'm facing him. "Is time travel possible or not, Hudson? Just answer the damn question."

I shrug again, tired of the whole good cop/bad cop charade. "You heard of Krikalev? The Russian cosmonaut who spent eight hundred-plus days zooming around the Earth? He traveled 1/48th of a second into his own future." I give a mirthless laugh. "So not the sort of time travel you could use to rig the lottery."

Picasso scrubs his hand across his face. "What about sending something into the past?"

"Yeah," I say, "there's no going backward in time. A portal to the past would require faster-than-light travel, and that contradicts causality *and* special relativity. And just for the record, my money's on Albert."

Dick looks confused.

"Einstein," I say. "He's almost never wrong." I direct my attention back to Picasso. "So yeah, a flying DeLorean, a hot tub time machine, or a TARDIS. In the movies, sure. In the real world, not so much."

"And a wormhole?" Dick asks. "What the hell is that?"

"A way to move quickly across spacetime," I say. "Like a shortcut from here to another galaxy."

Dick rubs his hands together, looking for all the world like a bald Grinch. "That could be valuable," he says. "Very valuable."

"Except it requires negative energy," I say, "and that's not a thing. At least, not yet."

Picasso lifts his chin. "Humor me for a moment, professor. Is there a way—any way—to get around the theoretical constraints? Maybe bend the rules a little while not technically breaking them?"

I scratch my head. "There are some physicists who think quantum mechanics lends itself to a many-worlds interpretation, but that's a bleedin' can of worms."

"Indulge me," Picasso says.

"It's the idea that every event that occurs—say the flip of a coin or the roll of a die—causes our universe to split into all possible outcomes. So in one universe, the coin comes up heads. In another, it's tails. Both universes pop into existence the moment the coin lands, and they're identical except for that one coin toss, including both having exact copies of everyone in it. And it's not just coin flips that create new universes. Every possible decision—from what you eat for breakfast to which coconut falls off a palm tree in Bermuda—pops out new universes like a bubble machine stuck on high."

"Bubbles?" Dick scowls. "What the hell are you on about, Hudson?"

"Let me give you an example," I say and hold up a finger, happy to switch into professor mode. "But please keep in mind that this is a fringe theory, so it's probably rubbish."

Picasso gives an impatient nod.

"Right now," I say, "we are in a universe where I said TARDIS a minute ago, but there's one where I said 'Heptapods', and one where I said 'Time Turner', and one where I suffered a massive heart attack and died without saying anything."

They both look bewildered.

"See what I mean about it being a dog's dinner?"

Picasso frowns. "Could this many-worlds theory explain why the logo is reversed on the sock?"

I think about that for a minute. "Sure. It's possible the sphere came from an alternate universe, using some currently unknown technology which clumsily hurls heavy metal spheres backward in time, all to provide us with Diego's name, one sentence of data encrypted fifty years ago, a foil-wrapped seashell, and a dirty athletic sock. Or," I say and let out a sigh, "the sock was made in a sweatshop where they printed the logo wrong to avoid copyright infringement." I let that hang in the air for a moment. "Wanna put a hundred bucks on which is more likely?"

"And in this alternate universe," Dick says, his ears perked up, "that loser buddy of yours,"—he glances at the paper— "Nadales. Could he be some sort of big shot capable of building advanced technology like this?"

I suppress a laugh. "Now that would be an actual miracle."

Madders' Log
Entry 13

Target: Isabel Sanborn
Nexus: Kirkland Enterprises World Headquarters
Chrono Tag: 1 Week Later

Veracity of suspected jinn objects confirmed.
Entangled parallel for seashell exists in this
timeline, and primary for athletic sock found in
Diego's possession, suggesting very limited
deviations in universe that sent Chronosphere.

Diego wheels me up to the heavy glass doors of the Kirkland Enterprises engineering building, and I hand him my ID card. He uses it to unlock the doors, props one open with his foot, and drags my wheelchair through backward, careful not to bump the foot that's sticking out.

I take a deep breath and let it out slowly, willing my hands to stop shaking. Solving the pollinator problem is one of the last big milestones for KE's NASA contract. After years of R&D, my custom bees are ready for their close-up—at least, I hope they are. Yesterday, my team did the run-through without me, and Sophie said it went off without a hitch.

Famous last words.

In half an hour, the governor and five congresspeople will witness the first public unveiling of my artificial honeybees. If all goes as expected, KE will be sealing my microdrones inside Eden-1 in a matter of weeks. Two years from now, my bees will be headed to Mars with Eden-2 and Eden-3.

Diego returns my ID and pushes my wheelchair across the glass-enclosed atrium, his eyes still glued to the huge biodome on the other side of the lake. "I didn't realize it was so big," he says. "You could fit a whole city in there."

I laugh. "There *is* a whole city in there. Over five hundred acres worth. It even has its own zip code."

"Unbelievable." There's awe in his voice.

When we approach the desk, the guard takes stock of my injured leg and then smiles. "Good to see you, Mrs. Kirkland."

"Nice to see you too, Lamar." I pat the unwieldy splint. "I knew you'd be impressed I found a way to skip leg day."

He chuckles and picks up an old-style phone. "I'll let Mr. Kirkland know you've arrived."

Diego clears his throat. "I'd rather not bump into the man, so I'm off." He squats down in front of me. "Go blow them away, Iz. From what I can tell, you've earned it."

Given what he thinks about my work, his words catch me by surprise, and I tear up.

"Don't look so shocked," he says with a laugh. "I'd tell you to break a leg, but you're way ahead of me on that." He winks, squeezes my hand, and stands up. "Text me when you're done. Absolutely no hurry." He leans forward like he's going to kiss me, then thinks better of it and hurries off.

"Thank you," I call out, watching him stride across the marble floor in his sexy jeans and Oxford shirt.

I miss you already.

The guard places his hand over the speaker of the phone. "Mr. Kirkland and his guests will meet you at the containment facility shortly. He's sending someone to escort you over." He clears his throat. "And he wants to know if you got the flowers."

I stare at him for a moment. "Yes, of course I have flowers," I finally say and lean back in the chair. "What sort of pollinator demo would it be without something to pollinate?"

The guy's face reddens. "He means, did you get the flowers he sent to the hospital, ma'am?"

"Oh. Yes." I swallow. "My bad. Tell him I said thanks and that I repurposed his gift into a zero-space storage solution."

As the guard is passing along my sentiment, Dave's bodyguard appears. His suit is too tight, and he's carrying a large paper cup.

"Good morning, Isabel," he says. "We're all thrilled you're on the mend."

I force a smile. "Always a pleasure, Vinny."

"The boss wants us to wait for him outside Isolation Room 3," the guard says. "And he says to make sure the A/C is cranked up so the heat charging thingy goes off without a hitch."

I resist the urge to roll my eyes. Dave micromanages when he gets nervous—that and starts promising miracles.

"Will do," Vinny says and grabs onto my wheelchair with one hand, and we spend the next ten minutes awkwardly navigating hallways and crossing through buildings. Between gulps of coffee, Vinny keeps up a steady stream of sports commentary which I nod at but ignore as I go over my spiel—and try to keep my hands from shaking.

After crossing a grassy courtyard dotted with oak trees, we enter KE's state-of-the-art Containment Building. The wheels of my chair glide smoothly across the reinforced, hermetically sealed entryway as the biometric scanner verifies our identity and records both our badges. The thick, bulletproof glass doors slide open with a soft hiss, revealing an airlock chamber that sanitizes any potential contaminants and generates a low-energy electrical pulse to disable errant bots. After the inner doors unlock with a reassuring click, Vinny pushes me forward, and we move past walls made of non-porous materials topped off with a filtration system designed to trap and neutralize airborne threats, both biological and micro-mechanical.

When we started work on making the bots capable of stinging, I insisted KE build a world-class containment area, and it may be the only time Dave followed my instructions to a T. At the time, you couldn't buy off-the-shelf isolation rooms for non-biological agents, so we had to design one from the ground up—more like from the sewer up. I shake my head at the memory.

"Just the plumbing took a year to get right," I say to myself, then realize we've stopped in front of the IR-3.

"Yep," Vinny says. "This place is buttoned up tighter than a nun's confess—"

The airlock clicks open behind us, and Dave strides through, his expensive blue suit catching the light. Except there's a large sticker on his lapel. And his face is red.

He must have forgotten his badge again.

Behind Dave is a small group of people also wearing temporary badges—and looks of amazement.

"Ladies and gentlemen," Dave says, "I'd like you to meet our director of microdrone engineering, my lovely wife, Isabel Kirkland."

Ex-wife, Dave. And I'm changing my name back to Sanborn.

I force my lips into a smile. "Welcome to Kirkland Enterprises. We're thrilled you could join us today."

Dave nods impatiently at Vinny, and the guy rushes to unlock the lab door, realizes his badge won't work, and stands there with a hangdog look on his face. I wait for Dave to color up again, then roll over and unlock it with my badge. Vinny muscles through the thick door and props it open with his folded coffee cup—totally against safety protocols.

Before I can say anything, Dave swoops in, grabs my wheelchair, and whisks me into the lab. He leans over so only I can hear. "Don't fuck this up."

"Relax," I whisper. "I already got that out of the way with you."

As Vinny looks around for a non-existent wall thermostat, the dignitaries file in. I shake hands and chitchat for a minute—I recognize the governor and two senators from TV—and then say we're ready to get started.

I double-check that everything is still in place from the run-through yesterday. The back half of the lab looks like a well-tended garden, a variety of stalks and flowers stretching up toward the powerful sunlamp. Next to the plants, chairs are arranged as if for a small wedding with a half-height podium in front. A suitcase-sized Hive Controller is open on the podium, twelve microdrone bees waiting inside.

Dave wheels me up to the podium as everyone takes a seat. Dave gives his standard spiel about mankind leaving the cradle and a new age dawning—and hands it over to me.

"Welcome to life on Mars," I say with a grin. "The future belongs to those who believe—and invest—in it." I insert my badge into the controller, wait for it to recognize my face, and type in the code to re-awaken the bots. "For one hundred and thirty million years," I say, "honeybees have been a crucial part of life on Earth. Without them, we would, quite literally, not be here."

A high-pitched buzz fills the lab as the artificial honeybees, about twice the size of their namesakes, power up and hover over the controller.

There are lots of *oohs* and *ahs*, and Dave, standing in the back, nods his approval.

"Now," I say, "thanks to NASA's ongoing funding, Kirkland Enterprises' 'Synthetic Autonomous Microdrone Pollinators'—or just 'bots' as we affectionately call them—are ready to create a buzz." I bring up the pollinating instructions, lean in for the face scan, and fire them up. The bees spring to life, zipping across the room toward the garden.

For half a minute, I let our guests watch them buzz around, pollinating flowers.

"See that clump of chili peppers in front?" I say, pointing out the plants with no bees. "The bots are avoiding those spicy shrubs altogether." I give an exaggerated shrug. "Can't say I blame them."

There are a few chuckles.

"Using state-of-the-art genomic information, the microdrones are programmed to pollinate some flowers while avoiding others—no detours into the weeds on my watch."

More chuckles. Dave gets a funny look on his face—like he's surprised the demo is going so well.

"These little guys are adaptive, too," I say and dim the solar lights. "They're powered by our latest innovation: a Heat Differential Charger or HDC." I give people a moment to watch the bots mosey over to a heat lamp on the edge of the garden. "You see, they're clustering around the warmth like a bunch of retirees in Florida."

The audience laughs, and I realize I'm actually enjoying this.

"Translation? Rain, shine, or Martian dust storm, our microdrone bees are on the job. They'll find a warm spot, recharge, and get right back to work." I turn the sunshine back up, and the bots start returning to the flowers.

"Now, before you ask, no, they can't reproduce, but they are capable of self-repair." There are some murmurs. "And, yes, they can sting. But the venom's harmless to humans."

Dave cuts in. "Don't forget, folks, the stingers are there for a reason."

I bite back an annoyed huff, nodding politely as the room turns toward him.

"As you know," he says, "we have a full suite of critters in the Eden biodomes, and artificial bees need to defend themselves, just like they do in nature. It's all part of our commitment to biodiversity, balanced ecosystems, and, of course, safety."

A senator in the front row raises her hand. "If they're not self-replicating, how will they scale up for larger biodomes?"

I open my mouth to answer, but Dave jumps in again.

"Good question!" He waits for everyone to turn toward him.

"We're investigating self-replication features right now. Once the design passes our safety protocols, we'll be set to deploy the hives on a massive scale."

That's total bullshit, Dave.

We haven't seriously considered self-replication. Where would the bots get the resources? How would they self-assemble? How would you control them? Even if we ignore all the ethical issues—of which there are tons—the engineering problems are staggering.

"Like I said," Dave continues, "it's all in the pipeline. With your continued investment, we'll be able to transform entire Martian landscapes. Let me add that we've programmed the bots to be adaptive and self-repairing, so you'll get a lot of bang for the buck."

The audience turns back to me.

I manage a smile, but it's thin. "Yes, we're exploring ways to reuse the microdrone base for other tasks: environmental monitoring, pest control, building inspections. The sky's the limit—but I promise, no mosquitos!" I get a few laughs.

The governor chimes in, "What about security? Could someone hijack the microdrones and turn them into, I don't know, murderbots?"

I meet his gaze, having practiced my answer to this all week—but Dave's voice rings out again.

"Governor, I share your concern. Given our decades of investment in this technology, we take any and all hacking threats very seriously. We've built multiple layers of security into every aspect of the system. The microdrones operate on an encrypted network with real-time monitoring, so any attempt at hijacking would be immediately detected and neutralized. The Hive Controller uses biometric locks and multiple, repeated authentications. Turning the bees into murderbots isn't just unlikely—it's practically impossible." He gestures back to me.

"Yes, that's correct," I say, trying to get my mojo back. "We pioneered the use of proprietary lattice-based cryptography for each and every bot. That's a fancy-schmancy way of saying we're on top of the post-quantum computing challenge—and years ahead of our competitors."

"And," Dave says, "if someone wanted to build autonomous war machines, starting with our microdrone base would be laughable. Like I said, the venom is harmless to humans. Even if a Hive Controller got into the wrong hands, the bad guys managed to break multiple layers of encryption, *and* they found a way to hack our software, what would they do? Tickle people to death? It would take literally hundreds of these to bring down a single mouse."

I take a breath, forcing myself to stay composed as I nod along.

"As you can see," Dave says, on a roll now, "we've got the world's top expert on artificial pollinators heading our project. Hand-picked her myself." He grins and gestures toward me, and the audience is subjected to more whiplash.

Well, let's hope this project doesn't need as much maintenance as you did, Dave.

"Within a decade," he continues, his arms spread wide like a well-dressed Jesus, "billions of these little guys are going to be pollinating genetically-toughened and radiation-resistant plants across the entire Red Planet. Hell, in fifty years, it won't even be the 'Red Planet' anymore. It's gonna be green."

Don't oversell it, Dave. So far, we've only built a dozen bots.

The bots are resting on a large, flat leaf right under the sunlamp now, done with their pollinating.

"The bees have completed their assigned tasks," I say, half expecting Dave to interrupt again, "and are charging their thermal batteries while they wait to be called back to the hive." I type in the recall command, and the little guys fly toward the controller.

"Haven't lost a single one," Dave calls out.

At least he got that part right.

"We haven't come up with a way to collect their honey," I say.

"But we're working on it!" Dave calls out. "Nineteen ninety-nine a jar!"

He gets a few chuckles.

That's when I notice that one of the bots hasn't returned to the controller. It's hovering over a forbidden pepper blossom and doing some sort of bee-like dance: two quick steps forward and one slow step back. Dave meets my gaze, and his eyebrows rise.

Have to look into that.

I repeat the recall order, and, this time, the little guy buzzes back to his hive.

"Thank you all for coming," I say before Dave can make more iffy promises. "There's a basket of strawberries by the door. Please help yourself. They were all pollinated by Kirkland Enterprises' micro-drone bees."

There's brief applause, and Dave herds the dignitaries to their next demo—and sends Vinny off to retrieve the forgotten badge.

After I lock up the microdrones inside the controller hive, I set the sunlight and sprinklers back to automatic, turn off the heat lamp, and let my team know the demo was a success. It's noon, and they're already gone for lunch. They've been working night and day to get the demo ready, so I tell them to take the rest of the day off, and that I'll be back in the office in three weeks.

I eat the last three strawberries, text Diego, and spend a minute trying to dislodge Vinny's folded paper cup from underneath the door. When I finally manage to get it out, I slump into the wheelchair to catch my breath. After the door shuts and the lock clicks, I turn myself around and creep toward the airlock. By the time I reach the lobby, I've banged my foot twice, my biceps are on fire, and I have a newfound respect for people in wheelchairs.

When Diego sees me, he rushes over to hold the door for me. "How'd it go, hon?"

"Well," I say, wishing I could throw my arms around him. "I think I answered the question: To bee or not to bee?"

Madders' Log
Entry 14

Target: Diego Nadales
Nexus: Diego's Cabin
Chrono Tag: 2 Weeks Later

Minor ripples detected around Kirkland
Enterprises ATHENA-1 project. Predictive software
indicates most, if not all, will dissipate.
Reduced involvement by Isabel likely source of
deviations.

I t's Isabel's last night at the cabin, and we're standing in the kitchen with our shoulders touching, washing the dishes.

Christ, if I could just freeze this moment and hold onto it forever.

We spent the day hiking up to the point with a picnic lunch in the backpack—Lucky riding on my shoulders and Tolstoy going the whole way on puppy power. Isabel made the climb with only a handful of breaks—and clearly doesn't need my help anymore.

Even though it was a beautiful fall day, I couldn't shake the feeling that everything was about to come crashing down on me. Isabel is leaving tomorrow, going back to her apartment and her job, and I'll be returning to a huge financial mess at work.

What am I going to do with myself once she's gone? This cabin is gonna feel painfully empty.

I let out a sigh and dry the last pan, sliding my hand across Isabel's back as I reach around her to stick it in the cupboard. She leans into my touch—and then takes an awkward step away and dries her hands.

"Do you mind if I start a fire?" she says.

It's dark out now, and snow is threatening. Despite the heater being on, there's a chill in the air. Something warm, bright, and hopeful is ending, and we can both feel it.

You need to come clean and tell her before it's too late, mae.

"Diego?"

"Sorry. Yes, of course." I shake my head, trying to clear the gloomy cobwebs. "I can bring in more wood if we need it." The phone in my pocket vibrates, and I pull it out to check the caller ID. "I probably need to take this. It's the head of legal, and he never calls unless it's important."

"No worries," Isabel says. "Did you want a little privacy?"

"No need. With the way I've been blathering on about work, maybe you can help." I accept the FaceTime call. "Yo, Hank. What can I do for you?"

"Hey, Diego. It'll be great to have you back in the office tomorrow."

"Looking forward to it," I say and point the camera at Iz. "Isabel is here too."

She waves and starts stacking logs to make a fire. "Hi, Hank. Nice to see you again."

"Pleasure." Hank's voice deepens. "Sorry to bother you both at home, but there's something I think you should know about, Diego."

"Uh-oh," I say, my gut churning. "What's up?"

"I just got a call from the trucking company," he says. "You know how the warehouse in Denver is chock full of boxed-up hardware ready to ship? Well, no one can find any freight reservations."

"Shit."

"Yeah. I called them to see if they could track down our order, but they don't have any record of it. And since you're wondering how I got involved, it's because the legal department at Water Is Everything has been all over my ass for three days. If our stuff isn't on their ship in Long Beach by Friday, they're canceling the contract. Without that money, we may have to file for bankruptcy protection."

"Christ," I say, thinking I should have taken this one in private. *Iz is gonna think you're incompetent.* "I'll get on it first thing in the morning, Hank. Thanks for the heads-up."

"No problem," Hank says and yawns. "Just doing my job."

I notice the dark circles under his eyes. "You holding up okay, *mae?*"

"Yep." He pops a couple tablets into his mouth and nods at Iz. "Glad you're feeling better, Isabel. As I'm sure you know, Diego was pretty worried about you." Hank reaches for the 'end call' button. "Ciao."

We sit in awkward silence.

Lucky jumps up on Isabel's lap, and Tolstoy lies down in front of the fire. Outside, thick snowflakes are falling.

I lean back on the couch and form my hands into a steeple. "Before you say anything, I have a proposition for you."

"As long as it doesn't involve yoga or cilantro."

I raise an eyebrow. "That leaves a lot of options, Ms. Sanborn."

The corner of her mouth twitches, and then she looks away. "If you need some financial help, I—"

"I don't," I say. "Hank is famous for saying the sky is falling. If worst comes to worst, we can rent some U-Hauls and drive the boxes out there ourselves. Probably cost less than the freight service."

She frowns but doesn't push back. "So what is it, Diego?"

I lean over and pet Tolstoy. "Since it's our last night together, I wanted to talk about something." I swallow. "Talk about us, actually." I turn to see her reaction, but her face is carefully composed. I force myself to continue, my heart pounding so hard it's difficult to think. "This time, I want to build our relationship on trust and honesty. So even if it's harsh or painful or embarrassing, for chrissake, I want to tell you the truth."

She strokes Lucky's fur, not meeting my gaze.

"I'm not promising to fix anything—far from it—but I was hoping you'd give me the opportunity to try."

She presses her lips together, and I can't tell if she's heart-struck or annoyed.

But the silence is almost painful, so I fill it with words. "That means from here on out, no twisting things or lying by omission. I'm going to share some stuff with you that might make you question my sanity. But I'm not going to lie to you. If I say I don't know, it's the truth. If there's something I don't understand, I'll say so, and you have to believe me."

"You're scaring me, Diego."

"Don't be scared. All I'm saying is, I think there are forces at play beyond the two of us, and we need to be able to trust each other." I look at her, studying her face. "Okay?"

"And if I say no?"

I stifle a smirk. "Since when could you turn down a good mystery?"

"Okay, you got me there." She taps her finger against her lips. "But the deal has to work both ways."

I scoff. "Absolutely not. What do you think I am, a glutton for punishment?" I wait for her to roll her eyes and then hold her gaze for a few seconds. "Of course it has to work both ways, Iz—even if I don't always handle the heat as well as you do."

She holds up her right hand. "Pinky promise?"

I wrap my little finger around hers, keeping my gaze steady. "I promise."

She lets go and ruffles Lucky's fur. "You go first."

Do it, Nadales.

"I knew you were trapped in the burning hotel because I got a text message telling me to save you." I hold up my pinky. "And I got the text while I was waiting for you to show up for dinner at the Top of the Rockies, the restaurant in Denver where—"

"—you took me all those years ago," she says and brings her hand up to her mouth. "I was on my way there after the divorce. How did you know?"

"You left me a note telling me to meet you there."

She pulls her chin back. "I did?"

"You left it in my car earlier that day."

She frowns. "No, I didn't."

"Well, maybe not yet, but you will. I have the note."

She scrunches up her nose. "What are you saying, Diego? Future-me will travel to the past and drop off a note for you? Did you forget to take your anti-psychotic pills this morning?"

I turn away, watching the fire crackle and pop. "I think the only viable explanation is that it *was* sent by a future you."

She makes a face like I just announced I'm Napoleon.

"Wait till you see the cat video."

"Can't wait," she says dryly. "How about we start with the note?"

I offer it to her, my hand shaking ever so slightly.

"Unusual paper," she says, rubbing it between her thumb and forefinger. "Handmade?"

"Yeah. And probably hand cut: the edges aren't perfectly straight. I bet the ink is handmade too." I get up to put another log on the fire. "Just so you know, I arrived at the restaurant at six-thirty and waited for over two hours—until I got the text message."

She reads the note telling me to reserve a table with a view, beware of Dave, and check out the viral cat video—and then she looks up at me. "'I don't know it yet, but I need to stop Dave?' If I don't know about it, how could I write about it?"

"Good question." I get up. "And it's *we* who need to stop Dave."

"Yeah. That's kinda ominous." She watches me lift a heavy log and set it on the fire. "Why would I write that?"

I take a metal poker and nudge the log into the hot coals. It bursts into flames, casting a warm flickering light across the room. "I was hoping you could tell me." I sit down next to her on the couch again. "If you can come up with a rational explanation for the note, I'm all ears."

"Some weirdo faked my handwriting to prank you?"

"Okay. Why?"

"I don't know, Diego, because he's worried about Dave's biodomes?"

"Possible," I say and hand her my phone, the *Furrari* clip queued up. "But I don't think anyone could fake this." We watch a live newscaster congratulating some local group called the Bluecoats on their 1st place win—when a cat jumps up onto the woman's head, curls his tail around her neck, and starts purring. On live television. In Canton, Ohio, for chrissake.

Isabel's face pales.

"I found the note five hours before the clip was *recorded*. You can see the timestamp in the lower-right corner." I bring up a screenshot of the text messages. "It gets worse," I say.

She reads the messages out loud:

> UNKNOWN
>
> Plan changed: Find her.
>
> UNKNOWN
>
> Tell the professor: cut the red wire, double-check the maths.
>
> Kid says wear socks in the coffin.
>
> And the world's about to shit itself.
>
> Now move!

When she's finished, she hands me the phone, her eyebrows

furrowed. "Why would anyone need to wear socks to their funeral? And who's the professor?"

"I don't know," I say. "But I think it must be some sort of code."

She gives me a look like I actually might be crazy.

I exhale. "Now do you believe me?"

She harrumphs. "No."

"Yeah," I say with a sigh. "I guess I wouldn't believe me, either."

"Although it does look like my handwriting," she says, running her finger across the paper. "But I didn't write it." She looks up at me. "Did you try calling the number?"

"Of course," I say, my voice too loud. *Tone it down, Nadales.* "I tried the next morning. Some friendly middle school teacher told me she'd let an elderly man borrow her phone after the Brown Palace went up in flames. She watched the fellow send the texts—noticed he was typing with one finger too. When the guy finished, he handed the phone back, thanked her, and hurried off *toward* the fire."

Something in her expression changes, softens. "An old man wearing red high-tops and a fedora?"

I stare at her. "How did you know?"

She spends a moment gazing out at the snowstorm. "I ran into him the night of the fire."

Tolstoy gets up and barks to be let out, so I pad across the living room and open the front door.

"Make it quick, buddy. It's freezing out there." I shut the door and wait, all sorts of crazy thoughts banging around in my head. When he barks again, I open the door and he bounds back in, getting snow all over the floor. I wipe it up with my socks and steal a glance at Isabel.

She's rubbing her hands on her arms, still looking a bit shell-shocked.

I will myself to stay calm. "How about some hot cocoa?"

"That would be fabulous," she says and cranes her neck around to look at me. "Do you have more of those little marshmallows?"

I suppress a smile. "Comin' right up."

A few minutes later, I hand her a steaming mug and sit down again, sipping a cocoa of my own.

She clears her throat. "Okay, so I'll play along." She taps at a floating marshmallow. "Why did me-from-the-future tell you to wait at the restaurant?" She lowers her chin. "If she *was* from the future, didn't she know I wasn't going to show?"

"Better yet," I say, "why didn't she just tell *you* not to enter a burning building?" I pin her with my gaze. "Like someone needs to tell you that. Christ, Iz, what were you thinking?"

She ignores my jibe and blows on her cocoa. "Why didn't future-me tell the Adopt-a-Pet people not to leave the pets overnight? That would have solved everything."

"Except for the hotel being destroyed."

She raises her eyebrows. "Kinda heartless of future-me, no?"

I chuckle. "I imagine you had your reasons."

She holds her mug with both hands and takes a sip of cocoa. "Ye gads, I hope so."

"Maybe future-you *did* tell the Brown Palace," I say. "And that's why it was closed for renovations."

"Right," she spits out. "I just fired off a telegram from the future warning them that someone was going to set off a bomb." She scrunches up her nose. "It doesn't make any sense, Diego."

"Yeah, I know," I say. "I can't wrap my head around it, either."

We sit and drink our cocoa, both of us watching the fire.

I turn toward her. "If I hadn't gotten that note, Iz, I would have been here that night."

She nods. "And I would have died in the fire."

"But if you died in that fire—"

"—I couldn't have sent the note from the future," she says. "It violates the Grandfather Paradox."

I rub the back of my neck. "So, maybe you did survive—without me, I mean. Maybe you just got hurt."

She shakes her head. "If you hadn't found me when you did, I would have been killed, Diego. End of story. The ceiling collapsed moments after they got me out. We all saw it on the news."

"Yeah."

She looks down at her hands. "I should be dead," she whispers.

"I'm glad you're not," I say and stare at the fire. "Elated, actually."

She makes a face.

"So maybe the multiverse is real," I say. "In one universe you went to the restaurant. But in another, you didn't. Maybe all these conflicting events are happening in different timelines, and they interact somehow, play into each other?"

She laughs. "Are you proposing the note was sent from the future *and* a different universe?" She scratches her nose. "I feel like we're going in the wrong direction, Diego."

"What about the old man?" I glance down at my cocoa. "How do you explain him?"

"I don't." She runs her hand through her hair. "But just because something is strange doesn't mean it's aliens or Bigfoot or effing time travelers. There has to be a rational explanation. We just haven't figured it out yet."

"I think whoever sent the note believed you'd show up at the restaurant, but something unexpected happened. When the old guy realized things had changed, he sent the text and followed you."

"He didn't follow me anywhere," she says. "I watched him walk away in the other direction. There had to be someone else in the hotel."

"Someone else?"

"Yeah. Someone younger. He called my name and pushed me down next to the piano right before the staircase fell." She swallows. "I hope he made it out."

I nod, remembering the broken piano and someone crushed beneath it like the Wicked Witch of the East.

"No one knew I was going to be in Denver that night," she says. "Not even Sophie."

I raise an eyebrow. "Kirkland did."

"Well, we both know it wasn't Dave who saved me," she says.

I scrub my hand across my neck. "But it could have been someone he paid to follow you."

"Yeah, right," she says. "And Dave's henchman crawled into a burning building, hung out while I evacuated stray pets, and then threw himself under a piano when things didn't pan out. What are you saying? That Dave knew the building was going to blow up?"

"No," I say and sip my cocoa. "Don't get me wrong, Kirkland's an ass, but he's not some psycho lunatic."

She crosses her arms. "So maybe I made different decisions in different universes, and future me, or you, or whoever, had to guess if I'd spend the evening sipping champagne or getting crushed by a piano." She looks like her chest hurts. "I *did* have a reservation at the restaurant. It was going to be a hurrah-for-jettisoning-Dave celebration for one. But as I was walking to the restaurant, a flyer for the Adopt-a-Pet thing blew down the sidewalk and caught on my shoe."

"And you decided to blow off dinner and get a kitten." I exhale. "That's what changed."

She shivers. "This is getting creepier by the second."

I give an evil laugh. "Welcome to the dark side. We have marshmallows."

"So," she says, suppressing a smile, "we're back to a note from the future, possibly from a different universe." She fishes out the marshmallow and pops it into her mouth. "I can't believe I just said that."

"So you do believe me." Relief rushes through me.

"No." She glances down at her hot cocoa. "But I'm too dumb to think of another explanation." She shrugs. "Aliens, Bigfoot, and time travelers for the win."

I polish off my cocoa and set the mug on the coffee table. "So tell me about the old man," I say. "What was he like?"

"He was wearing a hat, a fedora, low over his eyes, so I couldn't see his face. And when he walked away, I noticed he was wearing faded red high-tops." She gives an awkward laugh. "Just like you used to. I used to wonder if you wore them to bed."

I consider a joke about ways she could find out—but restrain myself and wiggle my eyebrows instead.

And then her mouth falls open, and she almost spills her cocoa on her lap. "It was you, future-you." Lucky skitters into the bedroom, and Tolstoy barks.

"Now, who sounds crazy."

"Omigod," she says and sets the mug down. "You were the old man who kept me from tripping on the sidewalk. You grabbed my arm, and then you picked up the divorce papers for me." Her hand flies up to her mouth. "I thought it was you when he first spoke, but I refused to believe it. He was so old and wrinkled, I didn't think it was possible."

"It's not."

She turns to face me, her eyes huge. "But it was. How could that be?" She lets her gaze fall across my face, down my shoulders, and onto my hands. "He was... ancient."

"Ancient?" I give her a hurt look. "I was going for distinguished."

The corner of her mouth curves up, and she picks up my hand, tracing the lines across my palm. "And when he picked up my shoe, I remember noticing he had your hands." She stares at me, her eyes filling with tears. "It was you, Diego. I'm sure of it. And I let him walk away."

I rest my hand on her knee, imagining what it must have been like for him.

Unimaginably painful.

"Tell me what happened," I say as Lucky jumps back into her lap.

She blinks a couple of times and then takes an extended drink of cocoa. I get up, grab a box of tissues from the bathroom, and set it next to her.

"Thanks." She blows her nose and takes a slow breath. "As I was walking toward the Brown Palace, I tripped in those stupid high heels and nearly fell. The divorce papers spilled all over the sidewalk, and this old man stopped to help me. He told me to get in my car and keep driving."

"*Mierda*, he knew about the explosion," I say. "He knew it was *going to happen*. Why didn't you listen to him and get out of the city?"

"He was a million years old, Diego, and I thought he was a bit woolly upstairs." She sighs and strokes Lucky. "He gave me something with the divorce papers, slipped it in when he handed them back to me. I didn't realize it until after he disappeared."

"The puzzle box."

She nods. "It was wrapped in handmade paper that had my name on it. My *maiden* name."

"*Mierda*. Recognize the handwriting?"

"No." She sets Lucky in my lap and stands up. "But there was something inside it." Tolstoy trots after her into the bedroom. I hear her open a drawer, say something to Tolstoy, and pad back to the sofa. The puppy settles next to her feet.

"It's *Nazareno* wood," I say. "Purpleheart. Native to Costa Rica."

"Why didn't you say something when you rescued it from my car?"

"Didn't want to pry."

She huffs. "Next time, Mr. Nadales, pry." She starts sliding the puzzle box edges, and when she takes out an orange seashell, my heart skips a beat. She turns the shell over in her hands, running her fingers across the rich swirls and delicate white spines. "It's beautiful," she says, "but why would he go to all that trouble to give me a seashell?"

"I don't know," I say, "but I have one *exactly* like it."

Madders' Log
Entry 15

Target: Matt Hudson
Nexus: Warm Springs Military Complex
Chrono Tag: Next Day

Hudson's pace of innovation continues to
accelerate ahead of expectations. Likelihood of
pre-Doomsday development of Trans Temporal Viewer
and Spacetime Bridge itself increased to 44 and
23 percent, respectively.

I slide the two biohazard bags into the safe and let the young woman guarding it know I'm done for the day.

"Monday at eight?" she asks as she closes the door and locks it with an actual key.

I pull off my gloves. "Yes, thank you." I watch her wheel the safe out of the lab, wondering if her family knows she's been guarding a dingy white athletic sock and a pink sticky note for the last month.

Despite the fact that I'm the resident materials expert, it took me a week of begging to get permission to run tests on the damn things—and don't get me started on getting access to anything else from the Einstein Sphere. All I'm allowed to do is look at photos, and even *that*'s controversial.

Anyway, it wasn't until Wednesday that I got access to the power tools: a mass spectrometer and a drift chamber.

After spending the better part of yesterday getting my permission slip signed by every adult in the building, this morning I hit the road running. I took the sock out of the safe, clipped a few balls of fuzz off, and stuck it in the drift chamber. It'll take at least a week for muon tracks to appear, but when they do, they'll reveal any atomic weirdness.

Once the muon detector was chugging along, I ran a bit of sock fuzz through the mass spectrometer and got back exactly what I expected: ordinary cotton with traces of other organic compounds—probably from dead skin cells, sweat, detergent, dirt, or even rubber.

Next, I got the pink sticky note out. After shaving off a narrow strip of paper, I stuck the sample in the mass spectrometer and fired it up. This time, what I got back was a bit odd, so I set up another sample for processing and ran it using a longer gradient. Thirty minutes later, I got the same baffling result:

Unknown isotopic signature detected.

So, I sliced off a third bit of paper, prepped it for full analysis, and told the machine to compare the sample to *everything* in the known universe. That was three hours ago.

I check my watch. "Should have the results soon."

After updating my logbook, I go over to the drift chamber to make sure it's working properly—and discover the machine has gone bonkers.

Instead of one or two straight lines, the scan looks like a bowl of spaghetti. Muons are twisting and zigzagging and folding over on themselves, a few even vanishing mid-run.

The drift chamber must be malfunctioning.

"Bloody hell."

I stop the experiment, reset everything, and run the full set of diagnostics again. Once I'm certain it's working, I stick in the sock and restart the test.

And the exact same thing happens again.

I take a closer look at the zigzags and whirls, trying to imagine them in 3D.

It's as if the lines have been folded over on themselves, bent backwards into squashed curves. It's like the muons are stuck in a...

Loop.

The damn thing's from the future!

"Nah, it can't be," I say aloud. "You've been watching too many sci-fi movies."

I plop down in my desk chair and rub my hands across my face.

Time to call it a day.

I unconsciously reach into my pocket to call Cassie—only to have my hand come away empty for the hundredth time. Usually on a Friday afternoon, we'd be chatting about the week, and she'd be telling me about her plans for the weekend.

I miss hearing your voice, pumpkin.

I yawn, remove my glasses, and rub my eyes, wishing I was heading to the pub with Sam and the lads.

Instead, I'll be sitting alone, gobbling down mass-produced food, so I can spend the evening locked in my hotel room, reading moldy physics journals and kicking myself for not eating slower.

It's that or *Star Trek* reruns—and I've already watched all of them twice.

Blimey, that's the hardest part about being stuck in here: the loneliness.

We get almost no news in here. Last I heard, the Americans were bickering over which TikTok influencer should be the next president. Meanwhile, hurricanes the size of the national debt ravage the East

Coast, inflation skyrockets, and crops all over the Northern Hemisphere fail for no apparent reason.

Maybe that wonder fertilizer Kirkland Enterprises has been flogging everywhere can make a dent?

Unfortunately, as the planet heats up—between the fires, floods, and wars—things are only going to get worse.

Perhaps it's better not knowing.

My stomach growls as I start shutting down the other machines in the lab. Picasso should be here any minute to escort me to dinner. Hopefully, he'll have an update on my request for a lab assistant— and my application for a phone with internet access.

I'm trying, Cassie.

I keep telling him that the rule requiring all outside contact to go through "proper channels" is a huge pain in the arse, and it's slowing down my progress.

It is, of course. But more importantly, it's breaking my heart.

Picasso just tells me I'm preaching to the choir, but I'm not sure I believe him.

And sure, Sergeant Major Richter seems like a decent bloke, but I have no doubt he'd put a bullet in my head if he thought I'd gone rogue. You don't get to be in charge of the most top-secret project this side of Roswell without being hard as a bloody Abrams tank.

I rub my hand across my face. "Kinda puts a damper on the social life, to say the least."

The mass spectrometer dings, the pink paper results fall into the hopper, and I pick them up, expecting to see the usual smear of organic elements. But there's only a single line of text:

`Atomic composition not in database.`

"What? How can paper not be in your bloody database? Every element in the known universe is in there."

Maybe I buggered the input parameters?

I double-check, but nothing seems amiss.

Blimey.

I print out the individual traces and scan through them, my heart pounding in my chest.

On the macro level, the note looks and acts like ordinary paper. But on the subatomic level, things are all over the shop. It's like learning that when no one's looking, your dog sings opera in Latin. So yeah, something about this sticky note is not just foreign, it's downright *alien*—literally from outside known physics.

Christ, the sock's from the future and the note's from another universe?

What would you call them? Extraversal? Paraphysical? Xenocosmic?

I cringe. All those sound vaguely pornographic.

Let's borrow one from science fiction.

"The sock is a *temporal* jinn object," I say aloud, trying out the sound of it. "And the sticky note is a *xeno* jinn, both of them artifacts out of their natural spacetime."

And then it hits me.

"The Einstein Sphere came through a wormhole," I blurt out. "From the future of a different bloody universe."

No physicist would say that and ever expect to be taken seriously again.

You included, mate.

With a shaky hand, I write down the impossible results in my lab book, stick in the printouts, and snap the journal shut. What I wouldn't give to have Cassie here right now to help me work through this. She'd probably think up a clever way to test my hypothesis.

Except she'd hate being stuck in this place—and who could blame her?

What about Sam? For as much as I complain about him running his mouth, he'd be good to bounce ideas off of.

And Sam loves conspiracy theories. He'd eat this place up.

I chuckle to myself. "Figuratively and literally."

I did ask Picasso to kidnap him—this place's version of a job interview—but so far, no luck. As far as I can tell, whoever's running this show doesn't care if we make any progress—as long as nobody finds out about the Einstein Sphere. I said as much to Picasso last week, telling him I'd be making a lot more progress if I was allowed to build a team. He just gave me the usual spiel about *working on it, security,* and *powers that be.*

I let out a heavy sigh and collapse in my desk chair, the phrase "jinn objects" bouncing around my brain.

You should tell Picasso.

What if it turns out the machines are misconfigured? Imagine announcing I've discovered something from the future *and* something from another universe—only to find out I forgot to reset the doohickey on the thingamajig.

What you need are more samples from the sphere—and other people to verify your results.

I know the government has spun up other teams because I see new muggles in the mess every so often. Maybe I can find someone to check my results? Of course, Dick made me sign a form saying I'd keep my head down and my mouth shut—and he has a habit of poking his nose around corners—so for now, probably not.

There's a knock on the door, and Picasso walks in, looking knackered. "Ready, professor?"

I nod. "Can I ask you something first?"

He steps inside, shuts the door, and sits down on the edge of my desk. "Shoot."

"I need a small sample from the shell and punch cards. I'm getting some unusual results, and I'd like to see if the other items display the same, uh, weird behavior. I wouldn't need more than a few molecules."

He sighs. "I can try. I'll see if I can arm-wrestle Johnson for it tomorrow."

"Also," I say, trying to keep my heel from jiggling. "Would it be possible to acquire high-grade tungsten carbide and access to an industrial-quality smelter? I want to build a sphere, stick some paper inside, and use a magnetic field to protect the contents while I blast it with plasma. See what happens."

He groans and starts massaging his temples. "The military has access to a smelter in Kentucky, and I can requisition the ore. How soon do you need it?"

I shrug. "Soon. Once I have a sphere, I'll need an autoclave to test it. That should give us a better idea of what we're working with."

"Okay. Get me the specs. Anything else?"

"Well, I could use a muon tomography machine," I say, feeling like a kid asking Santa Claus for half the store. "And I'd need a lab assistant to run it. At this point, I'd take a trained chimpanzee. But Sam Maxwell, the postdoc I was telling you about earlier, would be perfect."

He gives me a tired smile. "Well, then you're in luck. Dr. Maxwell has been here all day."

I let out a whoop, and Picasso actually laughs.

"If you're ready," he says and sets his hand on my shoulder, "let's go say hello. He's asked to see the artifacts before he commits, so I expect Mr. Johnson will be joining us."

My excitement dies right there on the vine. "Lovely."

He stands up. "Shall we?"

I pick up my lab book and follow him down a maze of hallways and into a windowless conference room. Sam is sitting at a table, flipping through photos of the artifacts, while Dick leans against the wall and scowls at his phone.

"Doc!" Sam says when he sees me. He jumps out of his chair and gives me a bear hug. "I thought you fell off the face of the Earth, old man."

"Me too," I say and give him a couple good pats on the back. "Good to see you, Sam."

He plops back down in a chair. "You gave up teaching freshmen for this shit?"

"Not exactly," I say. "Have you talked to Cassie recently?"

His eye twitches, but he shakes his head. "Not since the—you know what—happened."

Dick holsters his phone and steps closer to Sam. "I don't want to spoil your little reunion," he says, then sneers at me. "But we have a fucking job to do here. You said you could contribute, Maxwell, so do it or stop wasting my time."

Sam cranes his neck, staring up at Dick like he's a serial killer.

I exhale. "What have you got, Sam?"

He turns to me, still looking worried about our resident Marquis de Sade. "It's the world's lamest encryption," Sam says and points to a photo in the notebook. "Rote thirteen."

Dick perks up. "Where is this Road Thirteen? Russia?"

"Not road," I say, "*rote*. As in *rotation*. And nobody uses it anymore. It was popular back before the Internet was a thing. Mostly to hide lewd jokes."

"They told me I'd be working with pros." Sam scoffs. "Any middle school kid could've figured out that code." He puts his hands behind his head and his feet on the table. "Who do you guys have in charge of encryption, Inspector Clouseau?"

I grimace, attempting to get Sam's attention and tell him to tone it down.

Dick kicks Sam's feet off the table and grabs him by the T-shirt. "One more smartass comment from you, Maxwell, and my patience is gonna run out."

"Hey," I say and stand up. "Let go of him!"

Picasso grabs Dick by the shoulder and pulls him away from Sam. "Cool your jets, Johnson."

Dick shakes off Picasso's grip, but he lets go of Sam.

"Sam's right," I say and slowly sit back down. "Who *do* we have working on this?"

"No one," Picasso says with a dismissive glance at Dick. "It was designated SCI—Sensitive Compartmented Information—and the DIA and NSA have been fighting over it ever since. Once one of them wins the turf war, the CIA will probably snap it up. At some point, I expect they'll let us have a look."

"With binoculars from five hundred yards?" I say and turn back to my postdoc. "Sam, do you have any idea what the message says?"

Sam, who's still holding his hands up in front of his chest, takes a tentative glance at Dick. "Give me back my phone, and I'll tell you."

Picasso shakes his head at the same time Dick says, "That's a 'no' so hard it could kick your ass."

I resist the urge to roll my eyes. "How about paper and a pencil?"

"Wow," Sam says, still looking wary. "This place is *super* high-tech." He quickly adds, "But I can work with that."

I raise an eyebrow at Picasso, and he nods. I set my lab book in front of Sam and turn it to a blank page. I offer him my mechanical pencil, and he smooths down the paper and writes the date at the top.

"How many punch cards are there?" Sam says without looking up.

"Ten," Picasso says.

"How'd they find that many?" Sam says, laughing. "Ransacked the Computer History Museum?"

I clear my throat. "They were inside the bogey we—I mean, I—was tracking the night of the big fire in Denver," I say. "The one that made all those neutrinos your detector picked up."

Sam sits up a bit straighter. "Really? How did the paper not burn up? That thing was hauling a—"

"We call it the Einstein Sphere," I say. "I've been studying its composition, manufacture, and origin for the last month."

"Holy shit," Sam says, his ears getting red. "I told everyone you were working on some sort of Acoustic Kitty."

Dick reacts like Sam just said *thermonuclear device*. "What is that? Some sort of black ops listening device?"

"Look it up," Picasso says. He pulls more photographs out of the notebook and lines them up in front of Sam. "What about the rest of the punch cards?"

"They all look to be ROT-13," Sam says. He prints out the

alphabet in a single line. "It's a simple Caesar cipher." He writes the letters again on a second line, offset by thirteen places. When he finishes, he starts decrypting the first card.

"We're missing something," he says and gives a nervous laugh. He looks up at me. "A couple of the words are recognizable, but the rest is gibberish."

"Punctuation?" I say. "ROT-13 only uses letters. Maybe they used another character set for punctuation?"

Sam bobs his head. "Yeah, good idea, doc." He scratches out some of the letters, and we both see it at the same time. "Shit," he says.

"It's a URL," I say. "A link to a web page. Only, they're missing the HTTPS that goes at the beginning."

Sam shuffles the punch cards around. "Here. These three. See how they start out the same? That's probably the domain name." He translates those cards. "Does *CodeNex.gov* ring any bells?"

Dick stares at Picasso, both their faces unreadable.

Picasso rubs his chin. "It's a biometrically locked vault containing hard copies and digital backups of top-secret government projects."

Sam giggles. "Don't tell me, the files are stored deep within a secret facility on an air-gapped network, and even the President doesn't know where it is?"

Dick looks like he might explode, but Sam doesn't seem to notice.

"What else?" Picasso says.

Whistling to himself, Sam spends another minute decrypting the rest of the cards. "Easy-peasy." He circles three groups of words and turns the lab book so it's facing Picasso. "Trans Temporal Viewing Device, Einstein-Rosen Bridge Generator, and Singularity Transit Device."

My chest is so tight it's difficult to breathe.

The sphere did come through a wormhole from the future.

Sam sets down the pencil. "Sounds like we're building an Alcubierre drive." He looks at Picasso. "That's a warp drive for you Trekkies."

Dick grabs the pad and turns it so he can read it. "What's a warp drive?"

Sam huffs. "It's a trope in science fiction that makes you go really, really fast when you're running away from the bad guys." He glances at Picasso. "That would be the Klingons."

Picasso taps on my lab book with his finger. "How do we get the full URLs, Dr. Maxwell?"

After taking a surreptitious glance at Dick, Sam leans back in his chair and crosses his arms—but keeps his feet firmly planted on the ground. "Given the three domain name cards go first, you'll have to try reordering the other seven until you get a hit. There are only thirty-five possible combinations, so it shouldn't take long."

Picasso takes a photo of Sam's work, types something into his phone, and then rests his hand on Sam's shoulder. "Good work, son."

Even Dick looks impressed.

Sam sits up and rubs his palms across his pants, glancing from me to Dick to Picasso. "Thanks. The real prize is gonna be building a spacetime bridge." He swallows and takes a surreptitious glance at me. "Cassie, that's the professor's niece," he bobs his head at me, "studies ERBs—Einstein-Rosen Bridges."

I gasp, unsure whether to applaud or strangle him.

"You should ask her to join the project," Sam says. "She's like the world expert on wormholes."

I'm expecting Dick to say something nasty, but he doesn't let out a peep.

Picasso clears his throat. "We are in the process of vetting Dr. Cassandra Hudson. For now, let's focus on the problems at hand."

Sam and I exchange a quick look, and I decide that bringing in Cassandra is an ace idea. If nothing else, she'd be safe here—even with Dick acting the maggot.

"What does an Einstein-Rose thing connect?" Dick asks. "Flower gardens?"

Sam meets his gaze. "It's the hoity-toity name for a wormhole. You know, like in the movie *Interstellar*."

"And *Contact*," I say.

"And the *Star Trek* reboot," Sam adds. "Best of class."

"And *Alien*," Picasso says. "Loved that one. I had a cat named Jonesy when I was a kid."

"Don't forget *Firefly*," I say, enjoying Dick's look of discomfort as he watches us play movie ping-pong.

"And *Dark Matter*," Picasso adds.

Sam moans. "Killed in its prime."

"So, yeah," I say. "Pretty much every sci-fi flick with a spaceship has faster-than-light travel."

"So," Picasso says and scoops up the photos. "Either of you know what a Trans Temporal Viewing Device is?" He puts the photos back in the notebook.

"*Leave It to Beaver*?" Sam says, grinning like a madman. "You know, the TV show about a kid in the 1950s that was nothing like the actual 1950s?"

Dick looks like he might start punching things, but Picasso ignores him. "Professor? Any ideas?"

"Not really," I say. "Although the name would imply it allows you to see things from the past—so pretty much every video camera ever invented."

"Maybe it can see into the future," Sam says. "That would be cool sci-fi."

Picasso picks up the notebook and tucks it under his arm. "What about a Singularity Transit Device?"

"That one's easy as pie," I say. "A device that can withstand the gravitational forces of a black hole."

"More like the forces of a wormhole," Sam says, still grinning. "Which would be much more fun." He swings the chair back and forth. "Wormholes are basically black holes with benefits."

I clear my throat, and Sam stops oscillating.

"I think our Einstein Sphere is one such device," I say. "And it would explain why all the fragments disappeared: They got pulled back when the spacetime bridge shut down."

Picasso narrows his gaze. "How?"

"Imagine the sphere is like a beachball being held up by a stream of water—the hosepipe's your ERB. When you turn off the tap, the ball falls back to earth."

"Why didn't all the artifacts disappear too?" Picasso asks.

"Yeah," Dick says. "I was just going to ask that."

"It's wild speculation," I say, tapping my finger on my chin, "but perhaps the spacetime bridge only transports tungsten carbide—and whatever it encloses. Once the sphere was broken, it couldn't pull the other items back with it."

"Back where?" Dick says. "Back to the future?"

"Great Scott!" Sam says. "If that sphere hit eighty-eight miles per hour, maybe it really did rip a hole in the space-time continuum."

Dick looks at him, then at me, then at Picasso—who's smirking. "You little—"

I jump in before Dick can get too worked up. "The sphere didn't come from our future—or our past. It came from another universe, one extremely similar to ours but perhaps a few years ahead of us."

Sam sits up straighter. "How do you figure?"

"The valentine note isn't from our universe." I nod at Picasso and lift my hands. "I discovered that a few minutes ago, and I was planning to tell you once I got a chance to run more tests." I shrug. "But it seems the bag holding the cat has vanished."

The corner of Picasso's mouth twitches. "What about the sock?"

"It's your bog-standard used athletic wear—only from the future." I smile now that all the pieces are falling into place. "It's probably the anchor they used to target the sphere to *our* universe. And I'll bet a hundred quid the punch cards are jinn objects too."

"Gym objects?" Dick says, looking like he's having a bad day.

"Jinn," I say. "The word comes from Arabian folklore: *a spirit outside of time*. Jinn objects are not in their proper place or time, like a penny would be out of place in the Jurassic."

"And the shell?" Picasso says.

"Ah, the foil-wrapped seashell," I say and hold up my finger. "My guess is it's a jinn object from a *third* universe that has something to do with TEGO—whatever that stands for. And I bet the foil is tungsten, not aluminium." I can tell by the look on Dick's face that I'm right. "It probably acts like a cloaking device, hiding the shell—until it's time to use it."

"Time to use it?" Picasso says.

Sam grins. "In *our* wormhole generator."

I point my finger at him. "Give the man a prize."

Picasso's phone buzzes, and he takes it out to read. A minute later, he looks up. "We've located the Singularity Transit Device project. It was started during the Cold War and abandoned decades ago."

"Well, blow me," I say and feel my face flush. "I mean, blow me down."

Sam snickers.

"As of right now," Picasso says as he types on his phone, "I'm reassigning Professor Hudson to lead the Singularity Transit Device team, with Dr. Maxwell assisting." He looks up at us. "I'll brief you first thing in the morning."

I nod. "What about the other two projects?"

Picasso glances at his phone and scrubs his hand across his mouth. "The Trans Temporal Viewing Device is currently under development at a public university."

"Berkeley," I say, feeling a little giddy.

Picasso whips his head around, his jaw tight.

"Have you contacted Sabrina Lovelace? I heard rumors she was trying to peek into the past—although at the time, I suspected it was an April Fool's joke. She's big on those."

Dick snorts. "Jesus H. Christ, Hudson, are you buddies with every goddamn nerd in the country?"

I ignore him. "What about the spacetime bridge?"

Picasso crosses his arms and steals a glance at Dick—who still looks, well, shell-shocked. "So far," he says, "we haven't found a goddamn thing."

Sam deflates. "Without that, we got a whole lot of nothin'."

"Not true," I say, the magnitude of the opportunity hitting me full-on. "We know a spacetime bridge is *possible*. And *that* may be the most important breakthrough of all."

We all sit in silence for a bit, lost in our own visions of time-travel grandeur.

"If all this stuff turns out to be real," Sam says, swinging his feet again, "it would make almost everything we know about physics obsolete."

Picasso raises an eyebrow.

I nod. "Welcome to the Twilight Zone."

Madders' Log
Entry 16

Target: Isabel Sanborn
Nexus: KE World Headquarters
Chrono Tag: 2 Weeks Later

Eden-1 demonstration occurring as expected.
Despite considerable primary target deviations,
no delays for the impending First Disaster
detected.

After I slide my badge through the reader and pull the door open, the unwieldy cat carrier bumps against the doorframe, and Lucky yowls.

I shush her. "It's okay, kitty girl. Once we get to my lab, I'll let you out. It beats sitting at home by yourself all day, doesn't it?"

She makes a soft meow and stares up at me, her eyes wide.

I lug her carrier into the engineering building and up to the guard desk.

"Morning, Lamar," I say and set Lucky on the counter.

He glances at the cat and then at me. "Good morning, Mrs. Kirkland."

"Just a heads-up," I say, my throat a little tight. "I'm no longer Mrs. Kirkland. I've evolved into Ms. Sanborn—like a Pokémon, but without the cool powers."

He chuckles. "Gotcha, Pikachu. What do we have here?"

"I'm running some experiments on how the bots react to predators. Figured my house cat would be a good first test."

He shifts his weight. "I'm afraid I'll have to run that by Internal Ops. You know how people can be about cat hair."

I give him a wan smile as a large group of high school kids crowd around the outside door. A teacher in a sweater vest knocks, looking a bit harried.

"Excuse me," Lamar says and hurries around the desk. "They're here for a tour with Mr. Kirkland."

"With Mr. Kirkland?" I say under my breath. "That's a new one." I reach over the counter and push the button to release the inner door. "Let me know what Internal Ops decides," I say and sweep up Lucky.

Lamar whips around and starts to protest but gives up and waves me through.

"Thanks, Lamar," I say and push the door open. "I promise no cat hair outside the containment lab."

On the way to my office, I stop by the microdrone engineering floor. Everyone in the sea of cubicles is busy as, well, a bee. A couple build engineers are milling around the QA manager tapping their feet—and everyone else is trying very hard to ignore them.

Something's up.

Dave is giving a small presentation in the biodome on Monday—our first public demo outside the containment lab—but everything was good-to-go yesterday.

Sophie, an old friend of mine and the software manager, sees me and comes over to give me a one-arm hug. "Congrats on the name change, Iz. You never did seem like a Kirkland to me."

"Now you tell me," I say, and she laughs. I flick my head toward the cubicles. "What's going on this morning?"

Her smile disappears. "Dave wants the new stinging behavior installed on the bots for his demo on Monday."

"What?" It comes out like a gunshot. "We haven't even started formal testing."

"Hence the fire drill," she says with an expansive gesture. "He told me he cleared it with you."

"Well, he lied." I turn toward the cubicles and say loud enough for everyone to hear, "As of right now, we're rolling back to the last certified build for Monday's demo. No stingers. End of story."

They all stop what they're doing and stare at me.

"But Mr. Kirkland said—"

"We only release fully vetted microdrones, people. No exceptions." I shift the cat carrier to the other hand, and Lucky meows. "I'll update Mr. Kirkland right now."

"Not this again," one of the new guys says under his breath. "Ain't hard to see why the boss dumped her."

I give him a razor-sharp glare, and he goes back to his typing.

"I'll talk to him," Sophie says, walking along with me. "What's with the cat?"

"Live testing," I say, my heart still racing. "Beast versus bots. I want to see how the bees handle the disruption. Exercise that adaptive code we've been bragging about."

"My money's on the cat," she says. "Sure you're not bringing him in just to keep you company?"

I chuckle, but it's forced. "To be honest, Sophie, I could use your help." I lean in closer and lower my voice. "Maybe you could keep an eye on things for me? Dave's just too damn reckless, and some of the team, well..." I glance back at the guy with the smart mouth, and he looks down at his computer.

"Benny," she says. "I voted against hiring him."

"Dave overruled you?"

She nods.

"I get it. It's hard when Dave's dangling fifty-grand raises in front of anyone willing to bypass safety protocols."

Sophie puts her arm around my shoulder again. "Don't worry, Ms. Sanborn, I got your back. And I'll read Benny the riot act. That attitude of his is totally unacceptable."

"Thanks, Soph. I'd appreciate it. If you need me," I say, grabbing the weekly list of KE headlines off my chair and stuffing them in my satchel, "I'll be in the lab—after I talk to Dave."

"Good luck." She watches me walk away. "You're gonna need it."

I'm rehearsing what I'm going to say when I'm blocked by a gaggle of students in the hallway. KE offers college scholarships to help attract the best and brightest for future Mars missions—and to recruit for Eden-1 internships. Usually the tours are led by actual interns, but Dave is giving them the personal touch.

Must know one of the students. Ten bucks says it's a girl.

Not surprisingly, most of the students, both male and female, are crowded around him, hanging on his every word. A petite Asian beauty is staring up at him like he's Ryan Reynolds and giggling every time he looks at her.

"Lani, is it?" Dave says, and she flushes bright pink. He grins like he's the wolf in *Little Red Riding Hood*, and I choke down a gag.

He places his hand on the small of her back. "Like I said, you and your friends could be our first-generation Mars colonists: scientists, engineers, teachers, doctors." He winks at Lani, and she beams like she already got the job.

Probably not in the position she's imagining.

In any case, my little conversation with Dave will have to wait.

Goddamn him for ordering my team around behind my back.

I consider trying to slip past them, but change my mind. When I get close to Dave, I step between the adoring students and whisper in his ear, "No stinging bots outside the lab, Dave. No exceptions." And before he can take another group into the containment building to wow them with the security technology, I give him my sweetest smile and say so everyone can hear, "And I'm sorry to inform you that the containment building has been permanently closed to tours. As Mr. Kirkland always says: When security leads, success follows."

Dave scowls at me but recovers quickly. "Ladies and gentlemen," he says and puts his arm around me, "meet our director of microdrone engineering, Isabel K—"

"—Sanborn," I say and step away from him. The pretty Asian girl gives me a rather hostile look, like she just figured out I'm Dave's ex and he's been telling her what a bitch I am.

If only you knew the truth, cupcake.

I gaze at their bright, young faces. "Welcome to Kirkland Enterprises. We're glad you could join us today. Enjoy the tour." I make my way through the crowd. "And be sure to order the dessert at lunch," I call over my shoulder. "Our pastry chef is marvelous, and it's included with the tour."

Might as well get something for all those application fees they're forking over.

By the time I get to the containment building, my arm is aching from lugging the cat carrier around—and Lucky's not too jazzed about it, either.

Maybe this wasn't such a great idea.

As I'm taking her through the airlock, I glance at the KE-related news.

There's a short article touting our plans to use the microdrone bees as pollinators on Mars, along with more news about low crop yields in China and Brazil—with a mention of KE's newly released GroSurge crop enhancer as a possible mitigator. There's a retouched photo of Eden-1 with a mention of the grand opening next month, and an article on honeybees mysteriously dying. When the reporter asked Dave about using artificial pollinators to supplement Earth's bees, he told her: "KE is doing everything in our power to help with the challenges facing humanity, both on Mars and here at home. Stay tuned."

"Here we go again," I say, and Lucky meows.

I've told Dave a hundred times there's no way I'm deploying bots outside a biodome without being sure the whole thing won't blow up in our faces. The bees need to be run through a million different test scenarios before releasing them into the wild.

Anyone who disagrees should read up on the cane toads in Australia, the kudzu grass in the US, and the Great Chinese Sparrow Campaign—just to name a few.

The thought makes my throat tight.

Despite my childhood exuberance for artificial pollinators, it would take great hubris to presume that natural bees could simply be replaced by robots.

That's not to say I think it's impossible, just that I think we should take extra care to do it right.

Which seems to be the exact opposite of Dave's "let's throw those fuckers out there and make a shitload of cash before anyone can copy us" plan.

Still, I'm not surprised Dave is looking to branch out. Besides the dollar signs in his eyes, it makes sense to use our technology where it can do the most good.

But it also doesn't take a lot of imagination to see how things could go terribly wrong, especially if one company ends up controlling a key element of world food production.

Not gonna end well.

Once I get to the lab, I release Lucky and instruct the Hive Controller to assemble a half-dozen bots. The suitcase-sized prototype comes with parts to build twenty-four programmable microdrones, along with a 3D printer to customize them for specific uses, but I won't need all of them today.

When the bees are ready, I send them off to record and pollinate flowers in our ever-expanding garden. Kitty girl watches them for a whole three seconds, then curls up under the sunlamp for a nap. I check that the cameras are recording and get to work on a plan to ensure that "security continues leading" for Kirkland Enterprises.

When you can't trust your CEO, it complicates things considerably.

I agree that long term, it makes sense for the bots to defend themselves. But, there are risks involved in any new behavior, especially one that poses a threat to people and livestock. So far, all our testing assumes the bots will be buzzing around inside a biodome, not free-roaming around a field. Of course we have safeguards in place for escaped bots, but if any get through an airlock on Mars, the atmosphere will destroy them in a matter of minutes.

Here on Earth, not so much.

Dave knows all that, but perhaps he needs a little reminding.

After checking his schedule, I text him that we need to talk—and that I'll be in his office in twenty minutes. He has notifications silenced, so I call his secretary, verify that he's at his desk, and ask her to let him know I'm on my way.

I call the microdrones back to the hive, stuff Lucky back into her carrier, "Sorry, missy, I'll be right back," and hurry out of the lab.

Ten minutes later, just as I'm leaving the containment building, I get his reply:

Can't meet today, princess. Have you down for a week from Tuesday at 4.

I'm still fuming when I get back to the lab. "Never marry a man you wouldn't want to be divorced from," I tell kitty girl as I let her back out. I run my fingers through my hair. "God did I blow that one."

Given that Dave is stomping all over my authority *and* avoiding me, I decide my only option is to remove the stinger code from the main build and password protect the lock-out. That way, he can't just order Sophie—or anyone else—to put it back in.

That ought to get his attention.

Once we put a robust test and deployment plan in place, we can have a meeting about how to reintroduce the stinging behavior.

But as I'm trying to move the offending stinger files, the system gives me an error.

Access Denied!

I try again, thinking I mistyped my password, but get the same error.

Damnit.

Thirty minutes later, I figure out the problem: My name has been removed from the approved-access list.

"That jerk," I say and bang my fist on my desk. "Why didn't he just fire me?"

Because he still needs you to finish the demo for the grand opening.

Lucky jumps up on my desk and flops down next to my keyboard.

"He's going to get more than he bargained for," I say and collapse back into my chair.

I could probably use Sophie's account to fix the build, but that would only work once—and probably get her fired.

You need a secret and permanent way to access the build.

An idea I've been toying with for months pops into my head. I can use the bots' DNA analyzer to create a special key for myself. Once the Hive Controller saves my key in the master list of known plants, it will be available everywhere. So whenever a bot recognizes my DNA, it will unlock the Hive Controller, and I'll get secret superuser access to the bots and the main build.

Even if all my accounts are erased, it should still work—and be very difficult to trace.

But how to unlock a controller without any bots flying around?

"The diagnostic port," I say aloud and smile. I can queue up commands on a thumb drive, plug it into the diagnostic port on the Hive Controller, and input my DNA key that way.

Gettin' kinda paranoid, aren't you, Iz?

"About time," I say and stroke Lucy's soft fur.

I get to work on the first step: getting a sample of my own DNA.

A couple hours later, I'm ready to give it a try. I set the controller on the floor and sit down in front of it. I prepare one microdrone to take DNA samples. When I activate it, the bot starts flying around in a search pattern—but completely ignores me. Even when I stick my hand in front of its sensor, the bee zooms around me.

"Damn."

I spend more time adding an extension to the "locate heat source" skill it already has, telling it to find something warm and *then* take a DNA sample. This time, I shut down the sunlamps—*don't want any competition*—and download the code to a bee. After I fire it up, the bot buzzes around, searching for a heat source. Finally, it rises up to the ceiling and raps against the clear plastic covering over the recessed lighting, making a sort of pecking noise.

"Bee two, Isabel zero," I say with a sigh.

I get up, turn off the lights, and sit down by the hive again. I can see the tiny blue LED of the microdrone as it flits around the room looking for me. Kitty girl comes over and sits in my lap, and I stroke her fur while I wait. A minute or so later, I hear the buzz getting closer, so I stop petting Lucky and reach out my hand. The little guy lands on my palm, tickling me a little. It starts scraping my skin with its sampler appendage, scratching and turning in a small circle. Only it doesn't tickle anymore, it smarts. A drop of blood appears, and it finally stops gouging me.

Ugh. That was a bit more aggressive than I envisioned.

The bot starts whirring again. Without warning, Lucky leaps out of my lap and swats it down with her paw.

The sting comes before I realize what's happened—a sharp pinprick right in the center of my palm. I jerk my hand back, surprised by how much it hurts.

"Shit."

The microdrone hovers there, metallic wings beating with a faint hum, its tiny stinger retracting.

Lucky takes another swipe at it, and it buzzes away.

I feel a dull throbbing spread from the puncture wound, an odd mix of heat and numbness. "Great," I mutter, "attacked by my own creation. I think that makes me Frankenstein."

I hurry to the bathroom, stick my hand in the hottest water I can stand, and wait for the heat to inactivate the apitoxin. When the pain is down to an annoying throb, I go back to the lab, flip on the lights, and call the bee back to the hive. It hovers in front of my face for three very long seconds, then floats over to the controller, lands in an open stall, and deactivates itself.

I'm embarrassed to admit how relieved I am.

But it seems to have worked.

I name my DNA key *Tecta faciens*—secret maker—and add a hook to call a script that plays a random sound when it unlocks the hive. I save the hacked DNA key to the master plant database.

After stuffing Lucky back in the carrier—her complaining the whole time—I reboot the controller into a demo account that has very limited permissions. I issue a general scan order for a single bot: Look for flowers that need pollinating and record any hits. This time, when I stick my hand in front of the bee, it happily lands on my palm, runs its genome sensor, and the Hive Controller barks like a dog.

A grin spreads across my face.

Now that the Hive Controller has my DNA key, I need to test the diagnostic port hack. I recall the bot, shut down the controller, and release kitty girl. Next, I grab a thumb drive from the parts bin, add my DNA key, and push the stick into the small port on the side of the Hive Controller.

The controller wakes up and barks like a dog.

"And Bingo was his name-oh."

I get to work on the commands to remove the stinger behaviors, Lucky curled up in my lap again.

This time, it doesn't take me long. I leave the bark sound and add the code to remove the files, encrypt them, lock them, and start up the automated tests required to deploy build changes. After copying all that to the thumb drive, I plug it in and listen for the bark.

"Woof!"

Dave is going to lose his shit when he discovers this.

The thought makes me smile.

My stomach growls, and Lucky flops down on my keyboard—cat language for "feed me".

While I'm waiting for the tests to finish, I get some yogurt from the fridge in the lounge and some beef jerky from the vending machine. Back in the lab, I crumble the meat on the yogurt lid and set it on the floor.

Lucky sniffs it and looks up at me like I'm an incompetent mouser.

"Can't say I blame you, kitty girl. Our meal quality has gone down substantially since we left Diego's."

After I finish the yogurt, I download the new build to the Hive Controller and launch the bots with a general scan order again to make sure I haven't broken anything. I start up the interactive testing and watch the bots swoop and rise and land on things. When all the tests have passed, I type in the command that matters the most: the kill switch.

The little guys fall right out of the sky, making tapping sounds as they hit the leaves and floor.

"Sorry, guys. Safety first."

Lucky scurries over to sniff one of the bots in the garden.

"Careful, kitty girl. They won't sting, but those babies still cost thirty grand a pop."

I shoo her away and reactivate the bots, satisfied that I haven't introduced any oopsies. The microdrones spend a few seconds spinning in circles on the ground and then right themselves and whirr back into the air.

"Even superheroes have to learn to tie their capes," I say and recall them, already feeling better. My watch buzzes, reminding me to put out the trash before bed, and I realize how late it's gotten. I take out my phone, my hand still smarting, and cancel the reminder. "Where does the time go?"

Lucky meows and peeks out from the cornstalks, a leaf stuck to her ear.

"Quitting time, missy." At least I won't get any hassle on the way out. I'm probably the last one in the building.

My phone rings in my hand, and I nearly drop it.

It's Sophie.

I jab the accept button. "Sophie? Are you okay?"

"I'm fine," she says and hesitates. I can hear hip-hop music playing in the background. "I mean, I wasn't in a car accident or anything. I'm sorry to call you so late, but I didn't know what else to do."

I switch my phone to my good hand. "Are you sure you're okay? You don't sound so good."

"Actually," she hesitates again, "that's why I called. There's something you need to know."

My heart leaps into my throat.

"Dave is planning to sell the microdrones to the highest bidder."

I let out a sigh. "Given that bee populations are declining, I can't say I'm surprised. I know we've been assuming the bots would be deployed on Mars, but if we can just slow him down enough to make sure the bees are safe out there..."

I can hear her breathe in and out.

"Sophie?"

"He's not selling bees," she says. "He's selling biological weapons."

For a moment, I can't speak. "Are you sure?"

"Dave has been paying people on the engineering team to show up nights and weekends ever since you took time off. I knew they were working on a pet project for him, but I didn't know what." She lets out a huff. "Until a few minutes ago when Benny—that handsy, drunken jerk—accidentally spilled the beans."

Benny's the new hire who was giving me lip this morning. "Fuck."

"Yeah."

I hear some muffled noises, and the music in the background gets quieter.

"Well," I say, "they're gonna have a hell of a time developing murderbots without us. Benny's code is one step up from spaghetti."

"Yeah," she says, "but he literally does anything Dave wants. And he already makes twice what I do."

I make an annoyed sound at the back of my throat. "But you're the best engineer on the whole goddamn team."

"Isabel," she whispers. "They're not making anything new. Dave's just having them take out all the safety protocols and run simulations on stripped-down bots with a ten-x apitoxin reservoir. You know that guy no one likes? The one that looks like Colonel Custer? Benny says he's working on a neurotoxin. If you put that together with the stingers, any idiot could make murderbots."

"Are you sure it's not just Benny shooting his mouth off?" I say. "Dave can be an asshole, but he's not evil."

She's quiet for a few seconds. "Maybe *Dave's* not, but the guys coming to the demo on Monday are. Since the meeting is inside Eden-1, the list of attendees is public—although no one but me ever looks at the security log," she says with a mirthless laugh. "The biodome is going to be filled with despots from every oppressive regime with spare money. You should go see for yourself."

I don't know what to say.

"Anyway," she continues, "I called to let you know I'm quitting—and so is most of the team. We can see where this is going, and none of us want to be a part of it." She blows her nose. "But there are other people at the company who need the money, so... I thought you should know."

I hear someone call Sophie's name.

"I gotta go," she says and blows her nose again. "Be careful."

I swallow. "I will. Thanks for the heads-up, Soph."

"Sure," she says. "Talk next week?"

"Definitely. Thanks. Stay safe."

She hangs up, and I stand there, lost in thought.

Lucky meows, and I tell her, "Just a few more minutes, kitty girl."

I plop down at my computer and bring up the security website. After scrolling through pages of mind-numbing log entries, I search for Monday's date. Dave's pre-approved visitor list pops up, and I nearly toss my cookies.

"Holy shit. Does the US government know about this?"

Lucky makes a little squeak.

"Yeah, you're right. They must. Dave must be selling them a better version of the same technology."

I consider erasing all the servers and installing some sort of worm to destroy all the backups. If I did that, the Kirkland Enterprises microdrone program would go down in flames, and I could walk out of here with my head up.

Dave would sue your ass off, but what's new?

I sigh. The truth is, it would be impossible to destroy every single copy. People have clones on their local machines, edited copies on Hive Controllers—and Dave probably has backups stored offsite in some high-tech vault.

It'd set him back a week, max.

And then I remember the warning in Diego's note: "We need to stop Dave."

If anyone is going to keep the technology out of the hands of bad actors, it's gotta be me.

But how?

"You need to talk to Diego."

I lock up the Hive Controller, put the sunlamps and sprinklers back on automatic, and try to stuff Lucky back into her cat carrier. She's adamant about not getting inside, and I eventually give up and let her ride on my shoulders like Diego does.

I run my fingers through her silky fur. "Wish we were going home to Diego and Tolstoy."

She yawns with a soft yowl.

Diego is probably at a bar with Hank and friends. Or worse, out with some non-work-obsessed woman who has time to shave her legs.

The thought wrenches my small, atrophied heart.

I take out my phone and check Diego's location, afraid he will have cut me off after two weeks of radio silence.

Why can't you just admit that you miss him? That your life is better with him in it?

I stare at Diego's flashing icon, tucked away at his cabin in the mountains.

Do it.

I type in:

> Still awake?

And then delete it.

He will be after he reads it.

I try again:

> You alone?

I stare at the glowing letters, my heart pounding in my throat.

Good grief, Isabel. Don't be so needy. If he wanted to hang out, he would have asked.

Lucky mews and bumps her head against my cheek.

"Okay, okay." I hit send before I can chicken out.

A second after he reads it, he replies:

DIEGO
> No.

And then a good ten seconds later:

DIEGO
> Tolstoy is here too. 🙄

"Bastard," I say and crack a smile. "You had me going there."

DIEGO
> Come stay the weekend.

DIEGO
> Tolstoy says to bring Lucky. He misses her.

Lucky starts purring, like she can read English.

I laugh. "He's invited you to the cabin—which makes me your chauffeur, I guess." I take a breath, a glimmer of hope forcing out the morbid darkness in my chest.

> Be there in an hour?

I wait nearly a minute for confirmation.
Finally, he sends:

DIEGO
> Mierda, I've missed you.

I wipe my face on my sleeve, shut off all the lights, and make sure the lab door locks.

Lucky and I spend a very long ten minutes getting through the airlock, past the scanners, and out into the courtyard.

It's dark, no moon tonight, and cold. Narrow strings of lights line the sidewalk between the buildings. Lucky huddles against my neck as I lug the empty cat carrier across the courtyard. When I get to the other side, I set the carrier on a concrete bench and fumble for my keycard to get back in.

There's a buzzing sound next to my ear, and a bug lands on my neck. I slap it with my good hand and watch it fall, a faint blue glow hitting the sidewalk.

What the—

It's one of my bots.

Madders' Log
Entry 17

Target: Diego Nadales
Nexus: Diego's Cabin
Chrono Tag: Next Day

Global news feed comparison complete: No deviations. Chinese blockade of Taiwan initiated at expected time and date. US response restricted to vocal condemnations and retaliatory sanctions. Kirkland Enterprises wins multi-billion-dollar contract for construction of Eden-4 from Saudi government.

At first light, I get up and dress in double layers, feeling like I could run a marathon in ski boots. After turning up the thermostat and throwing a couple of logs on the banked fire, I open Isabel's door a crack to let Lucky and Tolstoy out. The three of us pad into the kitchen to get coffee and breakfast.

Isabel arrived after midnight, and I could tell she was exhausted and stressed out. I fed her a peanut butter and banana sandwich, loaned her an old T-shirt, and sent her off to bed—trying the whole time to keep the huge smile off my face.

I don't know what prompted her to text me last night, but I hope it keeps up.

After letting the pets out to do their business, I write Isabel a note telling her the hot water is off. Then I put on my gear and head outside to install more solar panels. Gemini's panels are designed to be installed by one person with simple tools. After wrestling with them these last few weeks, I've got some suggestions for how the process could be way freaking easier.

After five hours of work, the wind starts kicking up—and my stomach is growling so loud the bears are worried. I put my tools away, reconnect all the panels to the batteries, and head back inside.

Hot shower, here I come.

The moment I open the front door, an icy wind comes barreling in behind me. I hurry inside, force the door shut with my back, and rest for a moment.

Mierda, it's cold out there.

"Lunch will be ready in five," Isabel calls from the kitchen. It's difficult for me to express how good it is to have her back at the cabin, even if it's only for the weekend.

But "out of my fucking mind with euphoria" comes close.

"Be right there." I pull off my boots, hang up my coat, and head toward the bathroom to tidy up.

When I enter the kitchen, Isabel is standing with her back to me, humming to herself. Her short, curly hair is a bit wild, and she's still wearing my old shirt and a pair of my sweatpants, but she looks... happy.

The thought fills my chest with a warm, tingly feeling.

"Sorry about shutting off the power so early," I say and walk past her to the sink, resisting the urge to kiss her on the nape of her neck. "But I only have six more panels to install, and we'll be good to go."

"Look at us, all energy independent," she says. "Power to the people." She opens the fridge. "Swiss or cheddar?"

"Surprise me," I say, unable to stop smiling. "Can I help?"

"Nope. I got this."

I grab a glass from the cupboard and fill it with water from the tap. "I was hoping to finish today, but it's too damn cold out there."

"Well, we both know solar power doesn't happen overnight." She gives me a wry smile.

Mierda, I want to kiss her.

Tolstoy is on his bed by the window with Lucky curled up on his belly. He's doubled in weight since I got him, and he towers over the cat now. Although the guy is super-sized, he's about as ferocious as a bowl of oatmeal. I give both pets a little love, and then I wash my hands and sit down at the kitchen table, happy to have Isabel bustling around the kitchen again.

"Tolstoy, watch," she says, and the pets both look up at her, the dog wagging his tail. "Come," she says, and Tolstoy carefully gets up, trots across the kitchen floor, and sits in front of her, his eyes pinned on her face. "Wow," she says. "He remembers."

Lucky follows Tolstoy over and sits between his front paws, and Isabel laughs, a sound that fills me with pure joy.

"It's only been two weeks," I say, although it seems like forever.

"Seems like eons," she says and then flushes. "Thanks for letting me stay over."

I consider telling her I want her to stay over every night for the rest of her life, but it feels obscenely pushy, so I shrug instead. "Thanks for driving all the way up here. Tolstoy's really been missing the two of you."

She gives them both a treat. "Place," she says, and Tolstoy hurries back to the window, the cat right behind him. "Tolstoy is smarter than most of the people I know," she says and tosses him a piece of cheese. He catches it in his mouth, drops the cheese, and lets Lucky eat a bit. "And more polite." When the cat's done, he laps up what's left.

"Did you train him to do that?" I ask, amazement making my voice crack.

"Nope," she says, washing her hands.

"I wouldn't have believed it if I hadn't seen it with my own eyes."

"I know, right? It's like they're soulmates or something. They take care of each other." She dries her hands on a towel and turns to me, her eyes glossy. "Lucky misses hanging out with Tolstoy too. I took her in to work with me yesterday because I felt so bad about leaving her alone every day." She fiddles with the hem of her T-shirt. "Actually, we both miss living here."

"Except for the time that raccoon snuck into the pantry. Can't say I've seen a better broom defense outside of Hogwarts."

She laughs. "Ten points for Gryffindor."

I watch her moving around the kitchen, her motions fluid and graceful, wishing there was something I could do or say to convince her to stay.

She sets a plate of sandwiches on the table along with sliced apples and two bowls of Mrs. Malloy's homemade yogurt, looking like she has something uncomfortable to say.

Please don't tell me you have a new boyfriend.

The thought makes my chest hurt.

The silence becomes unbearable, and I cough. "Wow, I'm starved," I say. "Thanks for making lunch."

She nods and shuffles her feet, and then she looks up at me, her gaze intense. "Remember the first day I was here?" She gets herself a glass of water and sits down opposite me. "It was the morning you went into the city for your board meeting."

I exhale, getting a bad feeling about this.

She drops her gaze, and a blush spreads across her cheeks. "I was searching for your muffin pan, and a note from 'The Hole-in-the-Wall Gang' fell out of the cupboard—along with wedding rings."

All of a sudden, it becomes impossible to breathe.

"I know I shouldn't have read the letter, but what can I say? I'm nosy."

I shift in my chair, my hands feeling unnaturally cold. For weeks I've been working to give her space, not make her feel trapped—and the whole time she knew it was a ruse.

She clears her throat. "And I got the text messages you sent the night of the fire." She scrunches up one side of her mouth, half smiling. "When I activated my new phone, they both came through."

"Oh, shit." I drop my gaze. "I was, uh, I mean, it was all pretty intense. I wasn't thinking properly. I didn't mean to—"

She laughs. "Don't worry, I'm not going to run screaming from the room—at least not yet." She stirs her yogurt, her eyes on the bowl. "To be honest, I'm flattered."

"Could you say that again, please? I'm not sure I heard you right."

She rolls her eyes.

We eat in silence for a bit, and then she sets down her spoon and pins me with her gaze. "You said we weren't going to lie to each other, Diego. So, why did you buy wedding rings that night?"

"I didn't," I say, my voice squeaking, and take a bite of my sandwich.

She stares at me. "So where did they come from?"

I rub my hand across my mouth. "A group of kids looting the jewelry store." I shake my head at the memory. "They helped me break the plate glass window and told me how to reel out the string the firefighters used to find us. Without their help, I wouldn't have gotten in. And I probably wouldn't have gotten out, either."

"And the pets?"

"While I was crawling around in circles looking for you, the kids got them all out."

She's quiet for half a minute. "So you told them I was your wife to get them to help you?"

I keep my eyes on my bowl. "I told them I had just *proposed* to you—which, as you now know, is the truth." I look up at her—and then right back down at my yogurt.

"Hence the stolen wedding bands," she says.

"Yeah, but the rings are in the clear now." I take another bite of my sandwich. "I was planning to return them to the jewelry store the following day, but I couldn't bring myself to give them back—sentimental value, I guess. So I stopped by the store, explained the situation, and got out my wallet. The couple who owns the place was cleaning up the mess, and they remembered seeing you on the news. Didn't want to take my money. But I insisted."

Isabel's quiet for a bit as she finishes her sandwich, the corner of her mouth twitching. "Diego, I—" She takes a slow breath, her eyes dancing around the room again. "Damnit, Diego, you *are* amazing." She lifts her hands into the air and lets them flop into her lap. "And this cabin is amazing. The view is amazing. The pets are amazing. Even the damn coffee is amazing." She tips her head to the side. "I love it here. Every time I come back, I don't want to leave."

"I don't want you to leave either, Iz." There, I said it. "I want you to stay. Tolstoy and Lucky want you to stay too."

"But I can't, Diego. I just can't." Her eyes are shiny. "I know it doesn't make any sense to you, but right now, I need to be on my own. I lost myself somewhere between the night I pushed you away fifteen years ago and the night you saved me last month. I need some time to find that person again—because I don't want to spend the rest of my life staring in the mirror at somebody I don't like."

I gulp, my chest getting tight. "Okay."

"Okay."

A compelling need to change the subject sweeps over me. "I wish I could find the kids," I say and scrape the last of the yogurt out of my bowl. "So I could thank them. But I don't even know their names. There was this skinny Asian kid—I thought she was a boy—who was the leader of the gang. Even though she thought it was a death wish, she helped me." I'm blathering a mile a minute now. "It's weird how bravery and compassion pop up in the most unexpected places."

"Yes, it is," she says, going along with my change of subject.

Relief spreads across my neck and shoulders.

"It's amazing," she says and pins me with her gaze, "how ordinary people turn into heroes when they're given the opportunity."

I feel uncomfortably warm.

"Thank you," she says, her eyes glossy again. "For risking your life to save me."

"Well, there goes my 'worst human ever' streak."

She cracks a smile.

I clear my throat. "Now that the panels are connected, why don't you take that hot shower I promised you last night?"

"You should go first. You earned it."

"Nah," I say. "At this point, I don't need a shower, I need a pressure wash. You go ahead."

After I hear the shower start, I get up and collect the dishes. But as I'm washing them, the doorbell rings. Lucky skitters down the hallway, and Tolstoy barks. I grab a dish towel and dry my hands, wondering who it could be. The Malloy's are visiting relatives this weekend, and I installed a lock on the highway gate, so even the UPS guy calls before coming up.

Whoever it is, they bang on the door like they plan to break it down.

Pump the brakes, buddy.

I unlock the door and open it a smidge. The same icy wind blows in around the doorframe, and I gape at the sleazeball I regularly see in my nightmares.

How the hell did Kirkland find us?

He's wearing a suit that probably cost more than my car, and the wind is blowing his comb-over into a farcical mess.

He grins. "Hey, Grizzly Adams! Good to see you. How's the water collection business going? Screw any wet ones?" He laughs at his comic genius.

"Who let you out of your cage, Kirkland?"

"Thanks for the warm welcome, bro. Hey, but seriously, if you're diddling a man's wife, the least you could do is be polite to him."

"She's not your wife—and I'm not your bro."

"So you *are* poking her." He chuckles. "Good for you. You always could get it up for the Golden Girls."

I don't even dignify that with a response.

He tries to stick his head inside. "I need to talk to Izzy-Bee. She around?"

"Nope." I push the door shut.

He blocks it with his foot. "Her fucking car's parked on the driveway."

That's when I notice his Tesla Roadster. There's a platinum blonde sitting in the passenger seat, typing on her cell phone. She doesn't look a day over twenty. If the carpet matches the drapes, I'm Elon Musk.

The woman glances up at us and then cracks her window, the wind whipping her hair into her mouth.

"You left your phone in the car, cupcake." She jiggles it out the window.

I laugh. "Cupcake? Really? You must not be paying her enough."

"Get out of my way, dickface." He shoulders past me. "Isabel in the shower? Damn if I don't have perfect timing. She always did have a nice ass—even if I could never get her to shut that mouth of hers."

I close the door and try to decide if I should hit him with a lamp, stab him with the fireplace poker, or just knee him in the balls.

Maybe all three.

"How'd you get through the gate?" I say to his back.

"Same passcode as the kegerator in college, dipshit." He glances over his shoulder at me. "You really need to up your game, Nadales."

The shower turns off, and Isabel peeks out her bedroom door, her hair damp. "Diego, do you have more shampoo?"

Kirkland steps between us, grinning like he's the world's next billionaire. "Hey, doll."

She recoils. "What are you doing here?"

"Came to see you, my love." He turns to me. "How about you do us a favor and go play in your room, big D? Mommy and Daddy need to talk."

I take a step toward him, my fists still clenched.

"Don't take the bait, Diego." Isabel is one thin towel away from naked. "He's not worth it."

Kirkland lets his gaze slide down her body, the corners of his mouth twisting up.

She narrows one eye. "What do you want, Dave?"

"To have a little chat, of course."

She steps back into her room and gives me a pleading look. "Make sure he doesn't steal anything while I get dressed?" She shuts the door and clicks the lock.

Dave strides past me and peers into the kitchen. "You guys get Wi-Fi up here?"

Tolstoy—whose favorite job is babysitting kittens—starts growling at him.

I smile to myself, as proud as I've ever been of that dog.

You just earned yourself a steak dinner, Tolstoy, my boy.

Dave reverses course and steps past me into the office. "Any idea where she keeps her work laptop?"

"At work." I pinch the shoulder of his suit jacket and drag him toward the front door. "But if you really want to hang around to ask, you can wait outside with the other riffraff."

"Hey, no need to be an asshole." He scoots past me, pausing to straighten a photograph of Isabel with the engineers at Boston Dynamics. "That trip cost me a million in lost revenue," he says, "and the board still wouldn't license me their day-old shit." He lowers his voice. "Maybe you could get her to tell you how to unlock the stinging bots. If you do, I'll throw you a bone." He crosses his arms, still looking at the photo. "Say four million for your share of Gemini?"

"I told you, my company's not for sale, so why don't you take your day-old shit and get out of my house?"

He looks at my rumpled clothes and unshaven face. "What is it you have there, two dozen employees you're steering toward the iceberg? I hear Hank Simon's medical bills are getting pretty steep, and your marketing gal-cum-truck driver is struggling to pay her mortgage. You just gonna say tough shit to them when the house of cards collapses?"

Christ, he's been doing his research.

He steps past me. "Thought you were a better man than that, Nadales."

"Gemini is doing just fine," I say. "I don't need your money."

He peeks into my bedroom, the asshole. "Really? Tell you what, kid, I got some cash burning a hole in my pocket, so let's say you talk to the little lady, get me that encrypted key before tomorrow, and we call it a nice round five million?" He spies the rocking chair and scoffs. "Where'd you get that piece of garbage? Looks like a preschooler stapled it together."

I step forward and grab him by the lapels.

"No offense." He holds up his hands. "I'm sure you can afford to buy her a mansion, what with all that money you're making driving shit to California." He snorts.

I shove him backwards. "Fuck off."

He recovers and gives me a once-over as if he's actually seeing me for the first time. "My secretary's garden shed has more charm than this rabbit hutch." He straightens his shoulders. "Probably driving that piece of junk in the garage just to fool the tax man."

I shove him backwards again. "Get out."

"Whoa there, Rockefeller. This ain't about you."

"It is now." Tolstoy slinks into the great room, his ears back and his teeth bared. The dog may be a pacifist, but Kirkland doesn't know that. "Easy, boy," I say. "No need to rip his arm off just yet." I turn back to Kirkland. "Get out, or I'm calling the police. And won't that bimbo in your car be impressed when they slap a restraining order on you?"

"That bimbo earns more in a day than you do in a year."

"Who knew sleeping with the boss paid so well?"

He laughs. "Christ, Nadales, I don't sleep with her. I just let her suck my d—"

"Get out, or I'm going to get blood all over that expensive suit of yours." I pick up the fireplace poker and brandish it at him.

Tolstoy barks, then lowers his head and starts snarling, a low and menacing sound.

"And when my dog tears your tiny dick off," I say, "the bimbo will have to go back to lollipops."

"Okay, okay." He backs up to the door, his eyes pinned on Tolstoy. "Just tell Isabel that I need the bot stingers working by Monday. That was a clever trick she pulled yesterday. I'll give her that. But if she knows what's good for her, she'll restore the behavior before things get nasty."

I take a step toward him. "In case you hadn't noticed, things have already gotten nasty." I poke him in the belly with the iron rod. "Shoo."

"Look, I'm trying to play nice with you, buddy, for old times' sake. Don't make me take off the kid gloves. Either Isabel removes the lock, or she's fired. And if you let that happen, amigo, I'll make sure you lose your failing company, your crappy property, and your shitty car. And in case you need a crash course in how the US justice system works, here's lesson number one: In the end, the guy with the biggest wallet always wins." He opens the front door and walks out. "Asshole."

"Bye-bye, cupcake," I say and force the door shut with my shoulder. "He would make a lovely corpse."

There's a chuckle from behind me. "That was impressive."

I turn around, still wielding the poker.

Isabel's leaning against the doorframe. "I see you handle your weapon well."

"I have been known to keep my tip up."

She blushes, and I put the poker back where it belongs.

Turn down the innuendo, Nadales. It's not earning you any brownie points.

"Thank you," she says and motions with her head toward the door. "For that. What did he want?"

"The encrypted key to unlock the bot stinging behavior. Says he needs it by Monday or you're fired."

Her face turns white, and she looks away.

I put my hand on her shoulder. "How about you start by telling me what happened?"

"Dave promised a gaggle of warlords a microdrone chassis with attack capabilities. He's planning to turn my microdrones into murderbots," she says, tears rolling down her cheeks. "And sell them to the highest bidder."

I raise an eyebrow. "How do you know?"

She wipes her face with her hands. "Sophie told me. She sent me some plans Dave has to make the stingers stronger and expand the neurotoxin reservoir."

"Christ."

She shakes her head. "It gets worse. Dave's giving a private demo on Monday with a Who's Who list of human rights violators. He's planning to license the murderbots to any despot who can pay."

"Can't say I'm surprised." I cross my arms. "Kirkland would do anything to make a buck."

She brings her hands up to her face. "I can't believe I was so naive, Diego. It was so obvious, all along, that he would do this. I just refused to see it." She takes a ragged breath. "The note was right. I have to find a way to stop him."

I stand there like a statue for half a second, and then I wrap my arms around her. "No, you don't."

She looks up at me, her lips pressed together.

"*We* have to find a way to stop him, Iz." I run my hand down her back. "And we will."

She shakes her head. "I have to give Dave the key to unlock the files. He'll find a way around it anyway—and I need to steal a Hive Controller before he fires me."

I raise an eyebrow.

"So we can fight back," she says and tells me about the DNA hack she installed yesterday.

"Clever girl," I say, holding her at arm's length and grinning. "But you don't think he'd actually fire you, do you? I mean, it's just an empty threat. The whole bot project is your baby. Nobody knows as much as you by a mile. He needs you."

She gives me a tepid smile. "Thanks for the vote of confidence, Diego, but I'm not irreplaceable. And most of the hard work for the stingers is already done." She exhales, her eyes downcast. "I need to find a way to buy some time," she says and looks up at me.

"How about this?" I glance back and forth between her eyes. "You text Kirkland the code right now. Between now and Monday, we come up with a plan to torpedo the stingers. I'll get Hank on the phone—he's Mr. Conspiracy Theory—and see if he has any ideas from a legal standpoint."

She nods, thinking it through. "Then I go in on Monday, meek and contrite, and start planting the dynamite." She presses her lips together. "Yeah, okay. It might work. Dave's not going to have time to negotiate any big contracts until after the grand opening, so I'll have a few weeks to set things up. I could probably get most of my team to come back with their tails between their legs and help me pull it off." The corner of her mouth curls up just a little. "And then I'll light the match and kick his sorry ass out of my life."

"Sounds like a blast."

She actually smiles. "I might as well go out with a bang."

Madders' Log
Entry 18

Target: Isabel Sanborn
Nexus: Eden-1 Biodome, Winter
Chrono Tag: Six Weeks Later

Failure to stop the First Disaster almost certain. David Kirkland himself believed all three Great Disasters would need to be avoided to prevent the Doomsday event. estimations for overall mission success reduced to single-digit percentiles.

I knew this day would come, but it still breaks my heart. The microdrone bees are my life's work, and I'm about to throw it all away.

Unfortunately, it's the only card you have left to play.

Ever since I mucked with the stingers, things at work have been tense. Of course, Dave ended up getting what he wanted, but now he knows I'm a liability—and that he can't control me anymore.

He doesn't know the half of it.

After his schmooze-a-thon with the desert despots, Dave started consolidating power. He had my office moved to the boonies and posted security guards nearby. He promoted Benny to tech lead and replaced the people who quit. They all report directly to him now, and no one's pretending we're building cute little honeybees anymore. They even have a catchy new acronym: ATHENA, for Autonomous Tactical Hovering Engagement Neutralization Agent.

Even with lipstick, it's still a murderbot.

Yesterday, Dave stopped by my office on his way out. It was the first time I'd seen him in weeks, and I had a hard time keeping it together.

"We may not be hooking up anymore," he'd said and run the back of his hand across my cheek, "but I can't have you turning up in flats and a lab coat at the gala tomorrow night. Capeesh?"

I'd grimaced inside—but managed a curt nod.

He'd responded with "good girl" and gone back to chasing teenagers—or whatever he does at night.

I'd spent the evening installing a custom kill switch on the demo that does absolutely nothing—and leaving plenty of fingerprints for Benny to find in the morning. I'm sure Dave suspects I'm going to try something, so why not throw out some bait.

Late this afternoon, I showed up to work in "halfway respectable" garb—fitted black skirt, turquoise silk blouse with a plunge neckline, and matching spike heels—and made sure to stroll by Dave's office on my way in.

You gotta admit, it was actually a little fun.

I check my watch and force my leg to stop jittering. The Eden-1 grand opening gala starts in less than half an hour—and then my life changes big time.

A few minutes ago, Lamar called to say the limo was here. I told him I had to touch up my makeup, so I wouldn't be riding over with the executive staff, and asked if he could send back the limo? Dave knows I hate schmoozing, so he won't be surprised—but he'll still be fuming.

I smile at the image.

It's tempting to just stay in my office and watch the demo on the livestream, but I need to be out of the building before the shit hits the fan. So I pack up my stuff, grab my sneakers, and stroll into the lobby pulling one of the new Hive Controllers.

"Good evening, Lamar," I say, "I'm off to the grand opening."

He looks like I caught him jerking off. "The main road is closed now so Mr. Kirkland said to take the golf cart down by the lake." He glances at his watch, his cheeks red. "He said not to be late."

"The golf cart? Really?" I put my hands on my hips. "What's going on, Lamar?"

He swallows. "Your company privileges were revoked ten minutes ago—by order of Mr. Kirkland."

"My company privileges?" I raise an eyebrow. "What the hell does that mean?"

"He fired you, Mrs. Kir—Ms. Sanborn. I'm sorry."

It's a struggle, but I keep the grin off my face.

You screwed up, Dave. You thought I wouldn't find out until after *the gala. Now you've given me the perfect excuse.*

Lamar shuffles his feet, eyeing my Hive Controller. "And I can't let you take that out of the building."

I turn on my Ripley versus the Alien face and pin him with a razor-sharp gaze. "I'm running the demo for the grand opening in less than thirty minutes, Lamar. I may be wrong, but I imagine Mr. Kirkland will go ballistic if I don't show up with the bots." I cross my arms, hoping my lie will work. "Who do you think he's going to blame, Lamar?"

The man can't get around the desk fast enough. "Good luck, ma'am," he says, holding the door for me. "It's been a pleasure."

"Thank you." I take off my high heels and slip on my sneakers. And then I walk out carrying a pair of cheap pumps and half a million dollars' worth of proprietary bling.

Lamar watches me stride across the parking lot and then goes back to his desk.

A cloud of guilt follows me as I hurry down the path to the pond. Dave's going to fire his ass, and it'll be my fault. I say a silent apology and keep walking.

The minute I get out of sight, I toss the heels into the trash and call the man.

"What's going on, David?" I make a scared whimpering sound. "My life's work is buzzing around inside your engineering wonder, and here I am, locked out in the cold wearing cocktail attire? I gave you the best years of my life. I designed and built the world's first stinging microdrones for you. I even busted my ass to create your little light show tonight."

"Yep," he says, a grin in his voice. "You sure did, princess."

He knows I hate it when he calls me that. "So to repay me, you disabled my badge?"

"I figured you'd flake out and try to steal shit after the show," he says. "Besides, what the fuck do I need you for now?"

"You fired me?" I squeak out, adding as much fake alarm as I can muster.

He laughs. "If you thought you could sneak that custom kill switch past me, you're dumber than I thought."

I roll my eyes.

Better have the real one handy, cupcake. Oh, and I added a thirty-second delay weeks ago. Should be enough to get people asking questions. Maybe someone in Congress—if there's anybody left who cares—will get involved and shut down your little illegal weapons den.

He snorts. "Nothing to say, huh? Well, that's a goddamn change for the better. Now you listen to me, buttercup. It's about time you realized something. For all your pretentious bullshit, you're no smarter than my left nut. You take me on, and you're gonna lose. Every. Fucking. Time. So, just a little bit of free advice, darling: Don't even dream of testing me again, or you and lover boy are gonna end up in the deepest of shit."

He hangs up.

I sit down on a park bench by the lake and pull my coat tighter.

So long, and thanks for all the clams, Dave.

Of course, I've been dying to tell Diego about my nefarious plans. But if someone's going to jail over this, it's just gonna be me. In fact, I almost spilled the beans yesterday when I called to tell him about the livestream tonight. It was the first time we'd spoken in weeks, and the sound of his voice made me feel all melty inside.

Out of the blue, he'd invited me to stay at his cabin this weekend —and offered to wait and pick me up after the gala tonight. I couldn't say yes fast enough.

I miss you, babe.

I've decided that life's too short to waste whatever time Diego and I have left. Tonight, I'm going to tell him the truth, and we'll see where that takes us.

But first, I need to get away before the shit hits the fan.

After I push the button to call Diego, a rush of warmth fills me.

"Hey, beautiful," he says, and my heart does a flip-flop.

"Diego," I say, my face flushing, "you have to stop calling me that."

Madders' Log
Entry 19

Target: Matt Hudson
Nexus: KE World Headquarters
Chrono Tag: That night

New deviations continue to appear around Matt
Hudson. While Diego Nadales and Isabel Sanborn
are creating minor fluctuations, the changes, as
of yet, are not propagating beyond the pair.
Likelihood of Trans Temporal Viewer development
now above 50%.

The first thing I notice is how huge the biodome is. The sun is setting behind it, making the glass and steel structure look like solid gold. We're still on the freeway—maybe five minutes away—but Eden-1 is blocking out a good chunk of the front range.

Can't deny it. That biodome towering over the surface of Mars is a powerful vision.

I'm sitting in the back seat of a brand-new black SUV, Picasso across from me diddling with his phone. Junior's at the wheel, sunglasses on, humming a tune to himself, while Dick slouches in the passenger seat, arms crossed, looking as aggrieved as ever.

Today is the grand opening of the Kirkland Enterprises Eden-1 Biodome, and word is they're going to be showing off their caretaker AI, artificial bees, and more engineering wonders. It's the first time I've been off the mountain since they kidnapped me. Despite the rumors of calamities—which mostly come from Sam—the world seems to be stumbling along without us.

Matter of fact, I did a bit of consulting for Dave Kirkland back before he became famous. When Picasso mentioned he was going to check out the competition, I asked to come along. To be honest, I'm not sure why he said yes.

Maybe he doesn't want to be stuck in the car alone with Dick and Junior?

"Crikey," I say, my forehead pressed against the window. "That thing's bloody whacking."

"Yeah?" Dick says. "Well, size doesn't matter unless you're compensating—which Kirkland definitely is. Probably can't get it up without a government grant on the pillow."

Junior snickers.

Dick scoffs. "Fuckin' terrariums."

"That *terrarium* will house four thousand people," Picasso says, keeping his eyes on his phone. His fingers flick across the screen in quick, precise movements. "And they're building a private one in Saudi Arabia that will hold twice that many. To the tune of twelve billion."

Junior whistles. "That's some chump change."

I continue staring at the biodome, trying to get a feel for how tall it is. "I thought it was just a prototype for the two they're sending to Mars."

The beast's twice as high as the pine trees around it, so maybe twenty stories?

"It is," Picasso says. "But Kirkland's lobbying the government to build forty more—at four billion a pop." He reads from the brochure announcement on his phone. "Earth's climate is changing rapidly, its ecosystems under historic levels of stress. Kirkland Enterprises' Eden-Class Biodomes offer a controlled and resilient environment to protect people, property, and critical infrastructure."

I cluck my tongue. "Even if they can cram ten thousand in there, that's over a quarter million per *person*. Any wanker who supports that'll get thrown out of office."

Picasso puts his phone away and crosses his arms. "I was in Washington last week, and the President is seriously considering it. You know what a political disaster the deficit is, so if he signs off, our funding will be slashed." He tips his head, giving me the side-eye. "So I need something compelling to show, professor. Something other than socks deflecting muons or whatever the hell you claim the jinn objects do."

"That *is* something compelling," I say, my voice cracking. "If you'd let me publish my—"

"Kirkland's going to use our funding to build three fully kitted-out biodomes in DC, Omaha, and Nashville. They're already working on the plans." He settles back into the seat, his eyes closed. "Those biodomes could save thirty thousand lives, forty-five in a pinch. How many lives is your multiverse hosepipe going to save, professor?"

I let out a huff. "You know that's impossible to calculate. But I can tell you for certain, if you kept me in the loop on the other projects, I might be able to do better."

Picasso doesn't even look up. "We're bringing the Trans Temporal Viewer project onsite soon. Assuming our funding isn't cut."

Dick slaps Junior on the shoulder. "Get off here, you moron!" He glowers at the kid. "Can't you follow simple directions?"

"Okay, okay." Junior cuts off a Prius as we swerve across two lanes and onto the exit ramp. "Why can't we just use Waze?"

The old lady driving the hybrid flips us the bird, and I feel my face flush—until I remember she can't see through the windows.

Hiding behind tinted glass, mate. What a wuss you've become.

I clear my throat and glance at Picasso. "Any luck finding the wormhole generator?"

"Don't take the bait, Richter." Dick directs Junior to turn left.

"How did the creators of the sphere get a sock from our universe to use as an anchor?" Picasso says, looking over at me.

I scratch the back of my neck. "Someone sent it to *them*?"

"Why?" Picasso barks. "How? When?"

I stare at him and then shrug.

He looks away. "What do they want us to do with it?"

"I don't know," I say. "But both universes must be nearly identical to ours, so it can't be much."

Dick makes a show of rolling his eyes. "Yeah," he says under his breath, "this wing nut is gonna get us more funding."

Picasso shoots him a look and turns back to me. "Why can't it be something big?"

"It just doesn't feel right." I let out a sigh. "Assuming the inverse square law, sending a sphere to more distant timelines would take astronomically more energy. Also, the more differences between the timelines, the harder it would be to predict, initiate, or control any changes. Even though we haven't figured it out, there's a reason the pink paper has Diego Nadales' name on it. In a world where he doesn't exist, it would be useless information—even if the *only* difference is his first name changed to James."

Dick laughs. "You needed three degrees and a doctorate to figure that out, egghead?"

I ignore him. "The real problem is figuring out how to modify another timeline so that the change will eventually propagate back to your own. Like I keep telling you, there's no way to get around causality. You can't kill your own grandfather."

"Hot Potato," Junior says and speeds through a yellow light.

Dick jerks his head around. "What are you on about, Smith?"

"It's a kids' game where you pass a ticking time bomb around in a circle." Junior keeps his eyes on the road. "No matter how many people play the game, you only need to know how to toss it to the next guy. Maybe all we have to do is pass the hot potato?"

I think about that for a moment. "With three jinn objects and some tungsten foil, a triad of universes could move the objects around in a loop forever: from the valentine timeline, to our timeline, to the shell timeline, and back to the first."

Junior nods. "In order to remove the foil from the next jinn object and put it around the previous one, you'd have to keep smashing the sphere. Which means you'd need to manufacture a new sphere for every jump."

Not to mention figuring out how to build, power, and target a bloody wormhole generator.

"What the shagging good would that do?" Dick says. "You can't just send a name in a circle and expect anything to change. You have to send some poor fuck to another universe."

"Yes," I say with some reluctance. "I think you could be right."

Picasso sits up straighter. "So if I wanted my grandfather dead"— he catches my eye— "metaphorically speaking, I'd have to get another timeline to kill him for me."

"And then *you'd* have to kill someone else's gramps," Junior says. "To keep the chain going."

"What do you think, professor?" Picasso says.

I shrug. "It wouldn't break causality, if that's what you're asking. But jinn objects—including time travelers—muddle the rules." I scrub my hand across my mouth. "And what happens to you after Dexter does in your grandpappy is up for debate."

"Nadales," Dick says. "They want him to go. We send him to wherever the jinn thing takes him, and he does the deed."

I resist the urge to roll my eyes. "What deed did you have in mind?"

"Murder someone."

I scoff. "I seriously doubt that's it—especially killing someone who could have children. A change that big could cause the other timeline to go spiraling off into the Twilight Zone. The larger the change, the more unpredictable the result. So If you ask me, they only want us to make a tiny tweak."

"Like?" Picasso says.

"Introducing a minor traffic jam to delay an event, or misplacing a crucial memo for a day or two. Something like that." I give him a pointed look. "But the whole thing's moot without a wormhole generator."

Picasso bunches up his mouth. "We have people working on that."

"Maybe the wormhole project doesn't exist in this timeline," Junior says, pulling up to a stop behind a long line of cars. "Maybe whoever sent the sphere made a mistake."

"Or maybe it has a different title in our universe," Picasso says and runs his hand across his chin. "Like Diego having a slightly different name."

A couple blocks away, we can see security directing cars to park on an airstrip next to the biodome. As I'm admiring the jets parked at the far end, I notice exposed cabling running from the solar array to the main structure. "Looks like Mr. Kirkland still has a bit of work to finish," I say and point out the huge, unprotected cables. "Have they said when they plan to seal it up?"

Picasso shakes his head. "'Soon' is as much as he'll say."

"Go around them," Dick barks, gesturing at the cars in front of us. "Drop us off at the front entrance and wait in the car."

Junior, looking deflated, pulls out into the wrong lane and starts passing annoyed drivers.

After being waved past three checkpoints—the perks of being in a black SUV with tinted windows and government plates, I guess—we turn in next to a huge electronic billboard flashing "Eden-1" and "The world's first Bioregenerative Life Support Structure aka BLiSS!"

Junior rolls up to the crowded valet kiosk, and Dick swings his door open before we've fully stopped.

"Don't leave the car," he says.

Junior blows a raspberry. "Party pooper."

Dick shoves his handgun into the holster behind his back.

"Not gonna let you take any heat inside the biodome," Picasso says. "Controlled security environment."

Dick reluctantly locks the gun back in the glove box, and the three of us pile out. After Junior pulls away, we make for the entrance, climbing the wide, polished steps along with hordes of people speaking different languages. It's dark now and getting chilly, but the glass and steel biodome gleams like a jewel under the night sky, its angular surfaces reflecting a mosaic of vibrant color. At the top of the stairs, a warm glow spills out, casting a surreal, other-worldly aura.

"It's like the bloody Oscars," I say as we shuffle past a group of foreigners taking selfies. Reporters are leaning across ropes, stopping people to get their comments. Photographers are snapping poses of celebrities, and influencers are smiling into their livestreams. Once we get to the top of the stairs, we have to squeeze past the bodyguards of a woman being interviewed by CNN.

"Chouinard's daughter," Picasso says. "Gave away the entire company to fight climate change."

"Sort of," I say under my breath.

Dick elbows past them. "More money than brains."

As we step inside, I'm struck again by the scale of it all: trees, gardens, a park with a water fountain. Eden-1 is like a tiny slice of paradise. There are apartment buildings set in an open circle, with a medical center and school capping the ends. To our left, a floating staircase leads up to an open-air lounge. At the heart of it all, a round, glassed-in control center overlooks everything.

Picasso whistles low. "Impressive."

I can't disagree. "Wow," I say, running my hand along the wood railings directing us through security. "They've thought of everything."

When we get to the front of the line, Dick flashes our tickets and turns back to Picasso. "You clowns need to up your game if you're expecting to compete with this." We file through security scanners and into the main atrium.

"How the hell do they plan to get this to Mars?" Picasso says, half-distracted, as he takes it all in.

Before I can respond, a familiar voice calls out. "Matt Hudson, as I live and breathe!"

I turn and—bloody hell—it's Dave Kirkland striding over with a broad grin. I raise an eyebrow, half-surprised he recognizes me.

"Dave," I say, standing up straighter and shaking his hand. "Didn't know if you'd remember me."

"Are you kidding?" he says, laughing. "Your work on the dome's exoskeleton saved us loads of time and money." He claps me on the shoulder. "If you ever need a job, I can always use someone with your skill set." He winks at me and then glances over at Picasso, who's wearing a dress uniform today. "And we pay a lot better than the paper pushers."

"Thanks, mate," I say, feeling a mild prickle of heat around my neck. "I'll keep that in mind."

Dave glad-hands Picasso and then notices Dick—who's wearing his usual black suit and sunglasses.

"Nice place you got here, Mr. Kirkland," Dick says. "I've seen high-tech prisons with fewer layers of security. You might've just redefined 'unbreachable'."

Picasso and I exchange looks.

Dave beams and steps closer to the guy. "What did you say your name was?"

"Johnson." He shakes Dave's outstretched hand. "If I told you anything more, I'd have to shoot you."

Dave guffaws and punches him playfully on the shoulder. "Come work for me, Johnson. I'll double your salary. Throw in a nice sports car." Dave takes a business card out of his jacket and hands it to Dick. "Call me." He turns back to us. "Make yourselves at home, fellas. In fact, Matt, let me upgrade you and your friends to the VIP treatment." Before heading off to say hello to another group, Dave waves one of his guys over. "Take 'em to the lounge. My nickel."

I give Picasso the eyebrow, half embarrassed and half proud.

Picasso scowls. "Maybe I should invite him over so he can poach my entire staff?"

"Right this way, folks," the guy says and slips past the bouncers at the bottom of the stairs. He points out an escalator and waits for us to step on. "Enjoy your evening."

We are whisked up into a whole 'nother level of dosh.

Men in expensive suits and floor-length robes are surrounded by attractive young women in skimpy cocktail dresses and frighteningly high heels. Near the biodome wall, there's a full spread laid out: glass flutes sparkling under the lights and trays of hors d'oeuvres next to signs claiming everything is "grown here in Eden-1." I lift a glass of champagne, watching the tiny bubbles rise, and then take a sip. It's the expensive kind.

Dave sure knows how to make a good impression, I'll give him that.

"Generous guy," I mutter to Picasso, who grunts, his eyes already scanning the room for something more than the free drinks.

Probably totaling up the expenses.

I look around for Agent Johnson. He's holding a beer bottle under one arm and loading up a plate of food with the other. I join him at the buffet, and then we stand and watch the park fill up with people —a lot of people.

Down below us, Dave excuses himself from a group of men wearing white robes and colored headscarves, walks across the grassy park shaking hands as he goes, and jogs up a ramp onto a stage that's been set up between two lush gardens.

The crowd claps, and I glance up at the people in the control center, wondering what you'd do to get a little privacy in here. I don't like enclosed spaces, but I gotta admit, this isn't as bad as I expected.

In fact, it's proper nice.

Dave steps up to the podium, the biodome gleaming behind him. "Ladies and gentlemen, welcome to Eden-1—our first-ever AI-assisted slice of paradise. We built this not just to survive the future but to thrive in it! Think of this baby as Earth 2.0 but without the toxic politicians or endless traffic jams."

The crowd chuckles.

"In here," Dave continues, "no wildfires, no droughts, no sand-storms, just fresh air, green grass, and an AI that knows more about growing tomatoes than my grandmother ever did. Isn't that right, Eden?"

A sexy female voice—the biodome AI, I assume—replies, "Correct, Mr. Kirkland. Your grandmother overwatered her tomatoes by twenty-eight percent."

This time, the crowd laughs, and Dave beams. "Even the AI's a smartass."

He goes on for a bit about all the tech innovations and then has his team dim the lights. "Now, my wife's been warning me for years about the collapse of bee populations—pesticides, climate change, you name it. When I first asked her why she was so concerned about the bugs, she quoted Einstein: 'If the bees disappear, mankind's not far behind.' And that's where her brilliant idea for our artificial polli-nators came from. If you look carefully, you'll see our tiny blue microdrones buzzing around the plants, keeping Eden alive and healthy."

A murmur goes up as people turn toward the gardens. Little blue lights are everywhere. I glance around to see who his wife is, but she doesn't seem to be here tonight—which strikes me as odd.

The AI says, "Kirkland Enterprises welcomes you to the grand opening of our first bliss biodome, Eden-1."

The bots rise from the gardens and assemble themselves above the crowd, their lights spelling out "Kirkland Enterprises."

Kirkland lifts his arms like a Jesus statue. "Here's to innovation, hope, and a bright future!"

The crowd breaks out in applause.

A moment later, the bots start reassembling themselves into another phrase, and I don't think it's what Kirkland was expecting.

Dick tips his head. "What the hell?"

A hubbub breaks out, and Dave's eyes go wide.

He quickly recovers and laughs it off. "I told you," he says, "everyone's a practical joker here." He jogs to the edge of the stage, turns so he can see the control center, and mimes cutting his throat.

But the shocking announcement stays put.

A second later, the biodome is flooded with brilliance, and the message is washed away.

The AI chimes in again, "Mr. Kirkland, do remind everyone to recycle their champagne glasses?"

Dave looks a little rattled but quickly regains his composure. He grins, as if someone didn't just rat him out as an arms dealer. "See? Eden's even greener than I am. Enjoy the party, folks!"

Picasso and I exchange another look as upbeat music starts playing and the audience breaks out in loud chatter.

Dave hurries off the stage and has a heated discussion with one of his assistants.

"What the hell?" I mutter as I watch a woman below us swat at an artificial bee. I can see its tiny blue light. She manages to disable it, and it spirals to the ground. But there are ten more taking its place. "Shit," she yells after slapping another one. "They have stingers!" She stares at her hand for a moment and then starts running toward an exit, a cloud of little blue bullets chasing after her.

People start screaming and running for the exits.

Picasso crosses his arms, looking like he's enjoying himself.

"Just stand the fuck still," Dave shouts. "They won't sting unless you threaten them."

I look out across the biodome. Swarms of little blue lights are everywhere—but they don't seem to have discovered the lounge yet. I grab a tablecloth and wrap it around my head and shoulders, just in case.

"What's taking so long?" Dave shouts up to the control center. "Use the damn kill switch!"

The little blue bots freeze. After moment later, they fall to the ground.

People all over the biodome start stomping on Kirkland's very expensive bees.

Dave goes crazy and starts shouting, "Get 'em up in the air, damn it. Recall all the bots right now!"

It takes a minute, but a few bots rise and start flying toward the center of the biodome. But before they can get far, the music cuts out and all the lights fail.

The night sky is dark, stars visible above the biodome. A hush falls over the crowd, and I can hear the giant air scrubber fans slow to a stop. The sudden silence is eerie, broken only by the faint creaks of the girders and the gurgle of water draining out of pipes.

"Power failure," I say, and Picasso grunts his agreement.

Far in the distance, we can still see some lights.

"Maybe just us," Picasso says.

Emergency lighting snaps on, bathing the floor in a dim red glow.

The voice of the Eden-1 AI booms out across the dark biodome, "Warning! Carbon dioxide levels nearing maximum safe level."

Dave yells something about not panicking and that they'll have the power back on in a moment, but almost no one's listening. There are the sounds of chairs scraping and tables tipping over—and multiple shouts. "Watch out!" someone yells and chaos erupts as more people rush toward the exits.

Picasso grins. "What's that machine you wanted, Hudson? The muon thing that costs a fortune? I'm ordering it for you tomorrow."

I take the tablecloth off my head. "Thank you, I think."

Madders' Log
Entry 20

Target: Diego Nadales
Nexus: Gemini Solutions Office Building
Chrono Tag: Same Night

Limited nuclear exchange and resultant EMP events underway. Xeno Diego's incursion into this universe has made no significant difference on the world stage. Numerous minor divergences appear near Matt Hudson—but hope for success continues to diminish.

I t's almost eight on a Friday night, and I'm at my work, balancing the books and occasionally glancing at the livestream of the Eden-1 grand opening. Isabel's been crazy busy for the last few weeks—at least that's what I tell myself—and I've been sitting on my hands to keep from texting her. Yesterday, out of the blue, she called to tell me about the livestream. After my heart stopped doing the Macarena, I invited her over for the weekend and offered to pick her up after the big bash.

She didn't even bat an eyelash.

In fact, she sounded thrilled.

Tolstoy and I have been bouncing off the walls ever since.

"Haven't we, big guy?" I reach down and stroke his head, and he thumps his tail.

I glance back at the live video, but it's more of the same crap: a parade of celebrities I don't care about, influencers I've never heard of, and politicians I didn't vote for streaming into a sci-fi snow globe lit up like electricity's free. And, of course, Kirkland himself slithering around, pumping hands and grinning like a used car salesman.

Although, you have to admit, the structural engineering does look impressive.

Thirty minutes ago, I watched the great man introduce his executive staff as they strolled up the red carpet, but Isabel wasn't among them.

I know she hates crowds, so maybe she snuck in the back way?

Just as I go back to entering invoices, my phone buzzes. When I realize it's Isabel, my heart leaps into my throat.

I put her on speaker. "Hey, beautiful."

"Diego," she says, her voice wavering. "You have to stop calling me that."

I can almost hear her blushing. "Why? It's true."

"Because my hips are too wide and my arms are flabby and I have feet that could easily double as flippers."

"I knew it. You're a mermaid."

"You're incorrigible."

"Hey," I say, feigning offense, "I resemble that remark."

She laughs, and Tolstoy barks.

"Is that my favorite puppers?" she asks. "Tell him I've missed him a ton."

"Ditto," I say and then realize that might sound awkward.

"I've missed you, too, Diego." She takes a slow breath. "Are you watching the livestream?"

"Yeah," I say, then notice that the bots are forming into words. Lots of words. "*Mierda*. I'm watching it right now."

The microdrones keep rearranging into different messages:

KIRKLAND ENTERPRISES

SELLS MURDERBOTS

$25 BILLION DEAL

—and then they spell out a laundry list of human rights violators. The camera pans out as Kirkland tries to get his minions to kill the demo, but it doesn't seem to be working.

I laugh. "It's brilliant, Iz. Fucking brilliant."

"Thanks," she says. "Let's hope it does the trick."

A hot seed of anxiety explodes in my gut. "You need to get out of there, Iz. Now. Kirkland's going to go ballistic and have you arrested —or worse."

"I'm not in the biodome, Diego. I'm outside the engineering building, sitting on a park bench watching the show from across the pond."

"Christ. That's too close."

"Don't worry. Dave doesn't know I'm here," she says. "He fired me an hour ago. Canceled my badge. But I have a Hive Controller, one of the new ones with fifty microdrones."

"Holy shit," I say. "Nice going." I clear my throat. "Can I pick you up now?"

"That would be awesome. And I have something to tell you." She hesitates. "Something I should have told you a long time ago."

Don't even start, I say to the voices in my head. "See you in a few."

"Okay, but take the back way," she adds. "The whole Eden-1 area is a madhouse—and not just because Dave's there."

"Hah. Okay. Bye." I lock up the office and jog to my car, Tolstoy trotting along with me. I'm smiling so hard my cheeks are starting to hurt.

"Mierda," I say as Tolstoy jumps in the car. "Isabel's coming home with us." I hop in and start the car. "Maybe she'll stay with us for longer than the weekend, huh?" He licks my face as I back out of the parking space.

Just as I start down the ramp, all the lights in the garage go out. It's pitch-black, and I slam on the brakes—no lights coming from anywhere. My headlights are still working, obviously, but the whole city is dark. As I'm wondering what's going on, the lights blink back on—well most of them, anyway.

Weird.

I leave the parking garage and mix with thinning rush-hour traffic. A block before I get on the freeway, my phone blasts a loud, jarring sound that nearly gives me a heart attack. Tolstoy yips, but it takes my brain a second to recognize the noise: a flash flood warning.

I glance out my window into the clear night sky.

Or maybe an Amber Alert?

I stop at a red light and read the message:

EMERGENCY ALERT! POSSIBLE NUCLEAR
ATTACK IMMINENT. TAKE SHELTER NOW.
PRESIDENTIAL ADDRESS EXPECTED SOON.
THIS IS NOT A TEST.

What the hell? A nuke? In Colorado?

The message looks authentic, but I can't say I've ever seen an emergency alert before.

Maybe it's someone's idea of a joke?

I look up at the rearview mirror and then scan my surroundings. All around me, people are staring at their phones, a look of shock on their faces. And then two guys get out of their cars and start running through traffic. Someone lays on the horn, and a pickup jumps the red light, narrowly missing an SUV that skids into a stop sign.

And suddenly, it's pandemonium.

Get to Isabel.

I cut across three lanes and force my way into a line of cars going up the on-ramp. A minute later, I'm on the freeway, fifteen exits—and a lifetime—away from Iz.

As I merge, I glance at the frightened face of the woman in the car next to me, and then change lanes and accelerate past her. As the news spreads, cars start swerving in and out of traffic and driving way too fast.

This is not going to end well.

Not thirty seconds later, the Beemer in front of me slams on his brakes. I nearly lose control of the car as I avoid hitting him. He swerves into the median at the last moment, and I fly past. In my rearview, I see him whip around into oncoming traffic, nearly causing a pileup on the other side. Horns blare in a reverse Doppler as the guy tears off in the other direction.

Tolstoy lets out a soft whine.

"It's okay, boy. We're going to get Isabel. And then we'll get the hell out of Dodge."

With shaking hands, I flip on the radio and scan through the stations.

But the same message is being repeated everywhere: Take shelter; don't panic; the President will address the country in a few minutes.

Mierda, this is actually real.

If the President of the United States sent out an emergency alert, it would have to be something big, and he would have to be pretty damn sure it wasn't a red herring.

Somewhere in the back of my brain, I remember that it takes about forty minutes for a Russian missile to get here. I do the math and then put my foot down on the accelerator.

Please let it be a false alarm.

Usually, I can see Kirkland's plastic bubble from the freeway, but the place has gone completely dark.

"Thank goodness Isabel isn't in there."

Tolstoy barks his agreement.

When I finally get off the freeway, there are police everywhere stopping cars and telling people to take shelter. After being delayed twice, I put my head down and keep driving.

What are they going to do, arrest me?

The traffic is getting worse. At one point, I run a red light and cut across a lawn to avoid a long line of stopped cars. People honk their horns as I drive past, flipping the bird and rolling down their windows to yell obscenities.

"Sorry, sorry," I say but keep going. In my rearview mirror, I see people copying me.

It takes longer than I hoped, but I manage to get to the KE campus in just under fifteen minutes. I lay on the horn for a good five seconds, and then fire off a text message:

> I'm here. Where are you?

Across the lake, people are streaming out of the biodome from a side exit. They're lit up by swerving headlights, and I can see them rushing out in tuxedos and ball gowns, women stumbling in their high heels across the lawn.

For a second, I wonder if Kirkland was trying to seal it up when the power blew.

If not, he probably is now—although I don't know how much protection it'd give.

But even if the "possible nuclear attack" turns out to be false, people will be begging to move inside his biodomes now. It'll take months, if not years, for the panic to die down. Supply lines will be interrupted, prices will soar, and scared people will hoard everything from food to guns to toilet paper.

Mierda, not this again.

And if there *is* an attack on the US, life as we know it will be over.

Even if it turns out to be an accident, the hawks will be demanding that we bomb the culprits back to the Stone Age—and take out North Korea, Russia, and China just to be safe. That, and the rest of the world is not going to sit around and wait to be murdered by faceless despots.

Any way you slice it, things are going to get ugly—and fast.

I get out of the car and look around. The whole area is dark. I try sending another message and then look out across the city. The streets are packed with cars. Flashing lights are everywhere, and the cold evening air is filled with wailing sirens, skidding tires, and blaring horns. I imagine the grocery stores and camping outlets have already been overrun, and the freeways out of the city will soon be packed.

There's a plane heading over the Rockies, a contrail flowing behind it, making it look like it's a normal December evening.

Maybe you're wrong, mae. Maybe people will remain calm and face the future with thoughtful compassion. Maybe everything will be just fine.

The wind shifts, and I smell smoke. Across the street, someone comes out of a convenience store struggling with two large bottles of water. I watch the woman stagger toward her car, but before she can get there, two tall figures cast shadows over her. There's a scuffle and some angry words, and I see the two thugs jog off with the water while the woman stands there in the parking lot with her phone glowing in her hand.

A thoughtful and compassionate future, my ass. We're screwed.

It's getting downright cold, and I hop back in the driver's seat and turn on the engine, stroking Tolstoy and listening to the radio repeat the same grim message over and over.

Where is she?

Just as I'm reaching for my parka, I see a golf cart come bumping up the hill from the lake, one of its headlights out. I get out of the car and start running toward it. "Isabel?"

"Diego?" She jumps out of the driver's seat, lugging some sort of suitcase with her.

I sweep her into my arms, unable to speak.

"Thank you for coming," she whispers, her head pressed against mine.

I can feel her heart pounding, and an overpowering need to protect her fills me. "No worries," I say, struggling to keep my voice light. I kiss her temple. "But I'm never letting you out of my sight again."

She laughs and starts coughing, her eyes watering. "We have to stop meeting like this."

I take her hand. "Let's get out of here."

Madders' Log
Entry 21

Target: Matt Hudson
Nexus: Eden-1 Biodome
Chrono Tag: Same Night
Milestone: FIRST DISASTER

Primary target timelines diverge. Isabel's
disruptions swamped by First Disaster. Richter
and Hudson are causing extensive disturbances,
but no indications those will be sufficient to
avoid the Second Disaster.

Again, the voice of the Eden-1 AI calls out, "Warning! Carbon dioxide levels nearing maximum safe level."

The huge biodome is now a mass of panicked people in evening attire.

"Well this is turning into a clusterfuck," Dick says with a laugh.

Picasso's phone buzzes, and he glances at the screen. "Jesus

Christ," he says, his face going pale. "We need to get back to the mountain. Now."

I stare at him, incredulous. "I'm not going down there until they get all the killer bees locked up." At the base of the stairs, Dave's security guys are keeping people from coming up here, but the rest of the biodome is a mass of people absolutely having a wobble. The railings installed to direct people through security are piled with frantic bodies.

"There's something bigger," Picasso says, his voice low but urgent. Dick is standing next to him, his eyes glued to his phone as well. "The Russians may have launched an ICBM."

The words hit like a gut punch. I stare at him, my brain scrambling to keep up. "A nuke? At us?"

"Move, Hudson," Picasso barks and shoves me toward the back of the bar.

"What?" I croak as we push through a swinging door into the kitchen. "How do you know we can get out this way?"

He gestures with his head. "Follow them." People in white shirts and black pants are running down a small staircase in the back. The three of us plonk down the steps, Dick talking on the phone about "turning those doom tubes into glass."

When we get to the bottom, we jog through three sets of massive doors that have been propped open—and emerge on the east side of the biodome. There's a small road snaking up to us, but it's jammed with vans, delivery trucks, and buses.

"What happened to the electricity?" I ask as I catch my breath. Every last light on the property is dark, and there's no emergency lighting outside.

"Could be an EMP," Picasso says, scanning the horizon. "Or maybe Kirkland just fucked up and blew a fuse." He looks at Dick. "Where the hell's our ride?"

"An EMP would disable everything," I say, pointing to the distant skyline. "Wouldn't it?"

Picasso shakes his head. "Not if the blast was small. Remember the lines of unprotected cabling you saw coming from the solar array?"

"Right," I say. "No shielding. Not even a few feet of dirt to protect them."

"A bit sloppy on Kirkland's part."

"I don't care how you do it," Dick shouts at his phone, "just get your ass up here now." He looks out across the sea of cars and starts waving his arms. "Can you see us?"

Twenty seconds later, Junior drives up the grass slope, crashes through two rings of hedges, and bounces up ten or twelve small flower terraces, the SUV's headlamps sweeping up and down the side of the biodome. The car skids to a stop in front of us.

As we pile in, Johnson swears, half-impressed, half-furious. "What took you so long?"

"I came as soon as the lights went out," Junior says, throwing the SUV into gear. "What happened?"

"Get us out of here," Picasso says, pointing toward a road running along the airstrip. "Follow that and keep heading east until you see a sign for the freeway."

Junior continues driving across the expensive landscaping.

"How long to get back to the mountain?" Picasso asks, his eyes on his phone.

Junior gives a nervous laugh, and glances in the rearview mirror. "Are we talking Mario Kart or Grand Theft Auto?"

Picasso puts on his seatbelt. "Faster."

"Cool," Junior says and sticks some flashing lights on the roof. He floors it.

I tighten my seatbelt and close my eyes.

So this is how I die.

Sometime later, Junior pulls up in front of the blast doors—which I've never seen closed before—and Picasso hustles me out of the car.

It's below freezing, and a stiff breeze is blowing down from the mountain, so it doesn't take much prodding to get me to jog into the holding pen. Dick engages with the security protocol panel, and then the four of us shuffle into a huge airlock. Five minutes later, we enter a sealed chamber with radiation scanners and shower heads everywhere and wait for a red light to turn green. We go through five sets of thick, heavy doors, each with more security protocols, and enter a small waiting room filled with weird lime-green plastic chairs. Sam is lounging in one shaped like a smashed alien, munching on a bag of potato chips.

"About time you four showed up," he says. "I've been stuck in this furniture freak show for hours." He glances over his shoulder at two Marines standing outside the door. "Batman and Robin won't even tell me why I'm here."

"I'll fill you in once we get to the safe area," Picasso says. "Time is of the essence." Junior and Dick scurry toward the door, but the Marines block them with their rifles.

Dick recoils and whips around to face Picasso. "What the f—"

"One phone call each," Picasso says, pointing at an old-style rotary phone. "When you're done, wait for me at the portal." He turns to Sam and me. "Let's go. There's some paperwork you need to sign."

"Wait a minute," I say. "What about *my* phone call? I need to talk to Cassandra, make sure she's okay."

"The cell towers are down," he says. "All over North America, possibly the world."

"What the hell happened out there?" Sam says, his eyes darting around the room.

Picasso turns to me. "Is there someone on a military base you could contact, professor?" I shake my head and he turns to Sam. "You?"

Sam stares at him, dumbfounded.

"Then let's go." Picasso waits for the guards to lower their rifles.

We scurry out of the room after him.

After signing away a whole mess of rights I didn't know we had, Sam and I follow Picasso through a labyrinth of hallways into the heart of the mountain.

"Where are you taking us?" I say to his back.

"Somewhere safe," he says without looking back. "Everything in your rooms and lab will be moved for you."

Sam and I exchange a glance. "What happened out there?" I ask.

Picasso keeps walking.

"We have a right to know," Sam says.

Picasso stops abruptly, and I narrowly avoid crashing into him. He twists his chin over his shoulder. "Are you familiar with LGM-30 Minuteman III land-based nuclear missiles, Dr. Maxwell?"

Sam clears his throat. "Uh, big boom?"

Picasso raises an eyebrow and continues walking. "Three, possibly more, were launched this evening. The first was detonated two hundred and fifty miles above the Northwest Territories, creating an electromagnetic pulse that knocked out Canada's power grid and wreaked havoc here in the States. At least two more are inbound. If we are not inside the secure area before impact, we could be locked out permanently."

"Wait a sec," Sam says. "Those are *our* nukes. Are you saying the United States preemptively launched ICBMs?"

Picasso ignores him. "Although this military base was designed to withstand an EMP, it wasn't fortified to survive a direct nuclear blast. For this reason, we are entering an underground command post that was built precisely for this sort of fuckup."

"So the Russians launched nukes too?" Sam asks, his voice tight. "Are you kidding me?"

Picasso stops again—but doesn't turn around. "If you'd like to step outside and collect data on ground zero radiation accumulation, now would be the time to say so."

Sam looks like a wide-mouthed frog. "Nope. I'm good."

We exchange looks again and hurry after Picasso.

"Do you know where the nukes will hit?" I ask. When he doesn't respond, I stop walking and cross my arms. "I have a niece out there, Richter."

Sam copies me. "And parents."

Picasso glances back at us. "I get it. I have family out there too. At this point, the only thing I can confirm is that we've been hit by a weak EMP. The pulse matches the signature of an ICBM detonated in high orbit over Canada." He continues moving. "Are you coming?"

We keep walking.

Picasso softens his tone. "Intel says it was an unauthorized launch." Picasso uses his badge to unlock a heavy door and holds it open for us. "Right now, I don't have any more information." He waits for us to walk through, shuts the door, and leads on. "When I do, you'll be the first to know."

More enclosed spaces—and the deeper we go, the tighter my chest gets. When Picasso finally comes to a stop, Dick and Junior are standing in front of a door that looks like an airlock for a spaceship. Junior is playing a game on his phone, and Dick appears to be fuming still. Picasso walks past them and types something on a keypad next to the sealed portal.

A female voice says, "Special clearance required to proceed. Please identify."

Picasso inclines his head. "Sergeant Major Colton Richter. Clearance code: Woden Umbra."

"Thank you, Sergeant Major. What is the first treble clef note in Beethoven's 'Moonlight Sonata'?"

He thinks for a moment. "G sharp."

"Thank you. Please identify your companions, starting with the tallest."

Picasso nods at Dick, who clears his throat.

"Agent George Armstrong Johnson. NSA clearance Bravo Victor Tango twelve forty-one."

"Thank you, Mr. Johnson. What was your undergraduate degree, and where was it conferred?"

Dick's face flushes. "Hospitality Management from the University of Missouri at St. Louis."

"Thank you. You must be accompanied by Sergeant Major Richter to proceed through the portal."

The muscles in Dick's jaw constrict, but he says nothing. Junior glances at me and stands a bit straighter.

Picasso turns toward the younger man. "Agent John Jacob Smith. Clearance identical to Agent Johnson's."

"Mr. Smith," the computer says, "please state the name of your childhood pet and the color of your first car."

Junior looks flustered. "Ah, Poopsie, and, um, orange."

Sam snickers, and Junior gives a theatrical bow.

"Thank you, Mr. Smith."

"Samson Maxwell," Picasso says and gestures for Sam to step closer. "PCAST clearance pending."

"Hello," Sam says and gives a pretty good salute. "My name is Inigo Montoya. You killed my father. Prepare to die."

Johnson scowls, but a smile flickers across Picasso's upper lip.

The computer doesn't skip a beat. "Good evening, Dr. Maxwell. What is the airspeed velocity of an unladen swallow?"

Sam scratches his nose. "African or European?"

"Thank you, Dr. Maxwell."

"Matthew C. Hudson," Picasso says, nodding at me. "Physics Chair at the University of Colorado, Boulder. PCAST clearance pending."

"Working," the disembodied female voice replies. "Professor Hudson, what is a black hole?"

"What you get in a black sock."

Sam gives me a droll smile.

"Thank you, professor. Until your security clearance is confirmed, you and Dr. Maxwell must be escorted by Sergeant Major Richter. That includes exiting through this checkpoint, should the need arise. Do you understand?"

I gulp. "Yes."

"Dr. Maxwell?"

Sam shrugs. "Roger dodger."

The light above the door changes from red to yellow. "The portal will open three seconds after these instructions finish. It will remain open for eight seconds. Once inside the secure area, you will not be able to leave without proper authorization. In the event of an emergency, you must return to this location and apply for clearance to exit. Do you understand? Please state yes or no."

We all respond in the affirmative, although I'm starting to have second thoughts.

"Thank you," the female voice says. "You are cleared for entry."

The yellow light above the portal begins flashing and then turns green. The door slides open, and we step through. A few seconds later, the door closes behind us, and a panel with a red hand outline flashes next to it. The sign above it reads: "In case of an emergency, place your palm on the panel and wait thirty seconds for activation."

And hope to hell there's not an armed terrorist chasing you.

We follow Picasso past a second door, which opens automatically, and file into a large freight elevator. I struggle to keep my heart rate steady as the walls press in on me. Picasso watches my face but says nothing. When the floor begins to fall away, he takes a step closer and puts his hand under my elbow.

I recite a limerick under my breath, trying to focus on the silly wordplay.

> *There was a young lady named Bright,*
> *Who traveled much faster than light.*
> *She set out one day,*
> *In a relative way,*
> *And came back the previous night.*

Picasso lets go of me just a moment after the doors slide open.

We step out into another world.

I stand there with my mouth hanging open and my lungs burning. "Blow me."

"Me too," Sam says.

Buried deep inside the mountain is a huge underground city.

"So this is where they keep all the UFOs," Junior says, and for once, Dick doesn't shut him up.

Down a gentle slope, buildings—some as tall as three stories—line a lake with a Lady Liberty fountain in the middle, water pouring out of her light. Trees and grass fill in the open areas, and a wide pathway marked with glowing lamps snakes around the edge of the water. There's even a sign for a bowling alley. Hundreds, perhaps thousands, of people could live inside this vast man-made cavern.

All it's missing is a golf course.

I look up. The fake night sky is dotted with stars, but there's no moon. I get an uneasy feeling, and it takes me a moment to realize why: the constellations are wrong.

"Well," I say, "this pretty much explains the national debt."

Picasso chuckles. "They roll up the sidewalks pretty early, so let's get you over to the hotel before the lights go out."

We take two of the half dozen electric golf carts parked by the elevators and drive around the lake to one of the larger buildings. There is no lobby, and we're escorted to private rooms by men in crew cuts who appear uncomfortable in their civilian clothing. Sam's room is down the hall from mine. He waves at me as he disappears inside. Sitting inside the door of my room is a suitcase I own but didn't pack. A fake window looks out at the Eiffel Tower, stars twinkling in the phony sky behind it.

"Blimey, whoever built this place was daft." I step inside, and the lights come up.

My personal laptop is on the desk, the screensaver plotting distant galaxies in false color.

Picasso appears in the doorway, flanked by two Marines. "Home, sweet home—at least for now. Meet me in the lobby at oh-seven hundred for breakfast. If you need something, just pick up the phone." He turns and calls down the hall, "Did you hear that, Maxwell?"

"Yep," Sam says. "Nighty night."

I hear his door shut. "Is all this stuff for real?"

Picasso dismisses the men and then turns back to me. "You mean the city, professor?"

"Yeah."

"There's water in the lake, all right, but I wouldn't drink anything that didn't come out of a sealed container. This place was built about the same time as Disneyland, and I think they might have gotten the plans mixed up."

"That's reassuring." I collapse on the bed. "How bad is it out there, mate? Just between us?"

"Don't worry," he says. "You'll have plenty of time to ask questions tomorrow." He turns to leave and then looks back. "And if I were you, I'd hit the sack—and not spend too much time wondering about the trees, if you know what I mean."

"Yeah. I'll try. One more question?"

"Shoot."

"I'm worried about my Cassandra. She's an orphan and has no one but me. Is there any way you could check on her?"

"I'll see what I can do," he says. "Good night, professor." He shuts the door, and I listen to his footsteps fade down the hallway.

I count to ten and then check the door handle.

It's locked.

Crikey Moses.

A seed of panic forms in my chest, but I focus on the engineering marvel that is the Eiffel Tower, and my fear recedes.

"It's just 'Paris in Springtime'," I say and half-heartedly hum a few notes.

Like hell.

I flop down on the bed and eat my bruised banana, well past knackered.

Christ, I hope Cassie is okay.

I slip off my shoes, turn on a white noise generator from my phone, and fall asleep wondering what epic disaster has befallen the world—and how long I'm going to be locked up inside the Magic Kingdom's evil twin.

Madders' Log
Entry 22

Target: Isabel Sanborn

Nexus: KE World Headquarters

Chrono Tag: Same Night

Global financial meltdown in wake of nuclear
event happening as predicted. Despite early
fluctuations, Gemini Solutions' influence on this
timeline likely negligible.

The moment I open the car door, a furry monster streaks out and nearly knocks me over.

"Tolstoy!" I lean over and give him a bear hug. "I've missed you too, big guy." He's easily fifty pounds of fluffy happiness now, and he spends a moment licking my face as I ruffle his fur.

"I know you two haven't seen each other in a while," Diego says as he stuffs my Hive Controller in back, then glances around the parking lot, "but we should get going."

I make eye contact and nod. "Hup," I say to Tolstoy, and he

jumps into the passenger seat of the old CR-V and hops over the center console into the back. I notice the car's loaded with groceries, with a spot reserved for Tolstoy behind the front seats.

Once I get in and put my seatbelt on, Diego locks the doors and whips a U-ie.

"We have to pick up Lucky," I say.

"It's going to hit any minute, Iz."

I stare at him for a moment, and then he lets out a breath and nods.

"Thank you."

He goes out the back way, using his turn signal as he cuts into traffic. "Good thing you live close."

He slows for a red light and then floors it through the intersection. "After we grab Lucky," he says, "we'll head west to the old highway. Once we get to Aerie Town, it should be a straight shot to the cabin."

Ten minutes later, we pull into my apartment complex. It looks eerily normal for this time of the night, lots of windows lit up with the glow of a TV.

Diego brings the car to a stop in front of my building and turns off the engine.

"You can stay here," I say. "I'll be quick."

"Nope." He gives me a crooked smile. "I'm coming with you. Tolstoy will guard the car."

"Alright," I say. "Thanks." Something about his insistence makes me feel off balance, but I'm glad he's coming. I get my key out of my purse and open the car door.

"We'll be right back, big guy," Diego says. "You see anything, you start barking, okay?"

Tolstoy yips like he understands English.

Diego sets the back of his hand on my thigh. "There's a gun in a tackle box under your seat. Get it for me, please." His voice is dead calm.

I pull out the plastic box, pop it open, and set the cold metal weapon in his palm.

"Just in case," he says and puts it in the pocket of his coat.

We hop out of the car, shut the doors, and I hear it beep. After jogging up two flights of stairs, I unlock my apartment door.

Lucky meows and does figure eights around my legs as I flick on the lights and pet her for a moment. "We're going to the cabin, missy. And Tolstoy is coming too."

She meows again, and Diego leans over to pet her. "Hey, Lucky Lady. Long time, no see." He looks up at me. "What can I do to help?"

"Entertain her?" I say. "And maybe keep an eye on the car?"

He shuts the door and stands next to the window, holding Lucky and looking out.

The suitcase I took to the cabin is still in the den, and I roll it into the bedroom. I spend a few minutes stuffing clothes and shoes and toiletries into it. All the encrypted keys for my microdrone work are hidden on my personal computer, so I jam it into the middle of everything, and shut the suitcase.

Jacket.

I grab my down coat from the closet, along with a heavy scarf and mittens, and stuff them into the suitcase pocket.

"Ready." I drag the roller bag into the living room.

Diego takes the luggage from me, and I put Lucky on my shoulder and lock the door.

The lights go out all around us, and someone screams.

"Shit." I turn on my phone's flashlight and follow him down the steps, holding onto Lucky and wondering just how long we're going to be hiding out in the mountains.

He squeezes my suitcase into the back, shuts the rear hatch, and gets back in the car. "It's probably going to be a while before you're back here," he says and locks the car doors. "You know that, right?" He puts the gun in the center console and pins me with his gaze, his right hand on the ignition.

"Yes. Thank you for letting me stay with you."

A weird smile crawls across his face, and then he starts the car. "Anything else you need?"

I shake my head. "Not that I can think of." Lucky is standing on the center armrest licking Tolstoy's face. The pup lets out a soft sigh and closes his eyes, happy to have his best friend back.

"*Ohana* means family," I say, quoting my favorite line from *Lilo and Stitch*.

Diego puts the car in gear. "And family means no one gets left behind."

Our eyes meet for a split second, and something changes between us—something I can't quite name, but I'm pretty sure he felt too.

He runs his fingertips across my cheek, the first time he's offered any sort of physical affection since we broke up years ago. "It's going to be okay, Iz. We'll figure it out."

I press my lips together, feeling teary-eyed, and nod once.

He puts his hand back on the steering wheel and accelerates out of the apartment complex.

The streets are jam-packed with cars, and we have a good portion of the city to get through, but now that we're all together, I start to feel less stressed.

Lucky curls up in my lap, and Tolstoy rests his head on the center console as Diego drives over curbs and cuts through empty lots, always heading west toward the mountains. I pet Tolstoy's head and admire Diego's driving skills. The last time I spent this much time in a car with him, he was still learning to drive a stick. Obviously, he's upped his game. At one point, he turns down an alley to avoid a bonfire in the seedy part of town. Just as we're getting to the other end, a car blocks our path, its headlights blinding us. Diego lays on the horn, but the other car doesn't move, and we eventually have to brake or hit it. The moment we roll to a stop, all four of their doors open, and guys carrying baseball bats jump out.

Tolstoy starts barking like a madman, and Lucky's claws poke into my thighs. I toss her in the back and cover my ears, figuring the thugs might think twice about attacking a car with an attack dog in it. Diego jams the car into reverse, throws his right arm up on my chair, and backs down the alley as fast as the car can go. A couple guys give chase but give up when it's clear we're not going to crash.

Tolstoy stops barking and switches over to an anxious whine.

"Omigod," I say as the car shoots backward into the street. "It didn't take long to get to the post-apocalyptic part."

A truck honks and swerves around us, and Lucky meows.

I grab kitty girl and set her back on my lap. Diego whips the car around and heads in the other direction. We go ten or twelve more blocks on the backstreet and then cut over to a boulevard through a wealthier residential area. There are solar panels on the roofs and large lawns. In the halo of porch lamps, people are looking up at the sky. We finally get through the suburb and onto a divided freeway where the traffic is heavy but moving. Our radio is still on, but the stations are only broadcasting the emergency alert telling people to:

Seek immediate shelter. Stay away from windows and doors. Do not look at the explosion.

Diego leaves it on but turns the volume down.

I stare out at the patchy city lights. "Do you think they managed to countermand the missiles?"

"Well, if they didn't, we'll know about it any second now." He looks over at me and then squeezes my thigh. "It's gonna be okay, Iz. We'll be safe at the cabin."

I nod, wanting to believe him.

Over the course of the next half hour, the traffic gradually thins out, and our speed picks up. Most of the cars on the road are doing the same thing we are.

Getting the hell out of the city.

As we ascend, winding through an upscale suburb in the foothills, another emergency alert comes through, the loud jarring sound making my pulse race.

Tolstoy barks, and Lucky skitters off my lap into the back again.

I pick up my phone, but before I have a chance to read the message, my screen goes dark. I try to turn it on, and then I try to reboot it, but it's just dead. I turn the metal paperweight over in my hands, wondering why it's so hot. "That's weird," I say. "I'm pretty sure I had plenty of bat—"

"Oh, shit," Diego says, and I look up.

The whole city has gone dark, and the cars around us no longer have their headlights on. We watch in shocked silence as they roll to a stop in the darkness, forcing Diego to slam on the brakes. Our car sputters like it's out of gas but keeps going.

"Omigod," I whisper as Diego swerves around the car in front of us, our headlights illuminating the frightened faces of the people in the stalled vehicle. "What just happened?"

"A powerful EMP, I think," he says and starts driving on the shoulder, the sound of tall grass hitting the bumper loud in the eerie silence. "Probably a high-altitude one—at least that's what I'm hoping. HEMPs can travel thousands of kilometers, so the detonation could be very far from here, as far as Montana or North Dakota."

"Detonation?"

"Yeah." He turns the radio up and scans for a signal, but there's nothing except static now.

Not a single station is broadcasting.

I swallow and watch the stopped vehicles go by. "Why is our car still running?" I say, my voice hollow.

"I had it shielded." He adjusts the brightness of the dash down to almost nothing. "Right after I got the message about preparing for the worst." He looks over at me, and I nod.

"From the old man," I whisper. "He saved me twice."

"Yeah," he says. "You and me, both. But the shielding is not something you can test, so I didn't know if it would work."

"Well, it does," I say, sounding like an idiot.

"Let's hope it keeps working."

I hold my breath as he steers around people getting out of their cars. I feel like we're in the only working vehicle in the state. A minute later, he slows down and turns hard to the right. We bump up a concrete curb and crunch over a gravel median to get to a less-crowded frontage road.

A young woman carrying a baby and holding onto a toddler tries to flag us down. The wind is whipping her hair across her face, and she has to let go of the child to wave at us. Diego swerves, being careful not to get too close to them, but he doesn't stop.

"I'm sorry. I'm sorry," he whispers as we go past them.

I turn in my seat and stare at the woman standing in the middle of the road, her face glowing red in our taillights.

It's the end of the world as we know it.

Diego accelerates again, flying through the darkness.

Besides our headlights, the only illumination is an eerie bluish-green dome of light expanding in the sky to the north.

"What is that up in the sky?" I whisper. As I watch, waves of purple and red ripple outward from it. The edges shimmer and pulse, with streaks of lightning shooting out, bending and warping the night sky. It feels chaotic, unsettling—like the sky is tearing open.

"It's an aurora caused by a high-altitude nuclear detonation," Diego says, bending down to see out my window. "Beautiful and terrifying."

Ten minutes later, the aurora fades, and a night blacker than any I can recall descends.

"It's probably been over two hundred years since it was this dark outside," I say, scanning the almost unbelievable expanse of night.

Diego glances out his window but doesn't comment.

"Wait a minute," I say. "There's another car with headlights." I point at a long beam of radiance up on Lookout Mountain and then twist around to look at the city behind us. "And there are a few more behind us."

"Probably older cars without computer chips or electronic fuel injection," he says and lovingly pats the dashboard of the CR-V. "Betsy may be old, but she's a keeper."

"Betsy?"

He pats the dashboard again. "Seamus named her—he's the Malloy's grandson. Nice kid. You'll like him. He devours books just like you do."

We drive north across a huge overpass dotted with stalled cars and trucks, make a 270-degree loop using the old highway on-ramp, and start climbing in earnest.

"Thirty miles to go," Diego says and looks over at me. "I think we're going to make it home." He ruffles Tolstoy's ears and settles back into his seat, relaxing a little.

For the next few minutes, we sit in silence, following an old pickup truck as it weaves around stopped cars and steadily climbs up the canyon next to the river. I turn sideways, still petting Lucky. Diego downshifts and steers around more cars as we continue climbing into the night. In the dim glow of the dashboard, Diego looks the same as he did when we were dating. Only he's changed on the inside, transformed into a guy who knows what he wants and is willing to do what's necessary to get it. My father was a weekend car mechanic, and I grew up helping him change the oil, tune up the spark plugs, rotate the tires—things that got my hands dirty and my brain curious. When I first met Diego, he didn't know an alternator from an accelerator. Now he drives a stick like he was born to it.

Something about that makes me smile.

"I know I'm a handsome dude," he says, "but you've been staring at me for the last five miles with a goofy look on your face. What's up, hon?"

"Thanks for saving me again."

The corner of his mouth curves up. "We gotta stop making a habit of this—because it's killing me."

"You and me, both," I say and laugh. "I could have been stuck in that small apartment with no water and no electricity and nothing but cat food to eat."

"Probably better than a pantry full of Cheez Whiz and pitted olives," he says. "Which is what I had at my old place." He swallows.

"Let's wait till we make it through the first month before you thank me too much." He glances over, a forced smile on his lips. "But at least we'll have water and power—and plenty of food."

"And we'll have each other," I say and stroke Lucky's soft fur with my free hand.

"And we have the Malloys too," he says. "They have chickens and a milk cow and a herd of goats, and they've been teaching me how to store vegetables and shoot a rifle."

The old truck we've been following turns on its blinker. The driver rolls down his window and waves as he pulls off onto a narrow dirt road that winds around the mountain.

Diego honks twice, and the guy honks back.

A minute later, I can no longer see the truck's headlights, and a chill creeps up my spine. The temperature outside is just above freezing.

We drive through a small town in silence. There are a few abandoned cars here and there, but nobody is around. The windows of the local supermarket are all broken, and the doors are wedged open. We pass a candy store with smiling cartoon characters hanging in the window, the shiny finish reflecting our headlights in weird colors.

"Creepy," I say. "Where is everyone?"

Diego scans the shops and points to a building at the end of the street. There are flickering lights in the curtained windows.

"Candles," I say and then realize it's the local bar.

"And a lot of booze." He accelerates past. "Not a good combination."

We speed on into the dark night, strangely calm in a world teetering on the edge of disaster.

A few minutes later, Diego veers off onto another dirt road, and after winding back and forth a bit, he brings the car to a stop under a dim streetlight.

Dirt billows up around us, the sudden silence disconcerting.

It takes a few seconds for the dust to clear.

A couple of meters in front of the car is a heavy metal gate.

"Need to unlock it," he says and starts undoing his seatbelt.

"My turn." I set the kitty girl in his lap. "What's the combo?"

"Seventeen oh one," he says.

I laugh and open my door. "The registry number for the USS Enterprise?"

He shrugs.

"You're such a nerd."

"Live long and prosper," he says as I shut the door. He rolls down his window. "Be careful!"

The cold mountain air seeps into my thin skirt and blouse, and I shiver.

Tolstoy barks, and Diego shushes him. He puts the car in reverse and inches backward. The crackle of tires on gravel is loud in the still night. He repositions the car with the headlights illuminating the padlock. I enter the numbers, unhook the lock, and start unwrapping the heavy chain.

Should have put on gloves.

My breath makes wispy clouds in the freezing darkness as I struggle to untangle the cold metal links.

Tolstoy barks again, and I look up, blinded by the headlights. Someone grabs me from behind, and I let out a garbled cry.

Time slows down.

I can hear Tolstoy barking and scraping his paws against the passenger-side window. I try to twist around so I can knee the guy in the crotch, but he jerks my neck tighter, pulling my head back over his shoulder so my ear is next to his mouth. "Shut the fuck up, bitch." He holds a knife to my throat and pushes me toward the car.

Diego opens his door and shouts, "Let her go!"

"Stay in the car, lover boy, and put your hands where I can see them." He pulls my head up higher and brandishes the knife. "You let that dog out and the lady has an unfortunate accident."

"Okay, okay," Diego says and sits back down. "Don't hurt her."

The man snickers, and a fleck of saliva hits my cheek.

I let out a soft cry, and he presses the knife against my throat. "Shut up."

"Please," Diego says. "You can take whatever you want."

He puts his mouth up to my ear, and his stench makes me recoil. "Nice of him to share, ain't it?" He licks the side of my face.

And then everything happens at once.

The last bit of chain unwinds from the post with a loud clanging noise and releases the gate. The heavy metal barrier swings out, striking the guy from behind, and he lurches out of its path, dragging me with him. The gate sweeps past us, screeching with disuse and picking up speed, and then smashes into the grill of Diego's car.

I've read a hundred articles about why women don't scream when they're attacked, and now I know why.

You can't think and scream at the same time.

Fuck that.

I scream and grab the guy's wrist, jamming my heel down on his foot. I can hear Tolstoy go crazy, barking and banging against the window of the car. I tuck in my chin and twist away from the knife, biting into my attacker's hand.

"You bitch!" He tries to hold onto me, but I'm already free.

I knee him as hard as I can in the groin, and he lashes out with the knife as he doubles over, slashing me in the thigh.

"Get away from him!" Diego shouts.

I shove the guy down into the dirt and kick the grimy knife away, breathing hard. He vomits and makes a move toward the weapon, but I scramble across the road and toss it as far as I can into the weeds, the metal reflecting off the headlights. I hear the car door open, and Tolstoy bounds toward me, barking like crazy. He stops between me and my attacker with his teeth bared and growls, looking for all the world like a dire wolf.

"Get in the car!" Diego yells. I grab Tolstoy's collar and try to pull him back, but I trip and fall on my butt. The guy reaches out for my ankle, but Tolstoy bites his wrist and starts dragging him away from me, snarling now. The man shrieks as I scramble to my feet.

Diego pulls the car up next to me and pushes open my door. "Get in."

"Not without Tolstoy," I say and whistle. "Tolstoy, come!" Tolstoy releases the man, barks at him twice, and then races over to the car and jumps in. I dive in after him and slam the door.

Diego clicks the locks and looks over at me, his eyes huge. "How bad are you hurt?"

I take a ragged breath. "It's just a nick."

"Are you sure you don't need a doctor?"

I take a quick look in the dim light. It's bleeding but not a lot. "Yes. Go!"

The guy is still curled up, cupping his wrist.

Diego picks up his gun and eases the car forward. "This is going to be loud, so you may want to cover your ears."

I hold my breath, afraid of what he might do.

Diego rolls down his window, shifts in his seat so he can get his hand out, and points the gun at my attacker. "If I ever see you again, I'll kill you. No questions asked." He fires one bullet into the ground in front of the man. Rocks and dirt kick up into the man's face, and the shot echoes across the canyon.

Tolstoy starts barking again as the guy struggles to his feet.

"It's okay, Tolstoy," I say. "Shh."

The dog gives a long, low yowl but obeys.

Silence fills the night, dirt and debris still swirling around in our headlights. We watch the man limp up the steep embankment and disappear into the woods. Diego rolls up the window, engages the gun safety, and sets the firearm back in the console.

I collapse back against the seat, my whole body shaking. "And here I thought there wasn't going to be any drama tonight."

He turns up the heater and switches on the dome light. "Let's have a look at your leg."

"It's just a scratch," I say. "Honestly, I've had scarier first dates."

He takes a first-aid kit out of the glovebox. "Good to know the bar is so low."

I roll my eyes.

When he's done helping me clean up the wound, he takes a slow breath and lets it out. "How 'bout next time we let Tolstoy out first?"

"Party pooper."

Lucky peeks over my chair and meows. I pet her head, and she meows again.

Diego switches off the light, puts the car in gear, and reaches for my seatbelt. "I gotta say, that move you made to knee him in the groin was excellent. You'll have to teach me that."

"Learned it in self-defense class." I buckle the latch and will my heart to stop pounding. "Wouldn't you know it, the one time I actually needed spike heels, I wasn't wearing them." I look over at him, my chest filling with butterflies. "You weren't so bad yourself."

He laughs. "It was all Tolstoy."

Madders' Log
Entry 23

Target: Matt Hudson
Nexus: Warm Springs Underground City
Chrono Tag: 1 Month Later

Considered Dr. Sabrina Lovelace, Dr. Cassandra
Hudson, and Dr. Samson Maxwell as primary
targets. However, given their tight orbit around
my parallel, required resources cannot be
justified. David Kirkland remains an option if
significant divergence is detected.

I shut off the water pouring into our four-hundred-gallon
aquarium and wind up the hose, careful not to drip any on the
cables snaking across my lab.

*Who would have thought a spacetime portal would require a
swimming pool?*

I double-check that the shoebox-sized tungsten pod inside the fish
tank is properly connected to all the leads, secure the lid, and switch

on the video camera. Sam's been complaining about the setup not being grounded, but we followed the Singularity Transit Device instructions to a T, so no grounding.

To be honest, I find it difficult to believe it's going to be that simple. Even the best scientists leave out steps they think are obvious.

When was the last time you saw a recipe that instructed you to make sure the oven was grounded, for Pete's sake?

On top of that, the project folder contained over a hundred files. When we finally tracked down the instructions, they were spread across 114 pages, each with cryptic instructions.

But I'm not complaining. If I knew Cassie was safe and sound, I'd be having the time of my life.

They did let me listen to a message from her a couple of weeks ago—she seemed okay, more concerned about me than anything else —but still, I worry.

"Ready, doc?" Sam calls from the adjoining room. He's firing up the huge power generator Operations wheeled in this morning. At first, Sam wasn't keen about being locked up inside this mountain. But now—given the alternative is wrestling the masses for beans and bottled water—I don't think he minds so much.

Of course, I continue to lobby hard to bring in Cassie, and Picasso claims he's still working on it. But I have a hunch there's more to it than he's letting on.

That bloke's a tough nut to crack.

In any case, Dick is all over Picasso's butt about compromising security and consuming resources, especially where family members are concerned. All in all, it's very disheartening.

Hang in there, kiddo. I'm trying.

I take a slow breath and release it, attempting to focus on something happy, just like my therapist recommended back when I still had all my hair.

But thinking about Cassie makes my heart hurt. I take a roll of fruit-flavored antacids out of my pocket and pop one into my mouth. Picasso does let me send letters—the kind that you write on paper and stick in an envelope—but after they get redacted, all that's left is:

> *Dear Cassandra,*
> *I'm fine.*
> *Write back soon.*
> *Love,*
> *Uncle Matty*

I snort. "Eat your heart out, Shakespeare."

After they told us about the cock-up with the nukes—and the resulting EMPs—folks in here thought the world was done and dusted. We could only imagine how difficult it would be to survive without power, clean water, and grocery stores.

A right nightmare.

But Picasso says the grid is slowly coming back up and areas that invested in renewables are doing okay. I don't think anyone believes him—especially since we're still stuck in here with no real news, no meaningful external contact, and no way out—but I'm hoping we're wrong.

I pop a second tablet into my mouth and get back to the business at hand: testing whether our one-fifth scale model of the Singularity Transit Device can protect its cargo from heat damage. According to the link that was inside the sphere, the Singularity Transit Device should be able to withstand the tidal forces of a black hole and keep its payload at a safe temperature. Of course, this seems impossible given the laws of physics, but then everything's impossible until someone does it.

We heard they brought in Berkeley's Trans Temporal Viewer a few days ago, but until we get our hands on the wormhole project, there's no way to fully test "the coffin," as Sam calls it. But we're doing the best we can.

I tap Sam's button on my phone. "Are you ready, mate?"

"I was born ready," he says. "But the generator wasn't. Give me another minute." His stomach growls. "Can we get some lunch after this? I'm running on fumes, doc."

Ever since we did that *Back to the Future* marathon, he's been calling me doc—that and saying jigawatts every chance he gets.

"Roger, that." I strap on my safety goggles. "I'm switching on the Raspberry Pi." I wait for the tiny computer to beep three times. Sam came up with the idea to use the microprocessor to control the flow of current until the wormhole generator is built, and it's proven to be very useful. He also suggested we put a banana inside the Singularity Transit Device instead of frying one of our dwindling supply of sensors every time a test fails, and he was right about that too.

Our testing metric: a cooked banana is bad.

"The flux capacitors are at full power," he says and puts his eye close to the camera. "Did you remember to press the big red button, doc?"

"Yes, Sam," I say with more annoyance than I feel.

Crikey, I only forgot to hit the record button once.

I check the viewfinder.

Suspended in the middle of the large aquarium is a smooth metal submarine. It's a lot smaller than the Singularity Transit Device specified in the decades-old top-secret project, but otherwise comparable. Sealed inside the pod is our next test subject, a ripe banana. Now that I'm about to run a lot of current through a metal prolate spheroid immersed in purified water, I'm not sure it's such a great idea to be in the same room.

Too late now.

I triple-check that the record light is on. "Singularity Transit Device test number one hundred and seventeen," I say and add the date and time. "First test with hydro enhancement of the field."

"Let's hope four hundred gallons of water does the trick," Sam says. "I'm firing the pulse... now."

I involuntarily lean away from the glorified paddle pool.

Nothing happens.

"Jesus, it's sucking down the jigawatts," Sam says. "Where's it all going?"

The water starts glowing an ethereal blue, and I smell sharp, metallic ozone.

A moment later, I hear the ventilation system kick into high.

"Uh," I say into my phone, "something's happening in here. Can you see it on the feed?" The glowing water in the tank starts to boil, producing an impressive cloud of steam. "Cut the power," I bark and consider disconnecting the cable—but I don't want to get electrocuted.

"Great Scott," Sam says from behind me. "Is that Cherenkov radiation?"

I scoff. "It's a sodding fish tank, not a particle accelerator." But even as I say it, I know he's right.

He scratches his head. "What could be zipping around faster than light?"

"I don't know, but we need to shut down the power before it overloads the system."

"Already did, doc. Somehow, the Singularity Transit Device is storing the charge. Kinda cool, if you ask me." He steps closer and crouches down, peering into the boiling aquarium. "That banana is going to be toast."

I take off the goggles and give him an annoyed look. "Thanks for the heads-up, Einstein."

He shrugs. "Not that it wouldn't be fun to see what happens, but this whole thing could blow up big time." He says it like he's reporting the weather. "We should dump more water in there so the cables don't catch fire."

"Good idea," I say, wishing I hadn't watched that Chernobyl documentary last week. I grab the plastic bin from underneath my desk and dump the rubbish onto the floor. He picks up the one next to the door and does the same.

"Showers," I say.

The two of us race down the hall and push through the only

unlocked door in the building, nearly knocking down the woman coming out.

"Sorry," I say, hurrying past her. I shove the bin into a stall and turn the water on full blast.

"Matt?"

I pick up the heavy bin, Sam on my heels. The woman holds the door for us, her eyes wide.

"It is you," she says in a slight German accent, and my heart skips a beat.

"Sabrina?" I say and slam on the brakes. Sam crashes into my back, and I slosh water all over her. She leaps out of the way, dodging the worst of it.

"Oops. Sorry," I say, trying not to dump the whole bin. I meet her gaze for the first time. "Crikey, you haven't aged a day."

She laughs. "It's good to see you too, Matt. Been too long."

"Fire in the hole," Sam says and shoves me forward. "Or there will be soon."

"Don't let me hold you up," she says and flattens herself against the door.

We rush back to the lab, spilling water everywhere. Sam kicks off the top using his foot, and we dump the water into the aquarium. The liquid pops and sputters—and starts boiling into steam. When the tank's nearly empty again, black smoke starts wafting out, and I realize the cables must be melting.

"Bloody hell," I shout. "We're going to set off the sodding fire bell."

Sabrina jogs in carrying a fire extinguisher, takes a quick look at the setup, and starts spraying foam into the overheated aquarium. The froth bubbles and makes weird sucking sounds, but no more smoke escapes.

"Mischief managed," she says, her pants damp and her hair a bit wild from all the steam. "Hope you like your goldfish crispy."

Sam and I laugh.

She glances around the lab, looking impressed. "Is this what I think it is?"

I set down the trash bin, resisting the urge to hug her. "Damn, it's good to see you, Sabrina." I stick my hand out. "When did you join the circus?"

She puts down the fire extinguisher and pulls me into a hearty embrace. "They're watching us," she whispers before she steps away and then continues in her regular voice. "The government flew me in this morning. I was lucky enough to be on holiday when the tsunami hit."

"Tsunami?" Sam and I say together.

"Yeah," she says, staring at Sam and me like we've been living under a rock—which we obviously have. "Happened the morning after the nukes. The wave came in higher than the Golden Gate. Wiped out everything in the Bay Area. If I hadn't been sitting in a cabin in Tahoe..."

"Blimey," I say, relieved that Cassie's on the East Coast. "I'm glad you're all right."

"Me too." She runs her fingers over her unruly locks and bobs her head at Sam. "Who's your wingman?"

I introduce Sam, and they shake hands. "Sam's a postdoc in computational physics."

"And an Olympic champion in extreme water fetching," Sam says, wringing the water out of his T-shirt.

Sabrina looks impressed. "We could probably use your expertise —at least the physics part—on the Peeper."

"The Peeper?" Sam and I say like we're conjoined at the hip.

She scrunches up her nose. "They *really* don't tell you guys anything?"

"Compartmentalization," I say and make air quotes. I lean closer and whisper, "If they catch us talking to you, we'll all end up in the naughty corner."

Her eyes get big. "In other words, nobody knows what anybody else is building," she says. "So everything goes ten times slower."

"At least we've got dental," Sam deadpans.

She glances over her shoulder and then leans closer, keeping her voice down. "Peeper is short for Peeping Tom—what we were calling the device before the whole Bay Area went under."

"You mean the Trans Temporal Viewer?" I whisper, watching a small puff of smoke rise from the aquarium. "As I recall, that's what you were working on."

She pulls her chin back in surprise.

I swat it away. "You know the quantum grapevine. Gossip moves at the speed of light. Who else is on the project?"

She swallows and shakes her head. "They didn't make it."

I raise an eyebrow.

"Yeah," she says. "That kind of didn't make it. Yesterday when I snowshoed into town to get supplies, there was a letter for me, offering me a job with food and water and actual hot showers." She gives an exaggerated shrug. "Less than an hour later, I climbed into a helicopter. They told me the whole setup had been moved into a lab down here."

"Probably behind one of those locked doors down the hall," Sam says. "What's it supposed to do?"

"Well, our one-pager says it takes snapshots of photon pairs entangled across different spacetimes. To be honest, like a lot of other quantum mechanics, we don't really understand how it works."

"Well, we're building a spacetime bridge," Sam blurts out.

Sabrina and I exchange a worried look.

Sam plops down on my desk, his ears red. "I probably shouldn't have said that."

Sabrina's eyebrows rise. "Then I probably didn't hear it." She dusts off her hands. "Say, I was just on my way to get lunch, assuming that's allowed..." She points her thumb over her shoulder and takes a sniff. "If your carbonized banana can wait, would you care to join me? Maybe stop and grab some dry clothes on the way?"

Sam grins. "I thought you'd never ask."

"Just a sec," I say and turn toward the camera. "Test number one hundred and seventeen complete." I switch off the recording. "You ever seen a setup with a Faraday cage immersed in water, Sabrina?"

She scrunches up her nose. "Sounds hazardous, water being an excellent conductor. Might be an interesting way to hold the charge if you're using purified water, though."

"Ding, ding, ding," Sam says. "Give the lady a prize."

"Interesting," she says, her eyes widening. "And dangerous."

I start disconnecting things. "Won't be once we figure out how to turn it off."

Sam makes a whining noise.

"Right, right," I say. "After lunch."

When the three of us—sporting dry clothes—walk into the cafeteria, heads turn. There's been a trickle of new people over the last fortnight, and everyone's curious about the other projects—and how things are holding up outside. But just like Sam and me, everybody had to sign away all their rights, and each team has strict orders to sit at their assigned table. It might be the only thing that Dick and Picasso agree on.

But Sabrina's an old friend, and to hell with the bolloxing I'm gonna get.

What are they gonna do, lock me up in an underground military complex?

A few minutes after we get our food and sit down, Picasso strides in. He comes over to our table and shakes hands all around.

Crikey, he's gonna read us the riot act.

I clear my throat. "Sabrina hasn't been assigned a table yet."

"Yes, of course," Picasso says. "You two are old friends?"

"Yes," we say together, and I feel my face flush. I nod at Sabrina, and she continues.

"We were in grad school together back before the dinosaurs evolved into birds."

Picasso gives a polite chuckle.

"Sam and I ran into her by the showers this morning," I say.

"Yes," she says. "They made quite a splash."

Sam snickers and covers it with a cough.

Picasso raises an eyebrow but doesn't comment. "How are things outside?" he asks Sabrina. "I heard they're starting a biodome in Salt Lake City. Same design as the one up north of here. Did you see it on the way over?"

Sabrina nods. "Word is, there's one in Texas that has a water slide and one in Massachusetts with a movie theater. Anyone with a net worth over a billion should have plenty of elbow room once they're completed."

Picasso laughs. "I heard they plan to hold lotteries for service workers—nurses and teachers and such."

I sigh. "The whole damn world is gonna be like a *Logan's Run* remake."

"Loved that movie," Sabrina says. "Happy ending and all."

Sam rolls his eyes. "All of us are gonna end up like Morlocks, trapped down here in the dark."

Picasso groans like he's that one jock who got dragged to Comic Con—and then turns back to Sabrina. "I know things are pretty chaotic right now, what with the flooding and the fires. But as soon as the grid is back up, I think we'll be able to sort all this out."

I bump her foot, and she bumps me back.

"I sure hope so," she says. "I'm not keen on spending my retirement inside a cave."

"So, what do you think about our underground city, Sabrina?" Sam shovels a fork full of lasagna into his mouth. "I gotta thay it gibs me da creebs."

She glances at me. "I have to admit, it is a little out of the ordinary, but it's nice to have a semblance of normality again." She stirs her peaches. "That and hot showers. But I have a sister out there, and parents too. It's tough leaving your family behind, no matter the reason."

"If you give me their names and addresses, I'll see about getting you some regular reports," Picasso says and gives me a sideways glance. "We all have loved ones outside. Thank you for your sacrifice."

I set down my glass and turn to Picasso, but before I can get a word out, he holds up his hands.

"I'm trying," he says and looks at me. "That's what I came to tell you. Johnson is flying in from the East Coast as we speak. Your niece should be on that plane."

"Really? Blimey!" I say and shake his hand. "Thank you." Sam lets out a whoop, and Sabrina gives us a curious look.

"Cassie," I say, grinning. "My niece—and Sam's current crush. She's a theoretical physicist. Wormholes."

Picasso places his hand on my shoulder. "I showed the brass her research on closed timelike curves—the paper you sent me—and finally got the go-ahead."

I can barely contain the urge to break out singing.

Sam brandishes his fork at Picasso. "Didn't you say bringing in family members was a no-no? What gives? How do I get my family on the list?"

"And mine?" Sabrina says.

Picasso's face remains impassive. "When your Great Aunt Tilly gets a PhD in quantum field theory, let me know." His phone buzzes, and he takes it out and reads for nearly a minute, his jaw getting tighter by the second. "I'm sorry, but I've just learned that Dr. Cassandra Hudson is not on the plane," he says, not meeting my gaze.

"Wha...why not?" A sharp pain shoots through my chest, and I gasp. "Where is she?"

"I don't know. She evaded my courier."

"Who did you send?" I bark and then narrow my gaze. "Please tell me it wasn't Junior."

He raps his knuckles on the table. "Been nice chatting with you." He rests a hand on Sabrina's shoulder. "Welcome, professor. I'm glad you're here. Once your things make it through security, I'll fill you in on what comes next."

"Thank you," she says and drops her gaze.

He looks over at me. "I'm not gonna tell you who to eat lunch with, Hudson, but if I were you, I'd keep it to idle chitchat, if you know what I mean."

I bob my head.

He pins Sam with a razor-sharp gaze. "And next time you feel like telling someone you're working on a spacetime bridge, don't."

For once, Sam keeps his mouth shut—but Sabrina nudges me under the table.

She was right. They were listening.

"All of you are here on my say-so," Picasso says, "and that could change at any moment. Am I making myself clear?"

We all nod.

"Enjoy your lunch, people, then let's get back to work." Picasso strides out of the cafeteria.

Madders' Log
Entry 24

Target: Diego Nadales
Nexus: Diego's Cabin
Chrono Tag: Next Day

Global news feed comparison complete: During
First Disaster, 11 nuclear devices of varying
yields detonated: 4 above North America; 2 above
Europe; 2 in or near their silos in South Asia;
and 1 each above the Indian Ocean, Arctic Circle,
and Western Siberia. Resulting EMPs annihilated
global power grid. Subsequent shift in Juan de
Fuca Plate triggered tsunamis in Pacific Basin.
Downward spiral toward Doomsday on track with no
major deviations from virgin timeline.

I swing the axe down as snowflakes swirl around me. Metal bites
into wood with a sharp crack that echoes down the canyon. It's
been a month since the EMP, and there have been almost no

signs of recovery. I heft the axe and bring it down again, the dead tree splitting under the weight of my worries.

My gaze drifts to the leaden sky, imagining the world plunged into permanent darkness.

"Einstein was right," I say. "World War IV will be fought with sticks and stones."

As I fell another dead tree, I ponder the EMP's silent devastation: the darkness, the suffering, the cold grip of a new kind of winter. With hospitals looted and resources dwindling, each swing of the axe is a stark reminder of how fragile civilization is.

Focus on the things you can control, mae. Be thankful you have Iz.

After we got to the cabin the night of the attack, I cleaned and bandaged Isabel's knife wound. The cut hadn't looked too bad, but a week later, an infection took off. I had stockpiled plenty of first aid supplies but no antibiotics. So, I took my old truck down to town with a big wad of cash. But the only place open was the old bar—which had been turned into a pawn shop run by three rough-looking guys carrying rifles. When I asked how much money for antibiotics, they just laughed.

Up until that moment, I knew things were bad, but the reality hadn't really sunk in.

I stood in that dingy bar with a gun pointed at my back and rummaged through a basket of mostly-empty pill bottles priced in gasoline, ammo, and liquor. Had to trade my old truck, one of my last boxes of bullets, and nearly a full tank of gas for nineteen amoxicillin tablets.

After retrieving Tolstoy and my rifle from the cab, I tossed the chubby man my keys at the same time he tossed me the pills.

"Inflation's a bitch," he said and shrugged. "Where you headed back to?"

"Tahiti." I tucked the bottle in my coat pocket, and Tolstoy and I walked out. After we got up into the trees a ways, we waited behind some rocks for an hour to make sure no one followed us.

Of course, it was dark by the time we made it home, and Isabel was half-crazy with worry. Thank goodness Mrs. Malloy had brought over milk and butter that day because she had kept Isabel from jumping into the CR-V to come after me—and using up the little gasoline we have left. After Isabel finished hugging me, the two women gave me an earful about going down the mountain alone.

In hindsight, they were probably right.

The night of the EMP, I had thought about driving back into town. With all the looting and chaos, I probably could have taken whatever I wanted from the pharmacy. Now, it's like *Lord of the Flies* out there—only with rifles instead of spears and coconuts.

Considering how it could have turned out, you should consider yourself lucky. The antibiotics worked and Isabel's cut healed.

I wipe the sweat off my forehead and get back to chopping logs.

It's a challenge to survive in the mountains, especially in winter, but I'd take it over the city any day. At least here I don't have to worry about roving bands of looters—or worse.

In any case, Isabel and I are doing much better than most. In fact, if it wasn't for the state of the world, I'd say I've never been happier. We have plenty of food, clean water, and electricity. I have a garage full of solar panel parts and spare batteries, so we should be good for at least a couple of years. In exchange for flour and sugar—of which we have plenty—the Malloys keep us supplied with fresh eggs, milk, cheese, and butter. Once the snow lets up, I'll upgrade their solar panels and connect a spare battery so they can expand a little, maybe start a greenhouse in their barn. Molly's a nurse, and she could offer simple medical services in exchange for goods if things start improving.

Right now, I don't want anyone to know about the cabin.

Without the internet, it's difficult to know how the rest of the country is faring, but if my excursion into town is any indication, not great. I don't know how my family and friends in Costa Rica are managing, but at least they're not freezing to death.

Even with all the chaos, I have to believe there are rational, compassionate people out there working to put things back together. I figure if we can hold out until summer, things will start to turn around.

Once the snow melts, I plan to venture out to find gasoline and check on the Gemini warehouse, see what can be salvaged. Our products were designed to be used in remote regions and conflict zones but could easily be adapted for the home market. Right now, that could be doing a lot of good. Maybe we could hand out portable solar power generators, simple filtration systems, and induction-power hotplates. At the very least, our clean water systems could be supporting hospitals and other critical services while the government gets infrastructure back online.

It's not the world-changing impact you had imagined, but it's something.

I bring the axe down two more times and then switch to a left-handed grip, gratified to see the chips of wood accumulating at my feet. Now that the snow has started sticking, the sound of the axe is muffled a bit, making it seem like Isabel and I are all alone in the world. Back before the grid failed, that thought would have been full of cozy possibilities, but these days, it's a little scary.

I shiver and keep chopping.

When I'm done sectioning the tree, I stop and wipe the sweat off my face. The work is hard, but it feels good. I notice Isabel watching me from the kitchen window. When she sees me look over, she waves. With the back-lighting, the falling snow, and the huge windows, the scene looks like a photo from a ski magazine.

Like we're an old married couple, kids grown, out on winter vacation in the mountains.

The thought makes my chest hurt. Every night, I crawl into bed alone, wishing she was there beside me.

Don't rush the things you want to last forever.

I let out a sigh. "What if we're running out of forever?"

After I finish chopping the last bit of kindling, I put away the axe and start stacking the wood next to the rock wall by the garage. My stomach growls, and I remember that Isabel was making something in the crockpot this morning.

The thought fills me with warm anticipation.

Back when she first arrived, we had a light-hearted conversation about gender roles. I told her I'd be happy to cook and clean if she wanted to work outside, and I meant it. So I shouldn't have been surprised when she came out for a couple hours this morning—and wasn't half-bad at swinging the axe.

"I think that means I'm on bathroom duty," I say to myself and chuckle.

I toss the last two pieces on the stack and head back to the cabin, still smiling to myself. It's starting to get dark, and I'm covered in snow. My heart beats a little faster as I walk up to the door, looking forward to a hot shower, a home-cooked meal, and a cozy evening in front of the fire. Nowadays, there's nothing to do but read, watch old movies, and play boardgames.

That might be living hell with anybody else, but with Isabel, it's nice.

Really nice.

When I step inside, I'm surrounded by the most wonderful cooking smells. I hear giggling in the living room, and then Tolstoy yips.

I pull off my boots and peek around the doorway, my mouth watering. "Hello? What's for dinner?"

"Omigod, Diego, you look like a walking blizzard." Isabel is wearing silk pajamas with mismatched socks and a beanie that threatens to fall off her head. "Did you have a brawl with some snowmen?"

"Nah, those guys are chill," I say and take off my coat and gloves. I hang them up by the door and then dust off my hair in the kitchen sink. "Whatever you're cooking smells magnificent. I'm starving."

She smiles. "The dumplings need about ten more minutes. Wanna take a quick shower?"

"Yes," I say, letting my eyes wander a bit. Her nipples are visible beneath the silk pajama top. I swear she does that on purpose, and I force myself to look away. "Make that, *gads yes.* I haven't sweated this much since I had to make a funding presentation to World Aid."

"Well, I'd say hard work suits you." She crosses her arms and leans back against the kitchen counter, still smiling. "If you want to give me your clothes, I can stick them in with the last load. Use the extra water before it freezes overnight."

"Okay," I say, unsure what the protocol is here.

Should I go into the bedroom and put on a robe first?

You have nothing to hide.

I start unbuttoning my shirt, proud of the hard-earned muscles beneath it. She watches me, the corner of her mouth curving up. I slip my arms out of the sleeves, walk in front of her to the washer, and drop the sweaty flannel shirt into the machine. I pull my undershirt over my head and step out of my jeans, tossing those in too. She pretends to busy herself at the sink, but I can see her sneaking looks. I tug off my socks and lob them in as well. Then I stand there in my underwear, contemplating the only thing between me and naked.

No harm in letting her know what she's missing.

I slip off my shorts, drop them into the washer, and close the lid. "Shall I start it up?" I ask.

"Oh, most definitely." She's looking out the window at the last bit of daylight over the peak, her chin raised and her lips twitching. "Please, do."

"Oh-kay," I say, knowing something's up but not sure what. After the machine kicks on, I pad across the kitchen in my bare feet.

She makes a show of keeping her gaze averted, but after I walk past her, she giggles. "You still have the world's cutest buns."

I wave over my shoulder, my body responding to her tone of voice in a way that is super awkward right now.

"Um," she says, "I hope it's okay that I opened a bottle of wine?"

"Only one?" I say without turning around. "And there's no need to ask."

"Oh, and I started doing an inventory," she says. "You've really got this survival thing down to an art. On top of the eighty-odd movies, there's a huge box of ibuprofen, two jugs of hand sanitizer, a dozen pregnancy tests" —she gives me a look like I've been holding out on her— "fifteen bottles of shampoo, and eight cases of wine. And that's just the first storage cabinet in the basement."

But no prescription drugs.

"Yeah," I say to myself. "It's like I have a PhD in disasters."

But hey, if we're gonna have front-row seats for the apocalypse, we might as well have plenty of moisturizer.

Once I'm in the shower, I spend a couple minutes soaping up, my mind wandering to places it has no business going. When I switch the water back on, I notice that she's watching me from the bedroom doorway, her head tipped to the side. I consider opening the shower door and inviting her to join me, but I can't come up with an invitation that doesn't sound desperate or creepy.

Wanna save water with me, one steamy shower at a time?

I close my eyes and rinse off, my body racing ahead of my brain.

Did something just change between us, or am I taking a deep dive into wishful thinking?

When I step out of the shower, she's gone.

Wishful thinking, mae.

But as I'm toweling off, she peeks back in. "I forgot to tell you, it's pajama night."

"What? Why?" I say, like I was born without a brain.

She lowers her chin and raises her eyebrows.

"Never mind," I say, wrapping the towel around my hips.

"Well, you can come naked, if you prefer," she says, taking a quick glance below the waist. "But I suspect it's a little chilly for that." She disappears.

"Why pajamas?" I say to the vacant doorway, my empty stomach talking.

"Because," she replies from the great room, "when I was a kid, anytime my parents had something important to say, we had pajama night." She leans against the doorjamb, her eyes roving across my chest, then meets my gaze. "It's how I knew my life was about to change."

That shuts me up.

I put on sweatpants and my least-ratty undershirt, hoping they'll pass muster. Then I hustle back to the bathroom and pat on a little aftershave—it's pajama night after all—and walk out into the fire-lit great room.

The coffee table is set with four places, two of which have pillows in front of them. Tolstoy, gentleman that he is, is sitting in front of a large bowl of kibbles looking like the perfect dinner guest. He's wearing a red bandana around his neck and wagging his tail. Lucky is nowhere to be seen, but her plate has an unopened can of tuna on it. There's a bottle of wine standing between two lit candles and the soft notes of a Latin guitar coming from the speakers.

"Wow," I say, my stomach growling. "I think we should have pajama night more often."

"Have a seat," Isabel calls from the kitchen. "I'll be right there."

I sit down on a pillow with my back against the sofa and pour the wine. Isabel comes in carrying a large pot and sets it on a trivet between us.

"Coq au vin with dumplings," she says. "Julia Child would be aghast, but necessity is the mother of invention, so I invented." She opens the tuna can, pours some of it on Tolstoy's kibbles, and dumps the rest on Lucky's plate. "Dinner is served, kitty girl." Lucky jogs to the table, hops up on her place, and proceeds to devour the fish. Tolstoy looks antsy but doesn't break his stay. Isabel serves me stew and dumplings, and then sits down and serves herself.

"School's out," she says to Tolstoy, and he tucks in.

"Wow," I say. "You're great at keeping the Nadales men in line."

She rolls her eyes. "Some are easier than others."

I pick up my wine glass and wait for her to do the same. "Here's to pajama night. Thank you for cooking—and for all of this."

She clinks her glass against mine. "Thank you for saving me, Diego, twice and counting."

I give a mirthless laugh. "Is that what this is about? You know you don't need to keep—"

"Nope," she says. "This is about"—she takes a sip of wine, not meeting my gaze—"the stolen wedding rings you have tucked away in your underwear drawer."

"Ex-stolen," I say, and she laughs.

"Go ahead and eat." She nods at my bowl. "Please." She picks up her spoon and takes a bite—and then sucks in a mouthful of air. "Hot. Careful."

I stir my stew, my mouth watering. When I finally take a bite, it's all I can do not to dump the whole bowl into my mouth. "*Mierda*, Isabel, this is amazing."

She beams. "It should be. You made it for me the first time you invited me over for dinner."

"How do you remember that stuff?"

"Oh, I remember it all: the day at San Gregorio beach and the rainy night at the Cuban restaurant, and the first night you stayed over when Sophie barged in on us." She laughs. "I thought you were going to die of embarrassment."

"I almost *did* die of embarrassment." I reach across the table and take her hand. "Remember the day my car broke down and you fixed it with masking tape and an empty yogurt cup? I thought you were the smartest person I'd ever met. When I told you so, you taped my mouth shut."

She giggles. "I think we used up a whole roll of masking tape before we managed to get our clothes off."

The memory makes my heart swell—along with another body part. I adjust my sweatpants and serve myself another bowl of stew.

She presses her lips together, her gaze distant. "And I remember the first time you kissed me. To be honest, I didn't think you'd ever do it."

"Yeah," I say. "*That* I recall." I chuckle to myself, remembering the surprised look on her face—and the way she kissed me back.

We spend the next hour reminiscing, cringing, and laughing.

I wipe up the last of my third serving with a piece of warm bread and wash it down with wine. "Damn, those were good times."

She nods, her eyes glossy. "The best of times"—she swallows—"and the worst of times."

"I—" We both say at the same time and then look down.

"I was such an idiot," she says, stacking up her dishes. "I was so afraid of—" She exhales and then meets my gaze. "I'm sorry I didn't tell you the truth, Diego. I've regretted it ever since. How could I have been so naive, so afraid, so selfish?"

I reach across the table and take her hand. "Iz?"

She shakes her head. "And in what universe does asking Dave for help actually turn out well?"

"I'm the one who ran away, hon, the one who threw in the towel. I had never met anyone like you, and I was all in, totally over my head, madly in love. And then at the first bump in the road, I panicked and bailed out. What sort of an asshole does that?" I swallow, my heart stuck in my throat. "Can you ever forgive me?" I squeeze her hand and wait for her to meet her gaze. "We missed out on so many good years, and it's all my fault."

"Oh, Diego, stop." She blinks back tears. "We were both young and stupid. God knows I'd have run away from me too." She takes a slow breath. "But we're together now. That's what matters."

"Now, in the worst of times," I say, "we've found the best."

She takes a breath and lets it out, fiddling with the corner of her placemat. "That's what I wanted to tell you tonight." She sits up straighter. "I've been waiting for you to make the first move—assuming you have plans for the ex-stolen rings." She laughs through her tears. "But you know how impatient I get."

I stare at her, unable to believe what I'm hearing.

"You really gotta learn to take a hint, Mr. Nadales." She looks down at her hand in mine. "I don't want to sleep alone anymore, and I'm hoping you're okay with that."

I stand and pull her up, holding her at arm's length. "I have loved you since the first time you snickered at my frog pun." I sweep an errant lock of hair away from her face. "And I've wanted to ask you that damn question for years."

She glances back and forth between my eyes. "So ask?"

"Will you marry me?"

She nods, tears streaming down her face. "In the summer, when the wildflowers are in bloom. We'll invite the Malloys—and Sophie and Hank if we can track them down. No fancy clothes or anything, just the two of us and a few close friends."

I wipe a tear from her cheek. "Seamus can play the bagpipes."

She laughs. "And I'll teach Tolstoy to carry the ex-stolen rings."

I pull her into my arms and kiss her. Just for a moment, everything in the universe is perfect.

When she breaks the kiss, I hold her gaze. "I love you, Iz."

Her eyes dance across my face and hair. And then she takes my hand and leads me into the bedroom. "I love you more."

Madders' Log
Entry 25

Target: Matt Hudson
Nexus: Underground City, Spring
Chrono Tag: 2 Months Later

Sudden jump in ripples around Spacetime Bridge detected. Cause coalesces around Cassandra Hudson (tragically deceased during Second Disaster in virgin timeline). Odds of wormhole generator being operational pre-Doomsday adjusted to 53%.

My phone makes a strange ringing noise, and I almost drop the hot soldering iron. "Bloody hell. I didn't think this cave had cell service."

Sam takes out his phone and looks at it. "It doesn't."

My phone rings again.

"Maybe you should answer it," he says.

I've had trouble concentrating ever since Cassandra disappeared from that plane. Picasso assures me she wasn't harmed, but there's a part of me that just can't let go of it. I have nightmares of her running away from me.

I exhale and try to think calm thoughts, but it's not working very well.

You should have insisted they bring her in ages ago.

I said as much to Dick in the loo last week, and he made some snotty comment about Cassie being a nepo baby. That blew my top, and I tried to slug him. If Picasso hadn't been there, Dick probably would've shoved my head in the toilet.

"Doc?" Sam says. "You okay?"

"Yeah." I take the phone out of my pocket. "Hello?"

"Hudson, we got a problem here, and it's your fuckup."

"Who is this?" I say. The guy's huffing and puffing like he's being chased by a lion.

"Who do you think it is?" Dick replies. "Lady Gaga? Get your ass over here. Now."

I glance at Sam, and he mimes shooting himself in the foot. "Dickwad?"

I nod and switch the phone to the other hand. "It'll have to wait until I'm done rewiring the pod controller."

"Are you clear on what the word 'now' means, doctor?"

"No," I say, feeling my hackles rise. "You hired a complete idiot to build your time machine."

"Christ," Dick says. "They don't pay me enough to deal with you twits. You've got five minutes, Hudson, and then I send out the MPs —with handcuffs." He disconnects.

"What a lovely man our Mr. Johnson is," I say to no one in particular.

Sam chuckles, bless his soul. "We could stuff tissues into his shoes or short-sheet his bed. Maybe switch out the frosting in his Oreos with toothpaste?"

I laugh, despite myself. "Remind me not to get on your bad side. Could you finish up here?" I hand him the soldering iron.

"Don't let 'em take you without a fight, doc. Or at least a few choice words."

I nod. "I'll be back after I'm spanked and my parents are called."

When I go to knock on Dick's office door, it flies open.

"Get in here," he says.

"How kind of you to ask," I say and stroll in. "And yes, I'd absolutely love some tea and biscuits."

He snarls and points at the flat-panel display on the wall.

I turn, and my heart leaps into my throat. It takes me a moment to recognize her, but Cassie is standing on disintegrating concrete wearing a cowboy hat and mirrored sunglasses, a rifle in one hand. I let out a full-throated cry as tears stream down my face. "Thank the gods you're okay, pumpkin." I hurry closer to the TV. "I can't believe it! I thought you were—"

"Cut the crap," Dick says, "and tell me who she is."

Cassie looks straight at the camera and holds her jacket open so you can read the message on her neon-yellow T-shirt.

I read it out loud, my eyebrows rising. "Where is Matthew Hudson?" I laugh, almost giddy. "Christ, she's been out there for months traipsing through an apocalypse. That's why Picasso couldn't find her. She was out there looking for me."

Behind her stand two horses, a brown one with a saddle and a spotted one loaded up with supplies. She's standing with her feet apart, a holstered handgun visible on her right hip and the wind blowing wisps of her hair like the rogue in a gritty Western.

To be honest, she looks about as badass as I've ever seen her.

That's my girl.

"Crikey," I say, recognizing the crumbling concrete and the sign on the wall. "She's just outside the main blast doors." I let out another explosive laugh.

Dick grabs my shirt, but I pull away and step closer to the display.

"Blimey, is this live?" I glance over at him and then back to the screen.

"I said,"—there's menace in his tone— "who is that?"

"My niece," I say and take off my glasses to wipe my eyes. "She must have ridden all the way from Massachusetts."

"She's the other Hudson?" There's a catch in his voice. "The wormhole genius?"

"Got it in one." I put my glasses back on. "The question is, how did she find me?"

"With this." He tosses a small round button onto the desk. "Maxwell must have planted it in our vehicle."

Sam, you paranoid genius, you.

"Our secure location has been compromised."

"Guess it wasn't that secure after all," I say, my voice cracking with emotion.

"Yeah, well, it'll be real impressive when it lands her in the slammer. This morning, she flew a drone in restricted airspace, cut through three fences, and brought unregistered weapons onto a military base." He harrumphs. "Richter is the one who brought you and Maxwell in here, and I'm going to have his balls over this."

I laugh. "She's a theoretical physicist, for chrissake. Picasso's been trying to find her for months. She's on the damn manifest. Unless the horses are named Russia and China, I don't think you have anything to worry about."

The look of glee disappears from his face. "Why wasn't I notified about the manifest change?"

A voice from the TV says, "You are trespassing on government property. Drop your weapons, put your hands in the air, and identify yourself."

"About time," Dick says. "She's clearly armed and dangerous."

"Wait a minute." I glance at him and then back at the display, holding up my hands. "They're not going to hurt her, right? She's done nothing wrong."

"On the contrary," Dick says. "She's breaking seventeen federal laws just by standing there."

Cassie steps closer to the camera. "I know you have Matt Hudson in there. The neighbors saw the plates on your gas-guzzling SUV when you frog-marched him out in the middle of the night." She crosses her arms. "I'm not doing anything until you let me talk to him."

"Who are you?" It's another voice, and it takes me a moment to place it.

Picasso.

"You go first," she says, tipping her head to the side and putting one hand on her hip.

"Sergeant Major Richter," he replies. "US Marine Corps. I repeat: You are trespassing. Put down your weapons and identify yourself."

"Let's just say I'm a friend of Sam's. You got him, too, right?" She shuffles her feet. "And I'll put down my weapons when I know you aren't keeping them here illegally."

I hear a metal door slide open and see Cassie step back, her eyes wide. A line of Marines jog onto the screen. They kneel in front of the door, their weapons aimed at her.

"Oh, shite," I say, my words catching in my throat. "Let me talk to her!"

"Shut it," Dick growls.

I hold up my hands. "Put the gun down, Cassandra."

The horses start pulling away, and one whinnies.

"It's okay, guys," she says, glancing over her shoulder, a waver in her voice. "They won't hurt you." She takes a slow breath. "At least, I don't think they will." The horses continue twitching their ears and shifting their weight but stop trying to bolt.

One of the Marines isn't carrying a rifle, and he steps forward. The camera angle is bad, but I think it's Picasso. "Put down your weapons," he says, his voice firm but level. "And we can talk."

"No," Cassie says.

I let out a gasp. "Oh, Cassandra, don't do that. He's one of the good guys."

Dick snorts.

Cassie lifts her chin. "I came here to find Matthew Hudson and

Samson Maxwell, and I'm not leaving until I do. If I put down my weapons, you'll just lock me up in some extralegal jail cell and call it a day."

Picasso sizes her up. "I give you my word as a Marine that Professor Hudson and Dr. Maxwell are fine. If you'll confirm who you are, I'll see if they're available to speak with you."

Cassie's eyes get big. For once, I don't think she knows what to say.

Dick starts shaking his head. "Oh no, no, no. You are not letting that self-righteous little bitch in here." He picks up an old-style telephone and starts punching numbers.

Cassie brushes a lock of hair away from her mouth. She glances up at the camera and then back at Picasso.

Just put your rifle down, Cassandra.

"Ma'am," Picasso says, his palms held up in front of him. "Put down your weapon."

"Ma'am?" Cassie's face scrunches up. "What am I, your grandmother?" She holds the rifle out so he can see she's not going to use it, and then she turns, walks back to the horses, and puts the long gun back in the holster. After she secures it, she walks up to the line of Marines, stops in front of Picasso, and reaches for her handgun.

"Sir!" one of the guys shouts.

Cassie freezes.

"Hold your fire," Picasso says.

She looks up at Picasso, her head tipped sideways and her eyebrows raised.

He exhales, keeping his eyes on her. "Slowly, miss."

The corner of her mouth curves up, and I can see the guys with the rifles glancing at each other like she's some sort of superhero. Nobody crosses Picasso, let alone a woman.

Except, apparently, Cassandra.

"Drop the weapon," Picasso says again.

She may be stubborn, but she's not stupid. This time, Cassie follows orders and lifts the handgun out with her fingertip. She grabs it by the barrel and offers the butt to Picasso. "The firearms aren't mine, so I didn't want to get dirt in the barrels." She shuts one eye, looking him up and down. "I figured you'd understand."

Picasso takes the handgun, gives it to one of the Marines, and then frisks her.

"Usually, that'd get you kneed in the balls," she says. "But I'm feeling generous today."

Of course, it's hard to see, but I swear Picasso smiles. "Appreciate that, miss," he says and steps away, satisfied that she's unarmed. He glances at the Marines. "At ease."

They lower their weapons and hold them diagonally across their chests.

He inclines his head toward Cassie. "What did you say your name was?"

"I didn't, Sergeant Major Richter. But I thought you might have guessed it by now. You spent enough time trying to kidnap me."

Picasso narrows his eyes, his lips pressed together.

She takes off the hat and sunglasses, shakes out her hair, and glances to the left, waiting for him to catch up.

"Dr. Cassandra Hudson," he says, enunciating all the syllables.

"At your service," she says, and then her expression turns dark. "Now, what the hell have you done with my uncle?"

"He and Sam work for me—and the US Government," Picasso says. "If you hadn't run away from my courier, he would have told you that. And saved you the cross-country trek."

"I'm not big on taking candy from strangers or getting into unmarked black SUVs. Call it a quirk."

He gives her a wry smile. "Now that you're here, would you like to come inside?"

Dick is roaring into the phone, and I shush him.

"Piss off," he says and goes back to castigating whoever is on the other end.

Cassie turns to the line of Marines. "Do any of you have experience with horses?"

I can see one of them moving his eyes back and forth.

"Speak," Picasso says.

"I have, sir." The guy glances at Cassie. "My family breeds Morgans."

Cassie meets Picasso's gaze. "May I?"

"Be my guest," Picasso says with a tip of his head.

She turns toward the horse breeder. "The mare hasn't had a rest in five days, and her hoof pad is blistered. Also, her tack is wet and she doesn't like to be tied, so just easy over the bar, and she'll stand for you. The gelding needs a farrier and a new halter lead. And they could both use a bran mash and a rubdown."

"Yes, ma'am," the kid says, looking like Cassie just made his day.

"And don't take anything out of my pack."

The Marine looks to Picasso for approval, and he nods.

"What are you waiting for?" Cassie says. "The keys?"

"Dismissed," Picasso says, and the guy hands his rifle to the woman next to him. She and the others jog back inside.

The short, chubby kid walks over to the horses. "Hey, there, girl. Let's take a look at that hoof."

"Oh," Cassie says, turning back to him. "The raisins are in the left saddle bag. The gelding will do anything for a handful. Maybe you could refill it for me?"

"Yes, ma'am. I'll do my best."

Picasso suppresses a smile as Cassie turns back around.

"What is this place?" she says. "Some sort of low-security government playground?"

I let out a giggle, and Dick shoots me a look that could kill.

Picasso gestures with his arm. "After you, Dr. Hudson. I'm sure your uncle will be thrilled to know you're here. Perhaps you'd like to freshen up and join us for lunch?"

Madders' Log
Entry 26

Target: Isabel Sanborn
Nexus: Diego's Cabin
Chrono Tag: 1 Month Later

First notable deviation by Kirkland Enterprises.
News reports show ATHENA-3 self-repair attempt
resulted in hundreds of non-functional
microdrones. However, no significant delay
detected for ATHENA-7 catastrophe.

I t's been snowing for almost a week straight, and we're low on battery power. Thankfully, the sun came out this morning, and Diego is up on the roof clearing the solar panels. After I do the weekly inventory, I push melting snow off the deck with a broom while Lucky and Tolstoy romp around behind me, all of us happy to be outside.

A wave of nausea hits me, and I lean over the handrail and vomit into the snow.

When my stomach's empty, I pad into the kitchen, rinse my mouth with water, and grab a box of snacks. I sit in the kitchen, nibbling on crackers, and run my palms across my growing belly, wishing I could feel just one little kick.

Mrs. Malloy says soon.

Except for the fact that I'm a walking barf machine and my breasts feel like they're going to explode, I've never felt better.

When my stomach settles, I feed the pets, check that the cabin batteries are charging, and lug the Hive Controller out from under the spare bed. I set it on a deck chair with a clear view of the sky, plug it in, and deploy the antenna. Diego has high hopes the Starlink will start working again soon, but right now, the Hive Controller is our only connection to the outside world.

And a pretty sorry one, at that.

When Diego's outside, I've been testing the bots to better understand their behavior under threat. Of course, I never load them with apitoxin, but I've discovered that once they recognize me, they won't sting. So today I'm going to introduce Diego's DNA to the Hive Controller—and I'll do the baby's once the little nipper arrives.

Smarter to ask for forgiveness than permission.

I spin up a bee. It takes a bit of trial and error, but I eventually manage to get the bot to sample Diego's fingernail clippings. On a lark, I have the bot sample fur from Lucky and Tolstoy too.

Better safe than sorry.

I recall the microdrone bee, save the DNA snippets to the controller, add my authentication hack, and tell the Hive to sync the data to the main server via satellite link.

When the Hive Controller starts scanning the sky, I release Lucky and Tolstoy and grab my crocheting. I sit down in the sun and start on my second set of booties—pink this time—occasionally tossing Tolstoy's ball and letting Lucky bat around a ball of yarn.

High above us, a peregrine falcon circles over the ravine, her harsh cry cutting through the chilly air, her smaller mate watching from a treetop. I listen to them call back and forth while counting stitches and munching on crackers. When I finish a bootie, I pick up a wooden toy tucked in with my yarn. The day we found out I was pregnant, Diego started carving a set of farm animals for the baby, and they're the cutest things: a cow, a chicken, and a lamb, so far.

I put the wooden cow back in my bag and wipe away a tear.

I still can't believe we're going to have a baby.

The night of the pajama party—more like early the next morning—Diego offered to go dig up condoms from the basement.

"I'm too old to get pregnant," I told him with a mirthless laugh. "Haven't had a period in over a year."

He'd made some cheesy comment about women saying that right before they get pregnant, but he didn't insist.

And then right there in the middle of the best sex of my life, Diego lifts me off him and sits up. "How would you feel if we got pregnant?"

I think I rolled my eyes, but he was dead serious.

"No really, Iz. I know things are messed up—and it's going to take a while to go back to normal—but Mrs. Malloy is a nurse midwife, and we have everything we need here."

"Except baby clothes, a grocery store, a school, a hospital..."

"Yeah, you're right," he'd said, the wind all gone out of his sail. "I'll go get the—"

"Diego, there's a snowflake's chance in hell I can get pregnant. But if I do, I'm okay with having a baby—assuming you are."

And here we are.

A bell dings on the Hive Controller, telling me it's finished syncing, and I return it to the spare bedroom. I stir the crockpot, grab the crackers, and go back out in the sun to start on the second pink bootie.

Lucky jumps into my lap and rolls over on her back, purring. Tolstoy noses her in the belly. She playfully grabs his nose, and he pulls away, looking like he has a cat-sized muffler on his face.

I laugh.

Thank goodness Diego and I have the cabin and the pets and the Malloys.

Despite being a pushover, Tolstoy barks at the slightest provocation—and would give his life to save any of us. And Lucky is a world-class mouser. Given the volume of food Diego has stashed in the basement, we'd be overrun by critters without her.

The weird thing is, in the universe where I died in the fire, Lucky and Tolstoy died too.

Diego is surrounded by ghosts.

A strange feeling creeps over me. I swallow the acid in the back of my throat and gaze out into the pine trees, their branches drooping under heavy white blankets.

How much longer till things go back to normal?

Tolstoy drops his wet ball in my lap, and I rub his furry head. Lucky starts batting a pinecone across the deck, happy to be outside after weeks of cold and snow. I shut my eyes, listening to her skitter around and wishing I could muster her enthusiasm.

Being pregnant is exhausting.

Tolstoy jumps to his feet and barks, and I hear the lock in the front door turn.

"Isabel?" Diego's voice is shrill, and my heart jumps into my throat. "Where are you?"

"I'm out here," I call, my back wincing as I try to stand.

Diego hobbles out, holding one arm close to his body, his jeans caked with mud and snow. "I fell off the roof." Sweat trickles down his face as he gasps for breath.

"Omigod!" The knot of dread in my chest twists tighter. "Sit down," I say, scanning him for blood. "What happened? How bad are you hurt?"

He collapses into a deck chair. "Mostly just winded from the fall, I think." He takes a quick breath. "But I might have broken my wrist."

I take a closer look. His wrist is bent back at an ugly angle, and it's swelling fast. "Diego, you need a doctor."

"Mrs. Malloy," he says, his face getting paler by the minute. "She's a nurse."

A nurse midwife.

But I nod and jog into the kitchen to get a plastic bag. I fill it with snow from the porch, wrap it in a dish towel, and hand it to him. "Twenty minutes on, twenty minutes off." I get out our dwindling supply of anti-inflammatories and give him a double dose. When he's able to stand, I help him change into dry jeans, wrap a thick towel around his wrist to stabilize the break, and hang a down jacket over his shoulders. "Come on. Let's get you into the car."

When I click his seatbelt, I notice the giant solar battery in back.

"How did that get in here?" I roll up a blanket and wedge it under his arm to keep his hand positioned above his heart. He tries to act like he's okay, but I can see him grimacing with every movement.

"Block and tackle," he says. "But it took me a whole day to do it, so there's no way you're getting it out alone." He glances up at me. "The car's gonna drive like a tank with all the extra weight. Maybe we should send Tolstoy over with a note instead?"

"You're kidding, right?" I say. "Tolstoy gets lost on the way from the couch to the kitchen." I shake my head. "And even if he did make it, what would Mrs. Malloy do? Hike over here in two feet of snow? The woman's almost seventy—and they have less gas than we do."

He frowns, his face so pale, it scares me.

"I can do it," I say. "I grew up driving a stick shift on snowy mountain roads." I shut his door and then hold up a finger. "Just a sec. Let me get a splint from the house." I hurry back into the cabin, sort through the box of medical supplies, and take out an arm splint and a sling—and grab a box of painkillers too. Nausea twists my stomach, and I throw up in the sink, wash it down with water, and stuff a handful of crackers in my mouth. When I get back to the car, I toss the medical supplies in back, move the seatbelt below my baby bump, and shove the key in the ignition.

It takes a couple tries, but the starter finally catches, and the engine turns over.

I lock the doors, shift into first, and we slip and slide down the steep, snowy hill. At the first big turn, I veer onto an overgrown mining trail barely visible beneath a huge drift.

"Hold tight." I gun the engine and plow into the snow, creating a momentary whiteout.

"*Mierda*," Diego says and presses his shoulders back into the seat. When we burst through, he tightens his seatbelt. "Do you charge extra for that?"

"Only if you want to do it again."

He swallows hard.

"I'll take that as a no."

We follow the double track through the trees, the tires slipping and spinning in the deep, muddy slush. At one point, the vehicle lurches sideways toward a huge boulder. My heart skips a beat, and I brace myself, anticipating the worst.

But I manage to regain control at the last second. "Sorry."

"Next time you want to impress me," he says, "how 'bout we play Scrabble?"

I raise an eyebrow. "You always kick my butt."

"Do not."

I downshift and accelerate out of a fishtail.

"Okay," he says. "You let me win sometimes because you feel sorry for me."

I scoff. "You're confusing me with someone who doesn't mind losing."

He laughs, but it quickly turns into a grimace as we go over another bump.

"Sorry," I say again and belatedly glance at the fuel gauge.

Let's hope "empty" means we still have a gallon or two left.

I steer into the first hairpin turn, the car's rear end coming around hard as we head down a small, north-facing ravine. The snow is deep here, and it's challenging to stay on the road.

He winces as the car bumps and slides around more tight turns.

"Sorry," I say for the umpteenth time. "I'll slow down once we get through these switchbacks. I don't want to get stuck."

An elk comes bounding out of the forest and nearly lands on the hood.

Diego stifles a cry, and I jerk the car sideways to avoid it. "Shit. Hold on."

We bounce down an embankment, slide sideways toward a tree, and then bump over rocks and branches until we come out on the road again—facing the wrong way. "Whoops," I say, barely able to breathe. The urge to vomit grabs me again, and I open the door, barf crackers, and shut the door.

He looks over at me, his eyes wide. "You okay?"

"Am now."

"On the way back," he says, "just for fun, do you think we could stay on the road?"

"Hah." I manage to get the car turned around before fording an ice-covered stream.

"Brace yourself," I say and downshift for more torque.

"Do you ever get the feeling that the universe is—" His voice rises as we skid across the ice.

I glance over at him. "Trying to kill us?"

The tires find purchase, and we zoom up the other side.

"Hang in there, babe," I say and rest my hand on his thigh for a moment. "Not much farther."

It's mostly flat from here, and I relax a little.

Can't wait to have another go on the way back.

Mr. Malloy is standing in the doorway of the barn as I help Diego get out. "Good to see you folks," he calls out, tipping his hat. "What's up?" He looks like an old walking stick, skinny and gnarled. His left eye doesn't focus quite right since he ran out of blood pressure medication, and he doesn't hear so well.

"Diego fell off the roof," I holler. "And broke his arm."

"What's that? Problems with the roof, you say?" He closes the barn door and walks toward us.

I repeat myself, and his eyes go wide.

"Lord," he says. "Come inside, and we'll get the missus to have a look."

When we step into the small cabin, Mrs. Malloy waves from the kitchen. "What a nice surprise." She wipes her hands on her apron, and her smile fades. "Oh heavens, what happened, Diego?"

"Broke my wrist," Diego says, sounding like he got caught with his hand in the cookie jar.

She hurries over and lifts the bag of snow off his wrist. "That you did." She moves her hand gently across his arm. "Can you wiggle your fingers?"

He does.

"Good," she says and exhales. "No nerve damage. It's probably a Colles' fracture, but we can't be sure without an X-ray."

Diego looks a bit peaked. "What do you recommend?"

"Straighten it out and put a splint on it. You're young and healthy. If you rest it for a few weeks, it should heal fine on its own."

Diego nods. "Okay."

"I have a splint in the car," I say and go to get the medical supplies. When I come back in, Mrs. Malloy is wearing a clean apron and scrubbing her hands with soap.

I set the items on the table next to Diego and sit down. "What can I do to help, Mrs. Malloy?"

"Get the splint ready," she says. "After I straighten the bones, I'll need you to put it on to stabilize the break. And please, call me Molly."

"Okay, Molly," I say, not liking the sound of 'straighten the bones'. "I brought some painkillers, too, but I don't know if they're the right kind." I show her the box.

"Those will work." She looks at me and then Diego. "Are you sure they're genuine?"

"Yes." I take out a pack. "They're still sealed in foil."

"Good. Let's start with two." She hands Diego a glass of water. "We'll need to wait a few minutes for them to work."

Diego takes the tablets, polishes off the water, and hands the glass back to Molly. "Thanks."

She sets it in the sink and sits down next to him. "Tell me what happened?"

As Diego recounts how the snow shifted and he lost his footing, I look around their cabin.

There's a battered lantern on the table, smoke stains on the wall and ceiling, and burn marks on the floor. The room smells like musty wool and stale cooking oil, and a large plastic bucket sits on the kitchen counter, full of water I presume. Like us, the Malloys have a well, but without a battery, the pump doesn't work unless the sun's out and the panels are clear. And there's no washing machine or induction stove here, either. Instead, there's a blackened kettle on an electric hot plate, a pile of laundry in the sink, and a line of dingy clothes hanging in front of the fireplace.

Omigod, Iz, this could have been you.

Our cabin is a paradise by comparison. And with a handful of solar panels, the Malloys are luckier than most. Mr. Malloy fancies himself a "Doomsday prepper" and had built up a large supply of food and whatnot. But after four long months, things are clearly running low.

Diego puts his good hand on my leg and turns toward Mr. Malloy, who's still standing in the doorway. "We brought the battery, Richard, so after Molly gets me fixed up, maybe we can move it into the barn? I expect it'll be good to have a little electricity at night."

"That would be wonderful," Molly says and repeats Diego's words so her husband can hear. She pins Diego with her gaze. "But I don't want you using that arm today."

"There's a block and tackle in the back of the car," Diego says, louder this time. He turns to Mr. Malloy. "Any chance you've got something we can hook it up to, Richard?"

"Yep," Richard says. "And I think I know how to get the battery into the barn. Saw it on the TV a while back."

"I knew you'd come up with something," Diego says with a smile. "You always do."

Richard pushes the compliment away with his hand. "I ain't gonna be much use in here, so I'll go get things set up outside."

When the time is up, Molly places Diego's arm under her own and presses it hard against her ribs.

Diego looks a bit out of it—which I'm guessing is good.

"You ready?" she asks me. "It's usually less painful than people expect."

God, I hope she's right.

"Yes," I say, recognizing her nursing experience in the set of her jaw and the calm in her voice.

Diego lets out a soft cry as she uses trembling hands to realign his wrist. "Nearly there," she says.

I hear Diego exhale as the bone goes back into place.

"Finished with the painful part," Molly says, her voice breaking. She holds Diego's arm steady while I put on the splint. When I get it on, I let out a breath I didn't know I was holding. My hands are shaking, and I feel the urge to vomit.

"Perfect," Molly says and checks that the splint is snug.

She turns to Diego. "How does it feel?"

"Better," Diego says, still looking pale.

"Keep an eye on his fingers tonight," Molly says to me. "Make sure they stay pink." She notices the look on my face, gets a jar of breadsticks out of the cupboard, and sets it in front of me. "The nausea still bad?"

I nod and gratefully nibble on one of her homemade treats.

"Do you have over-the-counter pain meds?"

"Yes," I say, knowing they have even fewer than we do.

"Isabel, why don't we take a quick listen to the baby while you're here?"

I smile. "I was hoping you'd ask. Thank you."

She gives me a one-arm hug. "I'll be thanking you and Diego every time I turn on the lights at night. Let me get my things."

Diego tries to stand but looks a little unsteady.

"You stay right there," Molly says in her nurse voice. "Seamus is outside, so we can have a listen here in the parlor."

She has me lie back in a recliner, gets out her fetal doppler, and applies gel to my swollen belly. It usually takes her only a moment to find the baby's heartbeat, but this time she has to do a more thorough search, a look of surprise spreading across her face.

"You're having twins!" she says, grinning now, and lets us listen to both heartbeats.

Diego squeezes my hand, his eyes big. "Twins? I knew you were good, Iz, but *this* good?"

Molly laughs. "Have you felt the little ones move yet?"

I shake my head, still processing that I'm carrying *two* new lives.

"Might still be another month or so," she says to both of us. "Nothing to worry about." She wipes my belly clean. "And that explains the acute morning sickness, too. I'm afraid you're getting a double dose of hormones." She helps me sit up. "Congratulations! Won't it be nice for them to have each other."

I nod as all the possibilities spread out before me.

When we step outside, Richard and Seamus are lowering the heavy battery onto four small logs.

"I'll go give them a hand," Diego says and starts to stand again.

Molly sets her hand on his shoulder. "You most certainly will not."

We watch them roll the battery across the muddy gravel into the barn, moving the logs ahead one at a time. Once they get it inside, Richard hooks Diego's block and tackle up to the main beam, and they lift the battery into place next to a diesel generator that has long since run out of fuel.

By the time they put the block and tackle back in the car, Diego is looking a little better.

"When you hook it up," Diego says as I help him into the car, "be sure to shut everything off first."

"Will do," Richard says and closes the hatch, ruffling Seamus' bright orange hair. "Can't thank you enough, Diego. Take care of that arm."

Molly stands with her husband and grandson on the porch,

watching me turn the car around, and then they wave like happier versions of *American Gothic* as we drive away.

Not a minute later, Diego is sound asleep, his soft exhalations filling the car. It's still an hour until dark, but I stop and adjust his chair all the way back. Then I stuff the blanket between his body and the door and tighten up his seatbelt. Without the heavy battery in back, the car handles like a dream, so I stop worrying that we're going to get stuck in a snowbank.

On a lark, I turn on the radio, set the volume low, and push the scan button. Not that long ago, Diego and I used to search at least once a week.

I sigh.

Until it got too depressing.

I listen to the static rise and fall, wondering who else is out there listening and hoping. And then a voice says, deep and resonant, "—six hundred and fifty-two bodies were burned in all. You're listening to the Pulse of Eden radio network." The notes from *Close Encounters* play. "Now for the good news. But first a word from our sponsor, GroSurge."

"Diego," I say, shaking his shoulder. "Wake up. There's someone on the radio."

The ad goes on about crop failures and how KE's fertilizer is being used to increase yields and fight off famines.

I frown.

Trust Dave to find a way to make a fortune off this mess.

"Who is that?" Diego says, his voice groggy.

"It's some sort of broadcast from Eden-1. They must be up and running."

Apparently there are flocks of people camped around the biodomes—which were sealed a few weeks ago.

The announcer says, "Applications for permanent admission are accepted Tuesdays between nine and ten am. Highly qualified candidates in Hydroponics & Food Production, Mechanical & Electrical Engineering, Surgery & Emergency Medicine, and Animal

Husbandry are encouraged to apply. Our sister biodomes, Eden-5, 8, and 9, are nearing completion and are also in need of skilled labor. If you are within traveling distance of Salt Lake City, Annapolis, or St. Louis and can offer proof of needed skill sets, we encourage you to apply."

There's another ad for KE's universal pollinators—my bees! —and then the guy says, "We'll be back next week with more updates. Until then, this is the Pulse of Eden signing off. Stay strong, stay safe, and keep moving forward."

Diego locks a button on the station and turns the radio off. "That was weird."

"But hopeful," I say, climbing up the switchbacks that we slid down before. "If worst comes to worst, we can always get help at Dave's biodome."

"Over my dead body," he mumbles, and I pretend not to hear.

The sun is low in the sky as we drive up the steep, snowy hill to the cabin.

Once we get inside, I tape a plastic bag over his wrist so he can take a shower. Then I check the crockpot again and feed the pets their dinner. When I'm done, I put on a jacket and go out on the deck to watch the sunset.

A few minutes later, Diego joins me.

The night air is cooling quickly, and, above us, the paired falcons are hunting together.

And then I feel it—a flutter, like the soft brush of wings. My heart skips, and I hold my breath, waiting. A moment later, it happens again, more distinct this time, a little nudge from within.

"Diego," I say, my voice breaking. I reach over and take his good hand.

He turns to look at me, concern in his eyes.

I shake my head, smiling, and guide his hand to my belly. "Just... wait."

We stand there, perfectly still, Diego's hand cold against my skin. I watch his face as the seconds pass, his brow furrowing slightly as he tries to feel what I felt. And then, one of the babies kicks and the other follows suit. The movements are small but firm, right under his palm.

His eyes widen, and then his mouth breaks into a grin. "Was that...?" He looks at me, eyes shining.

I laugh, a mix of joy and relief bubbling up. "Yes! Can you believe we're going to have twins?"

Diego's face breaks into a grin so wide it makes my heart skip. "*Mierda*," he breathes, his eyes filling with tears. He crouches down, resting his cheek against my belly, his face full of wonder. "*Hola, mis bebés*," he whispers, his voice thick with emotion.

I place my hand on Diego's head and run my fingers through his hair.

For a moment, the outside world fades away, and it's just the four of us, forever connected by this little miracle.

Madders' Log
Entry 27

Target: Matt Hudson

Nexus: Underground City

Chrono Tag: 1 Month Later

Acceleration of Singularity Transit Device &
Trans Temporal Viewer confirmed. Unclear how
Diego Nadales' jump initiated dramatic shift, but
point to it triggering the Chronosphere event in
this timeline.

"**M**att, push that crystal toward the middle," Sabrina says and points, her voice clipped. Cassie, Sam, and I have been helping her configure the Peeper all week, but progress has been slow, to say the least.

I shift the chair I'm standing on and pull the artificial diamond closer to the center of the lattice, sweat dripping down my face.

Something is wrong with the ventilation system, and despite the propped-open door, the whole building is a sauna.

"If this works, I'll eat my lab coat," I mutter.

She huffs and wipes her face on her sleeve. "Any better, Cassandra?"

Cassie, who's lying on a suspended platform in the middle of the lattice, sets down a wrench, wipes her grease-covered hands on a towel, and takes the laser pointer out of her mouth.

"A smidge more toward the center," she says, and I comply. "Stop."

Sam's teetering on a ladder, securing one of the antenna wires hanging like cobwebs from the ceiling. "If they don't fix the AC soon," he says, "I'm gonna turn into a human puddle."

"Make that two," I say and bend over to wipe my face on my shirt. A drop of my sweat lands on the mirrored satellite dish below the crystal lattice. I climb down to wipe it off with my shirt, and Sabrina nearly bites my head off.

"Don't touch that!" she barks. "It took me weeks to get those mirrors aligned."

Cassie and I exchange a look.

Maybe we shouldn't have volunteered.

Sabrina scurries over, wipes the sweat off with *her* shirt, and hustles back to the computer.

"Hey, Sabrina," Sam says, "once we get this working, can we put in an order for alien pizza?"

"Focus, Sam," she snaps. "We're almost there."

I bloody hope so.

Sam mumbles something about not signing up to hang Christmas ornaments, but Sabrina ignores him. She goes back to typing on her computer for more than a minute. "Yes, that's better," she says more gently and motions for Sam to get off the ladder. "Everyone behind the radiation shield, please."

Cassie uses a button to raise the hanging platform and then scrambles down the geodesic scaffolding like she's a monkey.

Sam plods down the ladder and wipes his brow on his shirt. "You know, doc, if we just had a flux capacitor—"

"Not now, Sam," I say and stand behind Sabrina. Her display appears to be filled with the same static as yesterday. And the day before. And the day before that too.

"Are we making any progress?" Cassie asks and sits next to Sabrina.

"Of course." Sabrina twists another knob. "Trust the science."

"To do what?" Sam says and stands next to me. "Perform magic?"

She glares at him and then adjusts more dials. "Yes, that's better. Here we go." She presses a button, holds it down for a count of five, and releases it. "Good clean reset of the Goldstone dish," she says and bites her lip.

I'm not sure how, but Sabrina has the Peeper hooked up to a giant deep-space communications dish in the Mojave Desert.

"Good thing no one's using it these days," she says, twisting a numbered dial all the way around to twenty. "Okay, I'm starting the capture." She releases the dial, and we watch it tick down for ten long seconds.

There's a beep and a loud click.

The display is still filled with static.

"Damnit." She bangs her fist on the desk.

Cassie points to the screen. "Maybe we need to tweak the signal processing algorithm again? That looks too low."

"After lunch," Sam says. "Even aliens need food."

Sabrina ignores Sam and spends a minute updating more code. When she's done, she resets the dial, and we try again.

"Better," Cassie says, pointing at the new number.

"Wait a second," Sabrina says. "I think I know what's wrong." Her hands dance over the keyboard. "Matt, can you move that crystal down until I tell you to stop?" She points at a diamond on the other side of the lattice. Cassie starts to climb back up to the platform, but Sabrina waves her off. "Let's see if it makes any difference before we spend time aligning it."

I move the ladder, climb back up, and untie the fishing line attached to the ceiling. "Ready."

"Slowly," she says, her head bobbing. "Slowly." She turns another knob. "Stop."

I secure the line. When I'm back behind Sabrina, she resets the timer, and we try again.

As the seconds tick down, the static on the screen begins to shift, forming vague patterns.

"Holy alien donuts, Batman," Sam says. "It's doing something."

"Yes. Now we're getting somewhere," Sabrina says, rubbing her hands together.

On the monitor, the vague patterns have shifted to a fuzzy image.

We huddle closer to the screen.

"That's some sort of oval," Cassie says, pointing it out. "Not something you would get from the CMB radiation." She looks up at me, and I nod.

"Let me start the capture again," Sabrina says and reaches over Cassie to twist the timer. As we watch, the colors sharpen. Light rays scatter and bend, creating a shimmering effect. A frothy white line washes over the display, and tiny, glistening highlights flash and flicker inside—

"Bubbles," Cassie says.

"We're underwater," I say. "In the ocean?"

"Looks like it," Sam says, leaning in closer. "Those are waves."

Another wave passes over.

Taking quick, shallow breaths now, Sabrina adjusts the viewing angle, and everything goes dark. "Wrong way," she says, and makes more adjustments.

A shoreline appears in the distance.

Cassie gasps and points. "I think that's a palm tree?"

We all stare at the scene for a few seconds.

"It's cool and all," Sam says, his voice tight. "But how do we know it's not just some guy trying out his new waterproof camera, and we're just nicking his video feed?"

Sabrina huffs. "Because video cameras can't do this." She types in some commands, and we watch the view pan three hundred and sixty degrees, showing a small village down the beach and a whole lot of ocean. "Or this." We go back underwater, leaving no bubbles or even a ripple, and do another circle around. A turtle swims right through us. "Or this," Sabrina says as we dive into the sand and the picture goes dark. She does some more typing, and we float up through the water, then back into the air with a view of the beach.

"How do you know it's another universe?" Cassie asks.

"The Peeper only picks up photons with quantum quirks—little anomalies in their signatures—that don't match anything in our universe."

"Holy shit," Sam says, his voice rising. "So it *is* a Trans Temporal Viewer." He grabs on to Cassie's chair and gives it a shake. "Another universe. I mean, shit. We're gonna be famous!"

"Pipe down and keep still," Sabrina says—although she's smiling.

"How far can we move?" Cassie asks.

"Don't know," Sabrina says. "Let's see." She types some keys, and we move closer to the beach. But the quality of the image deteriorates. "*Verdammt!*" She types more. "Maybe fifty meters," she says. She tries a different direction and gets the same results. "There's some sort of anchor. The further away, the less we can see." She zooms back to the original position, sitting on the sand underwater, and the picture stabilizes. "The anchor's here."

Suddenly, a face appears, gazing down at us through the water.

All of us let out a startled yelp.

"What the—"

The bell dings, the electronics click off, and the image vanishes, replaced by familiar static.

There's a collective groan.

"Damn," Cassie says. "If we could get a good look at the face, maybe we could trace it?"

One of the wires Sam just put up comes loose and falls onto a lattice crystal, causing it to swing like a pendulum.

"Oops," Sam says. Cassie and I stifle a laugh.

Sabrina sits unmoving, her hands suspended over the keyboard.

"How is this possible, Matt?" She turns to me, her voice barely above a whisper. "Those photons don't exist in our universe, and yet we can see them, record them. I built the collector using the plans, but I have no idea how it actually works. And everyone who might have known" —she exhales— "is dead."

I touch her shoulder. "Do we know what universe that image came from?"

She shrugs. "Your guess is as good as mine. The key point is: not ours."

Sam looks thoughtful for a moment, then grins. "Hey, we use this thing to track down Jack the Ripper." He rubs his hands together. "Prove the moon landing wasn't faked. See who really shot JFK. Shit, we could stroll right into Area 51 and peek at the aliens."

Sabrina rolls her eyes. "Great idea, Sam—if you're braindead."

Sam's ears get red.

"Let's have a look at the recording," she says, bringing up a still image on her display. She runs it through an image processor to remove the static, and a face jumps out at us.

"Crikey Moses," I say, my heart jumping up into my throat. "I think that's Diego Nadales. In fact, I'm certain it is. Maybe a bit younger, though."

Sam frowns, his feelings still hurt. "Who the hell is that?"

Before I can answer, Dick bursts into the lab, his face dripping with sweat and his armpits looking like swamps. "What the hell is going on in here?"

"Science," Cassie says. "That shit you locked us up in here to d—"

"Shut your trap," he says, pointing his finger at her. "Or I'll shut it for you." He turns to me. "Who gave you permission to congregate? This is breaking regulations, and someone's head is going to roll."

"Tone it down, mate," I say. "We're all on the same team."

Sabrina sits back in her chair and crosses her arms. "You'll probably want to see this, Mr. Johnson."

Dick looks a little caught off guard by the invitation. "I thought I told you nerds to notify me the moment you got the T2V working?"

I let out a sigh—only Dick calls it that. "We didn't know the Peeper was working until two min—"

"Can it, Hudson." He scowls at me and Cassie, like we're attached at the hip.

He pushes past Sam and glances at the computer, his eyes widening as he takes in the photo. "Not effing Nadales again? Christ, I'm gonna have to drag his sorry ass in here myself. Get me a printout of that," he says to no one in particular.

Sabrina makes a face but obliges. The moment the photo finishes printing, Dick grabs it, turns on his heel, and strides out, barking into his phone. "Get me Richter. Now!"

We stand in uncomfortable silence, the image of young Diego still glowing on the screen.

"Well," Sam says. "There's our next kidnap victim."

Madders' Log
Entry 28

Target: Diego Nadales
Nexus: Diego's Cabin, Summer
Chrono Tag: 1 Month Later

Pre-Doomsday activation of Trans Temporal Viewer
confirmed. Acquisition of Einstein-Rosen Bridge
Generator lags virgin timeline. Cause of delay
unknown.

I stare out the window into the pouring rain. It pounds against
the cabin, a relentless drumming that mirrors the fear thudding
in my chest. Thunder roars between the peaks and echoes
down the canyon, leaving the damp air sticky with electricity. But in
here, there's a tension no storm can match. Isabel, my heart and soul,
lies on our bed, inconceivably asleep between contractions.

I cling to her feverish hand, a precarious connection by any measure.
The fever started two days ago and the bleeding, early this morn-

ing. I'll never forget the anguish in Isabel's voice when she discovered the blood. I stood there in the bathroom, pale dawn light leaking in through the windows behind me, heart pounding, as she wept, her hands bloody and her skin hot to the touch.

You could lose everything, mae.

Molly moves around me, a quiet force in the chaos, her hands washed clean with the soap I ration like gold now.

I wipe my face with the back of my healed wrist. "So, there's no hope for the babies?" I whisper.

She shakes her head. "The little ones went off to heaven before the bleeding started. I know it's not much consolation, but most women can get pregnant again. Once Isabel recovers, you could always try again."

Christ, I'd have to be an idiot.

Molly steps closer to me, her eyes not leaving Isabel. "We need to be strong for her, Diego. I hate to say it, but the miscarriage might be for the best. Carrying twins is an enormous strain on a woman's body."

The loss hangs heavy in the air.

We'd sung to the twins, made toys for them, talked about them having kids of their own. And now it's all gone. Isabel's eyes flutter open as a contraction starts, and her grip on my hand tightens. I lock eyes with her, trying to pour every ounce of my strength into her. "Hey, beautiful."

"Diego," she whispers. "I'm so scared."

I press my lips to her forehead, tasting salt. "I'm here, *mi amor*. I'm right here."

She lets out a whimper, her face twisted in agony. Her hair is matted with sweat from exertion, and her whole body is shaking.

Molly dabs Isabel's forehead with a cool washcloth. "Focus on your breathing, love. It'll help with the pain."

"Isn't there something we can do, Molly? Pain meds like you gave me, or liquor, even?"

"Anything we give her will only delay the inevitable," Molly says. "Now that the labor has started, her body needs to finish it."

Isabel's breaths come in short, jagged bursts, each one a shuddering reminder of the thin line between holding on and letting go.

"Stay with me, hon," I say, a plea to the universe more than to her. "Please. Stay."

The contraction eventually releases her, and she collapses back into the pillows. "Diego," she says, her voice breaking, "I'm so sorry." Tears glisten in her eyes, reflecting the dim glow of a single lamp. It's been raining for days, making the solar panels useless and leaving the batteries dangerously low again.

"Shh, Iz, you have nothing to be sorry for," I say, trying to keep my voice steady.

She shuts her eyes, and I stroke her hand, frightened by how hot she is. Molly thinks it's a bladder infection, but it could also be a problem with the placenta.

In either case, Isabel should be in a hospital.

You should have taken her to Eden-1 when you found out—maybe saved the twins.

"Don't beat yourself up," Molly says like she can read my thoughts. "The fact that she's alive is a testament to your heroism."

I swallow, not feeling the least bit heroic.

"Keep sponging her face and chest for me," she says and hands me the basin. "We need to keep that fever down as much as possible. I wish we had broad-spectrum antibiotics and an IV—and a ventilator and a dialysis machine while we're at it."

Isabel whimpers, her face contorted with pain. She's gripping the sheets so hard that her hands are deathly white.

"I'm sorry, hon. I wish there was something I could do to make it stop." I dip the sponge into the tepid water and touch it to her feverish skin. She convulses with the strain of another contraction, knocking the basin out of my hands and dumping water all over the floor.

"I don't want to go on without the twins," she says through tears.

The despair in her voice makes my chest tight, and I fight the urge to stand up and punch something. "Don't say that, Isabel. I need you. Stay with me."

Molly catches my eye and gives me an encouraging nod.

"Once you're feeling better," I say, going against everything I know to be safe and wise, "we can always try again."

She nods, her lips pressed together, and then her eyelids slip down, and she's asleep again.

I get up, take a clean towel off the dresser, and wipe up the mess on the floor. In the minute or so I have before the next contraction, I refill the basin. Over the last few months, the twins have become a powerful bond between us, a hopeful force pushing our lives forward into the future. There'd been so much laughter, so much optimism, I had come to believe in the dream.

I stare out at the pouring rain. No matter what I do, it's like the universe fights back, kicks me down—and there's nothing I can do to change things. Nothing.

I let out an angry sob.

Now that the twins are gone, I'm afraid Isabel will stop fighting, and I'll lose her too.

She should be in a hospital.

The frustration pushes me to act. I've let the fact that Isabel keeps begging me not to leave become an excuse. But there'll be no more excuses.

You can't save the twins, but you must save her.

I swallow hard and go back into the bedroom.

Molly is trying to get Isabel to sit up, but not having much luck. "I need your help, Diego." Molly's voice has an edge, and it scares me. "If you sit behind her and help her stay upright, the contractions will work better. She's close to exhaustion, and we still need her to push."

I lift Isabel's head and shoulders—she weighs almost nothing— and then slip in behind her, letting her back rest against my chest. Her head collapses against my shoulder, tears streaming down her cheeks.

I stroke her hair as lightly as I can, afraid that even this might hurt her.

Molly places her hand on Isabel's swollen abdomen. "We're waiting for the next contraction, dearie, and then I'm going to need you to push hard."

"I'm too tired," Isabel says. "Please. Just let me sleep."

The midwife looks at me, her eyes pleading.

I kiss Isabel's hot cheek, my heart breaking. "I love you, hon. And I need you. Don't you give up on me."

A few seconds later, I feel the next contraction seize her body. She lets out a cry, her whole torso shuddering with the exertion. Molly nods at me, her face pale.

"Push, Isabel," I say. "Push as hard as you can. For me. For us."

She grabs on to my wrists and presses back against my chest, her eyes squeezed shut. Sweat drips down her face and neck, and she lets out a high-pitched wail that morphs into a shriek.

The sound goes on for longer than anyone should have to suffer.

And then she collapses against me, sobbing and trembling.

A small head slips out of her body.

"Good work, Isabel!" Molly says, looking very relieved. "The second one will be easier." She lifts the tiny infant, cuts the umbilical cord, and wraps the baby in a small, hand-knit blanket.

Isabel reaches out. "Let me hold my baby."

Molly flashes me a concerned look and then sets the small bundle next to Isabel. "She's a beautiful little girl," Molly says, "but she's an angel now."

I can feel another contraction take over Isabel's body, less than a minute from the last. Isabel closes her eyes and then cries out as she bears down, her whole body convulsing.

Another head appears.

I hear Molly exhale with relief, and my own pulse slows its gallop.

"We're almost done now," Molly says, "and this last part won't hurt." She wraps up the second baby and lays it in Isabel's arms. "Perfect little boy, God rest his soul."

For a moment, the clouds part, and a ray of sunlight falls across Isabel and the twins.

"Her name is Soleil," Isabel says. "And his name is Lucas. I want you to bury them by the outcropping of rocks where they'll be in the sunshine."

Tears stream down my cheeks. "Okay, Iz. I will." I stare at their small faces and then run my fingertip across the girl's tiny chin. "She has your eyes."

Isabel picks up the boy's little hand. "And he has your fingers."

Molly lets out a soft sigh as she attends to the afterbirth. "They are beautiful babies."

Isabel collapses against me, still holding Lucas in her arms. "I'm sorry I couldn't save them, Diego. I tried as hard as I could." Her eyes flutter shut. I wrap my arms around all three of them and lean my head against Isabel's. She's asleep in a matter of seconds.

Molly tidies up the room. "I'll just be washing up in the kitchen," she says. "Take your time."

I lie there on the bed, Isabel's feverish body pressed against mine, and cry. She's lost a lot of blood, and the fever is still raging. We may have dodged this bullet, but there's another one already in the air.

If you stay here, it will kill her.

I carefully get up, tuck the blankets in around Isabel, and give her a kiss on the forehead.

After I wipe my face on my shirt, I pick up the two tiny bodies and tiptoe into the kitchen.

Molly's face is a mask of concern, her usual optimism dimmed in the shadow of Isabel's worsening condition. "I've done all I can," she says, her voice trailing off. But she doesn't need to finish. I know the unspoken words all too well.

Isabel's hold on life is precarious.

The thought is a cold fist squeezing my heart.

I look outside, the rain obscuring the once familiar landscape, turning it into a blur of gray and green. The world has shrunk to this moment, this decision.

Denver, with its dangers and its dwindling supplies, might as well be on another planet. But somewhere east of the city, amidst the chaos and decay, there's a biodome, a chance for Isabel. A chance for life.

The resolve settles over me, heavy as the rain-soaked air. Leaving Isabel now feels like a betrayal. Yet staying, doing nothing while the fever claims her, is a decision I can't stomach.

"I'm going to take the last of the bullets and trade them—and the rifle, if I need to—for a ride to the new biodome out east. I'll be back as soon as I can."

Molly's eyes fill with tears, but she manages a smile. "I'll stay with her until you get back."

I take the small bundles, get a shovel from the garage, and walk out to the point. There's a mist hanging in the trees, and the air smells damp and fetid. Raindrops splash on my hair and cheeks as I walk over the muddy ground. When I get to the outcropping of rock, the rain stops, and I stand for a minute with my face to the sky. Huge boulders loom above me, and I can hear the rush of the swollen stream a stone's throw away. I turn and face east, the sun shrouded by heavy clouds.

But on a clear day, you can see forever.

I set the tiny bundles down and begin digging, the sharp scrape of the shovel breaking the silence. It starts raining again, and I hear the patter as the hole grows deeper. When the pile of dirt is taller than I am and my shovel can no longer bite into the earth, I stop.

With tears streaming down my face, I climb into the grave and set the twins side by side. A part of me clings to the belief that there's a universe where the twins grow up to be strong and healthy, a place where Isabel and I grow old together and watch them fall in love and have children of their own.

I let out a cry of anguish as I throw the first shovel of muddy earth onto the clean blankets, rain soaking through my clothes.

I scarce know which part may greater be,
What I keep of you, or what you rob from me.

And after I cover them, I place a hand-carved toy on each pile of stones and stare up into the stormy sky, angry at the whole damn universe.

Just this once, let me make the right decision and save her.

I head back to the cabin, change my clothes, and throw some things in a backpack. Molly pushes a bowl of oatmeal across the table to me. "Eat. It may be the last hot food you see for a while."

"I'll be back as soon as I can, Molly. Thank you for staying."

"For later." She hands me a sandwich wrapped in a hankie. I stick it in a cinch bag and put both of them in my backpack.

"I can't thank you enough. For last night and for today and—"

"Go. And come back soon. She needs you, Diego." She motions with her head toward the bedroom. "But don't leave without saying goodbye. You owe her that."

I sit down on the bed next to Isabel and run my hand across her feverish face. "Hey, beautiful. I came to say goodbye."

Her eyes flicker open, and she shakes her head.

"I have to go, Iz. To Eden-1. I'll come back as soon as I can."

She takes my hand, her pallid skin hot to the touch. "Is it safe? To go out there?"

I smile at her through my tears. "I'll be careful. I promise." I stand up, but she holds on to my hand.

"I had a dream that you left me and never came back, Diego."

I push a stray lock of hair away from her lips. "Oh, Iz."

"And now you're leaving."

"But I *will* come back." I bend over and kiss her on the forehead. "I will always come back for you."

She squeezes my hand. "I love you."

"I love you more," I say.

Her eyes fill with tears. "I'm sorry I wasn't strong enough to—"

"Shh." I take her in my arms, terrified that this will be the last time I hold her. "It's not your fault, Iz. And it doesn't matter now. All I care about is you getting well." I place her gently back down on the pillow. "Molly is here, and she'll stay with you until I get back." I kiss her palm and then steal one last look at the only woman I've ever loved—then force myself to walk out the door.

I toss my backpack into the CR-V and drive out into the storm, my brain numb.

I'm not even halfway to the highway when the engine sputters and dies. I slam my hands against the steering wheel and pain shoots up my bad wrist.

"Damn it all to hell."

I sit in the car, the pounding rain making it impossible to see, and try to decide if I should stay on the road or cut down the mountain. Either way, it's a muddy mess out there, so I decide to take the shortest route and follow the stream down to the highway. After I shoulder the pack, grab my handgun, and pull the hood up on my poncho, I jog out into the downpour, already feeling exhausted and morose.

At the bottom of the ravine, I stop and take one last look at the cabin up on the mountain.

Please let her be there when I get back.

For more than an hour I hike downhill until I spot the highway on the other side of the ravine. I'll have to jump from boulder to boulder across a rushing torrent, but at least the rain has stopped.

I make a run for it and vault over to the first rock. Except my backpack is heavier than I anticipated, and its momentum nearly shoves me into the deep water. I balance on the slippery boulder, take off the pack, and then load the essentials into the cinch bag and put that on. I heave the backpack over to the opposite bank, but it lands short and is quickly swept downstream, taking my box of bullets, my sleeping bag, and all my food with it.

Shit.

I get to the opposite side, but not without landing waist-deep in the icy current and being forced to scramble up the muddy bank on my hands and knees, my wrist on fire the whole time. I peel off my jeans and attempt to wring them out, shivering in the cold. I consider starting a fire, but I don't want to waste any more daylight, so I change into dry socks, put my pants back on, and hike up the other side of the ravine, the cold, damp denim chafing against my skin.

By the time I get to the highway, my mud-caked clothes are almost dry, but daylight is fading fast. I start trudging down the cracked asphalt, trying to guess how far I am from town.

Maybe three or four miles?

I'm getting a blister from the wet boots, so I sit down in front of a burned-out Walmart and dig out my last pair of dry socks. Now that I've stopped moving, I'm freezing.

What are the chances that someone will drive by now? Six months after all the gasoline is gone?

I exhale. "*Nada.*"

I devour Molly's sandwich, put on my cinch bag, and start walking.

Ten minutes later, it starts raining again. I pull up the hood of my poncho and keep going. As the subdued light fades, the miles go by in slow, soggy monotony—Isabel's alarmingly hot skin pushing me forward.

And then, almost like a vision, I see headlights.

The memory of the incident at the gate fills me with dread, and I consider hiding.

What if it's a carload of looters? Or worse?

I reach inside my poncho to check the handgun. "Or it could be my last chance to save Isabel." I step out into the road and wave my arms.

The massive SUV stops ten feet away, the headlights blinding me. A male voice calls out in the rain. "Who are you?"

"I need to get my wife to the Eden-1 biodome east of Denver. She's dying, and they can save her."

"Put your hands up where we can see them."

I do as I'm told.

If they were marauders, they would have just run you down.

"What's your name, sir?"

I let out a sigh of relief at the honorific.

They must be military. And they have access to fuel and doctors and hospitals.

"Diego Nadales. I need help. Please." I lower my hands. The massive SUV inches forward and stops next to me, the engine louder than the pelting rain.

Someone shines a flashlight in my face. "Shitty night to be out walking, Mr. Nadales."

"Tell me about it."

The flashlight goes off. "Hand over your weapon and get in."

I stare into the passenger-side window at two men in white shirts and ties. "I don't have anything except wet socks."

The driver leans over to get a better look at me. "If you want to save that woman of yours, I suggest you follow orders, sir."

I hold up my hands again. "Okay, okay. I have a sidearm. But I want it back."

The guy riding shotgun snorts. "Yeah, and I want to ball Miss America. Hand it over and get in."

After I do, I duck into the back seat and toss my cinch bag into the cavernous rear. The moment I shut my door, the lock engages. Warm air buffets my face as I rub my hands together in front of the heater vent. "Thank you. Straight up the highway until you get to the gate on the right."

The guy in the passenger seat twists around. "Actually, we've been looking for you, Mr. Nadales."

"What?" I can't keep the shock out of my voice.

"I'm Mr. Johnson," he says and then gestures toward the driver, a guy who appears to be just out of diapers. "And this is Mr. Smith. We work for the government."

Smith glances over the seat at my muddy boots and then meets my eyes, his mouth tight with a fake smile. "Mr. Nadales." He puts the car in gear and makes a U-turn.

"Stop! What are you doing?" I say, panic leaking into my voice. "We have to get Isabel."

Smith accelerates hard into the downpour.

I lean over the seat, attempting to see what's on their computer. "Where are you taking me?" There's text on the display but no map.

Johnson picks up a three-ring notebook and tosses it over onto the seat next to me. "Like I said, we work for the government, Mr. Nadales, and you have been selected to assist in a top-secret project of grave importance to the American people."

"Selected to assist, my ass. I'm a Costa Rican citizen, and I need to get help to Isabel tonight." I push the notebook onto the floor. "Stop the car. I want out." I reach over into the cargo area, drag my cinch bag onto the seat next to me, and wipe my muddy boots all over Mr. Johnson's pristine carpet. "I said stop the damn car!"

The guys exchange looks. "We can't do that, sir. You're part of the project now, and our orders are to escort you directly to the mountain. We have the authority to do it by force if that's what it takes."

Johnson jingles a set of plastic handcuffs over his shoulder. "If you would just read the first few pages of that report, you'll understand why your participation in this mission is so critical."

I yank on the door handle. "Let me out of the fucking car!"

"Calm down, Mr. Nadales." Johnson glances over at the driver, and he nods.

The young guy peers at me in the rearview mirror, his pale skin and sharp nose making him look like a vampire. "In exchange for your full cooperation, we'll request that a medical team be dispatched."

"When?"

"Maybe tonight, maybe tomorrow," Johnson says. "I don't drive the damn trucks. In case you hadn't noticed, the whole fucking world has gone to shit."

I slam my hands down on their seat back. "She's dying from sepsis! Either send someone tonight or let me out of the goddamn car."

"Can't do that, sir."

I lunge for my gun, but the guy slams *his* into my face, and I fall back in a daze, blood trickling down my nose.

He glances over his shoulder at me. "I did advise you to calm down. We've been searching for you for days, Nadales, and there's no way I'm letting you out. Our orders are to escort you inside the mountain, and that's what we intend to do."

"If I'm that important, send a helicopter up to the cabin tonight. I'll give you the GPS coordinates." I wipe the blood off my lip. "Save Isabel, and I'll do whatever you ask."

The guy who calls himself Johnson types something into the computer. "I'd say the chances of that are negative zero percent, but I forwarded your request to HQ. What are the coordinates?"

I tell him, and a minute or two later, the console beeps.

Johnson reads the response and gives a mirthless laugh. "You must have some powerful friends." He turns so he can look me in the eyes. "They agreed. You give me your word that if we get medical attention to your wife tonight, you'll cooperate fully."

"Yes. But if I find out you lied to me, I will hunt you down and cut off your balls with a rusty penknife."

"Yeah," Johnson says with a snort. "Get in line."

Madders' Log
Entry 29

Target: Isabel Sanborn
Nexus: Diego's Cabin
Chrono Tag: Same Day

Major timeline divergence detected. Multiple
cascading events make it impossible to
extrapolate beyond imminent and previously
unrecorded Spacetime Bridge activations.

I'm awakened by a rhythmic thumping noise, and it takes me a moment to realize that it's not coming from inside my head.

The windows are dark, but blue and red lights flash across the ceiling and walls, casting eerie shadows that twist and gyrate into grotesque shapes. Kitty girl lets out a yowl, and Tolstoy tenses beside me, his ears flattening against his head as he emits a soft whine. I lie there, the sheets sticking to my feverish body and my heart struggling to find purchase.

I reach across the bed for Diego, but it's cold and empty.

Am I dreaming?

Lights flash like an alien probe, an otherworldly tentacle searching for victims.

I lie there, trying to make sense of the hallucinations that dance around me.

Just as I succumb to the residual tug of sleep, there's a loud bang. Tolstoy jumps off the bed and positions himself between me and the door, growling. Voices, low but urgent, converse in hushed tones outside my door. Tolstoy's growl deepens, a fierce, menacing sound.

Then I hear Molly's strained voice. "Thank goodness Diego got to you in time."

"Yes, ma'am. Please stand back."

"Forgive me," she says, her voice thick with emotion. "I'd almost given up hope."

Footsteps approach, and Tolstoy barks again.

"There's a dog in there," a voice says.

The bedroom door inches open, and Tolstoy snarls, his body stiff and ready to attack.

"Fuck. It's a goddamn dire wolf."

"He's a pushover," Molly says, slipping into the room. "Tolstoy, here." Her voice is calm and soothing. With a wary glance at me, Tolstoy stops growling and moves to her side. She grabs his collar and leads him out of the room, but the dog turns his head, keeping me in sight until the very last moment.

The door flies open, banging against the wall, and kitty girl lets out a long mournful yowl. A flood of blinding light washes over me, and I shield my eyes with my arm.

"Are you Isabel Kirkland?"

The question comes from a bulky silhouette framed in the doorway.

I stare up into the dazzling brilliance. "Diego?" My voice is hoarse but hopeful.

"Don't worry, ma'am. Your husband is waiting for you at the hospital. We have orders to transport you there immediately."

Husband?

Something about the word sets off an alarm in my head.

The light shifts, footsteps multiplying around me.

Lucky hisses from under the bed, someone swears, and I hear the cat skitter across the floor and race down the hallway.

"What the fuck was that?"

"Focus," a sharp voice says. "Get an IV started and then give her five cc's of clindamycin. When you're done, move her to the medevac and start oh-two. I'll get the hardware. Once we're airborne, you can take vitals. I don't want to be on the ground a microsecond longer than required."

"Yes, sir." The clinical detachment in the responder's voice chills me. Hands, impersonal and cold, lift my wrist. "Just relax, ma'am. We're paramedics."

That's exactly what the aliens would say.

There's a sharp poke in my arm and the sound of tape being torn. I try to pull away, but I have no strength.

Out in the hallway, someone says, "No, sir. We haven't found the Hive Controller yet, but we will." The same voice asks Molly if there's an office, but I can't hear her response. "Search the bedrooms," he says. "We don't lift off until we find it."

I hear something fall and glass break. "What are you doing?" Molly says, her voice tight.

"This isn't your concern, ma'am, so please step aside. We don't want anyone to get hurt."

Tolstoy barks.

"Got it," someone shouts. "Under the spare bed."

Rough hands lift me, and I'm jostled out of the bedroom and down the hall. Molly places her hand on my arm as I float down the front steps. "I'll take care of the pets, dear. You concentrate on getting better." Her smile is meant to be reassuring, but her eyes dart nervously to the shadows that are carrying me away.

Something is wrong.

I stare at her face, wondering why she's letting them kidnap me.

As we move through the darkness, cold raindrops hit my face, an icy contrast to my feverish forehead and chest. I'm maneuvered into a massive, indistinct shape that looms like a black behemoth against the stars. I hear Tolstoy bark again, and I turn my head as sinister shadows race toward me. The light shifts, and the shapes recede.

Dread fills my chest, and I try to sit up. "Stop." But I'm too weak to do more than lift my head.

A mask is placed over my face. Straps are tightened around me, making it impossible to move. More strangers crowd in around me, and the hatch slams shut, making my heart jump and my ears pop.

"Get us out of here." The order is barked from somewhere to my left, and I feel the airship lurch beneath me. The roar of gravity being beaten into submission blocks out everything else, and I eventually drift off into oblivion.

Sometime later—hours or perhaps days, I can't say for sure—I find myself adrift in a half-dream, half-memory of the Brown Palace Hotel fire. I'm lying on the hard atrium floor, the ornate tile hot against my cheek and the air thick with smoke. Next to me, the grand piano lies crushed, its keys scattered across the floor like broken teeth. Beyond the piano, a young man in a fedora stands in a circle of light, his features blurred and distorted by the smoke. Despite the cacophony of the firestorm around us—flames cracking, glass shattering, beams bending and snapping—we both remain still.

"Isabel?" The voice is distant, almost swallowed by the surrounding chaos.

I try to call out, but in the dream, I'm mute.

Fear surges through me, an icy spike cutting through the sweltering heat.

And then I remember I have to play the piano. I roll my head to the side, and the black and white keys scuttle back into place just beyond my fingertips.

A wave of relief crashes over me.

I strain to touch a key, but my hand is tangled up in something. I fight down panic as I try to pull free. But the moment my fingertips brush the cool ivory, my hand is jerked away and the dream shifts. Vines appear out of the smoky darkness, binding me like Devil's Snare. And the more I struggle, the tighter I'm held.

I try to scream, but no sound comes out.

Blinding white light fills my field of vision. Distant and unfamiliar voices whisper words I can't quite make out. I pull at my restraints, but there's no escape.

The dream shifts again.

I'm back on the floor in the burning hotel as the flames creep closer. The young man has vanished, and the wrecked piano is lying on top of my legs. Across the atrium, I can hear the animals barking and meowing for a rescue that will never come.

"Isabel? Can you hear me?"

The words rattle around in my brain like rocks in a can, unrecognizable.

I blink, trying to clear the cobwebs. The air smells of antiseptic soap and something musky, something it takes me a few seconds to place.

Dave's aftershave.

"Hey, princess. How are you feeling?"

I force my eyes open. The assault of too-bright fluorescents stabs my confused brain, and I raise my hand to block the light.

When my eyes adjust, Dave's face is hovering over me. "Welcome back, doll."

I let out a startled cry and try to pull away.

He laughs. "Nice to see you too, cupcake."

Epilogue
Eden-17 Biodome · The Not-Too-Distant Future

I force my eyes open, my head pounding and my mouth dry. It's dark, and there's a loud clicking noise behind me. I try to sit up, pushing against the wheelchair's armrests with my elbows, my lungs struggling for air. I cough once, twice, thrice, then gasp for breath.

When my head stops pounding, I fumble for the flashlight I carry around my neck and switch it on.

A bright red spray of blood covers my palm, and the memories come flooding back.

Dave is dead. Diego is gone. It's just you now, Isabelle.

You and your murderbots.

I swallow the lump in my throat.

Why of all people is it me they left alive?

There's that clicking sound behind me again, like a circuit tripping and resetting.

"Madders?" I call out. "Turn on the lights, please."

I sit there in the oppressive dark like a ninny—until I remember the AI is gone too, just one more of my hapless victims. It will be decades before the batteries charge enough for him to reboot.

If ever.

A shiver runs down my spine as I imagine seawater crashing through the broken walls of the biodome, thick vines hanging from the girders, the bots picking apart the precious metals inside. Madders' mainframe is buried deep underground next to the reactor for the frozen embryos, but I fear that won't be enough to save either of them.

Forgive me, Madders.

I turn my wheelchair around and fumble with the manual override for the emergency lights. The control room fills with a soft luminescence.

At least there's a little power left.

And then I realize what's causing the clicking noise. An electrical panel on the wall by the blast door has a breaker that keeps tripping and resetting.

And tripping again.

I wheel over to the offending panel, my arms complaining at the effort, and take a closer look.

There's a tiny bit of charge left in the main battery bank, but now that I've turned the emergency power back on, I can see the bar dwindling.

Houston, we have a problem.

The breaker trips and resets again, and I realize that's why the batteries aren't charging: the huge solar array up on the volcano is offline. A surge protector must have failed, cutting off the power. The biodome was designed with a large gap between the power cables and batteries to prevent an EMP from disabling the whole biodome.

Live and learn.

Some sort of system timer must be resetting the connection and attempting to bring the solar panels back online—and failing. Ironically, once the main batteries are drained, there won't be enough power to configure the system to recharge them. Humanity's last great engineering wonder will go dark.

Given what a mess we made of things, maybe it's for the best.

I take another look at the failing battery banks.

Madders.

He may not be alive in the traditional sense of the word, but I owe him a chance.

And more importantly, he's my friend

Between coughs, I wheel back to my desk, drink the last of my water, and haul out the printed manual for the solar array.

After the first EMP knocked out the Eden-1 generators, Dave double- and triple-engineered the replacement infrastructure to withstand anything short of a direct blast. I'm betting the cable from our solar array is no exception—and it turns out, I'm right. There's a manual pump that can be used to reconnect it. I just have to do it before all the battery power is gone.

Who doesn't love a life-and-death game of Beat the Clock?

The bad news is, the access panel is in the electrical room, a quarter of the way around the control tower. I study the instructions for a minute, including a map of the electrical room, until I understand what needs to be done, and then tear out the page and stick it in my bra, just in case.

I haven't been out of the control room or the attached living area in months, but I think there's a manual release on the blast door set low enough for me to engage. I take the electrical room key off its worn hanger and put it on the lanyard holding my flashlight. Helped along by the image of the dwindling battery, I make my way toward the blast door.

I unlock the deadbolts, turn the manual lever, and shove the heavy metal portal with my footrest. Thank goodness the door swings outward, or I'd be stuck. I try to push myself through the opening—but the damn chair won't fit. Too wide.

Of course, it is. Dave cut corners at the end, and "accessibility" wasn't high on his list of essentials.

I brace my hands on the armrests, willing my legs to work.

When it's the only option left, attempt the impossible.

I exhale and push up. My knees shake, almost buckle, but I manage to stay upright. One step, then another. My breath comes in gasps, pain shooting through my legs and back.

I grip the doorframe, steadying myself, and glance up at the biodome walls. Now that the door's open, the sound of the bots is loud.

I force my feet forward, clutching at the guardrails along the viewing area, my heart hammering in my chest. My legs want to collapse, but I keep moving, staggering down the curved corridor until I get to the electrical room. I lift the lanyard from around my neck and manage to get the key in the lock. I take a breath, turn the handle, and use my weight to push the door in—and end up slumped on the dirty floor, surrounded by darkness.

You left the damn flashlight hanging on the doorknob.

I consider going back for it, but there's no way I'm going to be able to stand up, let alone pull that door back open.

I sit there in the dark.

After a minute or so, my eyes adjust, and I can see vague shapes.

The emergency lighting must be on in here too, but most of the panels aren't working anymore. I crawl toward the closest source of dim light, take out the instructions, and smooth them out on the floor. I turn the paper until it matches up with the orientation of the room, then identify the manual reconnect panel I need to open—and notice there's a large door labeled "Emergency Supplies—Authorized Use Only" right next to it.

I'd kill for another drink of water.

While crawling and coughing my way toward the panel, I bump into an office chair—only to realize it has wheels! After shoving it against the wall and wedging the folded-up instructions under the wheels, I push and pull and swear my way up into it.

Sit happens.

I kick away the paper wedges and wheel myself over to the panel, pleased with my upgrade. The cover opens easily. Inside, there's a circular pump with a bellows below it. I push down on the top. As the air is forced out, I hear a faint mechanical click—like a pin moving in a turning cog. I push down again. Another click. I shift my weight to let more light into the box and see a gauge in back, a tiny slice of green visible at one end of a long red bar. I push five more times, wheezing and coughing between presses, and see that the green is getting longer. I rest for a bit, then keep pumping and coughing until it's solid green. When I collapse back into the chair, I hear a whole series of mechanical clicks and clanks inside the biodome walls.

Have to wait for the sun to come up to know if it worked.

I turn my attention to the emergency supplies cabinet, certain it will be empty. The door has nothing written on it, only a now-defunct access screen for the AI. I reach up and tap it, half out of habit and half out of sheer contrariness.

"Madders?"

But of course, he's not there. Instead, a keypad appears with six question marks above it.

"Damnit."

I know Madders' birthday but not what year. I try my best guess, and a message appears:

```
4 guesses remaining.
```

I try the year before and the year after.

"Okay," I say and sigh. "So maybe not his birthday." I know Matt raised his niece. She was killed during the Second Disaster, but I don't know which day, and besides, who would use a death date as a password?

And then I know what the code is.

I type in *Cassie*, and the door falls open a crack.

Inside the cabinet is enough food, water, medicine, books, toilet paper, and booze to last for months, possibly years.

Longer than you'll last. That's for sure.

I open a bottle of water and take a long, satisfying drink.

Probably an hour or so till sunrise.

I close my eyes, lean my head back against the chair, and rest.

The sound of a motor starting up awakens me.

I wheel over to the main control panel, my body stiff and my heart pounding.

But instead of the usual KE logo, the computer monitor has a small, white, blinking cursor in the top-left corner. I hit the return key, and a prompt appears, so I type in *status* and hit return again.

Characters, then words, spill across the display:

```
Battery Status: Charging…
Current Battery Level: 0.002%
Estimated Time to Eden-17 Guardian AI
Reboot: 8753 days, 6 hours, 21 minutes…
```

I wipe my eyes on the back of my hand and smile.

In matters of time, perhaps nothing is truly gone, only waiting to begin again.

Thank You for Reading!

If you enjoyed the book,
please, please, please...
Leave a Review!

(Yes, I'm begging! And if you let me know,
I'll gift you another book as a Thank You!)

dlo@dlorton.com

Also by DL Orton

Between Two Evils Trilogy

Crossing in Time

Book One

Lost Time

Book Two

Dead Time

Book Three

Madders of Time Series

Hive

Book One

Jump

Book Two

(Coming November 2025)

About the Author

The AWARD-WINNING & BEST-SELLING author DL ORTON
lives in the Tropics with her husband, a golden retriever mix,
a Siberian cat, and a bazillion geckos.

In her spare time, she's building a time machine so that
someone can go back and do the laundry.

Thank You for Reading!
dlorton.com
dlo@dlorton.com

———————

amazon.com/author/dl_orton
bookbub.com/authors/d-l-orton
threads.net/@dl_orton_author
instagram.com/dl_orton_author
goodreads.com/dl_orton

'